ALL THE LITTLE HOPES

ALL THE LITTLE HOPES

LEAH WEISS

THORNDIKE PRESS
A part of Gale, a Cengage Company

Copyright © 2021 by Leah Weiss.
Thorndike Press, a part of Gale, a Cengage Company.

Thorndike Press® Large Print Basic.
The text of this Large Print edition is unabridged.
Other aspects of the book may vary from the original edition.
Set in 16 pt. Plantin.

LIBRARY OF CONGRESS CIP DATA ON FILE.
CATALOGUING IN PUBLICATION FOR THIS BOOK
IS AVAILABLE FROM THE LIBRARY OF CONGRESS.

ISBN-13: 978-1-4328-9209-8 (hardcover alk. paper)

Published in 2021 by arrangement with Sourcebooks, Inc.

Printed in Mexico
Print Number: 01   Print Year: 2022

*Dedicated to the humble
bloodline of my rich history:
my mama, Lucy; her mama, Allie Bert;
and her mama, Minnie Brown*

THE YEARS

PROLOGUE:
LUCY

We are an innocent lot, my two brothers, four sisters and me, born on as ordinary a land as God ever made. Our tobacco farm in Riverton, North Carolina, is far from Oma's soaring mountains in the Black Forest of Germany, where tall trees dim the light of day and the tales of the Brothers Grimm grow out of the loamy soil. Where even a polished apple holds peril. Her stories raise the hairs on the backs of our necks, and fear prickles and chills our skin. Telling tales is Oma's best talent.

After, when prayers are said and we're tucked in our featherbed, and the house turns still as stone, I lie between Cora and Lydia, and we remember, and clutch hands until our grips soften, safe in this place, for our grandmother's stories live far across the sea.

But they are real.

Because of the *wolpertinger.*

Oma's grandfather came upon the creature

in 1881 while hunting, and he preserved it for all time. It is seventeen and a quarter inches long and is equal part rabbit, roebuck antlers, and falcon wings. Because wolpertingers thrive only in crisp air filtered through evergreens and washed clean in clouds, we'll never see wolpertingers in Mercer County. Our humid air is too heavy to conduct magic.

The creature came to America in a wooden box with a hinged door, and for the years Oma lives with us, it resides on top of her Bavarian armoire. We take turns cleaning it with a feather duster, but we never touch its eyes for they are hazy and off-kilter.

Of her seven grandchildren, I am Oma's favorite. In private, she tells me so. It's because I am curious and have a deductive mind. I collect obscure words like *misnomer* for contradiction, and *knave* for someone dishonest. My favorite word is *enigma,* for without mystery to challenge a curious mind, it starves. My brother Grady calls me high and mighty for using ten-dollar words in a ten-cent town. Out loud, I call him rude, but inside my head, I know he's a *chuff.* Mama says I can be insensitive. She says language is meant to communicate, not separate, so I mostly spend ten-dollar words inside my head.

Oma never returns to Germany. She dies in Riverton on the twentieth of May, and her granite tombstone is etched with a mountain sketch we've only seen on the page of a travel book in our library. At her passing, our hope for thrilling danger passes with her.

We fear nothing will happen here . . . here where a lazy river rolls by, outsiders are rare, and farming rules our days.

We think we are safe here, where nothing happens — until something comes that undoes us all.

■ ■ ■ ■

1943

■ ■ ■ ■

CHAPTER 1
LUCY: BITTERSWEET

The gray car with the faded white star slows at our mailbox, deliberates, then lumbers down our rutted road, raising dust. It interrupts my reading of *The Hidden Staircase* when Nancy Drew discovers rickety stairs leading to dark tunnels beneath mansions. I slip the bookmark in place and watch the arrival from the hayloft, curious.

The car stops under the oak tree whose leaves are limp from summer heat. The driver turns off the motor, and the cooling engine ticks like a clock marking odd time. He sits wide and tall in the seat and hasn't seen me studying him from on high, with my bare legs dangling over the edge of the loft. He checks his teeth in the mirror, flattens a cowlick with spit, and opens the door. The hinge creaks as he rolls out. If it's grave news this government man brings, news that is going to alter our family tree, I thought it would be delivered with more decorum. My belly turns sour.

At the coming of the car, Mama steps on the porch, wiping her hands on her apron. The screen door slaps behind, and she jumps. These days she stays wound as tight as Oma's cuckoo clock because of our men gone to war. *The not knowing is the hard part,* Mama says — like my thirteen-year-old self doesn't know that by now.

The government man is corpulent with flushed cheeks. He carries a battered brief-case and takes two steps while studying a scrap of paper. "I'm looking for David Brown," he calls out with a voice abnormally high for a heavy man.

"Is it Everett Brown or Wade Sully?" Mama's voice pinches, saying the names of my oldest brother and my sister Helen's husband.

"Oh, Lordy, ma'am." He clears his throat. "I'm sorry I scared you thinking that way, seeing this government car and all. No, ma'am. I bring good news."

Mama's body softens, and I turn curiouser.

She rings the dinner bell to call Daddy in from the tobacco field where the crop is already stunted from a dry spell this year. I come down from the loft, tuck Nancy Drew between hay bales, slip on my bee suit like I was supposed to when I wanted to read instead. I tie my sneakers and walk out of the barn in time to see the tractor chug this way on high. Grady stands on the frame, his shirt billowing in the air. When they get close, Daddy cuts the motor, and they jump down and move at a fast clip. Mama yells, "It's not our boys," so they don't race their hearts.

Daddy walks up to the stranger, sticks out his right hand mannerly, and slides his toothpick to the corner of his mouth. "I'm David Brown. My son, Grady."

Juggling the briefcase in his left arm, the good-news man wipes his right hand on his trousers before he shakes Daddy's hand, then Grady's. "I'm John T. Booker, sir, representing the United States government. Mind me asking how many hives you got there?" He nods toward the white boxes beyond the barn.

"Beehives?" Daddy was thinking bad news and is confused. He glances at me holding my bee hat in one hand and the unlit smoker in the other when it should be smoldering. I can't help that I love books with a passion and they can interrupt tending bees, but Daddy's forgiving. His eyes settle back on the fat man. "Bout a hundred, last count."

"Whew. That's a nice operation. Does that come to about a thousand pounds of beeswax and eight thousand pounds of honey a year?" Mr. Booker throws out figures I've never heard before.

"Thereabouts . . ." Daddy answers, but he doesn't elaborate on how often a hive absconds when the temperatures change, or the queen dies and throws the hive into a quandary, or their food source dries up in a drought like we had two summers back. It's rare to have all our hives in working order.

"I'm here to talk bee business with you, Mr. Brown."

"You want my honey?" Daddy frowns because with the war on and sugar scarce, honey is a prized commodity.

"It's mostly beeswax we need, sir. Is there somewhere we can talk? I've got a proposition for you."

Daddy nods to the table under the oak tree, where dinner is served at noon to field hands. "Here'll do."

Mr. John T. Booker brushes off twigs and leaves, sits on the bench, and plops his bulging briefcase on the table. Grady leans against the tree, chews on his toothpick, and adroitly rolls three glass marbles between his fingers. Mama sits between my little sisters, Lydia and Cora, shy on each side. I

18

sit, too, unzipping the bee suit for ventilation. Unexpected company takes precedence over chores. My older sister, Irene, is at her newspaper job in town, but she's going to be sorry to hear a proposition secondhand. And my oldest sister, Helen, stays inside the house like she's prone to do. Mama says it's melancholy that's taken hold of Helen since she got in the family way and her husband, Wade, is fighting in the Pacific. Even a stranger coming and sitting at our table won't bring her outside.

Mr. Booker looks nervous with so many eyes aimed at him. He is a rumpled mess, rifling through his muddled papers. He pulls out a wrinkled pamphlet, irons it out with his palm, and gives it to Daddy.

"This here will explain what I come to talk about." He uses his index finger to wipe sweat off his upper lip, leans toward Mama, and speaks low. "Ma'am, can I bother you for some water? I'm mighty parched." With a tilt of her head, she sends Cora to the well to fetch a cup. Mr. Booker stares after the pale and frail of my sister who has often been mistaken for an apparition. He takes the cup from her, but his hand trembles. Still, he drinks the water and nods his thanks.

Daddy reads aloud, "Honeybees and

Wartime," then studies the brochure while we study the government man. Mr. Booker wears a shirt straining at the buttons and a skinny black tie, like an encyclopedia salesman peddling knowledge a month at a time. His belt is brown, but his shoes are black with scuffed tips that have never seen a lick of polish. He has surprisingly tiny feet that don't look able to keep him upright when the wind blows. He squirms at the silence and starts talking before Daddy's done.

"It pretty much says *Worker Bees, Uncle Sam Needs You,*" and he grins like he told a funny. He adds weakly, "We could use your help, sir," then studies his chewed fingernails for somewhere to lay his eyes.

I've been holding back questions, so in the lull, I let loose in a polite way. "You a military man, Mr. Booker?" I say. I've never seen an unkempt military man.

"No, I can't be a soldier cause I got flat feet," he says and nods toward his briefcase. "I do paper stuff."

"Where you from?"

"Greenville," he says but not which Greenville.

"Did you know there are fifteen states that have towns called Greenville? Unless you're from Greeneville, Tennessee. That's different from all the others because of the extra *e* smack-dab in the middle. Which one are you?"

Mr. Booker mumbles, "North Carolina" without a crumb of interest in the insight I shared. He didn't even want to know the names of the Greenville states I can list alphabetically. I change course.

"Do you know rubbing beeswax on a fishing line makes it float?"

"No, I do not," he says.

"Do you like to fish?"

"No, I do not."

"Who's your favorite author? I love Carolyn Keene. She wrote the Nancy Drew books about a girl like me who solves mysteries and knows a lot about a lot of things. Do you like mystery books?"

Mama says quietly, "Enough, Lucy," and cuts off my litany of questions. "Leave Mr. Booker alone."

I comply, but I already know he's a dolt who's pitiful at conversation.

Daddy passes the brochure over to Mama and says, "Let me get this straight," and shifts his toothpick to the other corner of his mouth, and Grady does the same. "You want some of my honey and all my beeswax."

"Yes, sir, and we'll pay good money for it."

"And if we sell you beeswax, you'll give us barrels of cane sugar so we can supplement the hives with sugar syrup and sugar cakes. All the sugar I need, no ration coupon needed."

"Yes, sir."

"Say again what it's used for?"

"The war effort uses a million pounds of beeswax a year to waterproof canvas tents and lubricate ammunition, drill bits, and cables, stuff like that."

"You think it'll last much longer?" Daddy asks.

"Beeswax, sir?"

"The war."

"Don't rightly know, but we gotta be ready for what comes."

Daddy leans back on the chair legs. "Says on that piece of paper my boys won't have to enlist if they work the hives."

"Yes, sir . . . I mean, no, sir. They'll be doing war duty working bees. We know making sugar water to keep bees making wax will take a lot of man-hours. A hundred hives might need twenty-five gallons of sugar water a day. We'll give you the sugar, the scale, boxes, paper dividers, cutting tools — everything you need, even the postage to ship the wax — and send you a check."

"Is my son-in-law exempt, too?"

"Yes, sir. That release option applies to all the men tied to your family. Well, those who want to stay home, that is. It's kind of a sweet deal, don't you think?"

Daddy looks at Mama.

Our bees sign up.

With its departure, Mr. John T. Booker's car leaves another dust trail behind, and Mama's face has a flush of happiness in her sallow cheeks. She says, "I'll let folks know they won't be getting wax anytime soon." She turns to Daddy. "When will they let Everett and Wade know to come home?"

Daddy's eyes stay on the road where the dust settles. He doesn't look at Mama. "I don't think it works like that."

"What do you mean? Isn't that what you signed? That's part of the deal, isn't it? Our boys come home safe?"

"I know what you *think* it means, Minnie, but because our boys can come home doesn't mean they will."

"Why in the world not?" Her voice jabs. "Won't they feel lucky to work bees instead of fighting a war that's not ours?"

Daddy looks older than he did a minute ago, and he speaks low. "Civic pride's a powerful adversary, and it's had time to take hold. Everett's been gone a year, and it's been three months since Wade was home. I don't think we can mess with honor and hope beeswax wins."

"You've got to tell em what to do. Tell em we need their help." Her panic builds. "Tell em they won't have to live in mortal danger."

"We don't even know where they are." Daddy turns to face her. "The time they've been gone can change a man in ways we can't understand. If they don't choose to come home, we'll manage. Lucy can do more. I'll pull men from tobacco and hire extras when we render the wax. That's only two times a year."

She glares at Daddy. "You betrayed me, David Brown. You and that slick government man. Y'all were selling something I was buying, and now you're taking it back. Telling me it's not that simple when it is. We need Everett and Wade *here*. Not over *there* in some godforsaken land."

On one side, Daddy speaks the war-truth that's turned our days hard. On the other, Mama wishes on a star like a girl wanting to keep our boys safe. I wish that both sides would go away and today I'd see my big brother come around the corner of the barn. He'd be whistling and he'd swing Lydia and Cora high into the air, and they'd

24

squeal with joy, and he'd tell us a riddle. That's what I want.

Daddy is a peacemaker at heart so he lifts his arms for a hug, but Mama bats him away and locks her jaw. He says, "We'll let the men know, but the decision is theirs. They're old enough to go to war so they're old enough to make up their own minds."

Mama stomps off toward the house, and Daddy heads to the barn. We'll be keeping the two blue stars in our window representing our men in harm's way. Mr. John T. Booker's offer was a misnomer.

Lydia and Cora are near tears to see this argument. It used to be rare to witness fights between our parents. Now it's grown common. I say to Grady, "You gonna stay home and make Mama happy?"

He drops the toothpick on the ground and the three cat's-eye marbles back in his pocket. "I don't rightly know," he says, being honest. "I don't turn eighteen for twenty-six months and eight days. The war might be over by then. I don't want to look like a coward, Lucy. What kind a man chickens out of a war when his buddies are risking it all?"

I shoot back, "A smart man. A live man. A whole man who wants to stay that way."

"I got time to decide," he says, and he

walks to the barn where Daddy went. With only us three girls in the yard, Cora and Lydia stop crying. I push them on the swing while the tension in the air dissipates.

I wish Oma were here to comfort Mama, but she died a week back when I was in the hayloft stealing time, reading *The Secret at Shadow Ranch.* I looked up when the screen door screeched open and watched my mama bring German tea to her mama like she did every afternoon. But this time, Oma's head lolled to the side. Her mouth had gone slack, and Mama dropped the cup of hot tea and it cleaved down the middle, a good life split between Germany and Riverton. Nancy Drew slipped from my fingers, and I lost my place.

Mama lost her place, too.

CHAPTER 2
BERT: THOUGHTLESS

It's wash day on the last Wednesday in May. Sheets is heavy on the line next to overalls and flannel shirts, flapping in a breeze coming down from the highlands, heading for Asheville. There was this itty-bitty tear in Ma's old sheet, and it's what I'm in need of — a strip of cloth two lengths of a baby coffin. So being the thoughtless girl I am, I take the edge of that tear, rip it up one way then cross the other till I get what I want. Then I go to my room I share with my older sister, Ruth, and bolt the door.

Cause it's in plain sight, Ma sees that tore-out sheet and lets out a scream to her savior and her wayward daughter, getting us a tad mixed up. "Sweet Jesus, what in tarnation got into you, Allie Bert Tucker," she shouts to the heavens.

I don't come outta my room. Don't answer in respect neither. I keep winding that stole muslin round my necked chest to cover my swoll breasts. I'm tamping down my bosom because it changes things. I ain't ready for change.

The rusty hinges on that screen door scratch open and slap shut. Ma's heavy feet flap cross the sticky linoleum up to my door, where her words slide through the crack. "I know you done it. Can't be nobody but you. Ruint the cloth you sleep on, like we rich as kings and can buy what we please. You gonna be the death of me."

Ma stops her talking, breathes like a mule run hard, and moans low from the baby growing heavy in her belly. Her voice turns to mush when she says, "What's got into you, Allie Bert?" and I yell back, "My name is Bert. Plain Bert," then I jump when Ma hits the outside of that door with the flat of her hand and says, "You a thoughtless girl. I pray the good Lord will punish your selfish ways. May he break your willful spirit."

I still don't open the door. I git up on tiptoes to look in the cracked mirror on the wall to see a chest flat as a boy. The muslin makes breathing hard. I don't worry bout the washing on the line. Don't worry bout shelling peas or scrubbing a sticky floor. I let Ruth do the worry stuff, since she's fifteen to my thirteen. I pull on a shirt and overalls, climb out the open window, and drop to the ground quiet as a cat.

Ruth comes walking round the corner of the house cause she knows I'd be crawling out the back window for a getaway. She says, "Where you going?"

I whisper, "I need to skedaddle."

Ruth says, "Ma's upset at what you done. And Sam Logan's come for a visit. He's talking to Pa but waiting on you to take a walk with him."

Sam Logan don't make me pause, but I peek round the corner and see him tall as Pa, him sucking on a sassafras branch cause of his stinky breath. He's got ideas I don't like one bit, but I don't say such things to Ruth. I run. I run on bare feet cross the clearing with a circle of blue mountains all around. Through the apple orchard where blossoms are mostly spent. Past the grave-yard of my people into the dark of the woods. I'm heading to my thinking spot back in the holler. Grapevines thick as my wrist hang from tall trees that grow outta cracks in boulders. Moss covers felled logs and is so green it pains my eyes to gaze upon it.

In the bend of the narrow trail lined with ferns, I see a tiny ball of fur. It's lying still, and I walk up to it and nudge it with my toe. It's a baby rabbit, no more than a week old. When I pick it up, the little head falls to the side. It fits in the palm of my hand, and I tuck it against my chest and feel grief stab my heart for a death I got no part in. It's still warm, and I carry it and walk through my quiet woods. Patches of sunlight move on the ground and light up lichen and mushrooms and mica.

The rumble of falling water comes to my ears first, and when it comes into view, the spray soaks me clean through. I still hold tight to the dead rabbit, too precious to cast off. I tuck him inside my shirt pocket so I can climb wet rocks and work my way behind the rushing water to the slip of a cave. Inside is dry enough and deep enough to snuggle up to the far wall. Its comfort seeps through my damp clothes into my bones. A rainbow sparkles through the water, and I think bout today and why I come here: I don't wanna change from a girl to a woman and work till the day I die.

That's the God's honest truth. That curse from blood between my legs don't mean nothing but heartache. A growed woman won't never come to my cave. Or fly high on a grapevine. Or jump in a swimming hole deep as tomorrow. Or grieve a dead rabbit that barely saw the sun rise and set a half-dozen times. A woman's feet is nailed too solid to the ground to roam, and I need to roam. I wanna go to places Teacher talked about in them picture books. Paris, France. London, England. China with a great wall that wanders forever. I want to see water as blue as a morning sky. Teacher says I'm smart enough, and I want to believe her. I rub the soft rabbit fur with my thumb cause it gives me comfort and hope I won't have to settle for a puny life. I dream of blue ghost fireflies that will rise up soon and dance in the dark . . .

When I wake it's late and I scramble outta the cave and scoot down the slick rocks, wondering if Ma and Pa's gonna be mad at me again for neglecting chores. I hope they don't send me to bed hungry. I run through the long shadows of the woods, clutching my dead rabbit, come out in the clearing, and stop confounded. Clothes is still on the line. No light is in the windows and no supper smell in the air. In the yard beside the chopping block, Pa faces the setting sun on the long slope of Mount Mitchell.

I get up next to him and say, "Pa?" but he don't answer, and I look over at the cabin that looks like nobody lives in it. Gloomy and sagging in the middle, it makes the innards of my belly clutch. I think to say, "Where's Ma and Ruth?"

He look down on me like it's great pain to pull his neck my way. "Oh, Bert. Hello, girl," he says polite as church, "Your ma's dead. Your baby brother, too. They inside growing cold. Ruth's gone to fetch help."

I can't hardly breathe from the shock. Ma's labor musta come on early cause I run away. Labor pains brought on by her girl who don't think of nobody but herself. A girl who give her ma grief every live long day. But I'm puzzled. Why would the Lord punish Ma and that little hope of a baby stead a me? I'm the one who shoulda got kilt or got struck blind. I look up at Pa, who acts like he don't know I'm here. I hold the dead bunny in one hand and try to take Pa's hand for comfort, but he don't take mine back.

Over the rise, Aunt Beulah comes marching in a flurry, and Uncle Bud behind, and the midwife from Baines Creek that Ma don't have need for. All of em is led by Ruth, who looks older than she did this morning. Nobody looks my way. They hurry to the cabin with mighty purpose, go inside, and commence to wailing over the dead.

CHAPTER 3
LUCY: LEGEND

Daddy signed the honey deal on May twenty-seventh, but Mama writes the letters to our soldier men. She doesn't trust Daddy to plead with Everett and Wade to come home, so she works to find the right words. Words that won't be censored in V-mail. She pours out a mama's love that will be seen by a stranger, copied on microfilm, flown to foreign lands, and printed off again. The letters will reach Everett and Wade in as little as two weeks. The next morning, she kisses the envelopes and hands them to me to take to the mailbox and pull up the flag of hope. Daddy doesn't ask what she wrote.

The next Saturday at first light, I help Mama load the truck with honey, eggs, and extra produce for market. Our customers know our honey supply has been cut down, so the selling won't take long. We'll make government money, but some folks will have to drink bitter tea and eat cake flavored with sorghum molasses.

Cora and Lydia stay home with Helen, and Daddy and Grady are in the fields, and Irene is already in town working, so it's only Mama and me pulling out of the driveway, crossing the bridge over the Roanoke River, past the Majestic where the much-anticipated *Lassie Come Home* starts today, past the Hollingston Pharmacy and Soda Fountain, the courthouse where on hot days you can chip ice off the block that sits in the shade under a tarp, and the *Mercer County Reporter,* where my sister Irene works. A small library is tacked on back, which Miz Elvira, the librarian, oversees. We cut down River Road to the docks and farmers market held on Saturday mornings. I heard somewhere that my town has five thousand citizens living within its confines, but I think some folks must have been counted twice or even three times. It's only at the opening of tobacco market that starts in late August and runs six weeks that my town swells with importance. Still, it holds six churches that maintain distinctions people love to debate.

Our market table is in the shade, and I'm lining the jars neatly when Tiny Junior shows up. He's a hard worker with a sweet disposition but a simple mind. He won't take pay for helping because his heart is pure. Today, Tiny Junior helps me unload the truck, then we sit on two weathered stools and watch the crowd grow. I slip him a new pack of Black Jack licorice gum Daddy bought for him. It's his favorite.

"Do you know chewing gum comes from the sapodilla tree? The gummy resin is called *chicle*. So you've got a tree in Central America to thank for your chewing gum."

Tiny Junior grins.

Though it has been nine days since Oma passed, Mama still collects condolences. Miz Elvira shops early so she can open the library at ten, and she's the first of a dozen who speaks kindly of Oma who stayed a foreigner all her days. She pickled everything and skewed her words peculiar. She was a gloriously odd soul, and I loved everything about her except when she'd poot in her sleep and smell of sauerkraut. The older she got, the more she pooted, the more she slept alone.

Another fascinating soul is Trula Freed, the consummate enigma of Mercer County, a mystery who is making her way among the market stalls on the far side. She is a butterfly among common houseflies. Tall and graceful, she carries her sweetgrass basket on her skinny arm that holds a dozen gold bangles. I wish she'd come to our table so I could study her up close. Today, she wears a long dress in purples and blues and an orange turban wrapped around her head. Gold hoops hang from sagging earlobes. Her skin is as smooth as an egg and her eyes the green of a regal feline. Everything about Trula Freed is rich and exotic. When she casts her glance my way across the crowd, I duck my chin and my cheeks flush. Mama doesn't allow Trula Freed's name to be spoken under our roof for reasons I honor but cannot fathom. The woman's magnetic pull is palpable.

Mama taps my shoulder so I stop daydreaming and help Violet Crumbie. The brim of Miz Violet's tattered straw hat is cocked over one side of her face to shield it. I'm shocked to see a nasty bruise and a split in her lip. One hand rests protectively on her pregnant belly and the other trembles when she picks up a jar of honey. "How much?" she whispers.

Before I can say, her husband, Larry Crumbie, wrenches her wrist. "Put It Down," he orders, and she obeys, docile as a child.

They turn away, but Mama picks up the jar and heads after Miz Violet. "Wait," she calls out and presses the jar into the shy woman's hand, saying, "It's a gift. Please take it. It's good to see you at market."

She doesn't even look at Larry Crumbie, and that doesn't sit well with him. He grabs the jar and says, "We don't take charity," and he hurls that pint of precious honey on the ground. The bottle shatters and honey splatters. Tiny Junior stoops and picks up the glass, and a mutt dog sleeping in the shade ambles over to lap up the sweet, shards and all.

I can't help myself but blurt, "Do you know that it took the labor of twenty thousand bees to make that one jar of honey?"

Larry Crumbie shoots a mean look at me, obviously not caring for knowledge or a girl speaking outright.

Mama pats my arm to calm me. She got talked to rudely, but my heart breaks extra for Miz Violet. To my way of thinking, Larry Crumbie is the worst kind of fancy man. A showy man who wears ironed shirts and pomade in his hair. Now that his wife is in the family way, instead of being kind and considerate to her, he's turned extra spiteful. I'm glad Mama was nice to her. Maybe that counted for something.

We sell out of eggs and honey and head home early because it's picture show day. The humid air from the open windows lifts the hair off my damp neck. I hear Mama sniffling. "What is it?" I say. "It's not that Larry Crumbie, is it?"

"No, no," she says.

"Is it worry for Miz Violet?" I try again. "There's nothing you can do for her really," I say like I know what I'm talking about.

When I say Oma's name, Mama nods, wipes her runny nose on her forearm, and gives me a watery smile. I miss my grandmother, too. She was wrinkled and wore flowered scarves tied under her floppy chin. She was soft and squishy and smelled of lilac powder she got every birthday and caraway used in cooking. With Oma gone, Mama needs something new and promising in her life.

I need something new and promising, too, and I think an enigma like Trula Freed might be just the thing to hone my empirical thinking.

As fate would have it, the very next week, our paths cross.

When Assassin gets set on fire.

CHAPTER 4
BERT: EXILED

The week after Ma and the baby get buried in the Tucker cemetery, Pa says he's sending me away. He got a letter from his sister Violet, who lives clear cross North Carolina. I don't recollect ever meeting his sister Violet, but Pa says she's kin and in the family way and needs help, so I'm going. He found money for a one-way ticket on a bus outta Asheville that leaves at first light. He let Violet know I'm coming so the deed is done and I don't have no say. I thought bout running away and living in the woods, but that would hurt Pa to have to look for me. He can't help if he's got a wayward girl. All the same, my heart aches.

When can I come home? I wanna know, riding that goodbye journey in the truck that bounces over ruts, with Pa looking straight ahead and his jaw set hard. We go down, down the mountainside, and the chill leaves the air, and the air turns mild and buildings grow close, then rise up, and electric lights on the hard road chase the dark away cause we're in Asheville. Pa's a shy man so it's me who asks strangers for the way to the bus station, and we find it.

How you gonna know I'm okay? I wanna know before I climb the three steps into the belly of the bus, hugging my paper satchel holding clothes and my treasure box, but I don't wanna sound weak.

You gonna miss me? I wanna know but don't say. I go to the dim back of the bus to sit beside an old lady with dark skin, but she says, "Your kind gotta sit in front of that line," and she points to a faded mark on the floor. I hurry to find another seat quick and look out the window, hoping to catch sight of Pa looking back waving, but he's already going back to where we come from.

My punishment is exile from my homeland — like the Nation of Israelites in the Old Testament. It's what happens when you disobey and disrespect. The Lord keeps score. Exile is worse than being dead or struck blind. I hold back my tears. I gotta turn brave.

CHAPTER 5
LUCY: OUR ASS

Mama pulls in the yard and toots the horn for Lydia and Cora to run to the truck. Every boy and girl in Riverton is buying matinee tickets at the Majestic for *Lassie Come Home,* because yesterday, Friday, June fourth, school let out for the summer. Lassie is the reward for finishing another year.

The crowd stretches clear down the block, past the Hollingston Pharmacy and Soda Fountain and the *Mercer County Reporter.* Grady and his best friend, Ricky Miller, got here early and bought enough tickets for Lydia, Cora, and me, so we head to the shorter line for folks with tickets. I walk past the Turner girls, and May Beth Johnson and Jeannie Branch, who live beside each other and gossip as much as old biddies. Today they shoot dirty looks at me because they're jealous. I have a guaranteed seat when the first-run tickets sell out. Cora, Lydia, and I stand next to the boys, waiting our turn, but I'll sit between my sisters so I'm not caught beside Ricky. In the lobby, Ricky buys popcorn and jujubes and a giant Sugar Daddy sucker because his daddy owns the gas station and makes more money than a farmer and beekeeper does. I buy one bag of popcorn to share with my sisters.

In the low light, we find good seats, eat our popcorn one piece at a time to make it last, watch the seats fill, and wait for the velvet curtain to slide back. We watch the newsreel about the faraway war that rages, and like always, I look hard to catch a glimpse of Everett or Wade. We see our president riding in a car, waving to a crowd, and watch the next installment of Flash Gordon, where destruction of Earth is imminent. But today it's Lassie we've come to see.

I cry when that sweet dog gets taken way from Joe and sold to the Duke. I cry with happiness when the beautiful Elizabeth Taylor helps Lassie escape and begin the arduous journey home across rough and unfamiliar land. I cry when Lassie is *finally* reunited with the people she loves. Finding your way home is a good and necessary thing. I think I see Grady get emotional, but I don't embarrass him. I don't even look at Ricky.

Later, back at the house, all us moviegoers sit on the porch with the rest of the family and retell the Lassie story and the magical marvel of Technicolor. Sugar Mayhew from across the way is there, too — she's a year younger than me. My words and Grady's overlap talking about the craggy landscape of Scotland and a dog as exceptional as Lassie. Sugar pretends she doesn't care one whit about missing the movie, but she missed a good one.

When we start repeating ourselves, Mama says, "Who wants lemonade?" and hands shoot up and I go inside and help her, and the others draw circles in the yard and drop to a knee to play marbles in the dirt because everybody loves marbles. Lydia and Cora divvy up their marbles so Sugar can play with them. Each of us Browns has a sack of marbles we usually carry in our pockets for playing plus our own mason jar full of well-used glass and clay marbles, but the best ones made by our German great-great-grandfather live in a padded box in Mama's bedroom. She says, "Y'all shoot rough with marbles, and you've got plenty to play with. Leave the good ones alone."

I come out with a tray of lemonade, and right off, Ricky Miller vies for my attention.

He tosses marbles in the air and deftly catches a dozen in his mouth and almost chokes on that many, but I turn my back on him and pay him no mind. He's always desperate for me to notice him because I never do, but what he does next is excessive to the extreme: he injures my favorite mule when Assassin's minding his own business.

That rapscallion lights a dried corncob, and when the mule is drinking at the trough, Ricky holds the flame under Assassin's tail. The hairs ignite, and the mule kicks Ricky into kingdom come, and Assassin takes off running across the field, tail on fire and me running after him, leaving sweet lemonade and marble playing, and running till my lungs almost burst. When the mule stops, the fire is out but his pitiful tail is scorched something terrible. I gasp for air and the mule breathes heavy, too. I look around and get goose bumps.

He ran to Trula Freed's yard!

What a strange and wonderful serendipity that the woman who is the pinnacle of my curiosity is in such close proximity. A voodoo goddess with unknown ancestry. A gypsy queen everybody reveres or fears. It was just two days back I was at Aunt Fanniebelle Hollingston's mansion — she's my rich relative who owns half the town and buys the newest Nancy Drew book for me. I was taking etiquette lessons Mama declared I needed, and I was the only one attending that day because Mildred and Peggy Turner said they were sick, but they fabricate excuses all the time. It was only Aunt Fanniebelle and me with Uncle Nigel off doing errands, and because my aunt is more open-minded than Mama, I took the liberty of saying Trula Freed's name out loud to see what would happen. She said, "That woman is not of this world, Lucy. She might be the most important friend a person could have."

My skin tingled with anticipation. "You know her?" I said, pouring tea from a china pot to the appointed depth in our cups.

"Known her all my life, child."

"Have you been to her place?"

"*Many* times."

I dropped a sugar cube in my tea and placed a cookie on my Wedgwood dish and carefully said, "What's she like?"

My aunt leaned in and whispered though it was only the two of us there. "I'll tell you a story, but you can't tell your mama. She's set her mind to dislike Trula Freed because the woman can't be explained. You're smarter than that, aren't you?"

I nodded my complicity but kept my composure.

"Trula Freed wasn't born around these parts. She was born in that other Carolina in the low country on a coast that's hotter than here."

My aunt's iridescent fan flipped open and fluttered like hummingbird wings.

"I believe her bloodline is a wonderful concoction of gypsy, Cajun, or Lumbee but wouldn't swear to any of that, because it's not important. What is important is to know Trula's mama found her way back to her own mama here in Mercer County, so at one time, three generations of women lived together off Davenport Road. There's never been a man associated with the women, although one had to be involved now and again. It's where Trula lives today, but it's changed past recognizing.

"That girl brought something unique with her, and that gift was revealed one day when she shocked unsuspecting folks and made a powerful friend. You see, the girl Trula had gone to town with her granny and was waiting in the mercantile store. With arms by her sides, she eyed the jars of penny candy when the judge's wife, Mavis Beecham, came in to pick up special-order fabric. Miz Beecham said hello to Trula and told her she looked pretty in her blue dress. That was when Trula lifted her hand and laid it on Miz Beecham's flat belly and said, *You got two baby girls in there.*

"The judge's wife near bout fainted and had to grab holt of the counter to stop from sinking to her knees. She gave Trula the strangest look and fled the store in a flurry. Miz Wilson, the store owner, said, *Lord'a mercy, child, what a terrible thing to say,* cause she knew Miz Beecham had birthed three stillborn babies and was out of hope of becoming a mama. The store owner took Trula by the shoulders and guided her out the door and told her not to bother the customers, then she ran after Miz Beecham.

"After that day, Trula's granny didn't take her to town. The girl stayed out of sight while Miz Beecham loosened the seams in her dresses and Doc Parker confirmed she was with child. The nervous waiting began. Seven months to the day after Trula's prophecy, twin girls were born. Mavis Beecham was overjoyed but also mystified at the foretelling.

"On a chilly day, a month after her babies were born, a handsome horse and buggy pulled up to the shack where Trula lived. The rich woman knocked on the flimsy door. *I'm looking for the girl,* she said with

47

arms full of packages and a small dress made from special-order fabric. Miz Beecham brought gifts that day, but more importantly, she brought *respect* to Trula. She saw the girl as a messenger from God, and their friendship saved Trula from being misunderstood. Instead there came knocks in the night and truth declared and payment received. The roof got new tin. Glass window-panes and white painted boards set Trula's house apart from other shacks. But it was her red door with a brass doorknob that locked that proclaimed this was the home of an important person."

Today, I'm looking at that red door. A yellow dog rests beside it. At my coming, he raises his head with mild curiosity. The door is partly open, and a voice I've only heard from a distance calls out, "Come in, girls." It's an accent different from soft Southern. It carries power. But *girls?* I hear the patter of running feet and turn to see Cora.

I whisper harsh, "What in blue blazes are you doing here? Does Mama know?"

I'm where I shouldn't be, and Cora's here, too.

Cora is the sister we got at church eight years back when a missionary brought her before the congregation saying she was in need of a family. The baby girl was pale as an angel, pure as spun sugar. Today, after all that running from home to here, Cora's face is as calm as the moon. There's not a drop of sweat on her alabaster brow.

"Come in, children," the voice calls out again. "For medicine for the mule. My feet be swoll today."

Assassin turns his big head toward the door and ambles over like he understands. I take Cora's hand and yank it hard because I'm miffed at her, and we follow behind the pitiful tail that hangs limp. The mule stops at the open red door, and I lean inside. I squint against the glow of yellows and melon and plank walls the color of pearls. The room appears to have its own light source.

"Hey," I say, shy.

The skinny woman sits in a high-backed chair. She's not wearing her usual turban, and her white hair is cropped short. Bare feet are propped up on a needlepoint footstool. Her ankles are indeed swollen, and her thin arm with those gold bracelets motions me inside, jangling like a wind chime. She points to a cupboard of polished wood.

"He need help. Top shelf."

Cora walks in easy as punch while I go to the cupboard. I open the doors to a lacquered red interior the color of the Chinese music box in Aunt Fanniebelle's curio cabinet. Out drifts lemon, mint, salt, vinegar, and the metallic whiff of blood. In the middle is a line of matching bottles labeled *Stump*, *Ditch*, *Willow*, *Lightning*, and *Urine*. Baskets of tiny silk bags tied with ribbons and dried roots are in orderly rows.

"Darrrk honey," the witchy woman says, rolling her *r*'s. "Top rrright."

Reluctantly, my fingers glide past the silk bags and clay pots with cork stoppers. Past bundles of dried herbs to the top shelf of honey jars that start on one end clear as spring water then darken to black. I stand on tiptoes and grab the farthest jar, careful to hold it tight. It looks more like molasses than honey.

"Great healer, black honey. From wild carrot but not from here. Pour on his tail. Don't be stingy, Lucy Brown." My skin tingles hearing my name spoken by Trula Freed.

I step out of the golden room with its own light, back into the soft Carolina pines that cast shadows on the smooth dirt yard. Assassin waits while I coat his injured tail. He doesn't flick it or stomp his foot in impatience; only the skin on his back ripples in acknowledgment of my touch. It's like he knows the honey will help. Some of the sweetness drips on the ground, and the yellow dog saunters over and licks it up. When the deed is done, half the black honey has been used. I rinse my sticky hands in the wash bucket at the door, wipe them on my overalls, and step back inside.

"He need once more tomorrow. But come. Let's visit like friends we can be."

Cora already sits relaxed in one of the silk-brocade chairs like I've seen at Aunt Fanniebelle's. She swings her white legs beneath her red polka-dot dress that used to be mine. I pass a quick eye over the place I could never have imagined. A place filled with precious things as special as her name. The white open shelves hold delicate figurines and quartz crystals and a line of ancient books with gilded spines held upright by jade bookends. I read the name *Plato* on one end and *Da Vinci* on the other.

The old woman says to Cora, "This for your eyes," and pulls me away from my scrutiny. She has given Cora a tiny tube of ointment and a pair of child-sized tinted glasses. My skin crawls. This is plain spooky. How would Trula Freed know Cora would have a condition that makes her pale eyes sensitive? And how did she know Cora would arrive on her doorstep today? Is this black magic? Maybe Mama doesn't like her because the woman intuits the impossible.

"What's in that stuff?" I take the ointment from Cora's hand and smell.

"Herbs to soothe. Castor oil, mint. Only good." Her voice is as soothing as the herbs and the oil, and I look into her green eyes and tumble through space though I hold on to Cora's brocade chair. The ten-dollar word for Trula Freed is *arcane*. The mystery of her can't be easily understood. She is as rare as the balm of Gilead.

But today, I don't take this chance to know her better. I break the spell because I fear Mama's consequences more than the answers I seek. "We gotta go," I say and reach for Cora's arm and pull her to standing, sad we can't eat the sweet treats I see and hear our good fortunes told, but I've got to get Cora back home. Will Mama believe I came here by accident? Will she believe Cora followed me without invitation?

In the dimming afternoon light, we march away from the cottage that tugs at me to *Come back, don't go, stay.* My mule follows with his head hanging low. I'm in a tizzy thinking in two directions: how to understand the puzzle of Trula Freed that's thicker than before, and what lie can I conjure to get out of trouble for coming here. I'm not a good liar and that's my downfall. When I tell a lie, I stumble over words midway and look culpable — sometimes without good reason. On the walk back, I practice how to begin. *Mama, you won't believe what happened today,* I might say and watch her face and hope for curiosity. Or maybe I'll state the obvious. *Assassin needed my help, so I didn't have a choice* and see if shifting the blame works.

Cora wears her tinted glasses when we get home, but there's nobody in the yard to bear witness. They're all on the back side of the barn, looking at the litter of piglets the sow birthed at an auspicious moment. The next morning, I pour the rest of the black honey on Assassin's tail, rinse out the jar, and hide it among our empties. Before the day is over, Cora loses her tinted glasses. She asks me where they could be, and I say *What glasses?* ashamed of my deception. She doesn't ask again.

CHAPTER 6
BERT: BUS RIDE

I never been on a bus, and it scares me riding fast down roads I never seen before. How am I supposed to find my way back home? Me and my big talk bout going places, wanting different, wanting more. It's hard to breathe with that strip of cloth wrapped round my middle. I sit on the edge of the seat and put my forehead against the cool window.

The man beside me says, "You want the window open, miss? Let me help." He reaches over, slides that window up, and fresh air rushes in with smells of rubber and gasoline and bread baking. It blows my hair back and dries my tears. I put my elbows on the window frame and watch people walking hither and yon on paved paths. A little boy on a bicycle waves at me and I wave back. A black dog chases the bus for fun, his tail up and his tongue out, loping along till he quits.

We pass the stink of manure from cows and hogs grazing in fields, then the hills grow soft. The man sitting next to me taps my shoulders. "Want half?" He points to his biscuit with jam. When I nod, he breaks it in two. I missed breakfast this morning cause my belly hurt and my thinking wasn't right.

"My wife made it," he says. "She always sends me off with a biscuit to make sure I don't starve." He grins and his teeth stick out, but he's got nice eyes. I bet he's got a nice wife.

On most days, I can talk your ear off, but today I ain't in a talking mood, and the man beside me lets me be with my thoughts. My spirit rises with the sun, and I start looking at the new world in a good way. I'm flying down the road to somewhere a long way from where I come. Part of my heart cries cause there's only Pa and Ruth at the cabin now, but part of my heart flies high. "What day is today?" I ask the man, cause it's a big day for change, and he says it's June second. I'm gonna remember this day.

Before the trip hardly gets going, the man says, "This here coming up is where I get off. Nice meeting you," and he stands and pulls his case off the top shelf, and when the bus stops he gets off. A pregnant lady with chestnut-colored skin gets on holding a cardboard box tied with twine. She struggles down the aisle, and I go to help her haul her things, half dragging it, and whisper, "You can sit with me," but a man says, "Coloreds in back behind the white line." The woman smiles sad and thanks me for my help.

I'm looking out the window thinking bout that faded line painted on the bus floor when another man comes down the aisle jostling from side to side, and plops down next to me. "Hey, pretty lady. What's your name," he says and makes my skin itch. When I don't say or look his way, he says, "You ever seen a two-headed coin?" and like the fool, I look, cause I ain't never seen a two-headed coin.

He's got hairy hands, and the edges of his fingernails are black. "See, there's a head on this side and a head on the other. Must have been an accident cause I never seen another one, have you? Want to hold it?" I shake my head. He says, "It's your loss. I'm not gonna push you but I bet you'll never see another two-headed coin."

And like a fool again, I hold out my hand. He presses it into my palm and holds it for too long, and my skin itches some more. I give it back to him and go to looking out the window. At the next stop, the driver tells us we'll be here fifteen minutes, and we can buy lunch at the diner. I don't have money, so I stay in my seat. The man with the two-headed coin gets off and goes in the diner and comes out carrying a paper poke. He sits beside me again and drops in my lap a sandwich wrapped in wax paper and a chocolate Moon Pie. "Hope you like egg salad," he says. "Figured you were a Moon Pie kind of girl."

I let em stay there, not liking that he touched the paper but liking that it's egg salad and Moon Pie. When he puts his head back on the seat, I think he's sleeping, and I open the sandwich real quiet. Without opening his eyes, he says, "Thought you was hungry."

I eat it fast and ball up the paper and stick the Moon Pie in my paper poke. He says, "Didn't your mama teach you better manners? You gonna thank me for thinking of you?" and now my skin don't itch. It burns.

I whisper, "Thank you," cause Ma did teach me manners.

He whispers back, "Let's have us some fun." His arm pushes me back in the seat and he goes to rubbing between my legs with his hairy hand. I shock him when I bite his bare arm and draw blood. He elbows

CHAPTER 7
LUCY: BEST FRIEND

I'm besotted with the mystery of Trula
Freed, and Nancy Drew is partly to blame.
Aunt Fanniebelle started it when she gave
me the first six Nancy Drew books that her
daughter Patricia cast off. Some of the
spines weren't even cracked open, so I know
my older cousin wasn't as bewitched as I
am over Nancy Drew's detective proficien-
cies. Now my aunt buys the newest ones
direct from Grosset & Dunlap publishing
house. The books with the full-color covers,
wrapped in brown paper and tied with
twine, come as special delivery to her front
door. The next day, she brings them to me.
The latest is *The Quest of the Missing Map.*
Number nineteen. For all her etiquette lessons and lace-collared dresses, my aunt
understands the desires hidden in my quix-
otic heart, for mysteries are everywhere —
the magic of Trula Freed, Cora Brown's
pale condition, the crisp on Mama's lacy

cornbread, and the lost city of Atlantis, to name a few. It was Socrates who said *To know is to know you know nothing;* I aim to know something.

I have a lot in common with Nancy Drew besides my clever mind: my hometown of Riverton sounds like her hometown of River Heights. My name, Lucy Brown, has the same number of syllables and letters as her name. Nancy is only three years older than me, and her father thinks she's brilliant. She drives a blue roadster. She faces danger with alacrity. *Alacrity* is one of Nancy's favorite words, so it's mine, too. We face challenges with eagerness.

It is into this wishful world of mystery that my new best friend comes the second Sunday in June. I'm sitting on the bridge that spans the Roanoke River because it's cooler here with the flow of water that stirs the humid air beneath my feet. I'm reading *The Secret of the Old Clock* for the third time when the clock at First Methodist Church strikes four, and at that precise moment, a stranger's shadow falls across my open book. I look up and shield my eyes against the bright.

First thing the stranger says in a dialect different from here is, "I'm gonna travel the world someday. I'm gonna fly in one of

60

them air-o-planes and ride on trains and boats that cross the sea." She plops down next to me on the bridge, and our bare legs swing in unison. "I'm gonna drive my own automobile, too," is how she concludes that introduction.

She declares her name is Allie Bert Tucker but that she only answers to Bert. I tell her Nancy Drew has a best friend with a boy's name, too. A girl she calls George. When I say my name is Lucy Brown, Bert sticks out her hand, grips mine firm, and says, "Glad to meet you, Lu."

And just like that, my whole world changes.

Bert Tucker goes on to say that first day that when she has babies, she's gonna name them places she travels to, like Paris and London and Nova Scotia. I tell her I hope she's not going to Amsterdam, and that makes us giggle so hard we almost pee our pants. I set my book aside and grab her hand, and together we slide off the bridge into the river and come up still giggling over Amsterdam. I invite the stranger to supper, and she comes home with me like she was meant to, us looking like drowned rats smelling of creosote from the bridge and rotten eggs from the fertilizer plant upriver.

When we walk up the porch steps, I hold

out an arm to stop Bert and warn her that we're bibliophiles. She says she doesn't mind cause her folks are Primitive Baptist. I say, "No, silly. Bibliophiles love books. Daddy got his family's book collection when most everybody except him died of influenza in 1918. That tragedy was the start of our library, but we add to it all the time. Daddy says it's money well-spent if a book broadens your mind."

When Bert walks into our home, my new friend is stopped still. She stares at the bank of tall bookcases on two walls holding our family's library, alphabetized by authors. She runs her fingers along the spines in neat lines, and I declare, "These books are your ticket to the great mysteries of the world, Bert Tucker. You can read any one you want while you're here, but wash your hands first. That's Daddy's rule we abide by." I see deepened respect on Bert's face.

"Every Wednesday evening when the weather's fair, we have story time for anybody who wants to come. They sit on the porch or in the yard and listen to tales we take turns telling. And once a year, we have a birthday party for a special book Oma gave us." I babble on. "It's *The Velveteen Rabbit,* and she even made a stuffed rabbit to go with it."

Bert's eyes glide from the books to the sheet music and the battered case for the guitar and one for the fiddle lying on top of the upright piano that's missing some of its ivories. Large maps of the United States and of the world hang above the piano. Hundreds of pins mark places we read about. When her eyes slide to the doorway and she catches sight of my ghostly sister Cora, she grins and whispers, "Y'all are different enough."

My new best friend sits in Oma's empty place, and my siblings take turns drilling her while she eats fried chicken and lacy cornbread and tries pickled okra for the first time. She tells us in her wordy way that she's living at her aunt Violet's place, helping her get ready for the baby though she's never seen one birthed. Mama catches my eye, because Violet and Larry Crumbie are not a happy family. I feel a rush of apprehension for my friend.

Bert's dialect murders the King's English and her table manners are atrocious, but nobody calls her out because we want to hear what she says. Even my older sister Irene, who works at the newspaper, listens without her usual disdain. Bert is a revelation that brings a welcome spark to our boring days.

She came to Riverton on June second from the other side of North Carolina. Rode a Trailways bus by herself that stopped nine or ten times at places like Mocksville and Graham and Cary. Uniformed soldiers were everywhere, some leaving home, some coming home missing pieces of their bodies, taking up nearly every seat on the bus. Said she could tell the worn-out ones from the fresh. Mama and my sister Helen's faces cloud over with talk about injured soldiers. Our thoughts are never far from Helen's husband, Wade Sully, and my big brother Everett, who we desperately want to come home and work the hives. We don't know if Mama's words of persuasion did the deed.

"We don't got wet heat back where I come from like y'all got here," Bert says fanning her face with her hand. Oma complained the same way about our summer heat.

"Where I'm from, folks still sleep under quilts at night and frost can sparkle on the mountains in the mornings."

Little Lydia says, "Oma came from tall mountains but she's dead" and goes back to eating peas one at a time.

I clarify. "Oma was our grandma. She was born in the Black Forest of Germany and lived with us all my days till she died. You're sitting in her place."

Filling such an important seat doesn't seem to intimidate Bert. Without pause, she says, "I don't know bout no black forest but all the same I come from tall mountains. We got panthers and black bears and eagles. Mountains rise up so high that some days they disappear in the clouds. If you was to climb to the top, y'all could wash your hands in a cloud. Dirt slides right off. Don't need no soap."

"You're lying," Grady mutters, because Bert's words are starting to sound like bragging, and that doesn't sit well with my brother.

Mama says, "Son, don't be rude. Have you been to the western side of our state?" and Grady shakes his head, embarrassed. "Then show Bert the respect she deserves."

Lydia says, "I'm four, almost five. Do y'all have wolpertingers there?" barely getting her lips around the multiple syllables. She adds, "We got a dead one in our attic."

Bert looks confused, shakes her head, and turns quiet, likely from Grady's hurtful remark or maybe her puzzlement over wolpertingers. She lets us quibble among ourselves, trying to impress her, when the cuckoo clock does the job for us. Her fork stops midway to her mouth, and she says, "What in blue blazes."

"It's our cuckoo clock," Lydia pipes up again.

"How'd it do that trick, popping out like that?"

I explain, "Springs and weights, Oma said. It was made a long time back by Hubert Herr from Bavaria. We wind it on Sunday mornings, and it keeps time all week."

"Well, I'll be . . ." Bert takes the last of her biscuit and wipes every trace of food off her plate. She helps clear the table and does the dishes. I scrape, she washes, I dry. The rest of the family heads to the porch to make butter from clabber and hear the next chapter of tonight's book. The porch is quiet except for Mama's voice. Bert wants to know what she's saying.

"She's reading *Twenty Thousand Leagues Under the Sea,* chapter four, I think. I already finished the whole book. It's a grand adventure about the *Nautilus* and Captain Nemo."

"They from these parts?"

"No, silly. Jules Verne *wrote* the book. Made it up from his imagination. He lived across the Atlantic Ocean in France in the seaport town of Nantes. We put a pin on the map close to where it is. Nantes would make a lovely name for one of your girls."

"You believe that stuff I say? Bout traveling to them places? Bout having babies I give pretty names to?"

"Why wouldn't I? You already rode a bus clear cross North Carolina. I don't know any lone girl who's done that."

Arms in suds up to her elbows, Bert grins lopsided and nods to the window ledge. "What's all them blue jars for?"

I whisper, "Vicks VapoRub. Daddy uses it for *everything.* Colds, bug bites, cuts, bee stings, dry skin, bruises, headaches, sore muscles. He goes through a *lot* of Vicks. Mama says it's his man perfume. The jars are too nice to throw away. Now they hold dried herbs and seeds and odd buttons."

"I thought I smelled something besides supper when I come in. Aunt Violet's got tins of Dapper Dan pomade. Says the pomade keeps Larry Crumbie's hair in place. He don't come home since I been there."

I say, "I saw him at market a week back," and drop my voice. "I don't understand how your aunt Violet and Larry Crumbie ended up together. They're as different as chalk and cheese, her being meek and him being of an angry nature."

"Pa said her being twenty-seven with no prospect in sight must a been the cause for her to latch on to Larry. He likely latched

67

on to her cause she had a farm deeded to her. All I know is that the days I been there, Larry Crumbie don't come home. My aunt's pitiful lost without him."

We finish the dishes in silence, me wanting to correct her grammar when Bert switches gears on me. "Your mama sure is a good cook. That was the best food I ever ate."

"Daddy says she can make sawdust taste delicious with enough crackling and butter."

"He's right."

"Your mama must be a good cook, too," I say to include Bert in the compliment, not thinking I was trespassing where I shouldn't. Her face scrunches up and her nose turns red and her shoulders slide up. She's *crying*.

I whisper, "What'd I say?" wishing I could take back what it was.

With poor timing, Mama yells from the porch, "You girls finish up. Bert needs to head on home to make it before dark."

My friend wipes her runny nose on her arm and yells back all composed, "Yes 'um."

Mama adds, "You stay here, Lucy. You'll see Bert another time."

I whisper again, "What'd I say?" as I hang the drying towel on the hook, but Bert shakes her head and sets her jaw in a way

I'll come to know as her *not ready to talk* look.

We come out on the porch, and Mama has her finger in the book holding her place. She says, "You know the way?"

"Do I walk the road or can I cut through the field?"

Mama points to the pine grove on the far side of tobacco. "It's quicker to cut through that way. You'll meet the road the Crumbie farm is on. Turn right and you'll be there before the sun sets good. Is everything okay over there?"

"Yes 'um. Thank you for the good supper."

"You're welcome here anytime."

I say, "Larry Crumbie hasn't been home since Bert came," knowing that's a good thing. The worry lines between Mama's eyes soften but don't go away. Bert and I step off the porch, and Mama starts reading again.

I walk Bert to the edge of the yard, past the line of beehives that have gone quiet for the night. She holds out her hand and shakes mine firm. "Good meeting you, Lu" are my new best friend's parting words, and I want to hug her but I don't. I want to know what made her cry, for tears coming that fast are a sign of trouble. I want to know she's going to be safe in a mean man's house. Instead I watch her walk into the June tobacco field. She turns around twice to wave farewell.

Like she knows I'll stand there and watch her go.

Till I can't see her anymore.

CHAPTER 8
BERT: EVERYTHING

Crickets, katydids, and tree frogs start their racket when I step off the heat of the field into the cool of the pines. I look back at Lu Brown standing on the other side in a patch of light. She's the luckiest girl I ever seen and likely don't know it. Why she took a shine to me I don't got a clue. They talk smart and got everything a soul could want — vittles, music, books, family. I like that ghost girl. She's got pink eyes.

I want what they got but I'm tainted. I finger the black button I stole. It was sitting on the windowsill, and it come from Miz Brown's housedress, the button at the neck. It was dangling by a thread when she snapped it off and set it on the sill for safekeeping. I snatched it when everybody went to the porch and Lu wiped crumbs off the table. Now it's mine. It'll go in my treasure box cause Miz Brown touched it. She's likely got more buttons in her sewing basket with proper thread and needles.

I walk on soft ground through tall pines, jump over the ditch onto the dirt road that takes me back to my aunt's place. My feet drag and my heart hurts for the difference between where I been and where I'm goin.

I don't say to the Browns that when I come off the bus in Riverton with my body and heart as empty as a June bug shell, nobody was at the station to fetch me. I sat waiting, hungry and parched, needing to relieve myself. The ticket man was locking the station door when he saw me and said, "Who you waitin on, girl?"

I said back, "Violet Crumbie. She be my aunt on my pa's side. I'm here on account of her having a baby."

The man took pity on me, drove me out to the farm, and left me in the yard. I knocked on the screen door for the longest time before my aunt showed her fat-bellied self. She said, "What business you got here? I got no handouts," like my coming was a surprise. In truth, we was strangers to each other. I didn't recollect what she looked like, and she didn't know me neither.

"I'm Bert. Your niece," I say. When she don't answer, I say louder, "My name is Allie Bert Tucker. Pa sent me. Your brother.

He wrote you a letter saying I was coming today."

She said, "I don't get no letter" but stepped closer to me. "Brother sent you? Why don't he tell me?" She unhooked the screen door, looking round for the boogey-man. "I reckon it's okay. Larry'll be home any minute from fishing. You can't stay here when he gits home. Larry don't abide out-siders."

That was my welcome to her house. It was as dirty a place as I ever did see. I held my breath for the stink. By oil lamp, I saw dishes piled in the sink, flies on spoiled food, soiled clothes on the floor. She went in her bedroom and shut the door. I put down my paper bag of belongings and got to cleaning.

This evening on day twelve since I come to Riverton, after meeting the luckiest girl in the world and eating at her fine table, I call out when I get back, "Anybody here?" but nobody answers. I head to the room where I been staying with its iron bed, stained mattress, bare walls, and a window that don't open. I reach under the bed for my treasure box to put Miz Brown's black button for safekeeping when I hear, "Where you been?"

Aunt Violet scared me. She sneaked up

like a spook. I don't pull out my box. I push it back deep and stand up and look at her.

"At the Browns. Lu asked me to supper. They got a cuckoo clock that tells time all day long."

"You was at the Browns," she says like she woke up from a long sleep and got cobwebs in her head.

"Yes 'um. You hungry? Want somethin' to eat?"

Her face twists all catawampus. Her eyes dart to the ceiling for answers, then she says, "I used to know me some Browns but I don't recollect from where . . ." and with that, she steps outta my bedroom into hers and closes the door. Her house holds sticky heat and lonely smells no matter how hard I clean on it. I'm lonely here, too.

The dark of night settles in, and I stretch out on the bed in the shorts and shirt I wore all day, them holding traces of the river I jumped in. I finger the smooth black button that belongs to me now. I smell the button and it makes me think of fried chicken, okra and biscuits, and a cuckoo clock. I think I smell Miz Brown's kindness on that button.

This confounded heat makes a body feel like a slug with the backbone turning to jelly. In the dark, through thin walls, I hear Aunt Violet's mattress creak, and she calls out, "What you doing sneaking in like that? You look a fright and stink of fish. I bout give up on you, is what I done. You hungry?"

Her bedroom door opens, and I stay in my room cause this is her and Larry's business, though I don't hear him yet. He's one sneaky man coming in without making a sound. Is he gonna throw me out tonight? My belly cramps with worry. I listen hard for Larry's voice but don't hear him. I listen hard for his manly footsteps on floors.

It's only her voice I hear talking.

It's only her footsteps I hear shuffling down the hall.

Nobody's here but us two.

CHAPTER 9
LUCY: FAMILY

The next day, I'm in a pickle. Will Bert Tucker come back, go to the river where we met, or not come at all? When I hear a knock on the kitchen door, my heart gives a leap — but it's only Sugar Mayhew. Across her arms, she carries the parlor curtains she's washed and ironed for the fifty cents Mama left on the table. I follow and help her hang them, her being half a head shorter and a year younger than me. Today she doesn't wear her eyepatch like she should.

"What you looking hard at?" She flashes and her good eye glares at me while her lazy eye looks over my shoulder.

"Where's your eyepatch? In your pocket? If you don't wear your patch, you can't cure your amblyopia. You need adhesive tape?"

Sugar fusses straightening the curtains, but she won't answer my questions. Instead she wears an air of righteous indifference when I'm only trying to help. She heads to the back door, scoops up the two quarters on the table, and drops them in her pocket. At the last minute, I get brave enough to ask, "Can you help me make beds?" and that stops her.

"Why you always whine bout makin' beds?" she throws back at me. It's true she's heard me complain before, and she's a forthright girl not scared to say things when the grown-ups aren't here to witness her attitude. She lives in the house across the way with her daddy, Yancy Mayhew, and mama, Gertie. Her brother, Whiz, enlisted two years back. His formal name, William Mayhew, was printed on the front page of the *Mercer County Reporter,* along with five other colored boys who signed up. When Whiz was promoted from private second class to private first class, Gertie bragged on him, which was her right. All the Mayhews are people of quality — except Sugar and her sassiness.

I say like always, "The corners of the featherbeds are too heavy for me to lift," because they are.

"You best grow you some muscle, Lucy Brown. I got my own chores to do with daylight burning."

She rubs me raw, but I endure it. "It'll only take a minute," I fib, knowing it'll take more to make up five beds.

"Two," she counters, moving into negotiations.

"You'll help make two beds?"

"Two for two."

"You want *two marbles* for making two little beds?" The girl's small collection is growing, mostly because of me. Sugar turns to leave when I say, "I pick em. The beds and the marbles."

"Suit yourself but get a move on." She adds, "You a worrisome girl," sounding for all the world like a grown-up when she's but a girl herself. Sugar does not live up to her name.

We head to Mama and Daddy's room, fluff the feather pillows, and set them by the open window to air. I make light conversation, being friendly. "Do you know there are three hundred and twenty-five different kinds of hummingbirds in the world? They're the only birds that can't walk or hop. They only fly, and they can live up to twelve years."

Sugar gets on tippy-toes and smooths out the bottom muslin with her skinny arms, not caring a whit about the miracle of hummingbirds. She is tucking the top right corner in firm when a flat, square package falls out on the floor. It's a rubber wrapped in cellophane under Daddy's side of the mattress, something I've seen before, and I know it keeps babies away. Sugar picks it up, paying no mind, and slides it back under the mattress. Maybe her daddy has got the same thing on his side of the bed. She unfurls the top sheet and cracks it in the air, and it settles like a picnic blanket. Sugar makes this dreaded job look easy.

Without a curious glance around my parents' bedroom, she moves to Grady's, where his bed looks like a battle was fought and the sheets won. She snaps his bed in order with me a weak observer, then she leaves, carrying my two plainest marbles. I shout, "Thank you," and watch Sugar cross the yard with her head high, her boney shoulders back, and her stride long. She once told me that we were uppity rich white folks and she wasn't my maid and for me not to forget. I said I never think of her as my maid, that she was free to do what she wanted with her life, but the look on her face said different. She said, "You a blind fool, Lucy Brown."

I know some uppity white folks, but that's not us.

After Sugar leaves, I make the other beds, finish my chores while the sun slides west, and deliberate what I should do about Bert

Tucker, when it takes care of itself. She makes her way through the same tobacco field down a row that's been suckered, looking at her feet, watching for snakes. I wait in the shade of the oak tree.

Bert looks smaller than I recollect. Maybe it's because her wild hair is tamed under a brown bandanna and her shirt is too big. Maybe because the tobacco field is wide and she's but a flint of a figure. Despite looks, Bert Tucker is already a giant in my mind.

She walks up to me, and I turn shy. "Hey" is all I say before she starts.

"She bout worked me to death today cause she thinks Larry is for sure coming back from fishing in that Dismal Swamp, and this time, she wants him to stay home for a spell. Last thing I done was put on a mess of beans and ham hock with new potatoes, then she told me to skedaddle so she could clean herself up best she can. I was mighty glad to get outta there and extra glad to see you."

I grin, tickled, and say, "You sure keep a pile of words inside that mouth of yours." I take her hand and pull her toward the barn and into its shadowed interior with rough beams and dust mites and the pungent smells from stalls and tools and leather. We climb the worn ladder and work our way out to the open loft doors and the iron pulley to the bails of fresh hay. We sit with a plop. I pick a strand of hay and stick it between my lips. Bert does the same and leans back and puts her hands behind her head. I feel light-headed to see our bare feet side by side, almost the same size, with dirt around the toenails.

Bert says, "I never seen such a brood of brothers and sisters as you got. There's bodies *everywhere*. You ever get em mixed up? Forget their names?"

"No, silly. I can name my brothers and sisters."

"Let me hear," Bert challenges me, and I start at the top like I should, taking my time to help them stick in her memory.

"My big brother Everett's in the army, and we speculate he's to the east fighting Nazis since he speaks a little German because of Oma. Mama's got a picture of him in uniform she keeps on her bedside table if you want to see what he looks like. Everett tries to see humor in everything, and he closes every letter with a riddle I figure out right away, but it takes the others longer.

"Helen is next. She's twenty and married with a baby coming around Thanksgiving. Her husband, Wade, is in the Pacific, so she moved back home for comfort and to help at mealtimes. It's on account of Everett and Wade we got two blue stars in the front window that show our war sacrifice but hopefully not the ultimate one, the gold stars, if they die. Don't think Mama could survive getting a gold star. Two weeks back, Daddy signed a beeswax deal with the government that said our two army men could come home and work bees, but I don't think that's gonna happen. Daddy thinks civic pride will win out."

Bert looks perplexed at so much information, but that's okay. We've got all the time in the world for her to understand.

"Next is Irene who, at eighteen and a half, is old enough to court, but she's picky and hard to please and has a know-it-all side that gets tiring. Men are not beating a path to her door." I tell it like it is. "She works at the newspaper doing advertising work but wants to be a real reporter someday.

"Grady's the only boy living at home, and he's quiet enough. He's the one who called you out at supper but got a warning from Mama for being rude. He's almost sixteen to my thirteen —"

I pause and ask, "How old are you?"

"Thirteen."

"Me, too. When's your birthday?"

"January twenty-second."

"Mine is January twenty-ninth. We were born one week apart." I can't hardly breathe from such a propitious coincidence. "We're almost birthday sisters."

When I sit there like a bumpkin, Bert says, "Go on with the naming."

"Well, I'm number five, and you know my name is Lucy. Cora's next. She's the one with pale skin. She was an orphan in need of a family, and we all voted to turn her into a Brown. She's a thinking child short on words."

I wait to see if Bert pokes fun at Cora's milky skin and watercolor eyes, but she doesn't. If she did, it would taint our friendship. I stand up for my sister. We all do. I tell folks that Cora is the only one who's got her own entry in the *Encyclopedia Britannica,* Volume I, page 218: ALBINO.

"And last is Lydia, who'll turn five in a month and wants a butterscotch cake and is still defining her personality."

Bert surprises me when she says, "Which one's Nancy Drew?"

"She's not family."

"You said her name special."

"When?"

"At the bridge."

"You don't know Nancy Drew?" I work to keep my shock contained, for I thought

Nancy Drew was world famous. When Bert shakes her head, I say, "Well, she's about the most brilliant girl detective in a book you'll ever know. I've got every Nancy Drew book that's been published, thanks to Aunt Fanniebelle. Mama thinks the books are banal, but I think a real girl can be that smart and successful. At least I aim to be."

I try to keep self-pride out of my tone. My strong kinship with my literary heroine borders on worship. "I believe solving mysteries is a virtuous endeavor." Then to include Bert, I say, "For example, how did your meek Aunt Violet — a woman without a mean bone in her body — get tied to the likes of Larry Crumbie? Now that's a mystery we can solve that could make a difference, don't you think? At least we'd understand better."

"I never seen him."

"That's a good thing. He doesn't have any redeeming qualities I can tell."

"He might send me away when he come back."

I pat the back of Bert's hand and say with conviction, "If that happens, you come here. You always got a home with us. Did I tell you Mama was a schoolteacher before she got married?" and Bert's face lights up like I hoped it would. "She'll correct your grammar all the live long day but don't take offense. She fell in love with Daddy because he loves books and plays the fiddle and raises bees." Right then one flies in the barn to check us out then darts away.

Bert says, "Is that what's in them white boxes?"

"Yep. Millions of em in a hundred boxes making honey and baby bees and beeswax. Do you know a bee only lives forty-five days and that only the female honeybee stings?" I shift so I face Bert and ask the question that's got me curious about her sense of adventure. "Why do you have a hankering to see the big wide world so bad?"

Bert shocks me when she blurts out, "I kilt Ma and the baby, so Pa exiled me from the family as punishment. Like the Israelites."

My jaw drops. What can I say to that? My friend sits there with her face locked tight, her eyes hard, her lips pinched. She looks out the loft at a normal day that suddenly isn't normal anymore. She goes on matter-of-factly. "It's not like I kilt em directly, but they dead all the same . . . cause a me. And Pa knows. He bought me a one-way bus ticket to here."

My common sense returns. "Bert, you're talking silly. You're not a killer. Maybe you have a one-way ticket cause your pa didn't know when your aunt's baby would come. Did you think of that?"

Bert stays quiet. I'm confounded as to what to do next. Maybe if I know more, I can help my friend sort things out, so I say, "If you want to tell me what happened, I'll be glad to share that burden with you. That's what best friends do."

"Well . . ." she says, tempted.

"You want to tell me. Otherwise, why would you have confessed and confided?"

So high in my hayloft, a dark slice of Bert Tucker's life crawls out of her parched heart that seeks relief. I hear about a torn sheet two lengths of a baby coffin, flattened bosoms, a dead rabbit, a secret cave behind a waterfall, a hope to stay a girl a little longer, and a child birthing that went bad. I listen up to where Bert's pa leaves her heartbroken at the Trailways bus station.

I'm crying and Bert's crying, and Daddy hears us in the hayloft. He calls out, asking if we're okay, but he doesn't climb the ladder and confront female tears. I yell, "Bert's telling a sad story, that's all."

"Well, long as nobody's hurt . . . You know where the Vicks is if you need it."

That makes us snort-laugh right in the middle of crying the same kind of ugly, with puffy eyes and red noses and swollen lips with spittle thick in the corners. We're worn out when the crying stops, and we lie back against the hay, damp clean through.

I whisper, "You still got on that strip of cloth?"

Bert lifts her shirttail to show dingy muslin stretched across her ribs and raw skin around the edges.

"Does it hurt?"

"Like hell."

I feel a pang of jealousy cause I don't need a strip of muslin.

CHAPTER 10
BERT: PLUM CRAZY

I been at Aunt Violet's two weeks since forever, and every day she loses another piece of her mind. I go to washing clothes in the yard pot and hanging em on the line when a big man comes by on a bicycle. He knocks on the screen door and steps back polite. Aunt Violet opens the door right off, so I know he's no stranger. They talk but I can't hear what they say cause I'm too far away. When he turns round and points to the woods at the back, she screams and beats on his chest with her fists, then runs inside. The big man, who's got the air of simple, waves at me like nothing's wrong. This buffaloes me with her getting upset at his coming. He rides away on his bicycle.

I come inside to find my aunt looking at the wall, hands by her sides, knocking her noggin against that wall. *Thud. Thud. Thud.*

"Why you doing that?" I say, cause what she's doing is plain stupid.

She don't stop. *Thud. Thud.* I take her by the arm and pull her to the chair to sit. Her forehead's done swoll and turning bruised. I was planning to go see Lu when I finish chores, but I can't leave Aunt Violet like this. I hold a wet rag on her bruise and stroke her shoulder, soft like my sister, Ruth, does me when I'm outta sorts.

Fat tears run down my aunt's cheeks and drop off her chin, but she don't make a sound. She don't move. She's pitiful and a sad that breaks my heart. I stand beside her for the longest time as the day passes and my feet grow numb and I gotta relieve myself. I run do my business fast, and when I come back from the privy, she's changed. She snaps her head round fast as a rattler and points a skinny finger in my face. "You got to git so my Larry comes home. He wants to take care of me but you scared him off."

All my pity for her fades like fog. Her eyes don't settle right, and for sure she's turn plum daft. What was Pa thinking sending me here? Why would Larry Crumbie want to come back to this?

"You that floozy what run him off," she mutters.

I throw back, "I'm your brother's girl. I'm Allie Bert Tucker." I reach in my pocket and rub hard on Miz Brown's smooth button for comfort, touching a long nail I snatched in Lu's barn yesterday when I told her my troubles. The nail is rough and crooked. I could gouge her muddy eyes out with it. Stick it all the way into her eye socket, into her puddin brain if I had a mind to be mean.

"I seed the way you cut your eyes at him."

"How can that be? I never laid eyes on the man."

"You want him . . . You want him," she sings and yanks her hair.

"You old dingbat."

She hums and tugs at the shoulder of her housedress. She catches a loose thread, picks at it so the seam starts coming undone, and I see pasty flesh. Then she turns on me like a nasty rooster. "You gotta git, git, git," she says and pokes hard at my chest.

I'm tired of this foolishness. I'm tired of sticky heat, but I say. "Where you figure I can go?"

"Back to where you come from."

"That's a long way from here. A day's ride on a bus I got no ticket for."

"Go back, go back, go back," she says over and over and starts giggling like she made a funny.

I get my hackles up like Ma warned me

not to. "I'd leave you in a heartbeat, you ugly pig. If I got a ticket, I'd leave you high and dry to fend for yourself."

Her face shifts and slides into something vile, and I git scared.

Something bad is coming.

CHAPTER 11
LUCY: GOVERNMENT WORK

The day after Bert confides her exile of biblical proportions, we start our beeswax business. The big difference between *before* the government job and *after* will be making sugar syrup for the bees to eat every day. That will trick our bees into staying in the hive longer to make more honey and subsequently more wax. When left on their own, they can travel five miles searching for nectar and pollen. If we deliver the sweet to their door, they stay home and make wax for new babies.

Daddy and Yancy Mayhew already cleared a corner of the barn, and Grady built two long worktables waist high and put in a wall of shelves for new mason jars. Today, two wooden crates covered with government stamps were delivered, and a small crowd of the curious watches Daddy pry open the crates with a crowbar. One holds a scale, the wax molds, cardboard shipping boxes, labels, wax paper dividers, and a book to record quantity and shipping dates. The other holds hundreds of quart jars and lids.

Fifteen barrels of cane sugar have already been delivered, with the astonishing promise of more every month. For the last two years, ration stamps have provided limited sugar, and for Southerners with a daily hankering for sweet tea and cakes, the challenge has been tantamount to cruelty. After today, the Browns no longer have to worry about running out of cane sugar.

Gertie Mayhew has been hired to boil sugar water, and she stands beside us looking at those glorious barrels. Mr. John T. Booker assured Mama she could use some of the sugar for private consumption and nobody would arrest her. Because of Gertie's work, the Mayhews are included in the kind gift, but that's where the generosity stops.

"We're gonna need a lock on that sugar room, David," Mama says wisely, understanding a sweet tooth denied to our neighbors makes for an incentive to steal.

"I got that covered," he says. "Yancy and I are securing it today."

Daddy starts explaining. "The process is simple," and he nods toward the back corner. "We put in that old four-burner woodstove where Gertie's going to make sugar water, but she needs help. Grady is the firewood man and will load the stove every morning and keep wood stacked beside it. Yancy will haul well water and fill the four canning pots every morning.

"Gertie knows that for every gallon of water, she puts in a gallon of sugar and cooks it down till it turns to syrup. That one gallon of sugar water feeds four hives for one day. It doesn't take a math whiz to know you need to make twenty-five gallons of sugar water every day to feed a hundred hives.

"Lucy, you are the bottle washer. Every morning, take the empties from the hives when the bees have drunk it all, then wash and line them up for Gertie to fill again. Hopefully, Gertie can get ahead of the bees and have some extra.

"Making sugar syrup is the new part of the job, but nothing else changes. The bees still need checking for mites and beetles and healthy queens. We'll harvest the honey and wax in August and next June, but making sugar water is the new everyday job — with Saturdays and Sundays off. The almighty bees can fend for themselves part of the time. Questions?"

Mama grins and says, "I think I'm going

to take enough cane sugar to bake Oma's marble cake."

The day turns to a celebration of sorts, and I stay busy punching tiny holes in the tin tops with the ice pick and lining up hundreds of mason jars. When Gertie fills the jars with syrup, I take them to the hive and turn them upside down, and that sweetness drips out and the hungry bees eat food delivered to their door.

For hours, I forget to worry about Bert Tucker living with the likes of Larry Crumbie. When I remember to watch for her coming, it's suppertime. I set an extra plate in Oma's spot, but it stays empty. Mama says, "She's okay," but she doesn't sound sure.

At supper, Mama reads a letter from Everett that came this morning. As usual, he makes the war sound like a grand adventure, but we've seen the newsreels at the Majestic. We watched *49th Parallel* and *Five Graves to Cairo*. The soldiers who returned to Riverton are somber and broken. We know war is no picnic, but Everett tries to keep worry away.

Dear Brown tribe: Today I jumped out of a plane, climbed a rock wall taller than the oak tree, and saw the sun set over wide water. I ate canned rations and pretended they were Mama's fried chicken. I slept under the stars that look different from Mercer County. What did you do? I miss you more than ice cream.

Riddle: What goes up but never comes down?

I know the answer right off is your age because my mind is good at deduction. But I don't spoil it for the others while they come up with silly guesses — a cloud, a balloon. A year is a long time for Everett to turn war stories into escapades, but he never tires of trying. We know his world is different than he says, but he works to fill us with wonder instead of worry.

At bedtime, Everett and Wade are already on my prayer list, but I add Bert Tucker. She's in a dangerous place. When the first roll of thunder rumbles over the land, I bolt upright in bed with a terrible thought. What if she's hurt? What if Larry Crumbie came home and locked her up and that's why she didn't come today. How can I sleep if Bert's life is in peril?

I pad down the stairs and into the parlor. Mama has her mending basket on her lap and her glasses on the tip of her nose, sewing a button on a dress. Her nose is red and her handkerchief is well-used, likely thinking about our war boys or missing Oma. I speak what's on my mind.

"I think something happened to Bert." I scoot in the chair against her soft side.

She puts the threaded needle in the pincushion, then kisses the top of my head and clears her throat. "I'm worried, too, honey. We witnessed Larry Crumbie's temper, and we know Miz Violet is helpless to defend herself or Bert."

"She should have come back here today since she's been here two days in a row."

"Maybe her aunt was feeling poorly and needed her. Or Bert had a long list of chores to do like you did."

"Or maybe Larry Crumbie came back from wherever . . ."

"That's possible, too. How about this. After chores tomorrow, if she hasn't shown up, we'll put together a basket of goodies and take it over there as a neighborly gesture. That way, we can lay eyes on the situation and make sure Bert and Violet are okay."

"I guess."

"There's nothing we can do tonight, honey. You head on back to bed. Dawn gets closer every minute. Sounds like a storm's coming."

When I don't leave, she says, "Something else bothering you?"

"The change."

"Have you spotted?"

"No, and that's the problem. Nothing's happened."

"Don't rush it. When it comes, you'll be a woman for the rest of your days."

"It happened to Bert."

"It happens at different times for different girls."

"And she's not happy about it one bit. She even tied muslin around her middle tight so her bosom doesn't show in her shirt."

"It can't be stopped."

"What if I don't want to grow up?" I ask, thinking back on what Bert told me that sounded dismal. "What if I don't want the responsibility?"

"Well, you'd be in a pickle, wouldn't you? Do you want to take time tonight to worry on things you can't change? Or do you want to get some sleep?"

I see the wisdom of her questions. "Sleep, I guess."

"Good night, dear Lucy."

But up the stairs, back in my bed, lying in the dark that's splintered with lightning and the howl of the wind rising — with Lydia and Cora curled up under the sheet, trembling from the storm and pressed up against me for comfort — the unease in my belly won't die down. It isn't the change that's the cause. It's Violet Crumbie's despicable husband.

If Miz Violet thought she was getting a helpmate, that didn't happen. I've watched him clean his fingernails with his pocket-knife and study his reflection in a window glass. I don't think Bert Tucker will kowtow to the likes of a cruel man who treats his wife like leftovers.

Larry Crumbie is the bad in this whole thing.

CHAPTER 12
BERT: LOST AND FOUND

Aunt Violet barks like a coyote, *"Out out out,"* and pushes at me till I back against the doorframe. When the door slams and the wood latch catches, I'm on the other side in the place I hate: the dark.

I press against the door and whine through the crack, "Please let me in. Please." I knock timid like a pitiful fool. "I'll be good," I promise, and feel my false pride drain outta my feet. I'm scared. I step to the front yard and look back at the window that's gone black since she blowed out the lamp. There won't a speck a light inside. I wanna see that scrap of sheet pull back. I want her to open the door and let me in.

The wind screams and leaves rattle, and flying dirt stings my eyes. I walk the road, and the wind pushes my back, whips my hair, and hard rain comes and punches me. Pine branches slap my face and the storm turns mean. I don't remember the walk in the woods being this long. Water stands deep in flat places, and I stumble over a broke branch. At last, I come to the edge of a field and run through the tobacco row into the Browns' yard and up on Lu's porch. I beat on the door, but rain hits the roof and windowpanes and drowns out all sounds but the wild. Nobody comes, so I curl in a shivering ball outside the front door and wait out the night. When Mr. Brown wakes me, the morning is calm, and he carries me to the warm kitchen.

"Look who I almost stepped on."

Miz Brown says, "Merciful heavens" and starts giving orders. "Irene, get dry clothes and a towel. Lucy, fix a hot water bottle. Grady, go with Daddy till we get Bert settled." Cora the ghost girl and the little one I can't recollect her name stand in the corner.

Miz Brown pulls the bacon frying off the fire and the biscuits outta the oven, then looks at me straight on. She pulls my wet shirt over my head and goes to unwinding the cloth round my middle when my hand flies to my chest.

She whispers, "I'll wash it and give it back." I let her unwrap the tight strip and cast her eyes on my sores and my nipples the size of dark nickels on wrinkled pale mounds, me taking my first deep breath in weeks.

"Hold the blanket higher, Lucy." The woman washes mud off my legs and arms and drops a fresh gown over my clean body and finger-combs damp curls away from my face. I don't ramble on like usual.

"Is she hurt?" Lu picks up my wet clothes. The stole button and crooked nail fall out the pocket and hit the floor. Lu sets them on the table. I look at Miz Brown and know my thieving ways is found out, but she don't hit me with hands or switch or belt. She don't even say it's her button I stole. Instead she says, "I don't think she's physically hurt. No cuts I can see, only shock. We'll get the details later. Help her to bed, Lucy, and stay with her. I'll let Gertie know you'll be late washing sugar jars. Put the hot water bottle under the covers to help with her chills. Be patient. Don't push her to talk, you hear?"

This woman is goodness this thief don't deserve.

Lu leads me out the kitchen, up the stairs to her bedroom, and closes the door. We crawl in the high featherbed with the soft sheet pulled over my shoulder and light falling through clean windows, and Lu rubs the small of my back as comfort. I can't even look at her. I don't know I'm crying till a tear rolls out my open eyes and over the bump of my nose and wets the pillow. Lu cries, too, and don't even know why. We rest in this place while her family stays quiet. I sleep.

When I open my eyes, Lu's looking at me, not blinking.

"Wanna talk?" she whispers.

"Not much to say."

"Say what you can."

"He never come back, not in the days I been there."

"Larry Crumbie?"

"She's been jittery every night, wringing her hands, hoping for his truck lights to pierce the black and pull in the yard. She even talked to him once like he was there when he won't. I don't know when he come home last."

"Why'd you come out in that storm?"

"She done it. Throwed me out. One minute, she say 'Larry Crumbie, you damn man. Why I got to love you, run-around man?' then she scream 'I hate you, I hate you,' and I don't know if she's talking to me or Larry. She says it's me keeping him away cause I'm a floozy girl. And I tell her I don't even know the man, so how can it be my fault he don't come home? Then she throwed me out."

"Why'd she call you a floozy girl?"

"She's gone round the bend, I guess." We scoot up and stack pillows behind.

"Then what?"

"I was standing out in her yard with that storm coming and the door locked, thinking what kind of family throws a lone girl out in a storm? But then I remember Pa sent me away on a one-way bus ticket." My throat grabs at my next words. "Maybe the trouble is me."

Lu says, "You stop saying that right this second, Bert Tucker. Something or somebody *is* wrong here, but it's not you." She pats the back of my hand and says, "Go on. Let it all out."

"Not much more to say. The rain blowed and I got turned round a time or two cause the world looks different in a storm, but then I found your tobacco field and got here all the same."

She squeezes my hand. "You should have come inside. Our doors are never locked. You hungry?"

I nod, cause I *am* hungry and don't think I ate good since supper here two nights back.

On the kitchen table are rows of blackberry jelly jars cooling — and my stole button and rusty nail. My sins are plain as day, and my belly grips. Miz Brown says, "I saved biscuits for you girls, and bacon and potatoes." She adds, "Don't forget your things on the table, Bert."

I pick em up quick, thinking maybe Miz Brown don't know the button belongs to her. The nail digs into my hand.

Lu loads two plates and pours coffee and adds a big dollop of cream and real sugar and sets breakfast on the table. I never been so hungry. Lu starts with, "Miz Violet threw Bert out of the house" and ends with "She had to git."

Miz Brown's kind face crumbles in on my account. "Thrown out during that storm. Oh, dear . . . Bless your heart." She puts her hand over her own heart. "Come here and let me love on you."

I look back at my food I'm hungry for, walk right into this woman's wide arms, and burrow my head against her neck and start bawling again.

She whispers, "You're safe here. We'll talk to your aunt later today and ask if you can stay here until life is sorted. Finish your breakfast, and you can help Lucy and Gertie with the bees and sugar water."

I lift my head off her shoulder. "Them bees gonna sting?"

"No. You won't get hurt. Lu will make sure."

One night, I'm drowning, and the next morning, I'm saved.

In the barn, a woman called Gertie stirs big pots on a woodstove, and me and Lu line up jars and punch holes in tin tops. After noon dinnertime for the field hands, Miz Brown say, "Why don't you girls bake a pie to take to Violet? It'll sweeten conversation."

So Lu and me pit cherries and bake a perfect pie with a braided crust. It'll be for my aunt's supper. Maybe she won't be mad. Maybe Larry will be there. Maybe they can eat cherry pie together.

To save walking time on a hot day, Mr. Brown backs the car outta the barn, brushes hay off the hood with his arm, and shoos two chickens nesting inside. I see a man working on a fence gate — the same man I saw at my aunt's farm.

"Who's that big boy?"

Lu looks to where I'm pointing. "That's Tiny Junior. He helps people do things, especially if they have men serving in the war. Why do you ask?"

"He come see her and knocked on her door."

"Your aunt? He knows everybody. He

won't take pay, only fixes things and goes on his way." Lu lowers her voice. "He lives with his mama, Flossie, a kind lady who cleans houses and takes in mending. But Tiny Junior's uncle is meaner than a striped snake. If you hear the name Terrell Stucky, run the other way. That man hates everything and everybody because bad luck plagues him: his two sons got killed in the war, he lost his farm when he didn't pay taxes, his daughter ran off with a fertilizer salesman, and his wife moved back home with her mama. All he does is whittle on a chunk of pine, spit tobacco, and throw slurs at people passing by. Tiny Junior's different. Maybe he was helping your aunt Violet with a chore."

Mr. and Miz Brown get in the front seat while Lu and me sit in back. We put the pie between us with a towel under it to catch juices that might spill. The crystal sugar on top glistens. It smells divine. "This is the prettiest pie," I whisper with pride. I'm nervous to see my aunt and lay eyes on Larry Crumbie, but I won't be alone.

She's in the garden with the afternoon sun beating down. Miz Brown says, "Garden work is early morning work. Violet's going to get heatstroke if she's not careful."

Our slamming car doors make her raise

her head and shield her eyes to see who has come on her property without invitation. When she sees it's me, her shoulders slump, and she wipes her hands on her apron. She picks up the garden basket heavy with vegetables, and Mr. Brown runs to take the weight from her. She don't want him to carry it, but Lu's daddy won't be stopped.

I stand with the Browns on one side, looking at Aunt Violet on the other. Mr. Brown pulls off his Feed and Seed hat and clears his throat. "Miz Crumbie, I'm David Brown. My wife, Minnie, and daughter Lucy you know from market. Bert showed up at our place in that storm last night. Said you threw her out. What can you say about that?"

Lu's daddy declares a sad truth, but Aunt Violet don't say a word. She watches a bird in the sky. A housefly lands on the end a her nose but she don't swat it. What she does is go inside and start yelling Larry's name over and over, and that puzzles me. His truck ain't in the yard. Calling his name goes on in a house barely big as a chicken coop till Lu's mama goes in and fetches her. Her strong arm is round my aunt's weak shoulders. She stands there in her own yard, looking like she don't know who we are or where she is. Hoping to make things better,

I step up with the pie and say kindly, "Me and Lu baked this cherry pie special for you."

With no warning, she takes my cherry pie outta my hands and walks over to the chickens in the yard. She shocks us when she bends over best she can and drops our perfect pie on the ground. The chickens come a running and peck it to death while she stands there singing a song in a little girl's voice, twisting a string of hair. It's a terrible sight that has Lu's mama exclaim, "Lord'a mercy," and rush to my aunt's side, and take her by the arm.

The two women get in the back seat of Mr. Brown's car, and they head to the doctor. Lu and me carry the vegetables inside, wash dishes, sweep the floor, and give order to the little house. We don't look at the pie plate in the yard. Before we shut the door, I get my treasure box from under the bed and wrap it in my extra shirt. I ain't ready to explain it yet. We start walking and I say, "Wonder where he is? I never caught a whiff of him cept his leftover Dapper Dan pomade."

"I don't know, Bert. Your aunt isn't herself. You told me she talked to Larry like he was there but wasn't. I think we could use some help, and I know where we might find it."

We don't head to the Brown farm. We cross land Lu says is the Mosby farm, into a different woods and cross a wide creek with a deep pool and flat rocks. Lu points to a snail and says, "Do you know snails sleep up to three years? They're really in hibernation, but they're sleeping all the same," then she runs and I follow till she stops and whispers, "We're here."

Here is a white painted house as little as Aunt Violet's place but pretty and clean. It sits under tall trees with the yard swept. The windows sparkle, and flowers in a pot are outside the open red door. A yellow dog is by the red door. A voice inside calls out, "He named Biscuit." The dog thumps his tail, raises his square head to look at us, then lowers it with a sigh.

"Come in, come in," the woman says like she was waiting on us. We step into a room the late sunlight spun to gold. A shelf holds a line of fragile cups, and fabric hangs at the window and puddles on the floor. A fat jar of sunflowers sits on a black round table with fancy legs. Three cups and a teapot is on the table with napkins and cookies. I smell lemons and pipe tobacco. A glass bowl on a shelf is filled with marbles. Green marbles. The green of the old lady's eyes.

Lu says, "It's good to see you again, Miz Trula. May I present my best friend, Bert Tucker. Bert, this is Trula Freed." I hear in her voice that this lady is special.

"You Violet Crumbie's niece who come to help with the birthing," Miz Trula says so matter-of-fact like she already knows my sad situation. I hold out my hand, and she takes it with fingers as strong as grapevine. They wrap round my fingers and won't let go. A shock of current runs through my arms and out the bottoms of my feet. I can't move if I want to. Is one of her green eyes bigger than the other?

When she lets go, I'm dizzy.

She moves to her polished table and pours peppermint tea in the cups. "Come. Sit," she orders, and we sit at her fine table. The cookies are perfect circles with smooth yellow icing. Because they're sitting right there looking at me, I pick one up and eat it.

"Bert," Lu says, "where's your manners?"

"What?" I say, confused, cause I am.

Trula Freed says, "Cookies for you."

"For us? But you didn't know we were coming. *We* didn't know we were coming until a bit ago, so how can the cookies be for us?"

"Every thought rise into universe" is the

strange words she says as she raises her willowy bangled arms, opens them wide, and chuckles. "I listen good."

Sounds like foolishness she's talking bout, so to be sassy, I say, "What am I thinking right now?" and keep my face calm and eyes on hers so as I don't give nothing away.

"'Tis easy," she shrugs. "Dat box."

"What box?" Lu says.

Trula Freed keeps her green eyes locked on me while she drops a sugar cube in her tea, stirs it with a spoon, and takes a long, noisy sip.

"What box?" Lu says again, and I nod to the treasure box under my spare shirt sitting on the floor beside my chair. The witchy woman would have seen it when I come in.

But then she say, "We eat, drink tea, then talk about dat di-lemma what's bothering you girls."

"Dilemma?" Lucy asks and picks up a cookie and licks off the icing.

"Bout Larry Crumbie. He not go fishin'. He go nowhere."

CHAPTER 13
LUCY: PURPLE HONEY

We close the red door on our way out like Trula Freed instructs, and in the lengthening shadows, we head home, utterly perplexed. When we're barely out of earshot, Bert starts. "What in tarnation happened back there? How'd she know them things bout me, bout my treasure box and that no-good Larry Crumbie? And if that no-good man's gone nowhere, where's he been hiding his sorry self? Who's been feeding him and getting his Dapper Dan? Want a cookie?"

I glance over at Bert holding out two lemon cookies.

"You took cookies from Trula Freed without asking?"

"She made em for us."

"You should have asked first," I say weakly and reach for one. "That's only proper manners." We walk and eat cookies, and I pull conversation back to Larry. "A good mystery always has more questions at the start than answers. And if Miz Trula's right about Larry going nowhere, I was thinking maybe Irene can put a notice in the newspaper asking folks to be on the lookout for him. Everybody who's anybody reads the *Mercer County Reporter.*"

"Think she'd do that?"

"Don't know. I might ask her boss, Drake Cunningham, instead. He's easier to talk to." I don't tell Bert that sometimes I wonder if Irene's heart is too small. She isn't very amiable, and she's stingy with kind words, like she's scared she's going to run out. It must be tiresome being Irene.

We get home, but I don't see Daddy's car, so they must not be back from taking Miz Violet to the doctor. Irene's car isn't parked beside the pickup truck either, and Grady isn't in sight. I tell Bert to wait in the barn, and I sneak in the parlor for one of Mama's sewing needles, careful that Helen and the little ones don't hear me. Then Bert and I climb to the hayloft. There, in the waning light, I say, "Hold up your right hand, Bert," and she does. "Do you, Bert Tucker, promise to never tell Mama what we witnessed today? About Miz Trula reading minds, knowing a person's coming before they know it themselves, and saying with certi-

114

tude that a missing man did not leave town?" When she doesn't answer, I say, "Say I promise."

"I promise."

"Now you ask me."

"Ask you what?"

"The *do you promise* oath."

"The whole thing? That's too many words."

"Oh shoot, Bert. I'll do it myself. Do I, Lucy Brown, promise to never tell Mama what I witnessed today . . ." and I say, "I do."

"Now we make it official — hold out your finger," and I prick our index fingers, and we squish our blood together. Now my best friend and I are blood sisters with a secret we'll take to our grave.

As we climb down from the loft, I say, "What's in your treasure box?"

She says, "It's got bits and pieces that glue me together when I'm coming apart. For now, it belongs to me."

There goes Bert confounding me again.

The next morning after breakfast, we head to the barn where Bert will begin her beekeeping lessons in earnest. Daddy's already in the barn and has rubbed Vicks on his hands to ward off the bees. Tiny Junior is mucking out a stall without being

115

told, and Yancy has already filled giant pots with water for today's sugar syrup. Yancy's putting Assassin's bridle on. My mule's pitiful tail hairs never have grown back. We catch the end of a conversation.

". . . gonna hire you some?"

"May not have a choice. Being short-handed this long is wearing on us. And now with the beeswax demands . . . How do you think the other men would take it?"

"Don't rightly know. This world's done turned upside down crazy. Never thought I'd hear talk bout Nazis walking on Carolina dirt when our boys is off fighting the devils. No sir. Never did." Yancy and Assassin head to the fields.

What's Daddy saying? "You talking about Nazis? Coming to Riverton?"

He strikes a match on the bottom of his boot and lights dry pine needles in the smoker that will calm the bees. "Maybe so, maybe no. They're already in Scotland Neck."

"That's only forty miles from here. What in the world are Nazis doing there?"

"Working tobacco and peanuts and cotton."

"Out in the field? Right alongside free men?"

Daddy nods while he tests the smoker.

"Does Mama know?"

"She knows but doesn't believe it'll come to pass. We'll see, but if I get the chance to hire some, I'll probably take it."

"I can't believe it, Daddy. You'd bring evil Germans here? The kind of Germans Oma was scared of? They're like Mary Shelley's Dr. Frankenstein who created an abomination. Why would you do something like that?"

"You sound like your mama," he says. "Life's turned hard these war years. You know that. Everybody's stretched too thin. Too many things don't get done. It's mostly children and old people doing too much, when young'uns should be playing and the old ones should be rocking. Thank the Lord for the beeswax deal to help carry us through."

Daddy heads to the hives, and I feel ashamed for not trusting him. In quiet, I help Bert get into a bee suit too big for her. With one leg in the pants, she says, "They got horns on their heads, you know," without saying who. "Like devil men." The other leg goes in. "They keep em outta sight under their hats."

"Who would say such a thing?" I roll up the sleeves so her hands come through.

"An old man on the bus sitting catty-corner to me. He was quiet for the longest time, then got moved by the spirit and started preaching to the air. He said, 'Them murdering Nazis are birthed from Satan himself and wear his horns on their heads as a sign. They eat babies and steal souls.' He preached for a minute then stopped as quick as he started."

"What horrible things to say," I begin —

— but Daddy yells, "What the devil," and we run outside carrying our gloves and veils. Tiny Junior and Gertie come, too, hearing the worry in Daddy's voice. He holds a frame packed with honey. Not the usual amber honey. *Purple honey.*

"What the devil," I repeat. We've seen honey turn different shades of gold, depending on where the bees find nectar, but purple is not in the honey spectrum. I don't even remember purple honey in Miz Trula's collection.

"In all my born days . . ." Daddy says more to the bees than to us. Then he moves to the next hive, smokes it, and reaches in to discover the same odd thing in the center frame. Worry clouds his face. "What did you get into, little buddies? Where could you have been?"

"What could have happened? You've got the best hives in the county," I say.

"This is a new one on me. One time, I heard talk about purple honey but thought it was a tall tale. Maybe since it's been drier than usual . . . Maybe the bees have been drinking from elderberries." Daddy takes off his hat and scratches his head, standing beside a hive holding eighty thousand worker bees who have created a mystery.

Gertie has backed away from the opened hive for fear of stings. She calls out, "Is it the government sugar what's doing it?"

"No. We just started feeding them syrup. This honey took time to make, and I can't believe I overlooked it. Girls, put some in a jar so I can take a closer look. I'm going to check the books." Daddy places the lids back on the hives and the two racks on the table. Some of the bees follow their racks into the barn, so Bert and I quickly finish suiting up so we don't get stung. Daddy heads to the house hoping to find answers.

A rack holds seven or eight pounds of beeswax and honey. This honey is warm from the sun, and it flows easy as I cut a piece of wax comb out of each frame and drop the blocks into a jar. It's runnier than regular, and some has dripped on the counter. Tiny Junior has been inching closer, but no bees sting him. He reaches over to dip his finger in it, and I say, "No, don't eat that. It might be bad," because we don't know. We take the honey in a jar to the house to study on a conundrum as perplexing as the missing Larry Crumbie.

As usual, Mama has the radio on, and "Bewitched, Bothered and Bewildered" is playing on low. Daddy reads at the kitchen table, thumbing through his favorite reference books. One is written by the Reverend L. L. Langstroth, the apiarist from Pennsylvania who revolutionized the industry a hundred years back. The other is by Mr. Walter T. Kelley. If anybody knows anything about purple honey, one of these men should.

Mama wipes her hands on the dish towel, reaches for the jar, and holds it up to the light. "It looks like thin grape jelly, doesn't it?"

Daddy rubs his hands over his face and closes the books. "It's not here. If either of them saw it, they didn't write about it. At least not in these books." He holds out his hand for the jar, unscrews the lid, sniffs it, then dips his finger in and tastes.

"David," Mama cries in alarm.

"Tastes good. Like honey should."

Mama snaps, "And that's proof you're not going to get sick? Because it *tastes* good?"

He says, "Minnie, this honey might look

different, but it comes from the almighty honeybee. If it wasn't any good, the bees would have suffered, and they're as sassy as ever." Daddy stands, hugs Mama, kisses her temple, and turns up the radio. They dance, and Mama's tired face softens and she even giggles. He adds, "Girls, let's harvest some honey. I want to see how much is purple."

Over the next week, we find grape-colored honey scattered in a quarter of the hives and it almost fills a fifty-gallon barrel. We don't sell this honey to the government. We don't sell it to our regulars. Daddy sells it to moonshiners in case something's off. He tells Bert and me, "There's going to be some gentlemen, white and colored alike, coming from over Bear Grass way. They'll ask for this special honey, and you sell it to them. Full price. They'll bring their own jars. You collect the money."

"Does Mama know?"

Daddy doesn't say, but he adds on his way out, "Put one jar aside for us and six jars for Trula Freed."

"Does Mama know *that*?" I say.

He doesn't answer outright but adds, "It's business. All business."

"We'll be happy to take it to Miz Trula," I shout as an afterthought, hoping.

But he says, "Y'all stay away from there," and he cheats us out of a legitimate reason for another visit.

Bootleggers start coming right away. Polite men in rusty pickup trucks with hats in hands tap on our screen door. Mama ignores them, so Bert or I go to the barn and fill jugs that smell of corn liquor. The men don't seem put off by girls serving them. We always ask if they know the whereabouts of Larry Crumbie. Some say they know of him but nobody's seen him lately. At day's end, we hand Daddy a stack of money. Sometimes two hundred dollars. Then the honey is gone.

CHAPTER 14
BERT: GOOD FOR SOMETHING

Aunt Violet don't go back to her farm after that Cherry Pie Day. She stays at the crazy house and births a boy. Miz Brown hears he's claimed by a distant cousin in Tennessee, close to my mountains. Nobody knows what name they put on the baby, but I bet it ain't Larry.

"Would you like to go see your aunt?" Miz Brown says in the heart of July, after breakfast while Lu and me do dishes. "We can see how she's doing and let her know she's not forgotten." She adds, "Then you can write a letter to your pa so he knows what's happened."

Truth is I don't think much bout Aunt Violet cept to say good riddance. I don't miss her stinky house or her spiteful ways. And I don't think on Pa much neither, since I never hear hide nor hair from him. To be polite, I nod about the visiting part — but not about the writing part. I'm not good with letters.

"We'll go this afternoon, the three of us, after chores."

We leave in sunshine and ride through two towns and into hard rain when we get to Primrose Mental Hospital and no primrose in sight. The outside of the building is red brick, and the inside stinks of bleach and lost souls. Nurses wear starched uniforms with white caps held on with bobby pins the color of their hair. They walk down hallways in rubber shoes that squeak, going in and out of rooms in a flutter, never looking anybody in the eye. The barred windows are tall and narrow. These windows don't open to the outside to let in hope.

A sour-faced woman takes us up gloomy stairs to the third floor. Iron beds line each side of a long room, and some of the women moan or cry out or stare at the wall. They got on hospital gowns and not a scrap of dignity. It won't a place to heal a body or a mind. Lu whispers, "Remind me not to go crazy."

My aunt's got all the fight taken outta her. She sits on the edge of a narrow bed. Her bare feet dangle off the floor, and her hands stay in her lap. "Hello, Violet, dear." Miz Brown gently touches my aunt's shoulder. "We've come to pay you a visit. Bert and

Lucy are here with me."

Aunt Violet looks confused and don't recognize us. She says, "You seen my baby? I come in with my baby, but he ain't here and nobody's saying" are her odd words. "He's supposed to be right in here" — she pats her tummy — "but it don't feel like nothing's in there no more."

Miz Brown clutches her heart, and Lu's mouth drops open. All my hate for Aunt Violet's meanness dries up, and I wanna cry cause nobody should be this alone! Somebody shoulda told her she had that baby and it's a boy staying with her cousin in Tennessee. Told her that if she gets well, she can hold her baby boy. She looks pitiful sitting on the edge of that bed with its dingy sheets and flat pillow and not a piece of personal anywhere. Her hair is stringy, and her toenails is long. Her skin is the color of fish gone bad.

Miz Brown sits next to her, and the mattress springs creaks. She takes my aunt's hand and tells her what happened. When she's done, Aunt Violet say, "You seen my baby? I come in with my baby, but he ain't here . . ." and we know she's gone round the bend to where we can't go.

My mountain folks back home and Pa's sister in Riverton is broke in two. They can't give comfort like the Browns. If left on my own, I'd turn to dust and blow away. But I'm saved for no good reason I can figure. I don't fit. I ain't smart or mannerly. But I am good at one thing. I'm good at tending bees.

Lu says to me when I start learning, "You got a quiet touch and a gentle voice, Bert, and the bees like you. Do you know their wings beat two hundred times per second?" My mind can't grapple with figures that big or time that small, but if I'm gonna be good at something, I'm glad it's working bees, for they are holy creatures. The hum of their wings sounds like angels gathered round. So when I listen, I hear a tribe of angel wings beating in a hive.

Lu says worker bees are girls and drones are boys. They make our food grow and only live forty-five days and never sleep, then they die. The queen lives five years and lays three million eggs, and none of em whine bout their lot in life like I do. I can learn from bees. I give thanks to them every day. When the sun sets and the bees come home for the night, I go to the hives and lay my ear down and listen to them telling secrets.

I think they whisper bout me.

CHAPTER 15
LUCY: THE PLOT THICKENS

Through the summer heat, Bert and I wash jars, harvest beeswax, and steal time to read in the hayloft. But it's Larry Crumbie who still intrigues us. We know how many shirts hang in his closet (three) and how many bottles of half-filled liquor we find around his farm (seven). We know he smokes Lucky Strike cigarettes and only uses Dapper Dan pomade on his hair. These are small things I mark in a notebook until the day we find something big.

We've ridden our bikes to the bait shop on the river many times and questioned Mr. Otis, the owner, because our biggest clue is that Larry was a fisherman. Today, I lean on his counter, chewing bubble gum, and say, "What kind of truck did he have?" because I really don't know.

Without looking up from cutting worms in half — likely thinking they'll become two worms when they won't — he says, "Model

A, wood slats, wide whitewalls, and a crack in the windshield on the passenger side."

"How do you remember it so well?"

"Cause I sold it to him."

"When was that?"

"Bout seven months back."

"Did he buy it on time?" Bert thinks to ask.

"Yeah, he was buying it on time. Till he stopped paying on time."

"What did you do?" Bert says. When Mr. Otis doesn't answer, she says, "Weren't you upset bout a truck you sold not getting paid for?"

Mr. Otis looks up and says, "That's enough. I want you nosey busybodies to skedaddle. Both of you. Don't come round again with questions less they're fishing questions." He picks up his knife, shakes it at us, and gets back to cutting bait with a vengeance. We hit a nerve but we leave.

Outside the shop, Terrell Stucky — Tiny Junior's evil uncle — sits in his folding chair in the shade of a sycamore tree and cuts on a piece of pine. We ignore him like usual till he throws his pearl-handled switchblade at my foot and comes close to cutting off my toe.

Bert snaps, "You crazy old coot, watch where you throw that thing." He cackles and his open mouth shows rotten nubs black from chew. Bert leans back in the door to Mr. Otis. "Did you see what Terrell Stucky did?"

But Mr. Otis shrugs. "The world's a dangerous place. You little girls take care. Run on home to your mommy and daddy."

We leave the dock vexed at the men for their rudeness and disdain, ride a short distance, hit the brakes, and stop on the side of the road. I say, "I got an idea about that missing truck."

Bert grins, "I got one, too. Bet it's the same one."

I've never been to Mr. Otis's farm before, but I know the road it's on, and I've seen his mailbox. We're going to look for a missing truck because we feel inspired, righteous, and justified, like Nancy Drew would be if she had heard Mr. Otis's answers today and deduced his guilt. I feel her bold spirit guide us to a dented mailbox with *Otis* crudely painted on the side, down a rutted drive I've never traversed before, into the dark interior of a barn, to the dusty tarp covering a Model A Ford pickup with a crack in the passenger side windshield.

"Well, I'll be." Bert's whisper sounds small in the big barn. "We did it. We found us a real honest-to-god clue."

This lead feels significant, because no man leaves town walking when he could drive. Our backs are to the barn door when Mr. Otis's voice slices the air. "What in sam hill are you nosy girls doing? I thought your daddy raised you better than this, Lucy Brown. This here is private property. I could shoot y'all for trespassing, and nobody'd blame me one whit. I've answered all your crappy questions bout a crappy man who owes me money."

Bert raises her chin in confidence. "Then how come his missing truck is here?"

"Cause it *was* his truck. It was on his farm with the keys in it. I took it back to pressure him into paying what he owes me, but he never come for it."

Bert says, "Save your talk for the sheriff, Mr. Otis. If you ain't hiding anything, why's his truck under this tarp?"

Good question.

"The sheriff? Good grief. Why would you go bothering Cecil? And I don't need to drive this truck when my other one drives better."

"Let's see what the law has to say." I grab Bert's arm and pull her toward the door, but Mr. Otis steps in front of us, his silhouette dark and menacing.

"Answer me one thing: What's Larry

Crumbie to you? He's a nobody who don't live up to his word. A liar, a cheat, and a lousy fisherman who beats up on a crazy wife. Why do you give a rat's ass bout what happened to him?"

The truth is I don't much care about *him*, but I love our very own *Mystery of the Missing Man.* My best friend delivered that delicious mystery at the same time she told me six things that captivated me:

One, Bert proclaimed she killed her ma and the unborn baby.

Two, she was exiled and sent away on a Trailways bus.

Three, she rode that bus solo across the expanse of North Carolina.

Four, she found traces of a nasty man who beat her pregnant aunt.

Five, that aunt went crazy and was committed to a mental asylum.

Six, Larry Crumbie has the glorious audacity to go missing and stay missing.

So it's with prideful determination that Bert and I ride into town to tell the sheriff what we uncovered in Mr. Otis's barn and nobody thought to look for. We ride hard and are winded when we rush into his office. He glances up from his desk, listens politely, then only halfway thanks us for bringing this clue to his attention. But he doesn't grab his hat. He doesn't head out the door to see for himself.

Bert flings one last thought his way. "If you dawdle too long, Mr. Otis could get rid of that truck. You might lose your first real clue."

Sheriff Cecil leans back on his chair legs. "You don't really think Mr. Otis or that truck is going anywhere soon, do you?" Before we can answer, he says, "Appreciate you coming by," and stands and walks us to the door while I fume, thinking no officer of the law would ever ignore Nancy Drew's important clue served on a silver platter. We head home downcast. We ride up to Mama and Daddy sitting on the front porch, rocking in unison. Their faces are hard. They've been waiting.

CHAPTER 16
BERT: BIG CHANGE

Without a hello or howdy-do, Miz Brown starts. "What made you think it was your right to trespass on a neighbor's property and enter his barn?"

Mr. Brown takes the toothpick out his mouth and says, "You were lucky you didn't get shot. A man's got a right to protect what's his. Lucy, I thought you were smarter than this."

Miz Brown dives back in. "Is it those Nancy Drew books? Are they putting dangerous ideas in your heads? Is that why you girls are taking foolish risks?"

We look at the ground, not upset at snooping but upset we got caught.

Mr. Brown decides, "You're grounded. Both of you. You'll harvest beeswax then stay in the yard. No gallivanting. No fishing. No heading into town. No visiting friends. No exceptions."

"For how long?" Lu whines.

He says, "Till school starts. For now, go to your room. We'll call you for supper."

We march upstairs, slam the bedroom door, drop across the bed on our backs, and stare at the ceiling while I fume about school. Lu starts. "You'd think they'd be proud of us. Mr. Otis hiding evidence like that. If it wasn't for us, everybody would forget Larry Crumbie when a crime has undoubtedly been committed. You'd never hear Mr. Drew criticizing Nancy for doing the right thing."

My insides are riled. I say, "Stop saying dumb stuff like that. You talk like your pretend Nancy Drew and her daddy are real folk. They ain't real. You told me they was made up. They don't live in a real town. She don't drive a blue roadster, so she don't get grounded and get sent to school with the little kids so she looks stupid."

Lu turns away from me. I turn the other way. We stay like that for the longest time till Lydia comes in and says supper's ready and stands there waiting. I get up and start to leave, but Lydia says, "Wait for Lucy," like there's some rule bout us going down-stairs together. I wait. Lu finally gets up. Her hair's smushed flat on one side. We go downstairs.

After Mr. Brown says the blessing and

134

food starts getting passed, I say, "I won't go."

Everybody keeps passing food, but nobody talks till Lu says, "I'll be going to high school since I finished two grades in one a few years back. Bert won't be going to high school yet."

I want to claw her eyes out and spit poison in her face.

Miz Brown says, "That's true, Lucy, and we all know that, but that sounded rude and unkind to your friend. Vanity doesn't suit you."

I say again, "Won't go."

"We'll talk about it after supper."

"Won't change my mind neither."

Mr. Brown butters another biscuit and asks Irene to pass the apple butter please, and Lydia eats her peas one at a time like usual, but I'm in a hurtful place and have lost my appetite. I don't eat cept to nibble at a biscuit. Lu picks at her food, too.

Helen holds her hand on her pregnant belly and surprises me when she goes to talking cause she's usually like a stupid bump on a log. "I'll be glad when this baby comes. It won't let me get a decent night's rest and nothing settles on my stomach right. Sure wish Wade would hurry home to work bees and be a good daddy."

I glance quick at Miz Brown. Nobody's heard diddlysquat from Wade Sully. Does Helen know something we don't?

"Dear, it will be wonderful when he comes home, but we have to be patient and say our prayers."

Them words make Helen slap the table, and our eyes fly wide at her upset. Her water glass turns over, she pushes herself to stand, and her arms tremble. "I am sick and tired of being patient and saying stupid prayers God doesn't hear and feeling fat and out of sorts and scared of what I don't know. I am sick and tired of being afraid and mad at everyone and everything."

Miz Brown stands and guides poor Helen to her bedroom.

Irene wipes the spilled water and starts cleaning off the supper dishes while Mr. Brown and Grady leave the table and head to the barn where they go when Brown girls throw a tizzy fit. The cuckoo clock ticks loud. Lydia and Cora go outside, then it's Lu and me sitting there with Irene doing dishes.

"I'm sorry," Lu whispers.

"Bout what?"

"Everything. Getting you in trouble. Bragging on being in high school."

"What's gonna happen to me? I'm dumb

as dirt."

Irene butts in and says, "Bert, you are smart and beautiful."

I'm puzzled cause she's never said a kind word to me.

"You're a quick study, and you have as bright a future as any of us."

Miz Brown comes out of Helen's room, catches Irene's words, and adds, "And I'm going to homeschool you for a while. You and I will study together in the mornings, and you'll do homework with the children at night. Your reading has already improved but I was wondering if you'd like to read *The Velveteen Rabbit* at this year's birthday party."

"Is it hard words?"

Lu says in her know-it-all way, "Yes, it is hard words. Too hard for her. How could she learn to read that in three weeks? And to be a reader is an honor, Mama. I thought Bert and I were being grounded and punished for trespassing and endangering ourselves."

"It would be a lovely incentive." Mama moves to help Irene with the dishes. "We'll all help."

Lu storms out of the room, saying over her shoulder, "Suit yourself if you want to witness a colossal failure."

CHAPTER 17
LUCY: THE WRONG
SIDE OF RIGHT

Bert and I avoid each other this cataclysmic evening: first, for her having the audacity to argue whether Nancy Drew was real, and second, for her getting an honor for no good reason I can think of. After supper, Bert's gone to the beehives doing God knows what, and I find Mama on the front porch braiding Lydia's hair before story time. I stand and watch Mama's nimble fingers and wait for her to say something, but she doesn't. She makes me talk first.

"Mama, why are you doing this?"

"Because Lydia asked me to."

"I'm not talking about her hair. I'm talking about Bert reading."

"As I explained: It's a good goal. It will stretch her faster than anything can. You want her to succeed, don't you?"

"I guess."

Mama puts her hands on her hips. "Lucy Brown, what kind of weak answer is that?

She's your friend. Someone who has not had your blessings in life."

"But you don't even correct her when she uses that atrocious mountain talk. *Ain't* and *he don't.* You get after the rest of us with a vengeance if we have one slipup. Why is she allowed to talk white trash?"

Mama turns livid eyes on me. "Girl, what has gotten into you being so hurtful toward Bert? She has had everything disrupted in her life. The last thing I want to do is have her think she needs to change for us. Better grammar will happen over time, but I will not put pressure on her. And you won't either, you hear me? Go. Take a walk and find a better disposition to bring to story time. It's your turn to read."

I whine, "But she's going to read *The Velveteen Rabbit.*"

Oma brought more than horror stories, unnatural creatures, and sauerkraut to Riverton. She also brought us *The Velveteen Rabbit,* a cherished story for the ages. On the third Saturday in every September that I can remember, we throw the book a birthday party. Twice I've been the reader. Two years back, Miz Elvira, the librarian, was given the honor. Everybody in the family has had a turn reading except Lydia and Cora. For that celebration, we bake Oma's

German marble cake, light candles, and sing "Happy Birthday." This year, the book turns twenty-one years old, and the party will take place on September eighteenth at three o'clock. Front and center is the family's velveteen rabbit passed down from child to child. Lydia is the current guardian. And now we know Bert will read.

Oma made the rabbit from scraps of rich velvet and brocade. She made him years ago to honor the book that she loved for its wisdom. She made him for her grandson, Everett, when he turned six. He was a kind boy long grown into an army man who loves riddles. Oma brought the stuffed rabbit we love and the wolpertinger we fear.

After she died that last Thursday in May and we cleaned out her bedroom so Irene could have her own, the wolpertinger came down from the top of the armoire and was put away. It moved to the attic in its wooden box locked in Oma's carved trunk, out of sight.

Weeks went by, then Lydia and Cora began hearing things above their beds, in the attic. They said someone was crying when they were trying to sleep. They believe it's Oma's creature crying because it's lonely. They aren't afraid as much as they feel sorry for the thing buried in a trunk. I tell them the noise isn't the wolpertinger. The feathered and horned creature died sixty years ago, so how can it make a noise? One night, I set out to prove I'm right and the little girls are wrong.

Since the crying happens only at night, we wait until dark, then we unlatch the door to the narrow stairs that lead to the attic. A rush of stale air pushes out, and we stare into the gloomy cavern, into the shadowy peak of rafters. Bert says she won't go up there. She's afraid of the dark and doesn't care whether somebody's crying or not. So Lydia, Cora, and I stand at the bottom of the stairs and listen. We hear the wireless in the parlor turned low. We hear the wind whistling through the chimney flue. We hear squirrels skitter across the tin roof. But nothing cries. I carry the Eveready flashlight I got from Daddy's bedroom.

"Ready?" I whisper, and the little ones nod. I've never been in the attic at night, and I feel a moment's trepidation because the dark changes things. I climb the narrow stairs first. The flashlight pierces the shadows and the slanted eaves and washes across the dusty planks. Stored things loom tall. The three of us huddle and walk the line of light past a dress form, a rack of Oma's clothes, a stack of empty suitcases and carpetbags, and wooden crates of pots and dishes and empty jars. We move as one toward that darkest corner that holds the carved trunk that sits mostly forgotten. The light beam finds the trunk. The lid is propped open. The wolpertinger stands in front. Its eyes burn with fire. *Shit.*

I scream and struggle to breathe and grab Lydia's hand and push at Cora, and we knock over the dress form and the pile of suitcases and scramble down the steps to the safety of light. The noise brings Mama and Daddy upstairs where they find me shaking.

"Lucy said a bad word," Lydia tattles. "She said shit."

Did I?

"What were you doing in the attic," Mama asks, "and at night?"

I glance at the attic stairs and step back. "The little ones said they heard crying. Lydia thought it was the wolpertinger crying. I went to show her she was wrong." Then I whisper words even I struggle to believe. "But she might be right, Mama. It was out of the trunk and out of its box. *It was standing beside the trunk.* It looked at us with fiery eyes."

Lydia tugs at Mama's dress, but Mama looks at me like I'm the troublemaker.

"You're saying you believe the wolpertinger — the stuffed wolpertinger — climbed out of its box and out of the trunk on its own accord and was waiting for you."

Lydia tugs again, but Mama still doesn't look down.

"The wolpertinger that your great-grandfather found in 1881. And stuffed."

Daddy takes the flashlight from my hand and climbs the steps. Little Lydia is right behind him before I can stop her.

Mama goes on. "The creature that sat on Oma's armoire for over twenty years and never made a sound or moved an inch."

"Yes, ma'am. I know it sounds implausible, but I know what I saw," I say defensively.

Daddy's boots clomp on the floor above, then he comes down the steps with Lydia behind. She is carrying the blasted wolpertinger under her arm, along with the German paperweight of purple forget-me-nots. I back away, preparing for the creature to pivot its head and shoot fire at me. Instead, Lydia says, "I took him out. He didn't want to stay locked up, so I took him out. The other day. When Mama got jelly jars."

It takes a moment for me to understand. The wolpertinger didn't get out by itself. Lydia took it out. When Mama went in the attic to get jars.

"I tried to tell you, knucklehead." Lydia is mad at me.

Daddy latches the attic door and heads downstairs with the crisis over and done with. Mama takes the glass paperweight from Lydia and drops it in her apron pocket. "I wondered where that went," she says and steers the little girls and the dastardly wolpertinger into their bedroom. She smiles at me pitifully, like I'm too old to be gullible.

The wolpertinger now lives in Lydia's room. She is its caretaker. It makes an appearance on the porch or in the parlor when ghost stories are told. I have a smidgeon of doubt that it is fully dead, but I have more important things to think about, like school tomorrow while Bert gets homeschooled.

On that first day at assembly, Miz Pinkney declares, "Being able to read and write is our civic duty. Millions of men who want to fight in this war have been rejected because they can't do that very thing. Knowing how to read and write is necessary to keep our country safe." If there's another reason to love school, this is it.

Miz Pinkney brings in her biweekly copy of the *Mercer County Reporter* for our civics class. I feel a sense of pride that my sister

144

Irene works for the newspaper alongside the editor, Drake Cunningham. Occasionally, she writes a tiny article and always points out which one is hers. Some days, my teacher says, "We are living in tumultuous times that will change the world." Other weeks, the civics lecture focuses on bravery, not sacrifice. War tempers school and flavors everything sparse.

Bert causes a ruckus without even coming to school. All the boys know about Bert Tucker. They've seen her at the farmers market, at the soda fountain and the Saturday picture show where we saw *Frankenstein Meets the Wolf Man* and *For Whom the Bell Tolls* — and the bell tolls for Bert Tucker. Even I think she carries her own special oxygen. Her shadow always overpowers mine.

When she bathes shamelessly at the washbasin, comfortable in her splendor, she's slow to slip her nightgown over her head to spill down her perfect body. One time, she caught me staring and said, "You want to touch em?" and I blushed a heat that mortified me. I left the room, shocked that my first thought was *Yes.*

In school, I wasn't prepared for the interrogation from the older boys. Jamie Wichard, Russell Langley, Frankie Moore, and

Donnie Gibson are Grady's age. They rubberneck those first days, checking for Bert's arrival before the school bell rings. I don't give them the satisfaction of an answer, but that doesn't stop them from giving me notes to take to her. One day, I say, "She's getting homeschooled," then feel guilty about tattling on her. I thought distance between Bert and me would be a good thing, but it's more trouble than it's worth.

Bert works every morning under Mama's tutelage. She does homework with us in the evening. She's almost worn out the dictionary to check spellings, but numbers stump her. We use dried beans to teach her arithmetic. It's a game she's getting better at. She practices reading *The Velveteen Rabbit.* She's getting better at that, too.

I don't give her the love notes. I stuff them in a sock and tie a knot and hide it in the hayloft.

CHAPTER 18
BERT: DOING THE DEED

"I'm gonna puke. Right in front of everybody, I'm gonna puke or faint and mess up everything."

Miz Brown keeps brushing my hair and puts bobby pins in to hold the waves away from my face. "You'll do fine. It's only nerves. Once you start, it'll all come naturally."

"I can't remember what a single word looks like. My mouth's a cotton ball. I'm gonna puke."

"Pretend you're reading to family. You've read to us at story time before."

I peek out the front window at a terrible sight. The porch is full and the yard's filling up, too. Everybody I know and then some is here. Everybody waits, laughing and smiling, and I hate em all. Every dadgum one of em. I suspect they mostly come to eat cake, but they wanna see me make a fool of myself.

147

"I can't." I back away from the door. "No, no, no, I can't."

Miz Brown takes my face in her hands, locks eyes and declares, "You must do it. This is a big moment, Bert, not because you can fail, but because you *will* succeed. You've prepared fully. Everybody's rooting for you. Every person out there is a forgiving soul. They know this is a big step, but it's *The Velveteen Rabbit*'s twenty-first birthday, and I chose you for the honor. What more delightful foray into public storytelling is there? Now, I'm going to walk out with you and welcome everybody. There's a glass of water beside your chair. Take your time. Have fun."

My mouth is dry as ash. My hands shake with the trembles. For the first time since I got exiled, I wish I was back on my mountain and could run to the waterfall. I won't even mind Sam Logan trying to steal a kiss from me, him with stinky breath that don't go away.

But you want more, Bert, and here is more. Take it.

I follow Miz Brown and my legs carry me to the only empty chair, and I sit. One hand finds the book, and the other finds the water glass, and I sip. They wait. Somebody clears his throat. Their folding fans stir the warm air like the thrum of bee wings. A honeybee lands on my knee and looks at me, then flies off. My ears are closed off and I hear my voice come from far away. I don't stumble over hard words like *mechanical* and *government* and *uncomfortable,* cause Miz Brown taught me good. Then I turn the last page, and it's over, and they clap and Irene carries out Oma's German marble cake holding twenty-one birthday candles burning, and when it's cut, I get the first piece.

Lu comes over with the librarian, who shakes my hand proper. Miz Elvira is her name, and she says, "You did a swell job reading. Some of those words are real challenging. I'm glad I came."

Tiny Junior waits. He stands there beside me while I wait for Lu to say I did a swell job, too, but she walks away with Miz Elvira.

"What?" I say to Tiny Junior, still feeling giddy and lightheaded and smarter than before.

"Real. What do it look like?" He always picks a favorite word from a story he wants to see wrote down, so I tear a scrap from a notepad and write real at the top. I say, "I left room so you can practice," and he takes the paper, folds it careful, and puts it in his overalls pocket.

CHAPTER 19
LUCY: HUMBLING ENDEAVOR

"I hate everything about tobacco." I confide this to Bert as we stand at the edge of the field after supper, eating oatmeal raisin cookies.

"I know you don't smoke or chew, but how come you hate it?"

"Because it's the most demanding crop a farmer can grow. At least that's what they say. All the plowing and planting and pampering baby seedlings when Mother Nature sends too much or too little rain. The hoeing to hack out weeds and picking off fat green hornworms that can ravage an entire crop. All the bent backs of men and women stooped over in the hot sun and windless heat to pick leaves from the bottom first."

"You don't do that kinda work," Bert says and misses my point.

"No, but I see it. And I don't have to do something in order to know how it feels."

She said, "That ain't true. Doing and

knowing go together, but seeing don't go with knowing."

I feel a rise of annoyance that she doesn't grasp the importance of what I'm saying. I'm telling her a terrible secret I never spoke out loud before, and I'm making a pragmatic observation about my family's livelihood; she's talking about something else.

For a hundred years, my daddy's people have worked this farm, and it's never been easy. I can hardly remember when Daddy was pleased with the outcome and income when the tobacco market started late August and ended in October. He called the tobacco business a humbling endeavor. He said tobacco has been valued all the way back to the Chesapeake colonies. Back to the time when tobacco paid taxes to the British crown. It bought land and paid preachers to save souls. Daddy read it even bought used wives who husbands didn't want anymore. Mama thought that was a crying shame and told Daddy not to get ideas, but she couldn't deny it since he read it in a book. Those glory days for tobacco are gone, but the gold leaf is still the money crop for farmers in my Carolina. The crop of '43 is over, and Daddy said he made enough for us to get by. Now Bert talks about something different and gets my dander up.

She repeats, "Doing and knowing go together, but seeing and knowing don't."

"What does that even mean?"

"Well, I could *tell* you bout going hungry and missing breakfast and dinner and supper all day long. I could *tell* you how your insides grab and pucker for a scrap, for a crumb, and it's winter and the woods are mean, and your mind forgets how to get you back home before dark, but *telling* you those words don't let you *feel* it. Don't let you *know* hungry. One thing is words, the other's hungry."

Oh Lord. "Did that happen to you? Did you go hungry?"

"Maybe."

"It's nothing to be ashamed of, Bert. If that happened . . ."

We've been looking out at the field, but now she turns to me. "What do you know bout shame?" she throws at me. "If you got a smidgeon of shame, it's cause you picked it. Not cause it's real."

"I don't want to fight, Bert. I was saying I don't like tobacco. That's all."

We finish our oatmeal raisin cookies, and Bert says, "Tobacco don't bother me."

"Good for you." I lift my chin in defiance. "But I'm different."

"You might wanna keep your thinking to yourself." Bert walks away.

CHAPTER 20
BERT: DELIVER ME

There's a knock on the front door. I open it to find a government man standing on the porch with his hat under his arm and a telegram in his hand. He says, "I'm looking for Miz Wade Sully."

I leave the front door wide open with the cold November air rushing in and run to find Miz Brown in the kitchen. She gets Helen from the bedroom and walks her to the open front door with me and the little ones behind. The soldier holds out that piece a paper, but Helen won't take it. Miz Brown has to take it for her. The paper says Wade Sully is MIA, missing in action. Helen crumples in a heap, right in the open door, like her legs quit working.

Miz Brown says over and over, "He's not dead, honey. He's missing. It says Wade's missing in action." The government man leaves, and I run into the cold to ring the dinner bell for Mr. Brown to come, and

Grady and Yancy, too, and Gertie and Lu come from the barn, and I step back while they hurry to carry limp Helen to the empty bed beside the empty crib.

That woman don't cry out. It's way worse. Helen opens her mouth wide and grabs the sheets and twists in pain, but no sound comes out. The pain is outta reach, locked in deep.

Then ice comes falling from the sky like tiny beads. They clatter on the roof and the packed dirt and the oak tree, and Gertie rushes home holding her thin coat over her head. Grady, Mr. Brown, and Yancy run to get animals inside the barn and cover the chicken coop with a tarp and put more feed inside. Me and Lu tie a hold-on rope from the barn to the house, and stack firewood on the porch, and the falling ice don't stop. It's like the sky is shooting BBs at us.

It's a hard night, and the telephone line goes out but the electric stays on. I heat soup and slice bread Helen baked this morning. Irene and Miz Brown stay with Helen in the back bedroom. We eat and watch out the window and listen to branches break and trees fall.

Next morning, the ice is thick on every bush and tree, and broke branches lie on the slick ground, but the ice keeps falling.

When giggles come outta Helen's bedroom, I'm ready to stick my head in their room and say, "What's so funny?" but don't have to. I peek through the crack of the door and see Irene on her knees beside the porcelain wash pan. Steam rises from the pan, her helping Helen to a sponge bath. Irene says, "I'm gonna need a bigger washrag . . . waaay bigger," which gets them two giggling again over Helen's necked baby belly, big as a watermelon. Sour bile rises in my throat, this being my first time seeing a pregnant belly without a dress to shield the ugly.

"Bert?" Miz Brown comes up from behind, carrying fresh towels. "You alright, dear? You look pale." She steers me into Helen's room as Irene drops a clean nightgown over her sister's ruint body and commences to brushing her long hair. Helen's eyes are closed and her face stays tight.

Her mama and sister chatter like magpies bout ice from the north coating everything in the South. They chat bout baby clothes brought down from the attic and washed for this new child. All the while, Helen clutches her belly and sways side to side.

Then it happens. I witness pain hitting Helen like a train. Her eyes grow big in shock, and her body locks, waiting for that pain to let go so she can breathe. All I can think bout is the way that baby's gotta come out a hole no bigger than a half-dollar. Right then and there, I vow to never get in the family way, even if I do travel to foreign places with fine names to call a baby.

"Would you empty the wash pan, dear?" Miz Brown's voice is calm as a cloud, and I take that wash pan, glad to escape a room getting ready for a bloody battle. I know now I'd have been no good to Aunt Violet in her hour of need. What was Pa thinking, sending a girl to do woman's work?

"Should you call the doctor or somebody?"

"The phone lines are down and nobody can get out this far."

"You know what you're doing?" I don't mean to sound rude.

"Bert, we're all Helen has. We'll do fine. I helped when Sugar was born. The midwife did the hard work, but at least I witnessed it. And having birthed six of my own helps me empathize. We'll manage because we don't have another choice."

I'm backing away from the bedroom door when Miz Brown says, "I do need you to feed the stove and put on more water to heat and tell Lucy I need her. We've got a baby coming."

Helen's room is at the back of the house,

and I walk to the parlor at the front, still carrying that washbasin in my hands, forgetting to empty it. Lu is reading, Lydia and Cora play with paper dolls, and Grady and Mr. Brown fiddle with the radio, trying to get a signal. *Fibber McGee and Molly* bursts into the parlor, and Mr. Brown shouts, "Hot diggity dog."

I wish I was a man.

"Lu," I whisper till she looks up.

"What?" she mouths.

I tilt my head toward Helen's room. "Your mama needs you." She puts down her book. I empty the washbasin, load the woodstove, put on more water to heat like I was told, pop popcorn and melt butter to go on top, then brush and braid the girls' hair. I do anything to stay away from a woman bout to get tore in two.

Helen's wails travel to the parlor, and the girls tear up. *Fibber McGee and Molly* is no match for birthing pains. I reach into the bookcase for *The Velveteen Rabbit,* but on this hard day wrapped in ice, even *The Velveteen Rabbit* is no help. Cora starts crying, and that starts Lydia crying, too. "Is she gonna die, Daddy?" Cora wants to know.

He turns off the radio and gets down on one knee beside us. "No, sweet girls. Your sister's working hard, and the baby's working hard, and she's got help. Let's bundle up and go look at a wonderland."

We put on layers of sweaters, coats, and gloves and stand on the porch and stamp our feet that get near froze and watch our warm breath come out in white puffs. Me and Lydia and Cora stay on the porch while Mr. Brown and Grady take holt of the rope strung between the house and the barn. The rope will keep them upright on the ice so they can go milk cows and feed animals.

I look at those white bee boxes with icicles hanging off the sides. Lu told me the bees huddle together extra tight in cold weather and they make heat by beating their wings. They eat the honey they made in summer, and every forty-five days, the bees die and are kicked out of the hive, and new babies are born. I wish I could put my ear against them boxes and hear that hum like angel wings. The bees need to hold on till spring.

When we girls bout freeze on the porch, Grady and Mr. Brown work their way back across the icy yard with buckets of warm milk steaming and a basket of eggs. We come inside and I find Lucy at the kitchen table looking sick green. I don't want to hear bout what she witnessed. She says, "A baby has come into this world. It's a girl."

Poor thing.

I peek in the bedroom. Bloody sheets soak in the washtub, and Irene washes Helen lying on the bed. I stand in the corner and put my eyes anywhere cept on Helen. After another clean gown is worked over Helen's head, Lydia and Cora are called to come in to meet their niece. They count her fingers. They pull back the blanket Aunt Fanniebelle made and count her toes. They're all moony-eyed over the red-faced thing mewing like a kitten.

Miz Brown straightens the edges of the blanket over Helen. "Thank you, Bert, for taking such good care of the little ones. We had our hands full for a while."

Her goodness can't wash away my selfish sin. I was worthless birthing this child.

"What's its name?" I say to be polite but keep my distance.

"Helen's calling her Baby Girl until she gets a formal name from Wade," she says, like Wade's gone fishing and will be home tonight and they can decide.

I take tiny steps toward the two of them in bed. Helen's eyes are dull, her face as pale as smoke. I step closer. She looks out the window into the world of ice. Miz Brown says, "Let me take Baby Girl so you can rest, honey. Her granddaddy wants to meet her. Come on, girls." The little ones bustle out of the room like a brood following the hen.

I turn to follow when Helen whispers, "Stay." She reaches out for me, and when I step closer, she clamps down on my wrist. I lean in to hear. "Need you to do something."

"Now?"

"No but soon as you can." She pauses to catch her breath. "I need to know bout my Wade. If he's alive."

"How would I know such a thing?"

"Trula Freed."

I glance at the door to see who looms nearby. We're alone. I turn back to Helen.

"She knows?"

"I can only hope."

"Your mama won't like it one bit."

"She doesn't believe in knowing things, but I'm sick with worry. I don't even want to name our baby till I know her daddy's coming home."

"You and Wade didn't decide names?" I try to wiggle my way out of the situation.

"Nothing final enough to lay on her for life."

"Why don't you ask Lu to help? She knows the old woman more than me."

"I want to leave her out of this. I want *you* to do it. As soon as the ice melts."

I never been to Trula Freed's place on my own. I remember the scare of that shock that run through me when she took holt of my hand. And what if she says Wade Sully is dead? Can I deliver that truth to Helen? And if I lie to her and say he's alive, can she forgive me when she finds out different? And if Helen dies of a broke heart cause of bad news I bring, will the Browns still want me? And is Lu gonna tan my hide when she finds me going to Trula's place without her? What Helen is asking can change my world.

She reaches on the side table for the telegram and presses it in my hand and says, "Give this to Trula Freed. Please, so I know for sure. I'm counting on you."

I don't have a choice but to put the telegram in my pocket and pray for ice to stay forever. My belly aches over what I got talked into and the weight of that telegram grows heavy in my pocket. On the third day, the sun shines and the warm air comes, and the ground switches from slippery to sludge, and I pick a fight with Lu helping me with my numbers at the kitchen table. I say loud enough for Miz Brown to hear, "My head hurts from all this stupid learning. I hate numbers," then I grab my jacket off the peg, stomp out the door and down the steps, buying space to do Helen's deed.

Nobody comes after me. We been cooped up too long and tempers are flinty. Before I leave the yard, I head for one of the hives and put my ear on top of the box, scared I won't hear nothing like angel wings, but I do. Wings hum and they whisper. That hum turns my heart light while I cross the field and go through the pines to Trula Freed's red door, but the whole way I pray, *Don't be home. Don't be home. Please don't be home.*

I knock, and Biscuit whimpers inside. I call out, "Miz Trula, you in there?" and I look in the window and see her on the floor. The door with a lock ain't locked and I open it. A chair is turned over beside the woman on the floor. She has blood at her temple and one leg cocked funny. When did she fall? The cup of tea on the table is still warm.

I lean over her. "Miz Trula, it's Bert. Can you hear me?"

She moans. I dip a clean rag in the pot of warm water on the stove and hold it at the blood on her head. She opens her green eyes and whispers, "Bert, my good friend. Tis my knee. It sprain, not break."

"Want me to fetch the doctor?"

"No. We manage. You help."

"*Me?* I got a weak constitution."

But there's nobody here but me and the

yellow dog, so Trula Freed talks me through the steps. I kneel beside her, slide my fingers under her head, and put a pillow for comfort. She keeps her green eyes mostly closed, but when they open and look for me, they don't look at me straight on. They flit around the walls, searching. My hands shake, and the air in my chest rattles being this close to a witchy woman who knows things. "You do good," she says, and I wrap her hurt knee tight to keep down swelling.

"Help me up," she says, and she uses my arms to sit and struggle into her chair. This time, I don't feel the shock at her touch. I pull her cup of tea beside her.

I say, "How'd you fall?" and tuck a soft blanket around her legs and under her feet.

"Reach too high. Up there," she says and points to a silver baby's rattle.

I get the footstool so I can reach it. I pick it up, and the sound is a tinkling bell.

Trula Freed says, "Put this under Helen's pillow. It's for Baby Girl."

I want to ask Miz Trula how she knows such things since she got no telephone and no neighbors close by. I don't smell anything special in the air she breathes. But I don't ask. I do say, "Helen wants to know bout Wade. Bout him being alive and safe." I hold

165

out the telegram and she takes it from my hand.

I come in the Browns' back door, take off my muddy boots, and don't even get to hang up my coat before Helen calls out for me, and I go to her. Baby Girl is being loved on in another room, and it's only me and Helen.

"Well?" she says without giving me time to catch my breath. "Did you see her? Did she tell you?" There is a glisten of mad fever on her cheeks.

"I saw her."

"And? *And?*"

I never saw eyes that hard or hopeful.

"I give her the telegram like you wanted. She said Wade Sully is alive, but he . . ."

Helen's face crumples in relief, and her narrow shoulders shake as she turns to cry into the pillow. She don't give me time to say bout the old woman's fall and the bloody knot, the twisted knee and the green eyes looking wobbly. I don't say that believing what Trula Freed said today ain't the smart thing to do. Helen hears what she wants. I got no choice but to let it be. I slip the silver rattle under her pillow.

CHAPTER 21
LUCY: GALL-DOUBLE-DANG

On the heels of the bizarre ice storm that held us captive, a heat spell arrives. We open windows wide and kick the quilts off our beds and the shoes off our feet. It's week three since we heard Wade is missing, and Helen grows frail, and the fretful baby with no name gives none of us a night's rest. There's been no letter from Everett for a week of Sundays, and everybody is flushed and lethargic with no appetite.

On Sunday afternoon, Uncle Nigel and Aunt Fanniebelle show up for visiting day. Their chatter coming into the house carries too much energy. Their words are like broken glass to my ears. Uncle Nigel says, "David, I'm reading an interesting book about antigravity and can't put it down."

Daddy chuckles.

Aunt Fanniebelle says, "Had to lay eyes on Betty Gail to see if her colic is getting better." She calls Baby Girl by a real name

167

no matter how many times we try to honor Helen's wishes for neutrality. Today, she brings more baby clothes too prissy to be practical, a fruitcake, and a jar of pickled beets. Her words clack against my brain like a train run off its track. My eyeballs pulse and feel bruised behind paper thin lids.

Aunt Fanniebelle stops talking and looks at Mama up close. Passes her eyes over all our silent faces. "None of y'all look good," she says and puts a cool hand on Mama's forehead, then on mine. She yells to Uncle Nigel in the parlor. "Go fetch Doc Robertson — and drive like a maniac."

"On Sunday? Can't you let Doc and the Lord rest? The baby'll be fine."

"It's not the baby. The whole gall-dang bunch is sick."

Nobody thinks to call the doctor on the phone. We're too fuddle-brained to register efficiency or our situation. We thought the malaise came from strange weather in December and worry over the war that won't stop. Or is it simply something we ate? We can't think straight.

Doc Robertson comes with his black bag and a linen napkin stuck cockeyed in his shirt collar. We line up like school children. Only Daddy, Cora, and Baby Girl have no symptoms. The rest of us have high fevers, sore throats, body aches, and stomach pains. Maybe we have the scarlet fever Margery Williams wrote about in *The Velveteen Rabbit.* Pint-size Aunt Fanniebelle stands by the tall doctor's side, peering around him moving from one of us to the next, her concern growing.

"You think it's the influenza?" she whispers with a catch in her voice.

Mama repeats, "Influenza?" while the doctor fingers her swollen neck. "You mean like the one back in 1918?"

Daddy has been leaning against the kitchen wall, but at the mention of the epidemic that changed his family tree, he stands upright. He doesn't have to look it up in the *Encyclopedia Britannica* to know that influenza killed as many people the two years *after* the Great War ended as were killed *in* the war. Daddy's people paid dearly. Overnight, the plague took the lives of his parents, two younger brothers, and a string of cousins. There's a box of old photographs in the attic. In the box is a faded picture of my daddy taken in April 1919. He poses with a dozen school friends on steps. They wear muslin facemasks, hoping the material would keep the plague away, but their fear of the Spanish flu is evidently unstoppable: from the nose up, the children are scared. I can pick out Daddy by the cowlick at his hairline and his perfectly arched eyebrows only Grady inherited. Daddy says one of the things he remembers is the hammering of nails in coffins. The hammering went on all day and all night.

Today, I don't say what's niggling in the back of my mind: Maybe a world-killing disease comes when a war has gone on too long. Maybe the Brown family is the starting point this time.

Doc says, "Let's not borrow trouble yet and make it bigger than it is, Minnie, but we're gonna take precautions since it's affecting so many of you. First thing, we need to check your food to make sure nothing has spoiled in this heat. We can bring down the fevers with ice baths. Then all the surfaces need to be scrubbed with hot water, vinegar, and baking soda. Bed linens need to be changed often. Bottom line: I need to quarantine everybody here except the baby and Cora, who show no signs of sickness. And you, David."

Aunt Fanniebelle says, "Nigel, you take the well folks to our place. Bring back a stack of clean sheets and towels and put em on the porch. Don't come inside. And, David, do you think the Mayhews would mind helping out? They're close by, and Gertie is kind."

"I hate to expose them to sickness."

Doc says, "You need more help than the Mayhews."

My brain has a hard time figuring out who's sick. Mama and me. Bert and Irene. Helen, who we thought was brokenhearted, but it's more than her heart that ails her. Grady and Lydia, too? I use my fingers to count seven. I don't remember Nancy Drew ever being sick in all her escapades. She got kidnapped, hijacked, locked up, poisoned, knocked unconscious, and almost drowned, but I don't think she ever got sick.

The doctor goes on, "Seven beds in seven separate spaces. Seven pans of chipped ice. Clean towels. Air the pillows and blankets several times a day." Aunt Fanniebelle writes down the list he rattles off too fast for me to hold on to. She is one little lady with purpose who rides bravely on a sea of sickness. She rolls up her sleeves. Then I faint.

I come to lying on a narrow pallet without a stitch of clothes on. I'm so cold my teeth hurt. The light in the room is low. The bookcases rise up and around the room and swim in my murky vision. I shiver, and my joints clack like a bag of marbles. Wet towels lie on my naked body. I try to call out, but no sound comes. I'm too weak to cast off the wet towels when Sugar Mayhew comes into view. She says too loud, "Mama, she got her eyes open."

Gertie comes in on soft feet, making soothing sounds. "Hold yourself together, Miz Lucy. Your teeth is rattling cause your fever's rising." She strips off the wet towels and sheet and wraps me like a baby in a warm, dry blanket. She raises my head. "Sip this tea. Trula Freed made it special for y'all. It's got purple honey in it. Said it holds a world of cure."

My ears must not be working right to hear Trula Freed's name spoken under this roof along with purple honey, but the tea is a comfort. I sleep.

I wake burning up, parched, trying to unwrap this shroud that has me in its grip. The blanket and pillow are soaked with sweat, and I try to find the edge of the blanket so I can pull it back. I gasp for air and raise my head, and the bookcases swim again before my blurry vision. Why is Sugar Mayhew still here? She calls out loud, "Mama, she got her eyes open again," and I think I heard her say that before but can't be sure. I try to turn off my ears to find quiet, but I hear "Nancy Drew" being called in hard whispers, needing help, needing hot

172

water, needing chipped ice. Or was Gertie calling her husband, Yancy Mayhew? I never realized my Nancy and her Yancy sound close. I need to tell him of my amazing discovery when I can rise from this soupy depth and my tongue works again.

An angel with white cotton hair and green eyes leans close to my face with a cool washcloth and more "tea to make strong, purple honey to cure" and comfort in her voice. She lifts me like I'm a twig or a dried cornstalk and washes me with water that smells of mint. Fresh air fills my lungs and takes me under to a quiet place.

I open my eyes and keep them open, and my first words from my arid throat are, "How long?" I hear soft voices down the hall in the kitchen. "How long?" I croak again and hear a heavy rustling off to the side. I smell pungent Vicks VapoRub.

Daddy comes into view. "Hey, Lucy," he whispers so my ears won't hurt. "It's been eleven days you've been in and out of fever."

"It felt longer. Like a year," I croak.

"No," he chuckles. "It's been eleven days. Long enough."

"Others?" Stingy words come out.

"Everybody's fine. Everybody's thin and weak but fine. Thanks to a lot of saintly people working to bring you through. I've never been so scared or so grateful for kindness. This thing was big, but I don't want to tire you. Lie still. I'll be right back. I gotta get your mama. She'll need to see you with her own eyes."

I want to ask Daddy what day it is. Did we miss Christmas? Did the lot of us sleep and shiver and sweat through it all? Did Cora stay well and the baby get over the colic? Has anybody heard from Everett and Wade? I stepped outside time long enough for so much to have happened.

There is a flurry of energy coming, shuffling feet growing closer. Daddy says from far away, "Only a few at a time. Don't crowd her."

Mama comes in first, and I gasp. Her hair is *white.* As white as Trula Freed's. Her cheeks are sunken. Her navy housedress hangs from her shoulders, but the eyes belong to Mama. She takes my hands and kisses them over and over until we giggle. Then Bert steps forward, a shocking image honed bone thin, the gold in her skin and hair like burnished copper. She looks like a Greek goddess. She holds a walking stick. Helen, tiny Lydia. Such changed faces. What do *I* look like?

"Help me sit, Bert," I say, and she piles pillows behind me and scoots me up so I

174

don't have to hold my head up. "What happened to us?"

Mama says, "The best Doc Robertson can say is that we had our own brand of strange sickness. Nobody else in the county has had it. At least none reported. Your daddy's been calling it the Brown influenza, but I don't like our name attached to something sinister. Aunt Fanniebelle took to calling it the gall-double-dang flu. Whatever the case, we made it through. Every one of us."

"How'd we do that?"

"With help." Mama reaches over me, raises the window shade an inch, and lets in a slice of afternoon sun that makes my weak eyes squint against the bright. "Let me get you broth so you can start recuperating. You hungry?"

I nod. Mama and Daddy leave, and Bert helps Lydia up on my makeshift bed.

"You look terrible," Lydia says, grinning. "And you stink."

"Mirror, please," I say, and Bert takes the framed mirror off the wall and holds it up to reflect a stranger, a *waif* I've read about in English classics, with sunken chest and eyes burned deep, who has flown close to the sun and been spared. I pull back my parched lips and try to grin, but I forgot how.

175

Mama returns with a steaming cup of something that smells delicious and looks pale purple. My stomach rumbles. She orders Bert to put away the mirror. "We all look a fright, but we're here and we'll heal."

I open my mouth like a baby bird. I swallow the first spoonful. Then another.

"Take it slow. Only a few mouthfuls every quarter hour until your stomach remembers what to do."

I reach out and touch Mama's white hair. Without thinking of protection or deceit, I say, "You look like Trula Freed."

Mama says, "I do?" and her hand strokes her head softly like you do a kitten. Her wrist is frail as a reed. "It was Trula's cures that carried us through," she explains. "When the doctor couldn't get the fever under control, she brought the purple honey that showed up last summer. Said it was the cure waiting for the sickness it would heal." Mama says the mystic's name with respect. "So many good people helped. Flossie Rose and Tiny Junior. Yancy, Sugar, Gertie and her sister Clara, and Miz Elvira. Friends from church. So many souls turned something bad into goodness I can never repay." She tears up and leaves the room with Daddy behind.

Bert and Lydia turn quiet, and I'm tired

from little effort. Lydia leans down and whispers, "You still stink."

CHAPTER 22
BERT: CROSSING OVER

We take naps like Baby Girl. Mornings and afternoons and as soon as the sun sets, we fall into bed cause we can't help it. It took everything we had to fight the sickness. When we wake, food cooks in the oven. Washed sheets hang on the line. More wood is chopped.

But this last day of '43, it's only the Browns and me at the house. Miz Brown ties on her apron and starts making angel food cake, and I sit at the table, separating eggs and beating the whites for her. The cake goes in the oven, and she looks at me odd.

"What'd I do, Miz Brown?" I'm quick to take blame.

"It's what you haven't done. You've been a rightful member of our family for half a year but still call us Mr. and Miz Brown like visiting company."

"What should I call you? It don't seem

fittin to call y'all Ma and Pa."

"I agree. Those were your parents' names. The children call us Mama and Daddy, so is that different enough for you?"

I get goose bumps looking at this kind-hearted woman, and I'm glad I'm sitting down, cause my knees woulda buckled. "What will everybody think if I act highfalu-tin?"

"Dear Bert." She reaches for my hand, hers flecked with flour and minus her wed-ding band cause her fingers are too skinny. "They'll say *what took you so long*. We'll tell them at supper."

And we do. I try not to wear out their new names that first evening, but the temptation is strong. "Mama, would you pass the biscuits, please?" I grin when I say it. A few minutes later, I say, "Daddy, can I warm your coffee?"

While me and Lu do dishes, the radio plays "Everything I Love." Lu whispers, "That's their favorite Glenn Miller song."

Daddy pulls Mama into his arms, and they dance round the kitchen floor, and he croons my haven in heaven above.

We rest, then rise, and on this last day of the year, in the heart of the dark, we wrap up in blankets and sit in the cold on the porch. Lydia says, "What's the New Year

179

gonna feel like? How will we know it's *really* here?" She cuddles up on one side of me on the swing and Cora on the other. Oma's quilts are tucked all around. The brittle stars hang close to the ground. "Is there gonna be a glowing light? Will it make a funny sound?"

"I don't think so," I say, but I don't rightly know. I never stayed up to bear witness to a new year. Mama's white hair glows in the dusk, her sitting in a rocking chair with Daddy behind her smoking a cigarette, leaning against the house. Doc Robertson says her hair might stay white the rest of her days. He says some sicknesses take more out of a body than others.

Mama explains, "The New Year will come without fanfare except when we light the sparklers Uncle Nigel gave us."

"Which way is it coming from? Over there?" Cora yawns, then points to where the sun rises.

"It doesn't come from a direction," Mama says. "It settles over the land when it's time, and everything looks the same but is different."

There are long pieces of quiet for us to think or rest our tongues from talking, cause these ain't regular days. I think of the folks who took care of us being sick. Tonight, we ate chicken and dumplings from Gertie's sister, Clara. Then we ate the angel food cake that Mama and I made.

In my piece of quiet, I think back to those sick days making me worthless as weeds. Sometimes Sugar and Gertie tended to me. One time, Sugar cried and her mama spoke words meant for private. "You hush them tears, child. You don't help your brother Whiz one bit cause you cry. He smart and doing all he can to stay alive. When he come home, he'll look for the good you been doing. Like now. Helping these sick folks."

"Is he gonna die?"

"Where'd you get such a notion? He as safe as can be, hunkered down somewhere. Whiz Mayhew got more things to think about than sending us his words. He'll write when he got time. But keep him in every prayer. Don't want the Lord to forget bout our boy."

I been told Whiz Mayhew was a regular in the Brown house before the army had need for him. He would hunch over the kitchen table with a stack of books and wear down the lead in a pencil. Mama said he graduated top of his class. His army picture was in the paper for getting a medal for being brave, and Mama took the whole newspaper that day to Gertie. He's called Whiz cause he's a whiz at everything. I wonder if the Mayhews got a letter from him yet.

Grady talks first. "Now why are we sitting out here freezing instead of sleeping?" He yawns and pulls his blanket tighter.

Lu says, "It's peaceful. I hear my heart beating."

"Me, too. Me, too," the little girls chime in, hardly giving time enough to hear their hearts beat.

Mama says, "Right now, nothing stands between the ten of us and the miracles we've witnessed the past year. Nothing to distract us from a new beginning, perched on a pinhead of possibility. I believe the best year of our lives starts tonight."

"How you figure that?" I wanna believe her.

"Well, we're different now. A year ago, we didn't know you were coming, and now you're one of us. A year ago, we didn't know Baby Girl was even a wish. Or that the gall-double-dang flu would take us to our knees, or that our honeybees would make purple honey to cure us, or that our friends would fight hard for us. I believe this New Year will see the end of the war, and Everett and Wade will come home where they belong. I believe that with all my heart."

Helen says, "Amen."

Irene starts singing "Silent Night." Everybody sings except Baby Girl, who does her part as baby Jesus. The cuckoo clock chimes midnight. Grady lights sparklers. We stand in a line at the edge of the porch, looking out on a new world. The sparklers fizzle. We hear a hum. The hum grows louder. It can't be honeybees. They don't survive outside in the cold. But a hum is coming this way, coming from the east, coming across the field.

Grady sees them first. Airplanes. A line of them. They rumble over the land. They fly low in front of the buzzing sound behind. My stomach cramps cause this don't look right. Planes don't sneak low in the night in the Carolina dark. We hold hands tight. The New Year is here.

But what has come with it?

■ ■ ■ ■

1944

■ ■ ■ ■

CHAPTER 23
LUCY: RIDDLES
AND A MYSTERY

I haven't had a dream since the flu left me unbalanced, and I wondered if I ever would again. Then a dream comes and it's grim.

It's a pale day spitting ice when a man comes to the door and knocks three times. Through the curtained window, I see his ragged army uniform. He carries a dusty rucksack, and his boots are muddy. The man could be our Wade Sully, but his nose is smashed flat. Dried blood circles coal-black eyes. His mouth is sewn shut with coarse twine. The sour of rot slides through the cracks of the door. I work to let him in, but when I turn the glass doorknob, it spins like a top and won't stop. I shout through the door, "Wade Sully, I see you. I'm trying to let you in. Helen and Baby Girl need you. Don't go." But the army man turns and walks away, and the back of his head is a wolf's face with brittle eyes and teeth a tangle of bloody thorns. Suddenly, Tiny

Junior is there and presses a scrap of paper against the glass and says, "Miz Lucy, is this what B-A-D looks like?"

I bolt upright in the bed that holds Bert and the lumps of Lydia and Cora nesting between, and I clutch my pounding heart. My skin is clammy through my flannel nightgown. The faint smell of rot lingers in the air. Lydia mumbles from under the quilts, "What stinks?"

"Bad dream. That's all. Go back to sleep."

But I don't go back to sleep even though traces of morning are far away. Why did I dream about Wade now when it's been six weeks since the MIA telegram? He's been on the periphery of my family all my life, eating at our dinner table, shooting marbles with Grady, listening to Oma's odd tales, courting Helen like a lovesick puppy. He's Baby Girl's daddy, and now he's missing, and my sister is a hollowed-out shell of herself, different from the weakness left behind by the gall-double-dang. Helen was always shy, but now she's a turtle locked inside hardness.

When the sun comes up, I drag myself out of bed, but Mama still keeps us home from school till we're stronger. I feel so puny, I don't even miss going to school, and our days are lackadaisical and erratic. We are a quiet household until Lydia hears the crunch of the mailman's tires. She squeals, "He's here, he's here," and the coming of Mr. Jules changes things. Out of respect, he hand-delivers letters from Everett instead of leaving them in the mailbox to wait. Today, January tenth, is the first letter of the year.

Lydia is happy to have her favorite mark for one of Everett's riddles. She strikes as the mailman opens his car door. "What two things can you never eat for breakfast, Mr. Jules?"

The patient man plays along. "What can I never eat? Hmm . . . Ice cream?"

"What *two* things," Lydia clarifies, then adds, "and you can eat ice cream for breakfast. I did that."

Mama with the white hair steps out on the porch for the letter. She wears one of Oma's old sweaters, her thin arms folded against the chill. Mr. Jules finishes the riddle game and I listen through the door.

"Liver and onions? Two pigs feet?" the mailman guesses.

"You saying silly stuff. But you're still wrong. Give up?"

"I'm afraid so. If I didn't have mail to deliver . . ." was how he ends riddle time.

"The answer is *dinner* and *supper*. What you can't eat for breakfast . . . get it?"

189

"You are a clever girl," he chuckles, hands Mama the mail, and adds, "Thought you'd want to know I passed a government car half mile back. The uniform man was asking for the Mayhew place."

"Oh, sweet merciful heavens," Mama whispers, then comes in the front door with Lydia trailing behind.

"Mr. Jules likes my riddles, doesn't he, Mama? Lucy says I bother him."

"Did not."

"Did too."

Mama says, "It's good you tell Everett's riddles. When you stop, the riddle's life is over." Mama reaches for her coat on the hook. "Every time I hear you tell one, I feel Everett here with us." She taps today's letter in her hand. "And tonight we get a new one, and I want you to wear it out and spread it to kingdom come. Right now, I need to go see the Mayhews."

Lydia and I follow her into the kitchen. Helen is hanging washed diapers on the inside line. The outside lines are full. Seven-week-old Baby Girl sleeps in a laundry basket padded with a blanket.

"Want me to come?" I say.

"Where?" Helen wrings out another wet diaper.

"The Mayhews. Gertie and Yancy may

190

have had a visit from a government man. I'll be back directly."

Helen's mind is fragile, and with those few words, she starts shaking. Mama slips out the back, and Helen takes Baby Girl into their bedroom and shuts the door. I finish wringing out and hanging the diapers. They drip drip drip.

My little sister pulls a chair to the counter, climbs up, and reaches on the top shelf for Oma's glass paperweight made by our great-grandfather. The one he made a hundred years ago when he wasn't making marbles. The one brought down from the attic the night Lydia schemed to get the wolpertinger to live in her room. In the center of the paperweight are purple forget-me-nots made from glass caning. The flowers are the color of the rare purple honey Daddy found last summer in his hives. The purple honey Trula Freed found healed us from the sickness.

Oma used to explain how the paperweight was made, and it sounded impossible: chunks of glass melted in marble crucibles in wood-fired ovens so hot they turned glass to liquid. Then the molten glass was manipulated with odd tools called a blowpipe, tweezer, punty, jack, and shears. Illustrations in our encyclopedia explained the ancient process. But it still seems impossible.

Lydia looks inside the ball and says, "I don't hardly remember what she looks like." She rubs her stubby finger on the smooth surface.

"She was an old woman. You know what they look like."

"Yeah, but what made her special?"

"Everything about Oma was special, but that was on the inside, not what she looked like." I'm sad our grandmother is fading from Lydia's memory.

"Where is she? In heaven?" My sister holds the paperweight up to the window and brings it close to her eyes and turns toward me. Her eyes are magnified orbs, lopsided, deformed. She is five and a half years old, and most of her life has been flavored by war.

"Her body's in the cemetery, but her soul's in heaven with God."

"Can we go see her? I got a question."

"We can't visit heaven. It's not a place we go till we die, but what's your question? Maybe I can help."

"You don't know. You gotta be in heaven." Lydia licks the paperweight and wipes the ball with her sleeve.

"Don't spit on that."

"Why not? I'm only cleaning it."

"Use the washrag. That's all. Don't spit on it. That's being disrespectful."

"This is glass, Lucy. It doesn't have feelings."

"What's your question?" I ask again. My little sister looks serious. She's getting thinner and there's a residue of sickness on her perfect skin, but she's still the prettiest of the lot.

To avoid answering me, she drills me with old riddles. "What has a head and a tail, is brown, but has no legs?"

"A penny," I quickly say.

"What room do ghosts never go in?"

"The living room." Then I pull her back on point. "I think you're bluffing. You don't have a real question."

"I smell her sometimes," my little sister says and stops me cold when I remember the smell of rot in last night's dream and Lydia's whisper about stink.

"You mean the spices she cooked with or her body powder? Or is it the mothballs in her sweaters?"

"No, her chewing gum. Oma whispers to me. When I sleep. That cinnamon stuff. I smell it when she whispers in my ear."

I didn't think there was any Dentyne left in the house, but I must be wrong. Otherwise how could Lydia smell it? We children like Rain-Blo bubble gum and Mama prefers Chiclets. Only Oma chewed Dentyne, because it didn't stick to false teeth. Lydia must be confused.

She puts the paperweight back with great care and says, "I wonder if Oma saw Wade Sully yet. She's looking for him."

Lydia glows unnaturally, but no one's here to bear witness but me. She is backlit by the winter sun through the window, but there's light inside her that glimmers on high like a firefly, then it's gone. I stare at my tiniest sibling, this pure soul climbing down off the counter and putting the chair back in its place, her corduroy overalls patched at the knees, her cheeks now sallow and pale. Does she comprehend what she said? That reference to Dentyne gum and an intimate tie with Oma beyond death that I envy? Oma has never given me a sign from beyond, and I'm disappointed. I thought I'd be the one she'd reach out to.

Bert confided that she went to see Trula Freed on her own at Helen's request. That she got a convoluted message because Miz Trula fell and forgot Bert's name twice and said Wade was alive and then he was dead. Bert should've told me she was going. We should have gone together, but we didn't.

I feel like I'm on the outside looking in.

Now Lydia has created a different ruffle in time that confounds me. I'll keep her premonition to myself. The truth will come out one way or the other.

CHAPTER 24
BERT: BIRTHDAY BASH

January is special cause it holds me and Lu's birthdays. Mine is on day twenty-two, and Lu's is day twenty-nine, so I'm seven days older than her. This is our first January sharing birthdays, and we turn fourteen. Aunt Fanniebelle asks the two of us to come for tea and stay Saturday night at her big house on my real birthday. "It'll do the girls good to have a change of scenery after the sickness," she tells Mama, but I ain't so sure. I never been inside the big house at the end of Main Street. It's got gardens and a fishpond and a portico, but Lu says it's got secrets, too. I hope they ain't in dark places.

"Only need to bring your toothbrush," her aunt says, so it's us looking out the parlor window, watching for Uncle Nigel, after eating my chocolate birthday cake at noon dinner and me getting a new green coat that hangs to my knees. I got it on and my toothbrush in the pocket wrapped in a clean handkerchief when Lu's uncle Nigel pulls up front at three o'clock on the dot.

"Ladies, I am the chauffeur at your service," he says all stiff and funny and gets us to giggling. He opens the back door, and we climb in his fancy car.

Lu says to me, "Do you know that Chrysler in Detroit, Michigan, stopped making civilian cars two years back? That's when they switched to making tanks for the war effort, and poor Uncle Nigel hasn't had a new car since. The Hollingstons have been a Chrysler family since 1925, haven't you, Uncle Nigel? Tell Bert about the Chryslers you've had."

I wanna smack her upside the head, cause that's what Uncle Nigel starts doing the whole ride. "Well, let me see . . . that first Chrysler was a Model 70 with six cylinders . . ." I don't look at Lu, cause I'm miffed at her thinking I give two hoots about fancy cars, but I look out my side window as we glide cross the river, past the courthouse with the flag flying and the Majestic advertising *National Velvet* that me and Lu is gonna see next Saturday, past the Hollingston Pharmacy and Soda Fountain, cross the railroad tracks and First Baptist, then we there. Things look different from inside a Chrysler. My kind don't belong in a Chrysler.

Up close I can tell the house is too big for two people, and I think that's why Aunt Fanniebelle gets lost inside her head talking scatterbrained. We pull into the driveway easy, and their yardman rakes leaves from under bushes and cuts little bitty branches and puts em in a pile. He waves, and Uncle Nigel waves. We step outta the car, and I get a gander at the red brick and wide porch, and it hurts my neck to look up so tall.

We don't come in the front door like company. We come in the side door like family, and we hear a piano playing, and I follow Lu running through big rooms and find little Aunt Fanniebelle playing "When the Saints Go Marching In" on a long black piano. Me and Lu start singing, and my throat gets a knot in it from joy I almost forgot, and I sing to lift my heart, and Lu grabs my hands and we take to dancing, and we spin and twirl, and my chocolate birthday cake Mama made special gets agitated, and I puke on Lu and on the rug and on my new green coat.

The piano playing stops, and Aunt Fanniebelle lets fly. "Lord'a mercy, child."

I wanna die. "I'm sorry, so sorry." And

somebody from the back of the house comes with wet rags they hand me so I can wipe off my clothes, and we follow Aunt Fanniebelle up long stairs, me holding the rag to my mouth, leaving behind my mess on the floor for somebody else to clean.

She says, "A soak in a tub's gonna do y'all a world a good. Should've thought about that when you first came."

I wonder who's gonna haul hot water up these long stairs, then I see hot water come out a spigot in a white tub big as a Chrysler. Aunt Fanniebelle pours pink syrup that bubbles in the tub, and the water grows deep and sweet.

"Give me your clothes, and don't fret. I seen y'all naked as jailbirds and bout as helpless as a kumquat with that sickness. If the water turns cold" — she points — "turn this thingy here for more hot water. I'll fetch you robes and towels." She leaves, taking the mess with her and closing the door, and on the back is a mirror that catches me and Lu looking back, me with my mouth open, flummoxed at hot water from a spigot and pink bubbles, and seeing me and Lu necked side by side, looking different but the same.

Lu turns shy and says, "Let's get in before we catch cold." We sink into suds up to our necks and water that's warm. Then Lu says,

"Hold your nose and close your eyes." We go under to a silent place. When I can't help it, I come up for air, giggling like a fool. We wash each other's hair and each other's back.

"How rich are these relations of yours?" I whisper. "Do they make their own money?"

"No, silly. I've never heard what they're worth, but they aren't uppity, so that counts."

"You said this place got secrets. What kind?"

"A dead body. Buried in the wall."

"Who said that?"

"Aunt Fanniebelle's daughter, Patricia, who's up North at Cornell University. It's spelled like the Cornell who helps put in tobacco, but he doesn't have a thing to do with the university. It was when this house was being built in 1915. One of the workers got killed. They buried him in the wall."

"Which wall?" I look at the one so close I can touch and wonder.

"She didn't say, but he might be buried right here." Lu's hand trembles as she lays it on the wall, then snaps it back, scared.

"What? What'd you feel?" I might puke again.

"A heartbeat. I swear it was a heartbeat. An ice-cold heartbeat. *Lub-dub, lub-dub . . .*"

Right then, there's a tap on the door, and we near bout jump outta our skins. It opens a crack, and Aunt Fanniebelle reaches in to put towels and robes on the floor. "Y'all get out when you're ready. You can find me in my dressing room."

Lu giggles cause she scared me. She pulls the plug, and the water starts gurgling out, and I know she was fooling bout that heartbeat. "You a mean girl," I tease, and we step out on the softest rug and dry off with fat towels and put on white robes that hang to the floor and socks to keep our feet warm. I whisper, "I know the heartbeat was pretend, but is the dead body true?"

"Cross my heart and hope to die. That's what Patricia said."

We comb our wet hair and let it hang down the backs of the robes. We open the bathroom door, and Aunt Fanniebelle calls out, "I'm here, I'm here," over and over, and we follow her voice through rooms and rooms till we find her in one filled with girly things. Even the ceiling's got paper roses on it.

"What is this place?" I say.

"This here's my dressing room, and nobody comes in except by invitation, and you girls get an invite cause it's your birthdays." She sits at a gold table holding bowls of necklaces and brooches and bangle bracelets like the ones Trula Freed wears. A silver brush and comb are beside a hand mirror. A blue glass hand stands up, and every finger has got a stack of rings. There's hats lined up neat on shelves and silk scarves hanging on hooks. Dresses are on padded hangers, not pegs, and shoes are in boxes I can see inside.

I say, "You know where everything is? Where it come from? What you need it for?"

"I do." She reaches over my shoulder and pulls out a green shawl with fringe and peacocks made of sparkly beads and silk threads on the back. "Take this here. It came from the French District in New Orleans in a shop not much bigger than this dressing room. When the saleslady held it up and Nigel got a gander at these sparkly peacocks, he said 'Sold,' and he slipped it around my shoulders and kissed the top of my head. Thirty years have passed, and I can still see the gaslights on the streets, the lovely iron works on balconies with French doors open to humid air that's different from here. I still feel Nigel's sweetness. I love that possessions carry memories. Want to touch it?"

I rub my fingers over sparkly beads held tight by stitches tiny as quilting.

Two lamps hang on the wall beside the mirror that holds the three of us looking in, Lu and me fourteen and scrubbed clean, and Aunt Fanniebelle old. She watches us in the mirror, her eyes like dark dimes. "We near bout lost you," she starts soft. "It was a fright to behold, the sucking power of it," and we know she's talking bout the sickness.

"At the start, we went through a block of ice a day, packing all y'all in ice chips to bring down the fevers that could boil blood and burn a brain. Tiny Junior did the hauling every morning, and we never ran out of ice when we needed it.

"Then there was the everyday pile of bed linens and towels needing washing and drying, and wood chopped for heat, and every believer in Riverton praying for the Browns, and you wheezed through the nights and moaned through the days, but y'all wouldn't get better.

"Trula Freed never missed a day mixing teas and making broths, but one day when she came, she was carrying six jars of purple honey. She said, 'This honey came to this place for a reason,' and not even Doc Robertson spoke against her when she started giving each of you a spoonful three times a day till the fever went away and the rattle in your chest stopped.

"Y'all were like Lazaro rising from the dead. It was a miracle."

Lu quietly says "Lazarus," and even I know who that is.

Aunt Fanniebelle rises from the stool and stands between us, a half head shorter than us. She rests her knotty hand on my arm. "Bert, I'm sorry I threw too much joy your way and got you sick when you first came today. We need to start small, even with music and singing and dancing. Why don't you girls pick out a bauble for your birthday from these bowls, get dressed, and come on down when you're done. The real jewels are locked in the safe. It's teatime."

When only two faces look back in that mirror, we sift through jewelry, looking for the right one. "Wonder when we'll see the real jewels?" I whisper.

"Maybe next birthday." Lu grins and slides big rings on every finger. We sort through earrings and brooches, then find the perfect birthday gifts and go to Patricia's room to get dressed. A storm has been building while the puke on our clothes got sponged off and we were in Aunt Fanniebelle's dressing room, picking out our presents. We see the storm out the window when we walk down the stairs wearing our bangle bracelets like Trula Freed. Mine slides up and down my arm, rubbing the hairs. I ain't never gonna take it off.

We don't go to the piano room for teatime. We go to the sunroom with windows on three sides where we see the mean storm clouds up close. Tall candles burn, sitting on the window ledges all around the room in case the electricity goes out. Aunt Fanniebelle is at the table fit for a queen. She pours tea from a silver teapot that tips down to pour. It's got a chain sticking out the top like a necklace. When I touch it, Aunt Fanniebelle opens the top and takes out a silver ball. She says, "It's an infuser. It holds tea leaves. You put it in the hot water till the tea steeps right. The darker the color, the stronger the tea." She sets the dripping infuser on a dish where the brown tea pools.

Uncle Nigel sticks his head in the door. "We got a big storm coming. I'll take supper in the study, Fannie, then retire. Happy birthday, ladies."

On a plate with little legs, darling cakes are stacked. Chocolate, strawberry, and buttercream are decorated with sugar flowers. I count fourteen for me and fourteen for Lu. They the prettiest little bites I ever did see. Everything in this place is rich. Nothing looks like a war's going on and ration coupons matter and people go without. There's a birthday candle in each cake, and Aunt Fanniebelle lights all twenty-eight and sings "Happy Birthday" in a wobbly voice and tells us to make a wish. Like always, my wish is that I can be good enough. I wonder what Lu wished for, since she's got everything. Maybe she wishes she was Nancy Drew.

Aunt Fanniebelle pours tea and puts a pressed napkin in my lap. "Your tummy feeling better? You want to drink the tea first to settle it. We'll wait to dance another day."

"I'm fine," I lie, then blurt out Lu's secret. "Patricia told Lu a man died building this house and got buried in the wall." Lu glares at me for telling her secret without asking, but I need to know. A dead body buried in a wall means ghosts in the night. I can't sleep with ghosts close by. "Is it true?"

"Well, yes and no." Aunt Fanniebelle plops back and thinks. "A man did die building this house that I can recollect. He fell from the roof because his harness rope broke. It was a terrible accident that made me sad to come here for a while, but no, they didn't bury him in the walls. That would be cruel. He got buried with his people. Patricia is mistaken." Aunt Fanniebelle sets her lips firm. "You might be thinking of one of your

Nancy Drew stories about a whispering wall or wishing well."

"Or I might not," Lu says in a bit of a huff. "You know I love Nancy Drew dearly, but I'm not good at being a detective. I want to succeed at solving mysteries, but when Bert and I investigate and uncover a good clue, we find trouble instead of approval. Mama and Daddy don't understand how hard it is."

"Nonsense. You got an analytical brain that puzzles things out. What you need is a little help."

"What kind of help?" Lu says, and that hurts my feelings, acting like I'm not the help.

"Maybe Ouija can help."

"Weegee?" we both say when a bolt of lightning strikes and thunder claps overhead and the windows shake. That storm has arrived.

Aunt Fanniebelle says, "Go to the parlor and look in the bottom of that walnut secretary. Bring the box that's got O-U-I-J-A on top." Lu goes to look, and I go, too, while her aunt talks a little louder. "The name comes from the French and German words for yes. *Oui* and *Ja.* Do you see it?"

"We got it," I shout. Lu lets me carry it.

"Help me make room, girls," and teatime

gets moved. "Now this here is a spirit board that will give you answers from a mystifying oracle. Either of you seen one before?" We shake our heads while she opens the box and takes out a wooden board. Painted on it are the letters of the alphabet, numbers from zero to nine, and *Yes* and *No.* The sun is in one corner and the moon in the other. *Good Bye* is at the bottom.

"How does Weegee work?" Lu says.

"It takes two open-minded, curious souls to connect to the spirit world. Scoot your chairs so you're directly across from each other. This pointer, this planchette with the circle window in the middle, that's the key to enter the portal and get answers. Both of you rest all ten fingertips on it — but don't press down hard — and ask it a question. Let's start simple to see if the spirits are willing to let you in. Bert, ask it if it's your birthday."

"That's plain silly cause you know it is," I say, but when I see she means it, I do like she says. Me and Lu's fingertips barely touch the pointer, and I say, "Spirit, is today my birthday?" and the pointer goes flying across the board to *Yes* and shocks the be-jesus outta me. We both pull our fingers back like they got burned.

"Did you push it?" I say to Lu, and I can

tell she's spooked. She shakes her head but won't touch the pointer. "You sure?"

"I swear I did not push it, Bert. Did you?" and I shake my head, too.

"Okay, that's a good sign," Aunt Fanniebelle says. "The spirits have let you in. Now you can ask something you don't know."

Lu says, nervous, "I think Bert should go first since she's older by seven days," but I can tell she's scared to put her fingers on that runaway pointer.

I'm scared, too, but I don't quit. "Come on," I say. "Put your fingers up and don't be a sissy." When she does, I say quick, "Spirit, who's gonna be my first love?" and Lu rolls her eyes. A crash of thunder booms overhead, and I get the willies in my belly, but our fingertips stay on that pointer. It don't move for the longest time, like it's making up its mind, but then it slides over *F* and stops. Then over the *T* and stops. It don't move again.

I pull my fingers back and say, *"F T?"*

"Maybe they're initials. Like mine would be *LB* for Lucy Brown and *FH* for Fanniebelle Hollingston. Do you know any *FT?*"

"No, but maybe we ain't met yet. I got time."

Right then, hard rain bashes against the windows in sheets and startles my heart.

209

The electric lights flicker and go out. The room is lit only with the tall candles. It's downright spooky.

Lu says, "Let's ask about that dead body Patricia says is buried in the wall."

When the pointer goes to *No* right away, Aunt Fanniebelle says, "Told you so."

We got one question we need to ask. It's that missing man mystery what's bamboozled us for months. "You ask it, Lu."

She clears her throat and puts on her serious face, and we lay our fingertips down light. "Spirit, where is Larry Crumbie?"

The pointer acts like it's sleeping, and the rain beats down, and our fingertips barely touch the pointer, waiting for the spirit to do the job. I think the storm is causing trouble, but then it moves slow as a turtle to the letter *H.* Is that for a town? A fishing river?

Then it moves slow as cold molasses to the *O,* and Aunt Fanniebelle joins in the guessing part. "*H O.* Could stand for Hollins County, or Hopewell or Hogtown maybe."

Then, like it's tired of taking its time, the pointer floats to the *M* and to the *E* and knocks the living daylights outta us.

Weegee says Larry Crumbie is *HOME.*

Same as what Trula Freed said. *He go no-where.*

CHAPTER 25
LUCY: MIRACLE

Bert and I are enlightened, in awe, and mystified all at once. Later that night, we huddle under covers in that big bed at the top of the stairs at Aunt Fanniebelle's where the storm rattles windows and lightning rips the sky. This is the best birthday I've ever had because Bert and I have been granted entrance into a spirit portal. We now have a tool to confirm truths that will make detective work easier. But we learned this evening that petty questions are not worthy of Weegee's power, and the oracle might give us a trick answer. For example, when I asked her who I would marry, she begrudgingly spelled out *ARM,* which doesn't make sense. What does an appendage have to do with true love? But we now know where Weegee lives: in a box, on a shelf, in the belly of the walnut secretary.

The next morning, before we go down to breakfast, Bert and I pinky swear that we'll not abuse this power. We'll only call upon Weegee when we have serious need. And we promise to keep her existence to ourselves. If Mama struggled with the mystery of Trula Freed, how would she feel about a spirit portal we are willing to walk through for truth's sake? We are changed girls who return home with bangle bracelets on our wrists and a secret in our hearts. We wear an air of confidence as our health mends in the coming weeks, and we wean ourselves of afternoon naps. Only Lydia remains weak and still sleeps for long spells and worries us. Then Daddy remembers the last jar of purple honey in the barn, and now Lydia gets a spoonful every meal. The jar is half empty, and Lydia is half healed.

We are all well enough to yearn for spice to our winter days that drag into mid-February when a genuine miracle happens — Irene meets a man who's good enough.

What she tells us about him before we meet is flimsy: he's a captain transferred from Camp Butner to Riverton and is coming to Sunday dinner. As the arrival hour nears, we gravitate to the parlor like mites to honey. Lydia watches from the front window and shouts, "He's here, he's here — *and he's riding a motorcycle.*"

Irene rushes into the parlor, still primping

with her hair, glancing in the mirror by the door, checking her teeth for lipstick. "Y'all back away," she orders. "Shoo. He's gonna get scared by the sheer volume of you."

We step out of the parlor and into the kitchen and try to act natural but look plain silly trying. Grady leans against the wall, chewing on a toothpick, and stares at the ceiling. Lydia, Cora, and Bert sit primly with their hands in their laps at the table that's already set for dinner. I pick up a plate of biscuits from the table and stand there like a nincompoop — a word from the Latin phrase *non compos mentis.* I am definitely not of right mind. We're holding our breath on this red-letter day.

Irene is pretty enough and smart enough but she's persnickety. Of course, all the young men who have a lick of sense have gone to war to have their courage tried, and those left behind and out of uniform aren't worth salt on a potato. But we're intrigued by what kind of man in uniform could get Irene's attention and finagle a dinner invitation. She blushes at the mention of his name: Byron Toots. Captain Byron Toots. Captain Toots.

From his name, he belongs in a Walt Disney cartoon with Mickey Mouse in *Steamboat Willie.* Toot-toot. No matter how you say it, it comes out funny. Mama warns us not to tease this man who is special to Irene. We figure he must be movie-star handsome and smart without being pretentious. Bert and I think he must look like Cary Grant or be as kind as Jimmy Stewart or as steady as John Wayne. I have butterflies in my belly, waiting to know what charm will walk into our lives and bowl us over.

He knocks, and Irene opens the door right away and says, "You made it," sounding surprised even though we already know he made it. That's the kind of ludicrous way she's been acting. "So glad you could come to dinner. Let me take your hat and coat. You look positively frozen." Her words are sweet. Her usual hard edge is soft. Then Byron Toots walks into the kitchen.

We are stunned.

For starters, he isn't nearly as tall as Irene, who isn't tall to begin with. And despite his army training and his rank of captain, he has a softness about him that's almost girly. It's a lot of things making this so: his stumpy legs and round face and chubby cheeks blazing red from the frigid ride. His bushy eyebrows look like black caterpillars hanging above gray eyes. Sadly, everything about him goes with his name. *Byron Toots.* So far, nobody has giggled because we're in shock. Irene smiles down on Byron like she found the pot of gold.

Then he starts with Mama. He takes her hand in both of his and says in a rich voice sounding better than a radio announcer, "Miz Brown, I'm honored to join you today." Then Daddy. "Mr. Brown, it's a pleasure to meet you, sir." He greets Grady, Bert, and Helen, as Baby Girl gums a silver rattle. He calls us all by name without being introduced, and he looks us in the eye, and we feel honored to be caught in his gaze, like he knows us better than we know ourselves.

I feel important in the presence of Byron Toots.

He grows tall before my eyes.

Irene met Captain Toots at her day job working beside editor Drake Cunningham, whose fingers are permanently stained with printing ink. A sharpened pencil lives above his right ear and a lit cigarette between his lips. Drake Cunningham is always on the job, paying attention, asking questions. I have an affinity with Drake Cunningham's investigative mind. He's as close to a detective as Riverton has, and he decides what is newsworthy. Irene works in advertising and longs to write real journalism instead of working with local businesses like the

Majestic, Dixie Motors, Hollingston Pharmacy and Soda Fountain, and Yetta's clothing store, but they pay the newspaper's bills. Out of the six pages of newsprint, four are allocated to advertising. Some days, Irene brings home more than news about sales.

Last week at supper, she said, "I found out about those airplanes we saw at midnight on New Year's Eve."

That got our attention. We all looked up and waited. She took her sweet time buttering her cornbread, taking a bite, chewing slow, and swallowing, then went on to say, "I found out a while back but wasn't sure how much I should say, since it's sort of a secret."

Grady said, "It can't be that much of a secret if they told you."

Irene ignores his barb. "It wasn't told to me directly, but it came out at our newspaper meeting."

Mama said, "If it's confidential — if you aren't supposed to tell anybody — we understand. We never want to put you in an uncomfortable position."

I cut a look at Bert and Grady. We think differently.

"What *can* you tell us?" I asked to nudge her telling along.

Irene next ate her butter beans. She likes

to eat one food at a time. "Drake said I could tell you it involves Russian pilots and test planes." She shocked the bejesus out of us.

"Russian pilots and test planes?" Mama put down her fork and plopped back in her chair. "What are you talking about? Russia is our ally, but what are Russian pilots doing here?"

"They're in Elizabeth City."

"How far is that, David? Fifty miles? Sixty?"

"It's close. Real close. Especially by airplane."

Mama's voice grew tight. "But what are they doing in Elizabeth City? Why can't they stay in their own country? Keep the war over *there,* far away from here?"

Irene went on. "They're learning to fly a new kind of airplane that takes off and lands on water. When they're good enough, they can bomb German submarines," she whispered, "the Axis subs off our coast of Carolina."

Mama sucked in a bigger breath. "The Nazis are that close?"

"There are things the government isn't saying out loud. They don't want to hurt morale or endanger the war effort, but that doesn't change frightening facts," she said softly that suppertime last week. "I have friends in Elizabeth City. The Russian pilots are right out in the open. They shop in town and go to the picture show. They speak English, so there's no confusing why they're there. International waters are only twenty-four miles off our coast, but I don't think German subs are respectful of that dividing line."

And now Irene's man, Captain Byron Toots, has been brought to our table as a vital resource. He will be our inside man with inside information. He knows our names and smiles special at Irene. He can tell us what's true. We know how to keep a secret — or at least not tell too many people.

After dinner with polite conversation, Daddy and Byron and Irene stay at the kitchen table over extra coffee while dishes get done. They smoke Lucky Strikes, and to my way of thinking, the smoke floats above their heads like gathering storm clouds, fore-telling.

"So, Byron," Daddy begins, and Irene fidgets. "What's your take on this war? Is it going to end any time soon?"

"Wish I had a crystal ball, Mr. Brown, but I don't. Don't believe in guessing either."

"Irene said you're from Lynchburg, Virginia, and got your English degree from the university in Charlottesville. But why are you in Riverton? Don't we already have recruiters signing up our boys?" Daddy blows smoke rings. I love smoke rings.

"I'm not a recruiter, sir. I'm the first officer in charge of the soldiers that'll guard the POWs. The Germans will be for hire at thirty cents an hour. I'm here to get the camp ready for their arrival in two weeks."

The rest of us know the Nazis' arrival is imminent. We've heard talk since last summer about POW camps springing up as far west as Asheville and east to Wilmington. It's only Mama denying it's real. She quietly leaves the room.

Irene stands in the yard waving while Byron Toots rides away on his motorcycle, and Bert and I head to the hayloft. We wedge between bales of hay we've shifted to fit our bottoms and backs.

I whisper, "Something big is coming and we only have to be patient a little longer before the tinder box explodes and lights up our world and life won't be boring anymore."

CHAPTER 26
BERT: HERO

Me and Lu help Mama at Saturday market, and we ride by the prison camp coming and going, but Mama won't look. She keeps her eyes on the road. Lu says, "It's like a temporary town within a town with those neat lines of tents, isn't it?" She adds, "And I don't think anybody could break through that powerful gate, do you?" But nothing distracts Mama from her worry till she goes to planning a party for a bona fide hero.

Whiz Mayhew is the real deal. Even before he got a medal for being brave, everybody's got a tale bout him. Mama tells about him reading thick books from our library. Daddy tells of him lifting feed sacks like they was clouds. Grady remembers frog gigging in the Dismal Swamp when a six-foot water moccasin fell in the boat; Whiz grabbed it with his bare hands and throwed it twenty feet. He's smart enough to go to college, and he wants to be a teacher. That's what I hear bout Whiz Mayhew before I even set eyes on him.

Mama's thin face lights up with happiness. "I want it to be the biggest party — with everybody and anybody the Mayhews want to invite. It'll be our way of thanking them for their help during the sickness. We'll clean out the barn and string up lanterns, and folks will put together a feast to rival homecoming at church." She grabs her coat and heads to the Mayhew place. Me and Lu tag along.

There's a chill in the February day, but Gertie's got the windows and door open, chasing out crumbs and cobwebs and whatnots. Sugar is at the clothesline, beating to death two thin rugs. Divine smells come from the woodstove. When Gertie sees us, her face is bright with joy. She shouts, "Glory be to God. Can't hardly rest a minute before I think of something else that needs doing. I'm cooking his favorite foods, done scrubbed the floor, and gonna wash windows next."

Mama laughs. "It's his family he wants to see. No need to wear yourself out. But I have an idea and want your thoughts."

Next thing we know, Saturday, February twenty-sixth gets circled on the calendar, and we got a party to plan. Everybody wants to help, but Mama puts Aunt Fanniebelle in charge cause she's good at telling people what to do. We stay away from the Mayhew's private homecoming on Thursday, but on Friday, we make potato salad, two pans of brownies, two pecan pies, and a platter of ham biscuits. The barn is swept, and long planks are laid on sawhorses to hold the bounty that will arrive. Oil lanterns hang from ropes to light the shadows. Lu helps Cora and Lydia make an *OUR HERO* sign with stars and flowers, and Grady nails it to the rafter. On Saturday morning, armloads of cut pine greenery fill the corners and Mama's yellow daffodils she forced on the windowsill line the center of the table. It's as special a party place as I ever seen.

It will start at one o'clock in the kindest part of the day, and the sun shines like we hoped. Aunt Fanniebelle and Uncle Nigel arrive early, and he runs round to open the door. He spies Daddy coming outta the barn and says, "David, did you know I used to be a banker?" Daddy's already chuckling when Uncle Nigel says, "But then I lost interest."

"That's a good one," Daddy says, but I don't get it. How Lu's uncle makes his money is a mystery cause he's got a lotta free time for a working man. I heard tell it was the railroad and the river, but neither of them things ever give me a nickel.

I hug Aunt Fanniebelle cause we're friends after my birthday visit a month back when I took a pink bubble bath and got tea poured from a silver pot and met Weegee. Me and Lu don't say Weegee's name out loud when folks are around. We don't want to jinx her powers.

Aunt Fanniebelle tells us what's gonna happen. "We'll have the blessing and let Whiz talk first before we eat since he's the reason for the party. Then after dinner, folks can play baseball before the music starts."

Sounds like heaven.

They start coming, colored and whites alike cause the Brown farm don't have a faded white line people can't cross. Nobody's turned away from story time or this hero's party cause here is a blending place. In cars, dusty trucks, and farm wagons, on bicycles, mules, and by foot they come to celebrate. They come on time because that's what folks do, and I know a lot of em. Helen's got Baby Girl and talks to Cornell and his wife, Rosalee, with their baby girl, Amee. Gertie's sister Clara wears her go-to-church hat and stands with Preacher Perlie and Trula Freed. The children play tag and jump rope and hopscotch. When the cuckoo

224

clock strikes one, the yard is full and everybody's here — cept the Mayhews.

Mama shoots Daddy a look when we catch sight of Yancy coming round the house. They walk over to him so they can talk in private. Yancy points back to his house and shakes his head. The three grown-ups head toward the Mayhew place.

Lu stares at em walking and says, "Yancy Mayhew and Nancy Drew sound a lot alike, don't they? I didn't know that till I was sick and heard Gertie calling her husband's full name. Yancy, Nancy. May-Hew, Drew . . ."

The grown-ups stand there lost as to what to do when Aunt Fanniebelle asks Preacher Perlie to say the blessing and people to start eating so they're doing something besides waiting. A line forms on each side of the table in the barn. Everybody brought their best dishes. Our plates are way too small.

At dessert time, when gingerbread, pecan pies, and twelve-layer chocolate cakes are cut and make you forget about ration stamps, we see all four Mayhews coming alongside Mama and Daddy. Whiz is on crutches, and he's got a black patch on his eye. Sugar wears her lazy eye-patch, too, the one she forgets most days. Maybe now she wants to look like her brother. He's as thin as a rail and everybody wants to rush up on

225

him and pat him on the back or give him a hug, but his coming late makes em hold back. They part like the Red Sea when he walks through the crowd. He don't say a word and settles in a seat Daddy points to. He sets his crutches on the ground and his bad leg up on a milk stool. Nobody knows what to do, and they turn shy and say, "Glad you're home, Whiz." "You gave em heck, son." "Thank you for your service."

Sugar gets her brother some food, but he don't eat. I see a jagged pink scar on his brown cheek. He's twenty years old, but he's got gray hair on his head.

Lu drags me over to meet Whiz and pushes me right in front of him. "This here's my best friend, Bert Tucker. She came last summer, and she's family now."

Whiz nods, but his good eye don't settle on me.

Grady says, "Hey, buddy, what kind of guns did you shoot? How many Nazis did you kill? Did you bring home any souvenirs?" but Whiz don't say. He's looking somewhere else.

I whisper to Grady, "Leave him be. The man's got enough on his mind," and with that, Whiz's one eye latches on me like a frog on a fly.

"What kind a girl name is *Bert*?" are his

226

first words.

"Bout as good as *Whiz* for a boy."

My sass turns our group quiet till Whiz says, "Fair enough. Take a seat." Me and Lu sit on the cold ground beside Sugar, who don't leave her brother's side till he asks for a piece a pecan pie. When she's gone, he says, "This here's a load of horse crap. A lot of hoopla for nothing."

"That's not true," Lu says. "It's not for nothing. You're our hero."

That starts Whiz to laughing, and his laughing turns crazy. Tears roll out his good eye and from under the black patch. He can't hardly catch his breath. He snorts and slaps his skinny leg, throws his head back, and opens his mouth wide. Spittle strings like spiderwebs. Everybody's looking at him but not in a good way. His mama hurries over to his side, her shoulders and arms twitching. Whiz's head snaps toward her like a rattler, and his voice turns cold. "*Stop. Don't touch me, woman.*" The crowd steps back from the heat of his words. There's pain on Gertie's face and pain on Whiz Mayhew's face. He is a broke man.

Folks start collecting their dishes and head home. They'll give kind words to Whiz another day. Yancy puts his arm round Gertie's shoulders and leads her into our house. Lu, Grady, and me stay out in the yard with Whiz and Sugar. A cold wind runs over the ground and shakes leaves. Like a bad omen, a gray cloud blots out the sun.

Whiz reaches in his back pocket and pulls out a brown bottle. He takes a long swallow and makes a sour face. For the first time, he sees us. He talks low, letting us inside his pain. "Never touched liquor before the war. Wanted to keep myself healthy and strong . . . Then this war took me from a farm boy with a future to a shithole." He takes another swig of moonshine, and his good eye settles on dirt at his foot. "That's another thing I never touched before — cuss words. Now they run outta my damn mouth all rotten and putrid. I'm messed up, man. From Casablanca through the Strait of Gibraltar over to France then Italy. Places on a map I didn't know could hold such ugliness. Hellholes. Every one of em."

All I know about the war is what Daddy and Byron and the radio says, and they say we're winning. Nobody talks bout the bad stuff. It ain't nice to shine a light on the ugly, but the ugly came home with Whiz and sits in our front yard.

He rattles on. "I come up on the first and third ranger battalion — the whole lot of em dead on the ground, covered in maggots, and the putrid smell made me puke. I can still smell that rot. They been lying there so long their rifles rusted. Nobody gave a shit about em."

We are still as stones.

"One time, we got bombed by our own planes. Can you believe that? Them stupid American pilots dropped bombs on *Americans.* I hid in a farmhouse where an old couple sat at their kitchen table holding hands while the bombs dropped all around and the windows rattled. I crawled under that kitchen table and stared at their dusty shoes. The old lady had holes in her black stockings."

Whiz takes another swallow of hooch, then takes in a big breath and says, "One time, I was ordered to check a town to see if any Krauts were there. I went house to house. I busted through a door, holding my rifle at the ready, and found four Nazis playing cards like they were on holiday. I told em to git outside. Told em they were prisoners of the U.S. of A. But when they walked in front of me out the door, the Germans shot their own people so they wouldn't be POWs, but they didn't shoot me. Like I wasn't worth shooting. It's craziness in this war you can't make up. Insanity that don't make a lick of sense."

I wonder if Whiz knows Nazis are coming to Riverton. Will he get his gun and kill em? Shoot em like fish in a barrel?

The man's got hooch in one hand, and the other reaches for something in the air we can't see. His fingers lock in a spasm, then the arm drops. "You want me to tell you bout being a hero? What I did, huh? Me in France . . . crawling around on my belly in the dark, crawling under chicken wire trying to get to a barn so I can hide? In that foreign dark, I come face-to-face with a Nazi crawling on his belly. He was a kid like me. And what did we do when we saw each other all wide-eyed bout to soil our britches?" Whiz giggles. "We turned around like scared little boys and crawled away to live another day. Does that sound like a hero to you?" He looks in each of our faces for answers. *"Does it?"*

His one good eye is bloodshot, and I wonder what's under that black patch. A hole or a cloudy eyeball like a wolpertinger's? Tears streak down Sugar's face and drip off her chin. Her eyes can't look away from her big brother. Then quick as a whip, he slaps her cross the face. We scoot back, stand up. He slaps her again, and Sugar keeps her little-girl eyes on him. She takes his pain. The screen door flies open, and

Mama runs from the porch across the yard and picks up Sugar and orders us, "Inside. Now."

We leave Whiz in the chair, in the yard. He peed his pants and don't even care.

Gertie's gone home, but Yancy sits at our kitchen table, as old a soul as I ever did see. Mama puts Sugar in his lap, and he holds her. Her cheek and eye is swelling. Mama wraps chipped ice in a rag and lays it gentle on the swelling.

"Our Whiz don't come home, Mr. David. This *bitter* boy come home. We don't rightly know what to do with him or how to help."

Daddy says, "He's got to figure things out. His wounds might have healed in that hospital, but he's a hurting man nobody can help till he's ready. Give him room, but don't put your family in harm's way." Daddy leans in on the table. "If you need Grady and me, we're right here. And if anybody needs refuge" — he looks at Sugar — "know our doors are never locked. Whiz isn't the first man to come home from the war dragging the bad with him."

Yancy carries Sugar and leaves by the back door, but Whiz don't move from the chair in front. Mama give me a blanket to put over Whiz. I walk up to him, scared. The empty hooch bottle is on the ground. He stirs when he feels the blanket. He mumbles, "Cabbage soup . . . never want to taste that watery crap again."

Next morning in early light, I look out the window. Private first class William Mayhew is gone.

CHAPTER 27
LUCY: UNFEASIBLE

The newspaper headlines confirm the truth at the same time the camp springs to life. I'm glad Oma died before the Nazis arrive in Riverton. I wouldn't want her to see monsters reign over chaos here. But part of me wishes she could interpret our danger. Our library holds some German books, but the only ones I've opened are the tales by the Brothers Grimm. One holds English translations we read from, but I sometimes study the one in German. I put them side by side so I can make out the meaning. *Sie schrien vor Angst. They cried out in fear.* Will that happen to us?

Now, the *Mercer County Reporter* reinforces these horrors in paragraphs, and photographs show Nazi cruelty to Jews. They starve and murder innocents. They are organized evil unleashed on a civilized world, and we're ill-prepared against such Goliaths.

Byron Toots will be our key to sanity. The evening before evil arrives, he asks us to tour the prison camp. Helen doesn't want to go, but the rest of us do. Byron wants to assure us that the Nazis cannot escape. Tiny Junior tags along, too, the quiet big man in our shadow. Outside the prison, Tiny's uncle, Terrell Stucky, now sits in his old chair he brought over from the bait shop. He whittles aimlessly with his pearl-handled knife and spits tobacco in our direction. His bitterness never takes a break.

Captain Toots calls out, "Mr. Stucky, you need to move along. Find a different place to sit."

"I ain't breaking the law. I'm checking to see you keep the bastards pinned in tight."

"Watch your language around ladies, sir. The Germans aren't even here, sir. And we don't need your help doing our business. Find a different place to loiter."

"It's still a free country last time I looked. At least till the Nazis and Japs steal it from us and turn us into slanty-eyed Krauts." Terrell Stucky spits tobacco that lands an inch from Byron's polished boot, and he slides his pearl-handled knife across his throat in parody of a murder.

Byron says low, "I'm warning you, sir."

"Like I give a damn," Terrell Stucky

234

shoots back, confident he hasn't crossed the legal line.

We turn away from the tension and enter the camp. Terrell Stucky tries to come, too, but Byron closes the gate on him and locks it. The bitter man goes back to his chair.

Mama looks up at the fence topped with concertina wire that can shred human flesh. At the long, narrow mess hall made of wide boards stacked twenty feet high. She says, "Have you seen a live Nazi up close?" She shields her eyes from the afternoon sun to watch Byron's face.

"I've seen some at Camp Butner."

"Is it true what they say about them?"

"They're only men, Miz Brown. Men brought to their knees and captured by Americans. They're not invincible."

"But they're not regular men either," Mama says with pinched lips. "They're freaks without hearts. Abominations . . ."

Byron adds, "With horns on their heads? And pointy teeth? I've heard rumors about Germans, rumors likely started by the Nazis themselves to increase our fear. And I won't deny that their war crimes are heinous and their goals barbaric, but on American land, they are severed from their origins. We are the ones with the weapons. We have the power to give liberty and take liberty away."

Byron walks on and points to guard towers at each corner that have search lights and an alarm to signal if a problem arises. Forty-four tents will house eight prisoners in each. I wonder if Daddy's beeswax waterproofed these tents. There's space for exercise and a small infirmary. "Other than leaving camp to work during daylight hours, there won't be a reason for the prisoners to be outside. If anyone misbehaves, we have holding cells. If that doesn't work, they get sent back to Camp Butner for isolation."

"How many guards?"

"One hundred and eighty-nine officers and enlisted men. Some of them speak German. That's one guard for every two prisoners."

"Only if you work twenty-four-hour shifts, which you won't."

"Yes, ma'am. You're right. We rotate every eight hours."

"What will the prisoners do when they're not working?" Mama knows an idle mind is the devil's workshop.

"We'll offer English lessons, and there's a small library. We'll keep them occupied. But I'll be honest with you, this is a work in progress. We'll tweak the rules to suit our needs."

"Are you scared, Byron? Scared to be in

tight quarters with them?"

"No, ma'am. We've trained for war. This is merely a different kind of war. We'll follow the laws of the Geneva Convention, or we'll have the Red Cross to answer to if we don't. These prisoners will be treated humanely, but their liberty will be restricted —"

"Whether they deserve humane treatment or not," Mama adds. "Do you believe they're doing the same for our men? Treating them humanely? That our missing Wade Sully has adequate food and medical attention? That anyone is worrying about his fresh air and good food and rest time?"

"That's my fervent prayer, Miz Brown. I can't answer for other countries, but we aim to abide by the law."

"Do you really believe this will work?"

He says, "I solemnly vow to keep all of you out of harm's way."

If anyone else said that, it would sound pretentious or banal. But this is Byron Toots.

While we tour their camp and look for assurance, the prisoners board passenger trains in Tennessee and begin heading east through Asheville to Greensboro and Raleigh — into my small town.

That March of '44, when three hundred and fifty-five Nazi POWs arrive in Riverton,

Bert Tucker has become something I fear I'll never be: a full-fleshed beauty. She hasn't worn a strip of muslin to flatten her breasts since she came to live with us nine months back. Bert isn't a tomboy anymore. Even with limited male targets, she flirts close to impropriety. She has a wanderlust soul, a brazen temperament, and a body that even overalls can't disguise.

Mama has instilled as many ladylike parameters as Bert will tolerate but only so much sticks. At fourteen, Bert is still a virgin, because she told me so, but I don't think she'll wear white on her wedding day and be honest. Now here come devil men right to our door. It's a time of dangerous possibilities for my best friend.

Tonight, at supper, Daddy butters his biscuits and tells us the news he heard today. "The owners of the fertilizer plants are the ones behind the camp coming to Riverton. It was set to go to Windsor, but fertilizer won out because they do government work producing nitrogen. They'll take a third of the German prisoners right off the bat." Daddy takes a bite of his biscuit and licks the butter off his fingers.

"How did it come to this?" Mama has asked this more than once, and Daddy is patient.

"Byron explained the number of prisoners captured on foreign shores is growing too fast for our military to handle. We don't have money to care for them over there. Plus, it doesn't make sense to send food, clothing, and medicine to prisoners over there when those efforts won't win the war."

"But they're *Nazis,* David." Mama leaves out our German heritage, because we don't come from Hitler's Germany. Our Germans made glass marbles. They lived good lives. "How could you let them out of your sight or turn your back on one?"

"Well, we got us a problem, Minnie, and it's not going away." Daddy's voice grows firm. "Here in the South, we need help in cotton, peanuts, and tobacco, and now we need help with beeswax. Up North, they got trouble in the timber industry. We've got to take a risk to provide for us *and* our American boys. It's that simple."

"You'd let murdering heathens know where we lay our heads at night?" Mama mutters, not letting go of this bone of contention. My neck hurts from watching. Helen leaves the table, too upset to eat.

"Enough," Daddy flares back. "I don't have all the damn answers, Minnie, but we know Everett isn't coming home to help with bees, and Wade can't come home. It

CHAPTER 28
BERT: IT BEGINS

School is out for two weeks, and Monday, March sixth, is circled on the calendar: it's the day the Germans come to work. Mama and Daddy and Helen done fought, worried, and cried. The sun is a foot off the edge of the earth, and I'm at the water bucket when Daddy's truck comes down the road. Two men are perched on the wheel wells. At the familiar sound of his motor, Lu comes from the hives. She sets down the smoker, takes off her gloves and veil, and shakes out her blond curls. Grady comes from the barn holding a pitchfork, and Mama from the kitchen, but she keeps one hand on the screen door. Yancy stands at the edge of the tobacco field with Cornell, Sammy, and Purvis behind him. Usually they're easygoing and joking, but today they all wear their hats low. They watch the coming of the devil men.

I tuck limp hair behind my ear but don't

know why. I'm a farm girl now with dirt on my hands and my overalls, and there ain't a speck of feminine showing cept my bosoms. I look over at Lu. She's a china doll.

My heart sputters to see the prisoners climb outta the truck. Two grown men younger than any we've seen in these parts for a while but old all the same. I don't count Grady, who don't like me for no reason I can cipher. Or the goofy boys trying to outdo each other for my attention. Or the ones who can't read or write so Uncle Sam won't sign em up. Tiny Junior don't count neither with his grinning sweet.

There was that time behind the barn when I showed Tiny Junior my bosom. I made him keep his hands by his sides and stay three steps back. Lu saw us when we come around front, Tiny Junior scratching his privates and me buttoning my shirt. She flared up and said, "What did you do to that boy?"

I don't lie. I say outright, "Let him see my bosom."

Her mouth fell open, her cheeks got pink, and she looked toward the porch to see if Mama was in sight, then she grabbed my arm and pulled me back behind the barn. "You unhooked your *bra*?"

"Don't start, Lu. It was harmless. He

don't touch em. He looked."

"He looked and now he'll talk is what'll happen. And you know what that'll do to your reputation?"

"Tiny Junior won't talk, and biddies already talk bout me like they know what they don't. Tiny Junior was looking, all doe-eyed and mushy. He's sweet . . . and I like being looked at."

"How can you say something so *wrong*? I can't believe you're not ashamed. Why do you think that's okay? Weren't you the girl who tied a piece of muslin around her middle and talked about being exiled like the Israelites? You weren't so proud of your bosom then."

"I changed," I said. "And don't tell me I'm gonna burn in hell for my sinning ways. You don't believe that mush any more than I do."

"I do believe it. We've heard it enough times." Lu looked puffed up. "It's not the ladylike thing to do, and I don't know why you're not embarrassed. I can't imagine ever showing my bosom to a boy."

I don't say the truth: she don't have much bosom to show.

The morning the two Nazis come, I stand in the yard while Lu waits at the barn door.

The prisoners get out of the truck with hats in hands and their dark-blue pants and shirts clean and new. There ain't a single scary thing I can see. No horns on their heads. No pointy teeth. One's almost short as Lu with dark hair shaved close and a big nose. The other is tall and skinny, stooped at the shoulders, fuzzy brown hair and a Adam's apple big as a walnut. They look like Mutt and Jeff from the newspaper cartoon in Uncle Nigel's *New York Times*. They stare at our field hands like they never saw colored men before, and our men stare back. When the workers head into the tobacco behind Daddy, the Germans follow. After all the crying and worrying for months, I thought they'd look more devil-like, but they don't even look interesting.

Mama leaves the safety of the porch and Lu the barn and come to me. Mama says, "I don't want them eating at the dinner table. It'll upset the men's constitutions, specially Yancy. They eat in the barn. Put boards on sawhorses and get two chairs from the hayloft. They might look safe, but they're Nazis all the same." She walks away and adds, "And, Lucy, put your bee gear away and help Bert and me. We got dinner to make," without needing to cause we make dinner every single day and today ain't different — cept Nazis making her outta sorts.

It's women in the kitchen locked in our own thinking when Helen says softly, "I don't want to lay eyes on em. Don't want to see the monsters who captured Wade. Don't want to touch their food. Don't want to hear their voices."

"Well, dear, we've talked about this before," Mama starts gentle. "Wade went to the Pacific. He didn't go east to fight Germans. Everett did. And that kind of ultimatum is going to pose a problem, since these prisoners will be here every workday. We'll keep them segregated, but they have to eat, and I'm not cooking special food for them."

Helen speaks a little louder. "Why didn't you ask me if it was all right for Daddy to hire those heathens? Why didn't I get the deciding vote, since it's my husband who's gone missing?"

"It wasn't a voting matter. Your daddy does what's best for the farm. He wouldn't hire these men unless it was necessary."

Best? Necessary? Helen's voice rises. "If it weren't for this dastardly war, Everett and Wade would be here. They were *necessary.* They were *best* for this place. Who thought up this insanity?"

"I know, dear."

"Wade should be here where he belongs and not fighting on some worthless foreign land. Or locked in some god-awful prison camp being starved to death or beaten to within an inch of his life."

"I know, dear." Mama doesn't fight with Helen.

"Every spoonful of our good food these Nazis put in their mouths is gonna make me wanna puke. I could choke them with my bare hands till they die." She spits words like poison darts. The only sound is the *ticktock* of the clock. The cuckoo clock made where Nazis come from.

Two minutes before it strikes, Baby Girl cries. Baby Girl who Aunt Fanniebelle calls Betty Gail so she doesn't sound temporary. A child with no name because there's no word from her daddy. That scrap of comfort bout Wade that Trula Freed gave has grown stale.

Helen leaves the room and closes her bedroom door to tend to her baby. The clock chimes eight, and Mama says, "Having these men on the farm is going to be different, and y'all have a way of crossing the line, so I want to be clear from the start: you are *not* to talk to the prisoners. You may *not* go to the camp. Ever. It's off-limits at all times. Do I make myself clear?"

I say, "I don't speak German, so how can I talk to em?"

"Do *not* sass me, young lady."

"I'm being honest, not sassing."

Lu punches me in the arm. "Say *Yes, ma'am.*"

"Yes, ma'am," I say, but Mama ain't finished.

"These prisoners are enemies of America, hired workers in hard times to help us get by. They have been *killing* our American men. Everett and Wade are risking their lives to defeat horrible men like these. They may look normal, but they're murderers and heathens, and you are pretty girls who they can't help but notice."

Lu perks up. "What kind of foolish things you think we pretty girls will do?"

Mama turns stern. "You know what I'm saying."

Later that morning — after the platters of potato salad and deviled eggs and sliced ham wait for the men to come in from the field — I find Lu in her mama's bedroom, looking in the mirror.

"What'cha doing?"

"Looking for a pretty girl."

"Well, she's right there in plain sight. What can't you see?"

"It's you. I see *you* next to me, Bert, and

I don't look like you."

"Course not. You look like perfect Lu Brown."

Lu leans closer to the mirror, looks into hazel eyes with flecks of yellow and teal and thick lashes that curl. She smiles, and her dimples pop through and turn on a light in her face. "Is this what pretty looks like, too?"

I don't even bother to say, cause her question's pure stupid.

The workers come in from the field where they been planting tobacco seedlings like little soldiers in a row. Sammy, Cornell, and Purvis are as old as Daddy, and they wear overalls almost worn through. Our men take turns washing up at the water barrel with lye soap. They wet their bandannas and wash grime from their faces and necks, and the Nazis watch, their new blue shirts and pants covered in dust, their faces red from the sun. When everyone else has finished, they wash up, and Daddy points to the separate table in the barn. Mama fixes two plates on the skimpy side, and I bring glasses of water, not sweet tea. Sweet tea is for Southerners who belong here. I steal a look at the enemy. One of em looks up at me, smiles, and says *donkey*. What am I supposed to say to that?

We make it through that day and the next

till the POWs become regular as rain. But Lu and me think they're being sneaky. Taking their time. Working on a devil plan.

CHAPTER 29
LUCY: LAST DANCE

In the heart of April, when the Nazis have morphed into something benign, we get exciting news — a military traveling band is coming to town. The band is called the Top Hats and posters go up on telephone poles and in storefront windows. They play big band music, so we practice the swing and jitterbug with Irene. We turn up the radio, push back the table, and work up a sweat dancing to Harry James, Benny Goodman, and our favorite, Glenn Miller. Some local dances are held in the high school gymnasium, but this one will be in the tobacco warehouse because it's bigger. The warehouse is our community center when it's not auction time. Square dances and bluegrass music and local talent shows are held on some Saturdays. This is the first big band to play.

This Friday, we pile in the back of the truck, and Grady drives. The dance music reaches our ears before we even get there. Grady warns us to stay in the truck till it stops, then we're off for the time of our lives. I don't know half the people at the dance, and that makes it extra exciting. The musicians are men in white uniforms, and they play swing as good as the real thing. Irene pulls us out on the floor to dance in public. Byron Toots holds his own next to Irene. Cora and Lydia coax Tiny Junior from the corner, and he shifts from one foot to the other, moving to his own beat.

Why does that pest Ricky Miller stay so close to me? He brings me punch when I'm not thirsty. He asks me to dance when I'm already dancing. The only good thing about Ricky Miller is his last name. It's the same as my favorite music man, Mr. Glenn Miller, but that's where the similarities end. Ricky can't carry a tune in a bucket. Plus he should know I'm still perturbed at him for setting fire to poor Assassin's tail.

Bert is swept up in a cluster of admirers she could care less about. Nobody has her attention — till a new band member jumps up on stage.

"Hello, everybody. I'm Frankie Tender," he croons into the microphone, a man in uniform who is movie-star handsome. Women get up on tiptoes to see him better.

A spotlight shines on his perfect hair and polished belt buckle. He sings "You Made Me Love You," and girls rush the stage to watch him. They sway to the beat, singing, "I didn't wanna do it, I didn't wanna do it," and love on him with their eyes. His voice is as smooth as Bing Crosby's. He even whistles like Bing.

I watch his eyes land on Bert and lock in a possessive way. Bert possesses him back. The words he sings are for her. She is magnetic. The light from the warehouse rafters shines down on her. I feel a pinch in my breasts and pit of my belly from the chemistry I heard Irene talk about to Helen. Chemistry I'm witnessing but have never experienced first-hand. Even secondhand, it's heady stuff.

The first set of songs ends, and the musicians take a break. Most of them step outside for a smoke, but Frankie Tender walks off the stage and parts the sea of ladies who reach out to touch his arm, his back, his shoulder. He walks over to Bert Tucker. He's the perfect height, standing next to her looking down, making her look up. Her profile is luminous, and her hair spills down her back like the tresses of Lauren Bacall and Ingrid Bergman.

Frankie Tender reaches in his pocket and

pulls out a folded piece of paper. He brushes it with his lips before he hands it to her. Bert boldly tucks it down the top of her dress. That's when Ricky Miller sidles up chomping on peanuts, looking like a country bumpkin next to Bert's admirer, who's far too old for her but still the stuff of dreams. Bert has an honest-to-god singing military man under her spell, and it's reciprocated. But what is she going to do? What *can* she do? After the dance, Frankie Tender will move on to the next town, and Bert will stay here. Will tonight be enough for my friend?

The air inside the warehouse heats up, and the band plays their second set, and we never sit down. We see moves we've only heard about. We see ladies' underwear when they're flipped over heads and rolled over backs. We dance till our legs wear out. Through it all, Bert is in Frankie Tender's sight.

Then it ends. The musicians break down the bandstand, and the punch table is taken apart, and cardboard fans stir the humid air we churned up in this space. People drift away to their cars and trucks. Small children sleep on their daddies' shoulders. Mama is counting heads when she discovers Bert is missing. One minute, Bert is behind me, heading toward the door. The next, she's not.

Daddy says, "Who saw her last?"

I speak the truth. "She was talking to that singer, Frankie Tender."

"Heavens to mercy," Mama exclaims. "Was she fool enough to go off with him?"

I shrug because I don't know.

Daddy says, "She can't have gone far. Byron, grab a flashlight, and you and Irene check the cars, front and back seats. I'll find the band members to see what they know. Minnie, you drive Lydia and Cora home in the car." Mama and Daddy look worn out at the end of a long day that's turned longer.

This is the most selfish, arrogant thing Bert has ever done. She's worrying us for no reason but the power of chemistry. She's bound to know we're looking for her, that we won't leave without her. She knows that if she told me she was slipping away, I wouldn't lie for her. But I never saw that look on Bert's face before tonight. The look for the singer with the smooth voice and smooth words.

"You come with me, Lucy," Daddy says, and I follow his straight back and long stride into the humid night, looking for my wayward sister shredding her tawdry reputation to pieces . . . and likely loving every minute of it.

CHAPTER 30
BERT: FLOOZY

Meet me behind the bandstand after the last song. I'm glad I can read. I put my lips where his have been. I tuck it inside my dress top. It burns my skin. I been struck by lightning. Every word Frankie sings is for me. He tries to give his magic to other girls, but his eyes always drift back to me. He grins and winks and puts his hand over his heart while he sings. I dance the jitterbug, knowing Frankie watches. I dance a slow song with a country boy who wants to pull me close, but I push back. I know about a tinderbox, a volcano, a flashpoint, but I didn't know he would show up in Riverton tonight.

When the dance is over, everybody claps and whistles and wipes sweaty faces and necks with bandannas, then start toward the warehouse doors fanning their hot faces. I follow Lu for a bit before I go to Frankie. He's winding cords and folding chairs.

When he sees me, he smiles like Christmas and drops the cord and puts out his hand, and I grab it — the smooth hand of a gentleman who ain't a farmer. Without a word, we walk into the perfect night and weave among the cars and wagons filling with people going home until the sounds fade away. My heartbeat fills my ears, and my breath feels like the tickle of butterfly wings. I follow him like a puppy.

He pulls me into a dense copse of pines. I don't like the dark, but I feel safe with Frankie Tender. In the velvet shadow, he pulls me to him rough, tugs at my hair so my face is locked up onto his. His lips taste of liquor and cigarettes and something salty and pickled. One manly hand squeezes my bosom through the cotton dress and the other my bottom, then both hands are on my bottom, and they pull me into his hardness, and my knees buckle from the want of him. Frankie licks and kisses my damp neck under my long hair. He smells traces of Mama's perfume she dabbed behind my ears a lifetime ago.

"You taste damn amazing, baby."

Frankie Tender fumbles with the buttons on my dress and cusses wanting to get at my breasts, but Mama's buttons are sewn tight. One pops off, then another, and I'm sad the pretty dress is getting messed up. The skirt gets tangled, and Frankie growls, "Take off your panties. I'm about to explode."

I want him to slow down. I wanna say this is my first time. That a girl wants to remember her first time. But he's undoing his army belt with the brass buckle clinking, unzipping his pants, and I stand there. He mutters, "Come on, come on, come on. I've gotta get back," looking over my shoulder to where we came from.

A strange wind rushes through the pines and gives me goose bumps and cold feet in one sweep. I say, "I don't wanna do this."

"What?" His voice is strained and pained. "You wanna stop? What are you — a damn tease? I figured you for easy. You knew why we were coming out here, so don't pretend. Remember, *you* came to *me*. I didn't force you." Frankie Tender has turned cruel.

"I never done this before," I admit in a small voice. "I'm only fourteen," needing to say the truth but ashamed of it.

"Jesus H. Christ," he says and runs his hand through his short hair, then grabs my arms and shakes me. "You keep your mouth shut, you hear? You can get me into a heap of trouble if you start blabbing."

"Ow." His grip pinches. "You're hurting

me. I wanna go." I'm turning into a crybab
when he slaps me cross my face so fast
sucks the wind outta me. I stumble back
ward and land hard on soft pine needles
and he stands over me. Gone is magic.
Gone is desire. Gone is the flirting fun and
the building heat and feeling special. A
stranger stands over me, and I'm nobody to
him.

I scuttle back on the pine needles. His belt
buckle catches the slight light. Outta the
darkness comes somebody who grabs
Frankie Tender from behind, holds his arms
by his sides, and lifts him off the ground.
"What the hell . . ." Frankie mutters before
he's dragged away, kicking the air.

I get to my feet and run out of the pines. I
run by a wire fence. It catches my dress and
rips the cotton. I run toward the dance and
the sound of my name being called. "Here,"
I try to shout. "I'm here," but I'm crying
and filled with a shame that's gonna strangle
me.

I see Daddy first. Then Lu. They come
outta the dark and catch me as my knees
crumple. Daddy lifts me like I'm a baby. He
says, "Go tell the others we found her," and
Lu runs.

"You okay?" His voice is tense.

"Yes, sir."

259

"He do anything to you?"

"No, sir." I hold my dress together where the buttons are missing.

"Sheriff Cecil is still here. He was helping look for you. He can go after the man."

I blush heat, thinking bout the sheriff knowing. "No. I wanna go home."

"You don't wanna press charges?"

"For being stupid? What I want is to up and die and disappear."

"You're fourteen," he says and shames me more. Daddy stops as we get close to the warehouse and sets me down. "Let me see you walk on your own," he says, and I do, but my head hangs low. Through the open doors, I see the warehouse is mostly empty. I don't step into the telling light. Lu and me climb in the truck. Grady sits at the lead, looking straight ahead with his jaw locked, breathing fast. Daddy walks over to the sheriff and talks. A minute later, they laugh, and I think it's about my foolishness. It's a warm night, but I'm shaking, and Lu tucks a quilt around my shoulders. We go home.

The truck rattles into the yard, and Mama steps out on the porch in her nightgown. She waited up like I thought she would but hoped she wouldn't. I walk past her, hiding the slapped face from her eyes, and say,

"Don't wanna talk," and she lets me pass. In our bedroom, I undo the rest of the buttons with shaky fingers and step outta my dress. I turn toward the light and the water bowl to wash off the bitter of Frankie Tender.

"Bert," Lu whispers and points to the swollen cheek and bruises on my upper arms. "He did that?"

I don't even wash up now. I crawl into bed and turn my back and she turns out the light. It's bad enough to feel the shame of it all. It's another thing to have the shame show on my skin. Lu don't press me. I hear Mama and Daddy talking low, then turn quiet. I feel Lu's eyes boring a hole in the back of my head, so I turn to her.

"Don't say I'm a fool." My voice is scratchy and worn out.

"I wasn't going to say that."

"You were thinking it."

Lu doesn't answer back.

"I thought he liked me."

"How could he not? You're beautiful." Lu gets up on one elbow.

"Did you see him slip me that note?"

"What'd it say?"

"*Meet me behind the bandstand after.* It sounded romantic, but you want to know the terrible thing?" My sob chokes me. I

261

swallow. "He already had that note in his pocket. He was looking for a easy girl to give it to. He don't write it to *me*. He wrote it to give to somebody — anybody — who would go off with him. He picked me for a patsy."

"No. He picked you cause you were the prettiest girl there . . ."

". . . and a fool," I add and Lu don't deny it.

She says, "Then what happened?"

"He took me out back into the pines. He kissed me rough, and I liked it at first, but his breath tasted awful, and there wasn't a crumb of tender in him like his name. When he saw I won't ready to *do it*, that's when he slapped me so hard it knocked me down. I think he was going to have his way with me whether I wanted it or not when a shadow came up behind and dragged him off. That's when I run."

"A shadow? Who was it?"

"I don't see his face." And that's the truth. It was too dark to tell but I have a suspicion I don't even want to put inside my head.

"You try to sleep now. In the morning, you'll have to listen to Mama say this was a lesson that came with a cost but wasn't as bad as it could be. I love you, Bert Tucker.

I'm sorry Frankie Tender didn't treat you right."

Lu and me lay there quiet in the dark till I say what hurts most. "Wanna hear the terrible part of the whole stinking thing? Frankie Tender don't even ask my name."

CHAPTER 31
LUCY: CRIME OF PASSION

I sit on the bed and Mama sits in the chair beside me and we watch Bert pretend to sleep. She faces the wall with her back to us, but her breathing is tight and telling. The sun has been up an hour. Mama says in her quiet, no-nonsense voice, "You can't avoid this, Bert, so sit up and get it over with."

Bert sits up. She draws her knees to her chest and pulls her hair over her cheek where Frankie Tender hit her.

"I know what you're gonna say," she starts. "I'm a fool."

"You're young, Bert. And lucky."

"Lucky? How can you say that? I went off with a man and almost got . . . *compromised.*"

"But you didn't. You're here safe in your own bed. But we do need to talk about the lesson to make sure you learned it all. Part of the fault of this crime was the older, experienced man looking for a good-time girl, but part of the fault is yours. I'm not sure you know where to draw the line between flirting and danger. Why did you think going off into the dark with a stranger was okay?" Mama's voice stays low, but there's underlying tension and sadness. "Did his uniform make you feel safe? Was it because he'd been singing on that stage? Did that make him the good guy?"

"Course it did," Bert flings back. "It was all them things. Any girl there would've changed places with me if given half a chance. If he had paid attention to somebody else. Everybody was in love with him. But he picked *me* ...."

"Is he still the good guy?"

"You know the answer to that."

"And you do, too. Let me see your cheek." Mama leans over and pulls back Bert's hair. "You need ice for the swelling, but it's still going to bruise. But you hear what I say: a good guy never hits a woman or grabs her arm. He never crosses that line. A good guy doesn't even have that line in his vision. Ever. You better learn that for yourself, or next time, you might not get off so easy." Mama stands to leave. "I'll get some ice for your face, but do you want to know what disappoints me most?" She waits till Bert looks at her.

"How little you love yourself. You are a treasure but you don't know that yet. Last night, you treated yourself like a cheap trick. In turn, that man treated you like a cheap trick."

Bert is crying, and I'm crying for her. There's a knock. Daddy says through the door, "Minnie, can you come out?"

Mama steps to the door. I hug Bert, who looks so dismal.

Mama says, "Get dressed, Bert. Sheriff wants to see you."

Sheriff Cecil stands when we come in, his hat in his hand, his jaw set hard, his eyes weary. He holds a skinny notebook and a stubby pencil. He doesn't talk right away. He simply writes *F* and *T* on the paper and presses on the letters.

FT. Where have I seen that before? Then I gasp. Weegee gave us those initials on Bert's birthday. When she asked about her first love. Those letters stumped us that day. My mouth is dry knowing now what I know.

Sheriff doesn't keep us in suspense. "Bert, you were the last person to see Frankie Tender last night. He never made it back to the warehouse, and the Top Hats haven't seen him since. You need to tell me everything that happened."

The room gets smaller and the oxygen thinner.

Ten minutes later, the sheriff puts the notebook in his shirt pocket, and Daddy walks him out to his car. I grab Bert's hand and pull her up the stairs to our room and shut the door, trembling. She's crying, but I don't have time to give her sympathy. I shake her shoulders and say, "Weegee was right."

"What?"

"The initials of your first love. FT, remember? Frankie Tender," I whisper.

"He won't my first love . . .".

"But I bet you thought he was for a little while last night."

"Maybe. But not now. And he's missing, and I couldn't help the sheriff one bit."

"If Weegee knew his initials, maybe she knows where he is, and we won't need the sheriff or the military police. Let them check the crime scene, but when we get a chance, we're hightailing it to Aunt Fannie-belle's walnut secretary."

We make up the bed together and fluff the pillows, and I say, "*The Double Case of the Missing Men* is official. Nancy would approve."

CHAPTER 32
BERT: NO CLUE

We get on our bikes and ride. I wear Grady's old hat with my hair bunched under. After we cross the bridge, we cut to the back roads and don't ride down Main Street full of the Saturday crowd. We get to the Hollingston mansion, and the Chrysler ain't there. We knock at the side door, and the housekeeper lets us in. Lu says matter-of-factly, "We left something in the parlor. We don't need help. We'll find it and be out of here in two minutes."

We rush to the front room and pull out the box Weegee lives in, set the board on top of the black piano, stand across from each other, wipe our hands on our pants, and put our fingertips on the pointer. Lu stares at me, us breathing hard from riding bikes and seeing Weegee again. She says right off, "Where is Frankie Tender?"

There ain't no storm today whirling outside to mess her up, but she still starts slow like she was asleep, then she moves to four letters.

H O M E

Lu don't look happy. "What the heck does that mean? Does she mean Frankie's gone to his house or his army barracks? And if he did, wouldn't the sheriff check there first? Did Weegee get mixed up and think I said Larry Crumbie instead of Frankie Tender? Let's try again."

But the same word happens, and we ain't got no choice but to put Weegee back in the box and slip out the side door, buffaloed. Lu says, "I bet the sheriff's finished at the crime scene. Let's go look. Maybe you'll remember more being there."

We ride and when we get there, everybody's gone. In daylight, the place of shame don't hold a speck a passion. It's a place where a grown man can hide a wrongdoing. One that Frankie Tender found before he found me to go with him. You can tell somebody's walked on the pine needles, and I see two places where my hands might've landed when I fell. We follow drag marks outta the pines to a path, to a dumping spot for rusty tin cans and wore out tires.

"Remember to look with fresh eyes," Lu says then points. "See those tire tracks? Think they're from a bicycle?"

"There's lots a bicycle tracks. Boys must ride down here all the time to do boy things."

"But look at this one. It's deeper in the dirt than the others," Lu says. "It doesn't carry a boy's light weight. It carries someone heavier. Let's see if we can figure where it went."

I think the track is wide cause the tires are mostly flat, but I do like Lu says, and we walk away from the dump, down a path to railroad tracks. That deep rut don't cross over tracks, so Lu looks one way then the other. "Let's go away from town. It doesn't make sense for the attacker to head into town and chance being seen with an extra body on his bike. You walk on one side, and I'll walk the other."

We walk and look and swat at buzzing flies and sweat bees because the April day has turned hot, and we pass a shanty shack with three children in the yard in cutoff britches. They bat a tin can with sticks. "Hey, Miz Lucy. Hey, Miz Bert," they call out and run to us, children who sometimes come for story night and who go by the names Peanut, Popsicle, and Patches.

"Whatcha doing?" the tallest one asks.

"Looking for clues," Lu says.

"Like a mystery clue?" another one wants

to know.

"We think a bicycle came down this track late last night carrying two men. It was after the dance at the warehouse. Do you remember seeing or hearing something odd?"

They look back and forth and shake their heads. "If it was night, we was sleeping."

"You can do me a big favor. Keep your eyes peeled on this section of track. If you see anything strange or out of the ordinary, you remember it and tell me. Would you do that?" The children start looking right away, heads bent, feet scuffing up the ground.

We walk a little further down the track, but nothing looks like a clue anymore. Lu says, "You want to give up for today, or do you have other ideas?"

I say hopefully, "Maybe Daddy already got answers. Maybe Frankie Tender is with his band."

"That would be real nice."

Me and Lu are on the side of town that leads to Aunt Violet's empty place. I see it in the distance but don't have need to go. Instead, we go home, and we're almost at our driveway when a truck full of boys in the back drives by. One whistles, and another yells, "Bert Tucker, I love you," and another stands and makes a nasty gesture. The dust from the truck chokes us and burns our eyes. When we get to the porch, I'm madder and sadder than I recollect ever being. Daddy says Frankie Tender don't show up at the next town. Nobody's seen him since he went off with me.

CHAPTER 33
LUCY: BALLS

How can a grown man in a white uniform up and disappear? Where is a hiding place for a singing sensation known in every town in the state? Did the shadow man Bert saw hurt him? Did Frankie Tender disgrace another girl in another town that led to his disappearance? And why in heaven's name did Weegee give us the same answer for both Frankie's and Larry's whereabouts?

For days after the dance, military police and Sheriff Cecil comb Mercer County's streets and back roads and the reeds along the riverbanks. They talk to folks who went to the dance and folks who didn't. Bert Tucker's name is tied to the missing Frankie Tender, and she suffers. After our single day of sleuthing and the nasty catcalls from the truck boys, she stays in her room. She wears big overalls. She cut random chunks out of her thick hair to set her beauty off-balance. She takes to her bed because her pain is profound.

My best friend is in a dark and lonely place.

On Wednesday, day five after Bert was maligned and we could find no clues to help, two visitors come calling. Mama sends me upstairs to fetch her. Bert's lying on our bed with her arms by her sides, staring at the ceiling, looking like a used-up body waiting on a coffin.

"Got company."

She doesn't move.

"Mama said for you to come down." She still doesn't move, so I declare, "You won't believe who's here to see you."

She says, "Who?" like I hoped she would.

"Trula Freed and Aunt Fanniebelle. They're sitting side by side on our porch."

"What do they want?"

"To see you."

"Did Mama make em come?"

"I don't know, but ask em yourself."

"Don't wanna talk."

"Then let them talk."

Bert keeps lying there, so I say, "You gonna make those old ladies climb the stairs with their rickety knees? You know they won't leave without talking to you."

Finally, she relents and drags her pitiful self down the stairs.

Trula Freed is on our porch sitting next to Aunt Fanniebelle. They rock in unison and the runners creak. Today my aunt wears a navy dress with a lace collar, but Trula looks like a priestess from a faraway land sitting in our plain place. Today, she's got on an electric turquoise robe cinched with a gold belt around her narrow waist. The fabric flows over fancy slippers too delicate for farm life. She arrived in the back seat of Uncle Nigel's cream-colored Chrysler.

Without getting up from their rockers, the two women raise their thin arms to hug Bert. Mama leaves, taking Lydia and Cora inside to the kitchen and tells me to come, too.

Aunt Fanniebelle says, "Let Lucy stay, Minnie. This visit is for her, too. Let's pull our rocking chairs in a circle so we can hear better."

We scoot our chairs around, then Bert pulls her legs up and wraps her arms around them to make herself small. With chopped hair and castoffs the color of dirt, she has successfully camouflaged her splendor and lost sight of her bright future.

Aunt Fanniebelle starts. "Y'all are old enough to know some important facts Trula and I come to impart."

Bert says cynically, "This isn't about the

birds and bees, is it? Cause if it is, it's a waste of time."

"No, dear." Aunt Fanniebelle snaps open her iridescent fan and looks at Bert, then at me. "Y'all aren't babies. This is different. It's a story about Uncle Val. Valentine Pugh."

I don't recollect hearing that name. I would have remembered the name Valentine Pugh.

Aunt Fanniebelle says, "Well, honey, Uncle Valentine was a slimy bastard who was slow to die."

Bert and I snap to attention. I've rarely heard so much as an insinuated cuss word come out of my aunt's lips, what with her lace collars, powdered nose, monogrammed handkerchiefs, and proper etiquette. Today her face stays as calm as a pond.

"Uncle Val died in 1913, a month before he woulda turned forty. It was his pecker that got him dead and buried cause he had syllabus."

"Syllabus?" I'm confused. "What does a syllabus have to do with dying?" I say, thinking I know the meaning of the word, but maybe it has another one.

"That's what killed him. Syllabus. It's a venerable disease that comes from putting your pecker where it doesn't belong."

My aunt's candid nature can run rampant. It's one of the things I love about her. Bert slides her feet to the floor and sits up straighter. Aunt Fanniebelle may be mis-speaking, but she has our full attention.

At that moment, Mama comes out with a tray of hot German tea and china cups, remnants of Oma, who had a cuppa tea every day. How much did Mama hear? Bastard? Syllabus? Maybe she already knows this story. Maybe she's happy to see Bert rejoining the living. Mama leaves, and we sip our tea and wait to hear more about peckers.

"As I was saying, syllabus destroyed Val's body. It ate his brain. It made a mess of that noble nose on his face. Then lumps appeared on his skinny legs. It was a slow, ugly death that gave him a lotta thinking time." My aunt's lips have curled in distaste. "His death was a serving of justice."

I blurt out, "What'd he do to deserve that awful fate?"

"It was his penis that got him in trouble. He was a handsome, golden-haired man, practiced and smooth, but he set his sights on little girls. The summer I was six, Val shined his light on me. He was seventeen, and I was flattered to bask in his teasing but a fool all the same. How could I not be?

277

I was six years old and trusting.

"Uncle Val picked easy targets. When I was older, I found out he'd been up to no good with my other girl cousins: Debby and Marcella, Bonnie and Mary . . . It was a long list of names that changed depending on who you talked to.

"Well that summer I was six, he set his sights on me. On the sly, he brought me pieces of candy wrapped in gold paper, a new dress for my doll, butterfly wings pinned on a piece of board. He was as slippery as an eel till there came the day he almost had his way with me. It was my sixteen-year-old brother, Augustus, who saved me from shame. We adored each other.

"Later, Augustus told me he had heard despicable things about Uncle Val and little girls, but he didn't have proof. On the day Uncle Val planned to do dastardly things in the hayloft, he told me he'd found a litter of kittens. Precious little newborns with barely their eyes open, nesting in a dark corner of that hayloft. It was a ploy no child could resist.

"Augustus saw Val and me walk hand in hand down the lane to the barn, and he followed us up to the loft, where Uncle Val had dropped his britches and already lifted my blue gingham dress over my head. I was crying and wanted to see the kittens, but Uncle Val covered my mouth with one hand and tore at my undies with the other. Augustus pulled him back, hit him in the face, and tied him to a barn post with his britches still around his ankles. He was going to cut off Uncle Val's privates and he took out his pocketknife, and I knew he was gonna do it. Augustus told me to go on back to the house to spare me the gore, but I didn't leave. Instead, I begged my brother to spare Uncle Val, a half-naked man crying with a big worm flopping between his legs."

Aunt Fanniebelle stops rocking. She looks off toward our barn and waits so long we think she forgot where she is, till she starts talking again.

"I knew if Augustus cut off Val's balls, everybody would talk and nobody'd be happy one bit. I felt sorry for the half-naked man begging for my brother's mercy. I promised him I'd never be alone with Uncle Val again."

Her eyes glide over to Bert. "I was ashamed that day and didn't know why. Do you hear what I'm saying, Bert?"

My friend is crying, nose running, eyes puffy, and she nods.

"What am I saying?"

"Frankie Tender is like your Uncle Val," Bert whispers right off.

"Those kinds of devils are everywhere. When something like this happens, we girls got two choices: we can take the damage they do and let it turn us weak or we can forge it into steel. Cowardly men like Uncle Val and Frankie Tender do more damage on a girl's delicate sicko than can be seen on the outside."

Did she mean *psyche*?

"Over the years, I thought that my plea to save Uncle Val's testicles was why he died that awful death caused by syllabus. If he'd lost his balls early on, he wouldn't have gotten into more trouble. Losing his balls might have tamed him down and let him grow old."

Aunt Fanniebelle sits back and sips tea that has grown cold. It's hard picturing her as a little girl in danger. An oil painting of her by a New York artist hangs in their parlor over the fireplace. She was sixteen. Next time I go visit, I'll look for the steel beneath the privilege.

"So you see," Aunt Fanniebelle ends, "your story is as old as dirt. As common as weeds. You're different now because of your close call, but you will rise again. You will rise up, beautiful Bert."

"What if they don't find Frankie Tender? Weegee told us he was home."

"Not your problem, honey," she says, pinching her skinny lips tight and ignoring Weegee's clue.

"But if he stays missing, people are gonna talk."

"Not your problem, honey," Aunt Fanniebelle says again, but this time, she grins. "You can hold on to the hurt or let it go. It's that simple, but gossip *will* fade. You'll find out people got more troubles on their minds than you and Frankie Tender."

The whole time Aunt Fanniebelle has been telling her syllabus story, Trula Freed has rocked steady. Now her chair stops, and with Bert's help, she slides the side table between them, reaches into the pocket of her silk robe, and pulls out a scarf of delicate black lace. It's wrapped around a deck of thick cards that she shuffles adroitly.

They're *tarot cards.*

She fans the shuffled deck out on the table, facedown. The cards are worn around the paper edges. I wonder how many cards are in the deck?

"Seventy-eight cards in deck," Trula says, and I gulp at her reading my mind.

Pointing to the deck, she says, "Today, only choose one card."

Bert's fingers tremble as they pass over the cards, hoping to pick a good one. She pulls the one from the middle like I would, and Trula Freed turns it over and sets it faceup on the table. The unpicked cards are restacked and put on top of the folded lace. The mystic studies a far-off place.

"The Wheel of Fortune. A powerful card, your card," she begins, and Bert remembers to breathe. "One to signal change, this Wheel of Fortune. Transformation has come and altered you." She strokes the card with her finger, "And here . . ."

Bert and I lean forward.

"The devil — cunning as a fox with his smiling face of deceit. He is the sly Frankie Tender, stretched out under your wheel. He can do no more harm, but other sly devils may appear."

Bert wipes her runny nose on her arm.

Trula runs her fingers over the card. "Here" — she taps the Roman numeral X — "is the power. The number ten represents completion." Then to the corners. "The magical winged figures in the corners resting on clouds —"

I lean in and blurt out, "Are they holding *books*?" and Trula nods. I get goose bumps, seeing this link between Bert and bibliophiles.

"You do not yet know your power to overcome, Bert Tucker. Today, news is good news."

As if from some unspoken signal, Uncle Nigel's Chrysler glides down our driveway and into the yard, and Aunt Fanniebelle and Trula Freed rise from their chairs in unison. The stack of tarot cards go back in the deep pocket, the table is moved, and Uncle Nigel helps the two ladies down the steps.

I blurt out, "But what about *my* tarot card and *my* fate?"

"Today is for Bert."

I feel let down.

Then Trula Freed flings parting words that add to a day of mystery. "This I know," she says. "Frankie Tender — he will turn up."

CHAPTER 34
BERT: ASSASSINATION

Knowing Frankie Tender was being his sassy self somewhere else would ease my pain, but the sheriff don't bring that good news. Hearing Wade Sully is coming home to Helen would soften our days, but that don't happen neither. Instead, Yancy brings different news. "Y'all gotta come see," he says from the back door.

"See what?" Daddy stands at the supper table, wipes his mouth on his napkin, and follows Yancy. We come, too, cross the yard, past the barn, to the fence. Assassin is laying on his side, like he's sleeping.

"What happened?" Daddy says.

"Don't rightly know, Mr. David, but he's dead."

"You sure?" Lydia asks.

"As a doornail."

"Then how come his belly's moving?"

The Browns and me lean over the fence, and so does Yancy, him with his worn coveralls over scarecrow-thin legs and dusty work shoes like my pa wears. The mule's belly ripples like a mole under sod. Is something in there? A tape worm? When enough gas comes out his rear end to blow the hairs on his limp tail, the moving belly stops. I'd heard tell bout Assassin being a champion tooter.

"It's not old age, because he's got ten good years left," Daddy ponders. "Any of the other mules show signs of sickness?"

"I check em myself first thing. Teeth is good and so is the white of the eyes. They still got their attitude. But see that white foam and them sores round Assassin's muzzle?" Yancy points in the fading light. "That's poison for sure. Can't for the life of me figure how it could be, cause all the mules work and eat and rest in the same place."

Flies crawl on the mule's open eyes. Buzzards circle watching.

"Check his feed bag and open a new bag of feed for the others. We need Sheriff Cecil to weigh in on this thing. For now, cover him with a tarp so the buzzards can't get at him. Don't want to lose evidence."

The men and Grady go to the barn and we girls to the house. We've been hearing about bad things going on in Mercer

285

County, news that Irene brings home. Mr. Langley's barn burned down on a clear night. Prize hunting dogs and milk cows are dead, and now Daddy's mule's been poisoned. Daddy heard tell every farmer with bad luck hired a handful of Germans. That must mean something.

At bedtime, Lu brushes her hair one hundred times. Irene cuts on mine and tries to make sense of the chopped-up mess I made in my fit of despair. "What do you think of this short hair style?" Irene points to a picture in *Photoplay* magazine.

The girl don't look like me. The only thing special on me is my bangle bracelet I never take off. "It'll do," I say.

Lydia, who's coming up on six in July, waltzes in and says, "Assassin needs y'all's thinking help to find his killer." She's finally got her sass and smarts back after feeling puny from the sickness. Mama gave her purple honey tea every day till it ran out right when Lydia come round.

Lu keeps brushing her hair. "It's gonna take smarter folks than Bert and me. We'll leave it to Sheriff Cecil."

"No," Lydia says. "Our mule's counting on you." Lydia blows us a kiss and leaves. I can tell Lu don't think we're good enough to help with this crime, and we don't think

Weegee is so smart either, cause she thinks Larry Crumbie and Frankie Tender are HOME. But I already know who killed the mule.

Irene says, "How's that look?" and when I see myself in the mirror, I look better than I should.

"You done a good job with the mess I made," I say, sweeping up hair clippings to save for a pincushion.

"It was easy, Bert. You look pretty without trying." Byron Toots is softening her heart.

Lu and me get in bed with the lights out, and I say, "I know who done it."

"Who did what?"

"Killed your mule. It was the Nazis."

"What are you talking about?" Lu gets up on one elbow. "Why would you say such a thing? When would they have had time? And why would they kill an innocent animal?"

"When I take water to their dinner table, that first day in the barn, they call me a donkey. Maybe they don't like donkeys or mules. Maybe that's why they killed him."

Lu is quiet for a moment, then giggles.

"Why you laughing? I know what I heard. It might be a clue."

"He didn't call you a donkey. He was saying thank you in German. *Danke.*"

"Oh. I don't know that. How could I know that?"

The morning after Assassin gets murdered, we start harvesting the second load of beeswax for the government, and it's a gang of us working. Me and Lu and Daddy got bee suits on and are gonna take the honey racks outta the hives. Grady keeps fires going under fifty-gallon oil drums filled halfway with rainwater he's already toted. Wolf and Gertie will cut the comb out of the frames, extract honey, and throw the wax into the heated rainwater where it will melt and rise to the top. It's sticky, hot work, and I'm getting wore out. Then the dinner bell rings.

Lu catches my eye, us getting out of our suits, and says, "I got an idea. I want us to look for a pile of wood chips."

"Now? But I'm hungry and need to pee. Can it wait?"

"It'll only take a minute." She grins, "We're looking for wood chips made by a mean-hearted whittler." We check the back of the barn and look inside the stalls before heading to the hayloft. At the top of the ladder, I go one way and Lu the other. Then I see what she was hoping for. In the shadows. By the three-legged chest. "Over here."

288

Lu comes to stand beside me. "Would you look at that." A pile of wood chips.

Forgetting all about dinner, we get Daddy from the yard. When he sees the wood chips, he says, "Well, I'll be . . . Good work, girls. I'll call Sheriff Cecil," and I feel smart.

Yancy found ground poke berries and stems mixed in with Assassin's food. Now, thanks to good detecting by super sleuths, we have a prime suspect. Little Lydia says, "Told you so," and makes us puff up.

Later that day, the sheriff questions Terrell Stucky about his whereabouts the day before, but he's got an alibi: he says he was fishing with Tater and Spud. Even Mr. Otis recollects the men bought bait from him. The sheriff tells Daddy he can't arrest a man with an alibi over wood chips, even if that somebody whittles all the livelong day. Cause of that stupid alibi, Terrell Stucky gets a stupid warning. But me and Lu know he done it. We don't ask Weegee for help. We figured out *The Case of the Ass Killer* all by ourselves. Lydia calls us heroes.

CHAPTER 35
LUCY: SLUR

Assassin doesn't get dragged into the woods to mutate into a pile of bones. He waits in the distance beside a massive hole that Cornell and Sammy dug at the tree line. Lydia has organized his funeral, and the family and Yancy come, and so does Sugar. She carries a bunch of *Houstonia caerulea* that everybody calls bluets. Uncle Nigel brings Aunt Fanniebelle, and she wears that elaborate shawl with beaded peacocks she got thirty years ago in the French Quarter in New Orleans. They bring Trula Freed dressed in somber finery. Black feathers have been added to her midnight-blue turban. She carries a brass box that dangles on a chain. She opens the hinged top, lights the contents, and refastens the hook. Sweet smoke spirals upward. The smoke is the color of Assassin's coat. She hands the chained box to Lydia to carry, and my little sister says with authority, "Y'all git behind," and we make a line.

We cross the pasture — watching where we step — and we circle the mule's final resting hole and wait. The smoke from the brass box drifts over Assassin's body and lies like a wispy blanket. Lydia, Sugar, and Cora start singing "She'll Be Coming Round the Mountain," and we join in, taking our cues from Lydia, who sings mournfully about six white horses and chicken and dumplings, and ends with "We'll all go out to greet her." We sing six choruses for Assassin's passing. Lydia nods at Sugar, who throws the bluets into the grave, then my little sister blows a tin horn that sounds like a familiar toot. It's done. No mule has ever received a more regal send-off.

Cornell and Sammy finish burying Assassin and we head to the house to eat cookies. Lydia sets her sight on Captain Toots so she can spring Everett's latest riddle. "You know how to make a witch into a itch?" she says, and he looks like he's thinking hard but he gives up pretty fast. I know the answer is "You take away the *W*," and I'm always surprised at how good minds don't think in a straight line.

Captain Toots showed up for the funeral and acted dignified through it all. I'm happy he has a decent singing voice, because

Irene's voice is beautiful. Every evening he's away from camp is spent at our house. He and Irene always wind up in the swing, even if it's cold or rainy. Bert and I are obsessed with this romance, and we eavesdrop because we're good at it.

Our bedroom is on the second floor, and our window looks out on the porch roof. The window tracks are greased with lard, so they glide with ease. Loose floorboards have been nailed down. We couldn't ask for easier targets.

The evening of Assassin's funeral, after supper and after story time, the couple sits in the swing and we crawl to the open window. "I've got a situation," Byron says as the swing creaks with their united weight. With those magic words, we pay closer attention.

"A situation?" Irene speaks kindly to Byron. She's only started using that gentle tone.

LOVE RULE # 1 I LEARNED FROM MAMA: SPEAK KINDLY.

"It's hate trouble."

"Hate? Against whom or what?" Irene shifts in the swing, likely facing Byron.

"A daily problem is that pest Stucky —"

"Terrell Stucky?"

"He still sits outside the prison all day long, whittling wood for no reason. When he catches your eye, he pretends he's slitting your throat with that switchblade, and it's getting tiresome. Nobody likes him being there, but he's not on government property, so I can't do much about him. But the bigger problem is the prisoners. Two of them painted German words on the side of the mess hall that can be seen from the street. Probably nobody in Riverton reads German, but that's not the point. Private Jenkins knows German, as do a lot of the other guards. That's why they're assigned here. Jenkins translated the words."

"What did it say?"

"Jews and Dogs Stay Out."

"Why would they post that? There's only one Jewish man in all of Mercer County, and he keeps to himself. And what do they have against dogs?"

"I don't know why they wrote it, but it doesn't matter. Bottom line, these prisoners are not allowed to hate on my watch. At least not publicly."

"What did you do?"

"The guards inspected hands and clothes for paint traces. They found two culprits with incriminating evidence on them, the morons. We've put them in separate holding cells until we decide what's next. Obviously, they'll clean up the mess they made, but what do you think we should do?"

LOVE RULE # 2 MAMA SAID: ALWAYS SHOW RESPECT.

"The trick is to make the punishment carry a lesson, don't you think?" Irene sounds like Mama. "Begin to change them at the basic level if you can."

"How would I do that?"

"Well, they'll have to paint over the cruel words . . . but could something go there in its stead? Maybe something like 'Hate Is a Choice,' but in German. You don't want them thinking hate is their birthright or that it followed them across the sea."

LOVE RULE # 3 I ADDED ON MY OWN: MAKE HER GIGGLE.

The creaking swing stops. Irene laughs. I think Byron is kissing her neck. He says, "You are not only beautiful and intelligent and clever, you're also cunning," and his words drift over the tin roof and through the screen of our open window.

Bert sighs, and I rib her with my elbow to

keep quiet, but the action on the front porch has dulled Byron's and Irene's hearing. We crawl away from the window and get in bed. This unrest Byron shared doesn't bode well for the Germans adjusting to Riverton or for the lone Jewish man who's causing trouble without trying.

I've never given much thought to Mr. Asher Cohen, because I've never seen him up close. He doesn't come to town or the market or to the farm to buy honey. He lives on the fringe of our lives in a solitary place on the river, and I don't even have a clear picture of what he looks like. How did the prisoners find out about him? Why would they hate a little man with simple ways? What did he ever do to them?

Then I wonder if it's Asher Cohen they hate at all. Maybe the prisoners hate the idea of *Jew*. Like Helen hates everything foreign. Like Terrell Stucky blames everybody for his misery. Like we hated our German Nazis before we laid eyes on them.

I do know this — and I spend some of my ten-dollar words to make the point: hate is incendiary, provocative, dangerous. Can Byron hope to eliminate it? Or even keep it at bay? Or will it lie in wait like a glowing ember ready to ignite when the wind shifts?

CHAPTER 36
BERT: STOLEN THINGS

I been watching the calendar, and today's the day: June seventeenth. One year back, I come to this place in a storm and got turned into a bibliophile and an apiarist. Now I read and write and tend bees. I play a fair game of marbles with Lydia. Some days, I forget who I was.

But this morning nobody says a dang thing. I thought they'd remember without me saying. I thought Mama'd make me a pecan hotcake with whip cream on top. When that don't happen, I wonder if my coming is as big for them as it was for me. Lu and me walk to the garden to weed, and I finger the bangle birthday bracelet on my wrist I don't take off and say, "Today's one year."

"Since what?"

"Since I come here through the storm."

"It's *came*. Since *I came*. Good grammar isn't rubbing off on you at all."

"Whatever. Anyway, you forgot." I'm cranky cause she forgot and cause she called me on my words.

"It's been a year already? I didn't forget on purpose. I stopped counting days I guess cause you're one of us. That's all." She can tell she hurt my feelings. We sucker tomatoes and tie up beans and all the while stay quiet. That's how me and Lu fight. We don't say what's right in front of us, so I think today's the day I see if Lu's my true best friend. I say, "Wanna see my treasure box?"

"The one Trula Freed saw was on your mind?"

I nod but get a scared thud in my belly. If I show Lu my treasure box, she's gonna find out things she won't like. She'll know I can't never be a real Brown. To prepare her, I say, "I ain't good."

"Who says you aren't good?"

"Me. *I* say it. But let me show you . . . Then you'll know."

I leave the garden with Lu behind and head to the hayloft. I go to the dark corner stacked with broken chairs, crates, and a three-legged chest. The place we found Terrell Stucky's pine chips. I wiggle open the warped drawer and pull out the cigar box tied with twine, then we shuffle over to the light and sit on a bale of hay.

Lu don't rush me. I like that bout her. She knows this box holds ghosts. I say, "I used to think it was important stuff in my box so I could hold on to something good when things got bad. But . . . well, you'll see."

I untie the string and lift the cardboard lid with the faded gold on top. The first thing I take out is a woman's pin missing some of the red glass. "I stole this from Memaw," I say straight out. "I took it off her dresser when she lay dying. Slipped it in my pocket easy as pie to remember her by. It was the only piece of sparkle she had. Memaw's sister and Ma looked high and low for this pin. I never told em I took it, but they knew I done it." I set the brooch on the hay between us.

"This tiny bottle was Ma's. It's got her smell, but it's mostly gone. And this here button come off your mama's dress that first day. When it got loose, she put it on the window ledge to keep it safe. I took it when you won't looking. I fingered it in my pocket those next days, looking for comfort."

I keep my head low in shame.

"And this here green marble —"

"You stole from *Trula Freed*?"

"I was thinking I never saw such a pretty place and might never get to come back." I

298

sound righteous. "I know she saw it slip into my pocket."

"It didn't *slip* into your pocket, Bert. You *put* it in your pocket. Stop blaming the object when it's you doing the bad deed."

Her words stab me. Why am I showing her these things? Why did I think she could understand? The quiet is heavy until finally she says, "Go on and finish. Show me everything." And I do.

"This here pocketknife belonged to my grandpa, and it always lived in Pa's pocket. I stole it one wash day and put it in my box cause I had need for it. Pa never could find the dang thing, and I didn't help him look for it cause I knew where it was."

Piece after piece, I lay out my crimes for my best friend to bear witness. When the box is empty, I look up and declare, "I steal things, Lu."

She says, "What's the last thing you stole?"

"This silver thingy. When we had our birthday tea in the sunroom at Aunt Fanniebelle's."

"Well, that *is* six months back, so you're slowing down your stealing. Are you going to stop altogether? Is that why you're showing me?"

Her question stumps me. Is that why I'm showing her these things? I say, "I guess."

"You can't be guessing, Bert. You gotta know for sure. Are your stealing days over? Do you need this stuff anymore?"

She makes me squirm, what with her shooting hard words at me. "If I say okay, then what?"

"You'll give everything back that you can. Tell the truth. Ask for forgiveness."

Lord'a mercy, that won't what I wanted to do. "You mean tell Mama. And Trula Freed. And Aunt Fanniebelle what I done?"

"What I *did,*" Lu corrects me but with soft words. "It's the only way. Then you'll burn the treasure box, because you won't need it anymore."

I don't know if I can give up my comforts. I'm darn sure I can't confess out loud. I whisper, "They'll hate me. Mama's gonna throw me out."

Lu sighs. "That won't happen. Everybody loves a wrong turned right. Everybody loves *you.* I think your heart will fly high when you unburden yourself. You have no idea what your stealing's been doing."

Why can't she see these things are mine to keep for a mighty reason?

Lu says, "I'm gonna leave you here with your box of things. If you come down carrying the box, I'll know you chose redemption for yourself. I'll help all I can. If you hide it again, the time isn't right. That's all. Whatever happens, it's all gonna work out."

I ain't strong enough that day to give stuff back, but I decide to stop stealing. I still get a flutter in my heart to take something that don't belong to me. The last thing I wanna steal is Irene's hair comb, crusted with a line of rhinestones, that she hardly wears cause it's fancy. I tell Lu bout that feeling, and the two of us stand in Irene's bedroom when she's at work. We look down on that jeweled hair comb on her dresser.

Lu says, "Pick it up," and I do so I feel its fine weight in my hand, press the teeth against my palm.

She says, "Put it in your hair," and I do. I stand there looking at myself in the mirror over Irene's dresser. I twist my head from side to side so the light sparkles.

Lu says, "Stand there and look at yourself until those feelings go away. Until you can put that sparkly comb down and leave it there. Keep looking till it lets you go."

I do, and it does, but it takes a while.

CHAPTER 37
LUCY: KEY OF G

Like Bert going against her thieving ways, Mama has a softening of the heart. She told our workers to make room on the benches so the men could all eat dinner together, and we put away the makeshift table and chairs.

It's a lot of little things that makes this big thing happen. The tall one named Joe laughs easy like Everett. At the water barrel where he washes up, he splashes water on his face, throws back his head, and shouts, "Yah," with a big grin of crooked teeth. With each serving of food that goes on his plate, he says, "Yum yum," and tickles us.

Wolf is the short one who tends bees and whistles while he works. How that was determined came early when the two POWs were told to hold out their bare arms. Daddy held a chunk of ice on their forearms till the skin got numb, then held a worker bee between tweezers and let her plant her stinger in the cold patch of skin; the men went back to the field, rubbing their arms, looking confused.

The next day, Daddy iced their arms again in the same place and this time he set two stingers in the same patch of skin. Right away, Joe's arm got hot and itchy. Wolf's arm looked mildly irritated, so he was the one to work bees. Joe went back to tobacco. Wolf would say he got the sweeter part of the deal, stings and all.

Helen has not softened toward the prisoners. She stays inside at dinnertime and holds tight to her hate. Fearing she'll hear one of the Germans speak, when dinner starts, she turns up the radio to drown outside voices. Today, "Boogie Woogie Bugle Boy" fills the air. I hear seven-month-old Baby Girl start to cry in her crib in the bedroom Helen stays at the sink, and Baby Girl cries louder.

I shout, "Want me to fetch her for you?" but Helen doesn't answer. She keeps washing the same plate. "I can bring her to you if you like." She still doesn't answer.

Then the crying stops. Baby Girl never stops crying on her own. She stops when she's fed. She stops when she's picked up.

I run to the bedroom, and Helen is right behind. The crib is empty, and through the open window, we see our tall German, Joe, holding Baby Girl in his arms. He's smiling and cooing at her, but Helen goes crazy. She leans out the window with her arms flung wide and screams in a thorny voice, *"Get your filthy hands off her."*

Joe freezes, and his face fills with confusion and grief. Mama rushes around the corner all aflutter and takes the child from Joe's arms while he says, "So sorry, so sorry." Mama gives the baby to Helen, who grabs her too tight, and the baby squirms to be free. Helen pulls her inside. I lower the shade.

My oldest sister sits on the edge of the bed. She rocks and sobs in a private pain that words can't find. The radio is turned off, and Mama hurries into the bedroom and kneels in front of Helen. "Dear girl, my sweet girl," she croons and strokes Helen's arms. Baby Girl nuzzles Helen's breast, and her milk lets down. Mama gently pulls back the dress so the baby can nurse. Helen strokes the baby's soft hair.

"The man who picked up Baby Girl . . . he won't do it again," Mama says, because there is no reasoning with Helen's wounded mind. Mama doesn't say that Joe has a baby girl of his own he left behind. Byron told us as a courtesy.

Helen turns glassy eyes to Mama and

whispers, "What if Wade dies? What if he comes back like Whiz, broken and lost and no good as a husband or a daddy?"

"Then we'll help him heal. We Browns are a family of love, and love can cure most everything. But do you want to borrow trouble before its time? You have an important purpose right now, and Baby Girl needs you. Finish feeding her and change your dress. The men have gone back to the fields."

That evening, Daddy takes Helen and Baby Girl to Aunt Fanniebelle's house. She needs to heal in an easier place. I wonder if she met Weegee? Maybe she'll ask her about Wade.

While Helen mends out of sight, our tobacco grows high and peaches grow ripe, and on a regular Tuesday, Mama makes peach cobbler. To celebrate the first peaches and a reprieve from stifling heat, Daddy fetches his fiddle. Lydia, Cora, Bert, and I sing "Keep on the Sunny Side" full-voiced like the Carter Family while Daddy plucks the strings as background. When we finish, we bow, and everybody applauds.

Wolf steps forward and holds out his hand for Daddy's fiddle. Puzzled, Daddy gives it to him. Wolf deftly tunes the instrument and tucks it under his chin, and out flows a haunting melody in a minor key with the flavor of a gypsy soul about it. The skill is extraordinary. The final notes lie soft in the air. One minute, our German is a farmhand in need of a bath, then he leaves us breathless.

We learn that Wolf played a tune by Felix Mendelssohn written a hundred years ago in our mutual homeland. That evening, like I knew she would, Mama looks up Mr. Mendelssohn in our *Encyclopedia Britannica*. He was born in Hamburg, Germany, wrote romantic music, and started performing when he was Cora's age. This sounds like the good part of our German heritage, something to be proud of. Mendelssohn's parents were musicians, too, and Jewish, but when they were freed from the ghetto, they became baptized Christians and members of the Lutheran Church. I didn't know a Jew could become something different by saying so. "Did they do it to be safe?" I ask, but Mama says don't speculate, because that's a dangerous thing, and truth is something different. Mr. Mendelssohn was thirty-eight years old when he died.

"How old's Daddy?" Lydia wants to know.

"Forty-five," Mama says, then quickly adds, "But Oma was sixty-four. Your daddy's fine, honey."

After that peach cobbler day, Wolf plays when dessert is served. Daddy doesn't mind the minutes it takes to pause and refresh. He read a book by the psychologist B. F. Skinner, who believes positive stimuli elicit better behavior. Wolf's music is a positive stimulus. It makes our hearts happy. Happy hearts make everything better.

And for the first time in a long time, we get enough rain, and our tobacco grows strong. It's now time for the opening of market.

CHAPTER 38
BERT: MOVIE STARS

When market comes in August of '44, me and Lu are mostly grown at fourteen years and seven months. I been living with the Browns for fourteen months and fourteen days. Fourteen must be my lucky number.

Some of my mountain tongue has ripened into proper Southern, but for comfort, I hold on to pieces of twang. I read books without pictures now and I'm up to forty-one, sixth grade level. Lu is nearing eight hundred books but tells me it ain't a contest, so pay no mind to her number. Mama and Daddy don't even count their reading numbers anymore. Maybe numbers don't go that high. I feel smart compared to where I come from. I'm ready to hold my own with some college girls.

This opening of market, Patricia Hollingston and her three friends come down from Cornell University in Ithaca, New York. Lu points out Ithaca on the map, so I know it's a long way to come to rattle our farming town. Patricia is the late-in-life daughter of Uncle Nigel and Aunt Fanniebelle, and Lu says she has wanted for nothing. I saw lots of pictures of her in frames and on the walls when we stayed in the mansion. And it's there that Weegee stays in the bottom of the walnut secretary. We only called on her one more time to ask the same question bout Frankie Tender. She gave the same answer as she did for Larry. HOME.

Lu and me are six years younger than Patricia, and we've been invited to Friday tea, which is going to be served under the portico, not in the sunroom. The day before, we wash our hair and rinse it with lemon juice so it smells nice. Mama drives us to the mansion so we don't get rumpled. Daddy and Grady are already at the tobacco warehouse off Main Street. We'll meet them later and eat supper at Morningside Oyster Bar, then go to the dance. Or maybe I won't go to the dance. Nasty gossip about me has grown thin, but more than I can say, I wish Frankie Tender would be singing tonight and I could have a do-over. Frankie Tender would want a do-over, too.

We go to the front door like guests instead of the side door like family. When I first lay eyes on Patricia Hollingston, I get the gumption knocked out of me. She's a movie star like Ingrid Bergman and Gene Tierney, gorgeous and perfect. White teeth, ruby lips, polished nails, hair bobbed, and silk nylons in leather pumps with nary a scuff mark. Standing next to Patricia Hollingston, I'm a cow patty. A pig farmer. A pig farmer who wallows in slop. Next to Patricia Hollingston, I ain't moved a inch from my plain roots like I thought.

Patricia squeals. She gives Lu a perfumed hug. "Lucy Brown, you're so *dahling,*" she gushes, holding her cousin out at arm's length to study on her. "Turn around," she orders, and Lu spins, sending her skirt in a twirl, looking young and silly.

She remembers I'm here and turns to me. "And this is my best friend, Bert."

Patricia's smile shifts. "*Bert?* What kind of girl's name is Bert?" Her voice carries a thorn.

"Her whole name is Allie Bert Tucker, but she only answers to Bert."

"Well, Allie Bert Tucker, it's good to meet you." Patricia insults me a second time and gives me her weak hand to shake instead of a hug, but Lu don't see it like that. She's starstruck.

"Pleased to meet you." I sound stuck-up and shy in my homemade dress that looks every inch homemade next to Patricia's store-bought one that shows off her womanly curves.

Patricia introduces us to her friends I won't never see again. They got fancy names like I thought they would: Alice Madison, Ashley Johannson, and Annemarie Moss. They go together like puzzle pieces. I forget their names right away.

Lu gushes, "Alice, Ashley, and Annemarie — with all those A names, are they your A team?" and they giggle.

I think they're assholes. Asshole one, asshole two, and asshole three. Patricia is the queen asshole.

Lu gushes on, "Tell me about college. What are you studying?"

I want to pinch her so she stops acting stupid.

The A girl with the dark hair parted down the middle and rolled at the neck reminds me of Miz Elvira at the library but not as pretty. She says, "It's boring since all the men over twenty-one have been drafted in that godforsaken war. But Patricia is the lucky one," she says, and Patricia holds out her left hand to show off a sparkly ring that's way too big to be real, but I know it is.

"Oh, Patricia," Lu squeals. "What's his

name? Where's he from?"

"He's a second lieutenant in the Marine Corps. He looks dashing in his dress uniform, if I may say so. His name is Julian Sanders the Third from the New York *Sanders* family. He'll be a partner in his daddy's law firm one day. I can't think of a more perfect man for me. Our engagement will be announced in the newspapers soon." She whispers, "You two are the first people in Riverton to know — other than my parents and Helen. I don't know where he's stationed, but he writes every day. It's the hardest thing for us to be apart." She tears up perfectly.

"Is it true," one of the assholes whispers, "that you have *Nazis* in a prison camp at the docks?"

Lu says, "We have two that help on the farm. One works tobacco. The other bees."

"Oh my word," "Heaven help us," and "Good grief" overlap from the mouths of the prissy girls, clutching their hearts, their eyes big and wide.

Patricia whispers, "Helen said one of them *stole* Betty Jean right out of her crib."

I say right back, "He didn't steal her. He was comforting her. Cause she was crying and Helen wouldn't feed her. And we like em. The Germans. They our friends. Our

312

Nazi friends." I want to rile up this perfect world. I don't care that my words sting. I don't like these people. They act snooty.

The four college girls stare at me with cold eyes, and I have a pinch of regret for messing up our invite we've been looking forward to. Lu looks like she's gonna cry, and that surprises me. She likes Joe and Wolf, so why wouldn't she stand up for em and tell the truth?

Patricia takes my hands. She holds them tight so I can't snatch em away. She's strong for a college girl. She looks at me and from her perfect mouth says, "I'm going to forgive you that heartless remark, Allie Bert Tucker, knowing my fiancé is in some *godforsaken* place fighting for his very life and our country's freedom. And you forget that dear Helen's husband Wade is MIA, all because of dangerous enemies who are no friends of ours. But I did not come home to quarrel. I want to spend a lovely afternoon with my favorite cousin and her wonderful best friend. Can we call a truce and mend this awkward moment?"

I feel small.

I hate her and like her all at once for her bravery.

Nancy Drew would look like Patricia, only Nancy's got more brains.

I nod, and Patricia gives me a big perfumed hug and says, "Forget the tea for now. It'll keep. Let's go upstairs. I've been *dying* to doll you two girls up from the moment I saw you. Makeup, curled hair, fingernail polish, the works. You're already beautiful, but we're going to make you *irresistible.*"

The A team goes to work on Lu's hair, rolling the back and waving the sides. Patricia works on me. She sits me in front of a big round mirror. Daylight pours in from two tall windows on each side and makes me look bright and clean. She opens jars and taps fluffy brushes on her wrist and pats stuff on my face, saying, "Allie, you are a rare beauty."

I don't fight when she calls me Allie, cause this is a different girl sitting in front of the mirror.

"See how this blush makes your cheeks look sun kissed? You only need a little. A lady doesn't overdo. And this is my favorite perfume. Emeraude. You put a tiny dab behind each ear, like this." Her touch is like a butterfly wing. "I'm going to give you this little bottle, but use it sparingly. It is powerful."

Then she holds up a finger and says, "Wait, wait, wait. Let me get something."

I'm left with a stranger looking back at me. I smile, and she smiles.

Patricia come back carrying a dress on a padded hanger. "This teal-blue fabric looks exquisite next to your auburn hair. Look what it does to your eyes and the gold in your skin. Try it on."

"Now?"

"It's only us girls, and we've seen it all."

I feel shy in my slip that was Irene's hand-me-down, a little proud that my bosom is full and high, but a traitor to Mama's dress she labored over in the evenings. When I put on the taffeta dress Patricia don't want no more and she hooks the back, buckles the thin matching belt, and turns me around to look at myself, everybody stares. Lu comes beside me wearing a Patricia hand-me-down in purple with white on the edges that is perfect for her.

Patricia says to the A team, "May I present Miz Lucy Brown and Miz Allie Tucker, who will break hearts from one end of Mercer County to the other."

We stand like happy fools, grinning at ourselves. We are *movie stars.* We look as sharp as Nancy Drew on her book covers. Nobody can deny the girls in the mirror are smarter than they were before.

Patricia gets her Kodak camera and takes

a picture to remember the day. I forget I was mad and grin like the fool.

"This calls for a celebration." She reaches into a cabinet and brings out a brown bottle I seen before. She whispers, looking over at the bedroom door, "I want my friends to have a taste of Moon Pies and moonshine on their virgin trip South, and this moment seems fitting for the hooch." She pours the clear liquor in little glasses and hands one to each of us.

I look at Lu to see if she's gonna drink it. I don't think she's ever had a drop pass her lips. It's gonna knock her on her behind. Her smile is crooked, but she looks determined.

One of the A girls says, "Do that toast of yours, Patricia. The naughty one we love."

The college girls straighten their backs, lift their chins, and raise their glasses, and we do, too. We wait for Patricia. She looks serious and clears her throat.

"Here's to the girl in the little red shoes,
She'll smoke all your cigs and drink all
    your booze.
She doesn't have her cherry but that's not
    a sin
Cause she still has the box that the
    cherry came in."

The lot of them crack up laughing like Patricia said the funniest they ever heard, then they swallow the shine in one gulp, coughing, and gasping and tapping their feet. Lu and me laugh, too, but it's a pretend laugh, and Lu gulps her shine and gets in such a choking fit, she almost messes up her makeup. That makes the four assholes laugh louder. If I didn't look so good, I'd a slapped em upside the head.

We go downstairs, out to the portico, and drink tea and eat sweet treats. Lu and me sit taller and straighter on our chairs. Helen is there with Baby Girl, but Helen is so thin and so sad she don't say a word bout our newfound beauty. Baby Girl is nine months old and grins a lot.

We leave the Hollingston mansion and walk Main Street with a grown-up sway in our step. Our homemade dresses are in Bonwit Teller shopping bags with more dresses from Patricia's closet. Our hair is piled high, and our lips are painted strawberry pink. Patricia touched up the color before we left. A man on the sidewalk tips his hat. Ladies look us up and down and smile. I see our reflection in the pharmacy window. It's where we sat on stools at the counter and ate banana splits when Grady became marble champion of the world.

When we pass, Ricky Miller comes out. He's the boy two years older than us who has a powerful crush on Lu she don't see. The story goes he was the one who set Assassin's tail on fire, which carried Lu to Trula Freed's door that first time. I know he did it to get Lu's attention. When he sees us today, he grabs his heart and falls back against the wall like he's been shot, like he's bowled over by our new selves. I get the giggles, but Lu don't even give him the time a day. She's hard on him. He's cute in a country way.

Lu ignores him and says, "What do you think Patricia meant about a cherry in a box?"

"I think she was pulling our leg. Down here, we pick cherries by the bag. And it takes a lotta cherries to make a pie for Aunt Violet to feed her chickens."

Lu cuts her eyes over at me. "That's the first time you've mentioned that cherry pie day."

I nod. "She was crazy before, so she couldn't help it."

"That's a good way to look at it, and it's a shame." Lu hooks her arm through mine. "But today, we're beauties without a care in the world."

Lu's right. No movie star on earth ever

felt more power than we feel in our store-bought dresses. Our skin is dusted with blush, and hairspray keeps our curls in place. I feel different from the fool at the last dance who went off with Frankie Tender. This girl is better than that.

We see Daddy off in a crowd of his friends, smoking, laughing. We catch his eye. He smiles and tips his hat like he does to ladies. He don't know who we are till we walk up to him and say, "Hey, Daddy."

CHAPTER 39
LUCY: POWER

Bert and I are the stars of the day. I didn't know a change on the outside could make such a difference on the inside. We cause a ruckus walking down the sidewalk and up to Daddy's friends. Ricky Miller follows us from the soda fountain to the warehouse and acts the fool. I ignore him on principle. I ignore all the tobacco doings that afternoon, so aware of the attention Bert and I receive. We've crossed some invisible line into the land of beguile, and I feel a power I never knew before.

The camp Germans working inside the warehouse keep looking our way, us standing at the door as exotic as peacocks in a pigeon house. Two soldiers with rifles by their sides watch the POWs in case they get out of line. One soldier says, "Keep your eyes to yourself," but the Germans smile at us anyway. Maybe they don't know English. Maybe they do.

I almost forget to pay attention to my favorite part of market: the auctioneers. If it weren't for them, our tobacco wouldn't get sold for top dollar. Without auctioneers singing the praises of the brown leaf, the sweat of the field hands would be for less. Then Daddy might not call himself a tobacco farmer, and the family land we've owned for three generations might be lost. Daddy says auctioneers are the stars who make all the hard work *work.*

They wear tailored suits and silk ties and polished shoes. They slick back their hair with pomade. Their voices are mesmerizing. In the dusty cavern of Riverton's tobacco warehouses every Friday for nearly two months they will drift from basket to basket, pull top bid from the buyer, and give top dollar to the seller. Auctioneers love the limelight, and the limelight loves them.

Today, Daddy's tobacco gets sold, and the price makes him happy, but he doesn't say anything about how grown-up Bert and I look. Grady works to cut us down to size.

"How'd you girls get your hair in sausage rolls like that? Pass the mustard. I'm hungry." And "Where'd your freckles go, Bert?" Grady wouldn't know high fashion if it bit him in the butt. We hold our heads high.

Then things start to slide downhill.

The walk to Morningside for supper is three sweltering blocks from the warehouse. My scalp and face start to itch from the hairspray and makeup. I sit on a bench packed tight and eat fried oysters while the pads in my armpits soak through. I'm mortified to see sweat pooling at my waist. Bert looks as bad as I feel, and she uses a napkin to wipe her upper lip and across her forehead, but she smears the makeup so her freckles show through. Her lipstick is gone and her curls droop. From the look on Bert's face, I look as pitiful.

We excuse ourselves, but Daddy and Grady hardly notice. They eat another plate of fried oysters, and we find soap and water at a sink out back. We take turns on lookout and change back into our cool cotton dresses Mama made. The store-bought ones get stuffed in the bag. We pull a hundred bobby pins out of our hair to set it free. When we get back to the table, Daddy's paying the bill, and Grady grabs the last hushpuppy. They don't even notice we look like our fourteen-year-old selves again. We walk to the opening market dance held at the high school gymnasium. Bert lags behind.

She says, nervous, "You think he's inside?"

"Who?"

"Frankie Tender."

"Why would he be here?"

"This is a dance with a band, isn't it?"

"Yes, but I think Frankie played with the Top Hats. This band is the Romeos from New Bern. Says so right there." I point to the poster, and relief floods Bert's face. We start to walk in when Cousin Patricia and her college friends drift by, parting the crowd with their perfumed demeanor. Men backstep, hitch up pants, tip their hats. Country women with hair in hard buns shoot jealous darts to the pampered beauties. Despite the August humidity that soaks through the stiffest starch, the college girls are flawless. When they see us, they say nothing about our morph back into our adolescent selves. Instead, they hug us like it's been a month of Sundays since we saw them. Such is the charm of our visiting stars from Cornell University.

Patricia and her A team have barely left Riverton on the train when the prison alarm pierces the quiet shortly after three in the darkest part of night. It wails and wails and rouses the town people from their beds with hearts filled with trepidation. Of course, we only hear a modest wail two miles out of town, but we hear the sharp ring of the telephone. Daddy plods out of his bedroom to answer it, and all of us trail on his heels, sleepy-eyed, curious. A phone call before the sun comes up never means good news.

"David, got bad news" is how Uncle Nigel starts. "There's been killings at the camp. Some of the prisoners are dead, their throats cut clean through, but I don't know the particulars."

Every one of us has been witness to Terrell Stucky and his killing gestures, so it is to him that our thoughts fly for this reprehensible crime. We want to know if *our* Germans are safe. Uncle Nigel tells Daddy to come down to the prison camp, because that's where everybody who's anybody is headed.

We stand stunned in our kitchen with questions swirling. Irene says, "Don't forget Byron — please." We have tears in our eyes and knots in our bellies thinking about pandemonium at the camp. In the months the POWs have been here, our fear toward the Germans has changed. We've learned some are artists, and they hang their work on the prison fence. Some are singers and formed a choir that practices in the evenings. Others plant gardens of herbs and vegetables. Riverton should have been a safe place for them to work on farms and wait out the war.

"Come on, Grady." Daddy kisses Mama's temple and promises to call.

It's close enough to dawn that Mama starts breakfast and chores get done earlier than usual. On the other side of the world, millions of lives have been lost in this god-awful war that drags on, but today's crime happened in our backyard. At breakfast, Mama bows her head and says the blessing with greater fervor.

I'm doing dishes when the phone rings, and Mama answers, yelling into the mouthpiece, "David?"

"Minnie, it's Aunt Fanniebelle" is shouted out of the earpiece loud enough for us to hear across the room. "Your David wanted me to call so y'all stop worrying. He said Jim and Rolf and Merwin are fine. They weren't the ones murdered."

"You mean Joe, Wolf, and Byron?"

"That's what I said. Jim and Rolf won't the two Nazis kilt," she shouts like we're standing on the far side of a wide field. "It was two other fellers that was Germans. Heard tell the blood was everywhere. Like slitting open a hog on hog-killing day." She continues to shout details as if she's seen it with her own eyes. "They were lying in a pool of blood big as a lake. It's a wonder a man's got that much blood in him."

"Uh-huh. Is David coming on home?"

"Don't rightly know. He told me to call bout Jim and Rolf."

"Thank you."

"That siren was a frightful thing, waking a body out of deep sleep like that."

"I can imagine."

"You know my hearing's not so good, but I heard that blasted siren. Nearly gave Nigel a heart attack jumping up so fast, looking for his glasses so he could hear better."

"I can imagine," Mama repeats patiently, rolling her eyes. "Thank you for calling."

"They finally turned off the siren, and my ears got to ringin and won't stop. Might have to go see Doc Robertson bout that ringing but don't think he could help much."

"Thanks again." Mama finally hangs up the phone, shaking her head. Talking with Aunt Fanniebelle is risky business. We have to trust that Jim, Rolf, and Merwin are our friends and that they were spared.

Midmorning, Daddy and Grady get back, and Mama makes a fresh pot of coffee. She sets out ham biscuits and says, "We heard Joe and Wolf and Byron are safe."

Daddy nods. "They're safe, but two Germans were murdered, and one was that little man they called Ketchup who worked the kitchen."

Byron had told us about the man dubbed Heinz Ketchup. He was more poet than mercenary, older than most of the prisoners at twenty-nine, an engineer in a former life. He was undersized, and they assigned him to the mess hall instead of farmwork. He washed dishes and peeled potatoes. He got his nickname when he saw *Heinz* printed on a bottle of that sweet tomato sauce and said, "Das bin ich." That's me. He fell in love with the red sauce. He put ketchup on everything — eggs, potatoes, green beans, pickles, chocolate cake, vanilla pudding. We find out today that his real name was Heinz Grout, an educated man learning to cook Southern.

"Sheriff thinks Heinz was killed second. That he went to the latrine and interrupted the first murder. There was no blood tracked back to the tents. All the other prisoners were accounted for. Other than the guard who found the two bodies — who didn't have any blood on him except what he walked in — everybody was clean."

"How did the killer get inside?" Bert says.

"There were tracks out back of the latrine to a hole under the fence that wasn't there yesterday."

Mama clenches her jaw. We don't have to

say Terrell Stucky's name, but it hangs in the air like the stink of bad fish. And it's made Sheriff Cecil's job easy.

"One more strange thing." Daddy picks up his third ham biscuit. "When the sun came up this morning, Stucky wasn't in his lawn chair outside the gate. He never showed up at all."

CHAPTER 40
BERT: SURE THING

Different armed guards are outside the prison camp, and they don't know Daddy and Grady. The hole in the fence got fixed, but the prisoners are scared cause the crime can't be undone. This is what Grady tells Lu and me cause he comes and goes as he pleases while we're stuck on the farm. He says Sheriff Cecil had to give the case to the military police from Camp Butner since the killings took place inside the camp. I bet he's glad to step away, since the killer is likely Flossie Rose's brother, Terrell Stucky. Me and Lu think the sheriff and Flossie are sweet on each other.

Grady says it best. "It's a waste of time if they don't arrest Terrell Stucky," he says when we all sit down at supper after a day that started too early. "Everybody knows he did it. He's been advertising for months."

Irene brings fresh news. "He's their number one suspect, and they'd like to question him, but nobody's seen him since yester-day."

"What bout Tater and Spud?" I say, pass-ing a bowl of potato salad. "They bound to know where he is. They thicker than gravy."

"They say they don't know, and I think they're too dumb to keep a secret this big."

"Where could he be?" Mama wonders. "Is he hiding somewhere? In an abandoned building or barn?" Her eyes fly wide, and she whispers, "We better lock the house tonight. And everybody be on the lookout."

"Don't let your imagination grow wild," Daddy says. "Terrell Stucky knows better than to cause more trouble for himself. He's likely headed for an island in the swamps."

"He could be close and desperate. Look what he did to those boys in that camp."

What did Mama say? She's gone from calling the POWs *evil Nazis* to *prisoners* to *Germans,* and now *boys.*

Irene says, "Terrell Stucky wasn't in his lean-to when the soldiers went to arrest him. He wasn't in Flossie's little house either. They did find something disturbing where he's been living. They found a gun." Irene takes a bite of buttered biscuit, and we wait for her to chew and swallow. "The gun was lying next to a puddle of blood on the floor where Stucky sleeps. Looks like there was a fight there, too, with a chair turned over."

Daddy asks what we all wonder. "Did somebody shoot Stucky or did he shoot somebody?"

"Can't tell. According to Byron, nobody's been to Doc Robertson or the hospital with a gunshot wound. There was no sign of Stucky's pearl-handled switchblade either. It wasn't left at the scene of the crime. It wasn't in Stucky's lean-to. This situation isn't as simple as we thought it'd be."

"And what about the murdered men? What's going to happen to them?" Mama asks.

"Preacher from First Christian said the two could be buried at the back of their cemetery. Talk around town is that a lot of people are sad and shocked. Even people who don't like having Germans here one bit."

Mama says, "A lot more than lives have been lost with these murders."

The next afternoon after chores, Lu and me ride our bicycles over to Flossie Rose's place. She says, "Let's check with Tiny Junior first, then we can ask Weegee for answers." We want to see where Terrell Stucky lived his last days. It's gotta be a hole of a place but a sight better than sitting inside jail rotting for the rest of his days. When we get to the unpainted Rose house, two soldiers with rifles stand at the end of the driveway. I thought they would have left by now since they didn't find Terrell Stucky.

"This is off-limits," one soldier says.

"But Flossie and Tiny Junior are our friends," Lu protests. "We brought cookies to be neighborly."

The soldier repeats, "This is off-limits," and he looks at us with a hard face like we're the enemy. Tiny Junior stands on his porch. He waves and we wave, and Lu holds up the cookie tin so he can see we brought treats. He comes our way. The two soldiers got their backs to him, but when Tiny tries to get around him, he says, "Stay on this property, sir."

Lu says, "That doesn't make sense. Are they prisoners in their own house?"

The guards don't answer.

"Well, we'll talk to Tiny Junior standing right here in the road. Eating a cookie. You can't fault that." Lu opens the tin, and Tiny Junior and me takes one. We made sugar cookies this morning topped with extra real sugar that glitters on top. Our beeswax business spared the sugar most folks don't have.

The two soldiers cut their eyes to the tin

lined with wax paper and layered with golden cookies.

"Y'all want one?" I ask sweet as honey. "They're real good. We won't tell."

The soldiers are in a tight spot, being tempted by cookies but wanting to do the right thing. They look one way then the other down this empty dirt road with drain ditches on each side. They shoulder their rifles and take one. "Thank you," they say, grinning, looking young as us, licking sugar crumbs off their lips.

"When's the last time you laid eyes on your uncle?" Lu asks.

"Yesterday," he says with his mouth full of cookie.

"Yesterday? After the killings?" I think to ask.

He nods and takes another cookie without hardly swallowing the first.

"Were you close enough to talk to him?"

He nods again.

"Well, did he kill em or didn't he?" I get vexed cause talking to Tiny Junior can be like pulling teeth.

"He done it," he says, and the soldiers look at our friend for the first time.

"He said that he killed those poor men — for sure?"

When Tiny Junior nods a third time and

reaches for a third cookie, all our mouths drop open in shock at seeing the simple truth declared.

Lu says, "Did you tell your mama?"

"Yea. He done it."

CHAPTER 41
LUCY: QUAGMIRE

Missing men from Riverton have become a variation on a theme, much like the clever music of Johann Sebastian Bach that Wolf played for us. That German composer would shift a tune from major to minor and from fast to slow. After our resident violinist introduced us, that very day Mama had us look up J. S. Bach in the *Encyclopedia Britannica.* He lived two hundred years ago and wrote over a thousand compositions. He sired twenty children and went blind. He died at sixty-five from complications from eye surgery. He was a prolific man.

So far, our Missing-Man Theme has four variations: cruel Larry Crumbie, seductive Frankie Tender, unfortunate Wade Sully, and murdering Terrell Stucky.

We wonder if there will be more missing men to come, and if so, who will be next. We never dreamt it will be our favorite music man, who casts a spell over all of us.

One who inspires the swing and the Lindy Hop and the jitterbug — Mr. Glenn Miller.

Couples fall in love, say "I do," and make love to his music, but sometimes not in that order. Helen told me these things in private last year when she called me naïve, but I'm not. I know these days babies are born closer to the wedding date than they should, and Glenn Miller is one of the reasons. He makes twenty thousand dollars a year playing music and might be the richest man in the world. Songs like "Stairway to the Stars" and "Over the Rainbow" lift us above the tiring war life that has worn us down. When we got word back in November a year back that Wade was missing, Glenn Miller's music was both a comfort and a torture for Helen. She had memories, and when one was resurrected by a song, she stopped what she was doing, went to her bedroom, and shut the door.

One time, I followed her and sat on the edge of the bed, rubbed her back, watched her cry. Unlike Bert and me, Helen cried pretty. She dabbed at the corners of eyes made brighter by tears. Her nose didn't even run or turn red.

"I wish there was something I could do, Helen. I wish I had answers."

"We all wish we had answers, but we

don't. I have to hold tight to hope, this little teeny hope." She picked at a stain on her apron with her fingernail. "Hearing Glenn Miller's music makes it all raw and real. Did you know Wade proposed to me right after we heard 'In the Mood'? All the while it played on his car radio, I could tell he had something on his mind. He was antsy. When that song ended, he said 'You know what I'm in the mood for, Helen Ann Brown?' And before I could even guess, he said, 'I'm in the mood for you to be my wife.' "

What could I say to that? So I called out to the air, "Wade Sully, are you listening? We're in the mood for you to come on home now." That made Helen half laugh, and she patted the back of my hand.

"Thank you for that," she said, and we stood and hugged. I couldn't remember when I last hugged Helen. She had grown appallingly thin. If I squeezed, I would crush her bones.

Now, she's gotten even thinner.

We know the words to every song Glenn Miller recorded. "Pennsylvania 6-5000" is a favorite, named after a hotel telephone number. You'd think we'd get tired of shouting the chorus until we're hoarse, but we don't. "Chattanooga Choo Choo" won Mr. Miller his first gold record. He is loved by Americans in ways no politician or military man could hope to be.

When we think he can't do more to help morale, he joins the army and makes us extra proud. At the old age of thirty-eight, he becomes a major and leads the U.S. Army Air Force Band to dizzying success. I don't think Everett ever saw his orchestra play. He would have told us of that wonder, but Aunt Fanniebelle and Uncle Nigel did.

They saw him for real in New York City two months back. They took the first-class train up the coast and stayed at the Ritz-Carlton Hotel on Central Park South. Patricia's fiancé, Lieutenant Julian Sanders the Third, was on leave, and Uncle Nigel got tickets for them to dance to the Glenn Miller Orchestra performing in the ballroom. Patricia and Aunt Fanniebelle wore evening gowns purchased at Neiman Marcus, Uncle Nigel wore his tuxedo, and Lieutenant Sanders was dashing in his dress uniform. They had a picture taken standing next to Glenn Miller and had it framed. It sits on their baby grand piano. That trip made me understand that I had rich relations who boggled my comprehension. I was covetous to my core until they got home and gave us the new Glenn Miller record. They also gave Bert and me a silver frame holding our grown-up picture Patricia took on opening day of tobacco market. We don't look one bit like ourselves, but we keep it in our room to remind us of possibility.

Now '44 is coming to an end — the year Mama foretold the war would be over and Everett and Wade would come home. Instead, the bizarre vortex in Riverton continues to swallow bad men, and when asked, Trula Freed says the same nebulous thing: "They'll turn up." Weegee goes to the same four letters: HOME. They've both lost their telling touch. But the Missing Men of Riverton is a conundrum that pales in comparison to the loss that sinks us to our knees. It happens on Friday, December fifteenth, when we're going about our day without bracing for a disaster of epic proportion.

We don't know a single-engine plane took off from Bedfordshire, sixty miles north of London. A plane carrying precious human cargo in temperatures near freezing and icy fog at zero visibility. The pilot is confident they'll make the crossing, but he's inexperienced. The plane flies low over the English Channel, under the radar. It was supposed to land in liberated Paris in two hours, and Glenn Miller would step off and be greeted by adoring fans braving the cold to catch a glimpse. He was to be the star of the Christmas show for the Allied troops.

That was the plan.

The next day, the radio announcer tells us that Glenn Miller's plane never made it to Paris and we send prayers heavenward and beg God to spare our music man. The weight of our prayers is a palpable thing as we beg for a miracle.

But Glenn Miller stays missing.

Into the next day.

And the next.

Through the dark days of December.

Then the world begins to speculate. Maybe Glenn Miller was rescued but has amnesia. Maybe his plane flew off course and he's being hidden by a French family. Maybe the Nazis captured him and will leverage his life in exchange for our surrender. We study our maps on the parlor wall to see where he could have landed. We hold tight to hope. We hope with a fervor we didn't know we had. To our way of thinking, until they find his body, he can't be dead.

Then cruel rumors rise up, rumors we hear from Uncle Nigel who reads the *Washington Post* and the *New York Times.* Then the rumors are reported in snippets on the radio and become accusations. Did the British Lancaster bombers abort a mission? Did they drop their bombs in the English Channel before landing and hit Glenn Miller's low flying plane?

Glenn Miller tunes are played every day on the radio, but they've lost their sparkle. They are too lively. He stays missing.

We don't bother to ask Weegee.

■ ■ ■ ■

1945

■ ■ ■ ■

CHAPTER 42
BERT: REDEMPTION

This year, we don't leave our beds to watch the New Year come. Mama don't pretend the war will end anytime soon. She don't say Everett and Wade is gonna come home. Glenn Miller stays missing and hope has run thin. I make up my mind to mend my old ways. I'm gonna let go of the things in my treasure box cause they ain't special no more, but facing the people I wronged scares the bejesus outta me. I need a soft start, so I go see Aunt Fanniebelle.

She's in the sunroom drinking tea in a bright spot of January sun. A fuzzy green robe is wrapped round her like a peapod with her wrinkled face poking out. I'm nervous cause the sunroom was the scene of the crime that first time I come for me and Lu's birthdays. That stormy night, I wrapped the silver infuser in a pressed napkin and slid it easy in my pocket. Today I put that napkin and infuser on the table beside Aunt Fanniebelle's teacup. The silver's turned dull.

The old woman cocks her head to the side and says, "I once had me an infuser like that."

"This *is* your infuser. I took it." Then I say, "I stole it," cause Lu told me not to water down my sin but don't puff it up more than need be.

"We looked for that infuser for days but couldn't find it. We even beat the bushes looking."

"I had it. In my box of stuff," I say. "Stuff I stole."

But Aunt Fanniebelle isn't hearing good. "It needs a good cleaning from the look of it. Hand it here and go get the polish in the butler's pantry. It's in the drawer to the far right. You need to learn to polish silver right. This is an embarrassment. A lady never lets her silver tarnish."

I get the silver cleaner and a rag, and Aunt Fanniebelle shows me how much polish and pressure to use, and I wipe off the stain from that infuser and let the shine come back. She don't exactly forgive me. Instead, she tries to give back the thing I'm trying to give her. Finally, I say, "Can you keep it for me? If I have need for it, I'll come to you," and that pleases her.

Next is Mama's black button I took off the window ledge that first night. I want to sneak it back in her sewing basket and pretend it always lived there, but Lu said proper redemption don't work that way. Repentance is not sneaky. The hurt should ping my heart in order to heal. I don't want any of my family to witness my outright sin, so I pick a time when Mama's alone in the kitchen. I put the black button on the table and step back, ashamed. She don't throw a tizzy fit when she sees it. She says matter-of-fact, "I wondered when that button would turn up again," and drops it in her apron pocket.

"I'm sorry, Mama. So sorry." I don't want to get off easy.

"Bert, I knew you took the button, but for a while, you needed that button more than I did."

"Yes, ma'am, I did. I needed to hold on to something good, but that don't make it right."

"Stealing is never right, but sometimes it's necessary," she says and confuses me.

"Necessary?"

"You were uprooted, looking for solid footing. Like Helen, who's been in a dark place these months. But you've moved back into the light. You don't need this button

347

anymore, and I'm happy for you."

I wait. "That's it? You ain't gonna punish me? Take a switch to my backside? Give me extra chores?"

Mama ties on her apron and starts making a butterscotch pie. She says, "Maybe that guilt you've been carrying around has been punishment enough. You've already done the heavy work."

"How you figure that?"

"You've worried and reflected on your behavior and decided to right a wrong. There's the lesson." Then she adds, "But don't get the wrong idea. Thieving chips away at your character. If it goes on too long, it can't be remedied."

"You think my thieving ways went on too long?"

"No, I don't. You stopped at the right time."

So far, this letting go of stole stuff's been easy, but Trula Freed's green marble is the heaviest thing in my box. I know now I wasn't fooling her one bit when I plucked it from her bowl of marbles and tucked it in my pocket. Today, I decide to lay that burden down and head to the hayloft to fetch the marble and take it to her. I hope the marble don't carry bad luck that lingers.

When I come outta the barn, I see her. I

348

rub my eyes at the apparition, thinking I conjured her out of fear, but Trula Freed is real all right, walking up our road, wearing a red hooded cloak that drags the ground, carrying a burlap bag by a drawstring.

This kind of spooky stuff is troubling.

"Hey," I call out. "I was coming to see you. You here for a visit?" I sound silly cause I'm unsettled at her being so close to the stole marble that burns in my pocket. I say, "What's in the bag?"

She says, "Marbles," and bout stops my heart.

"Marbles?" My mouth is as dry as cotton dust, and I follow her into the house, back to the kitchen, where Mama has tea steeping in Oma's pot and the butterscotch pie is cooling on the table.

Mama lays her hand on my forehead. "You okay, honey? You look pale. Want some tea and pie?"

I stare at the burlap bag Trula Freed sets on the table. Marbles.

"Miz Trula." My voice is small, my hand sweaty around the little glass ball I pull from my pocket. "This belongs to you." I open my hand. My palm is hot and sticky, and the marble burns my skin. "I stole it," I say outright, because Mama already knows my wicked ways.

The sorceress takes the green marble, opens the burlap bag, and drops it in. "It's yours now."

Why'd she go and do that? How will I tell my stole marble from the other marbles? The marbles she had in her bowl that are now in that bag. Marbles the color of her eyes. Eyes that see through skin and bone and into my dastardly heart.

"I'm sorry," I say. "Real sorry."

"You are forgiven," Trula Freed says and puts a piece a pie in her mouth and chews slow.

"Mama says sometimes stealing is necessary," I say, and they nod and sip tea, and I rattle on. "But that don't make a lick a sense. Stealing's a crime. Back home, there ain't two ways bout stealing. You get a whipping. You get sent to your room with no supper. No breakfast the next day neither. Stealing is a sin against the Lord Jesus, so salt gets put on the floor, and you get on your knees on that salt and stay there till you cry out and your knees bleed, till you fall over and Pa says that's enough."

Mama stands in a rush and says, "Yes, that is enough, sweet Bert." She pulls me to her for comfort, but my body locks up on itself. She says, "You've carried unnecessary burdens for too long. You need to unlock these shackles that hold you down. Don't you understand that you're not meant to be perfect? None of us are."

"But you are. You're perfect. All the Browns are perfect."

"No, dear. We're only human."

But my body stays stiff against her softness.

Mama looks at Trula Freed. "Can you help her heal? My words don't seem to be working."

And the witchy woman holds out her hands, and mine quiver cause I remember that shock I got the first day, taking Trula Freed's hands without knowing. She waits for my hands, and the kitchen and the air and the light grow bright. She says, "I'll wait all day for you and tomorrow, too, if need be, because you are precious to us."

When I lay my hands in Miz Trula's, something buzzes in my head like the beat of tiny angel wings, and warm honey runs through me and fills up them empty holes.

CHAPTER 43
LUCY: MIBSTER

Trula Freed brought us a burlap bag of marbles. They were all sapphire blue except for a green one that puzzled my brother and sisters because they never saw the bowl of green marbles like Bert and I did. Bert stole one that long-ago day but gave it back. I'm proud of her.

All us Browns are better than average marble players. Even six-year-old Lydia knows how to knuckle down with a taw and shoot with precision, but it's Grady who was born with the gift of a champion. He draws perfect three-foot circles in the dirt without needing a yardstick. He shoots with the deadly aim of a rattlesnake. The rest of us play a fair game where we take back our marbles at the end and only hold bragging rights. Grady likes to play for keeps. He's the master mibster of Mercer County, but he's run out of challengers who'll take him on.

We know the Nazis prisoners come from the land of the best shooters, because Oma told us so. These men are older and experienced in ways our Southern boys and girls are not. Our feelings toward them have mutated into something abnormally different from what we thought would happen.

And they play marbles.

Prisoners and guards alike drop to a knee to play when challenged. Byron tells us such things and stirs our curiosity about new marble talent. We want to see these moves that defy belief. Mama reminds us of her order to stay away from the prison camp, but the passing of time is making that rule tenuous. Like a spider silk stretched to its limit, we hope the rule will break and we'll be liberated.

Playing marbles is the oldest game in the world. It started at the beginning of time with round stones and polished nuts and clay balls before marbles were made of glass. Then from the mid-eighteen hundreds, the center of the marble-making world was Germany, deep in the forest of my family's roots, beside the Lauscha River. Oma's father left the Black Forest to work in the factory that made a million marbles a day. The marbles filled a railroad car that was sent out into a world hungry for marbles.

Rich people paid an astonishing penny for one mib. It's because of our ancestor that playing marbles is as natural as breathing in the Brown family.

All the talk of marbles these days has Mama get out the locked wooden box she keeps in her room. Bert hasn't seen our great-grandfather's marbles. Mama spreads out a blanket on the kitchen table so the marbles won't roll off and possibly crack on the floor.

"There are forty-two marbles in that box, right?" Lydia says, because she's heard it so many times. Forty-two marbles that are almost a hundred years old — and all flawed but still priceless to us. These were marbles the factory rejected. We hold them up to the light and study them under Mama's magnifying glass. We look for bubbles, irregular lines, and our great-grandpa's fingerprints.

We have our own sacks of micas, sulphides, and latticino swirls. We're proud of our skill, but Mama reminds us we tread close to the sin of pride when it comes to marbles. I don't think we can help ourselves.

On the Saturday after my birthday, Grady is the lucky one. He gets to watch a showdown between the two best players in the prison camp, one a German and one an army guard from Warren, Michigan.

"Why can't we all go?" Bert says in her forthright way. "Cause we're girls?"

"Let Grady and Daddy go first, then we'll see about y'all going another time. If Byron thinks it's okay."

Mama uses this bargaining technique a lot: dangling hope to keep us in line with no real promise attached, and it works. If we throw a hissy fit, she can rescind any smidgeon of hope. Then where would we be? In a pickle, that's where. Mama is a slick negotiator.

When Grady gets back that marble-playing day, he has wonder etched on his face. His fingertips twitch. "Never seen anything like it," he starts. "First off, they call their game *ringers.* Stead of some puny three-foot circle like we use, they play on a circle ten foot wide with thirteen marbles in the crosshairs lined up on the axes. They play on concrete, and the taw flies and does good damage, but it can get away from you easy." Grady is flushed with admiration and adds, "And that's using hand-me-down marbles that are nicked. What could they do with good mibs?"

"How big's ten foot?" Lydia wants to know.

"Stay there," he says and steps back and

back and back. "From you to here."

"*Golly.* Are you fooling?"

"Nope. Daddy, Tiny Junior, and I witnessed the whole thing. The guard called Simpson is good, but it's that German named Didi who won today's match. He has moves I never witnessed. He puts a backspin on his shooter that keeps it right where he wants it to be. His control is phenomenal."

Bert says, "I bet you could beat him, Grady," which shocks me. She shocks Grady, too, from the look on his face. "Don't you wanna try?" she adds as a challenge.

Grady scratches his head. "I'd have to practice with the bigger circle on concrete to see which moves work and which don't. Uncle Nigel has that concrete portico. I could chalk a circle on that." Grady already sees it happening.

"Would you play fair or keepers?" Bert asks the question like she's interested when she doesn't even like the game. She came too late to us to be any good at it.

"Let me practice first. I'm a long way from beating the likes of Didi. They'll play another match next Saturday. I wanna watch again."

"You want company?" I say to Grady, then

look over at Bert, Lydia, and Cora. We're thinking the same thing: we're going to finagle us a trip to that camp.

The next evening, while I'm setting the supper table, I say, "Mama, about those camp mibsters." Her silence sounds amenable, so I go on. "We girls want to watch, too. You could come with us if you thought it was dangerous. Grady didn't feel scared one bit inside the fence, and you know Byron would make sure we're safe. Grady says it's playing the likes he's never seen."

And she astounds me when she says, "That might work out."

It might have been because of the glum of winter days that could use a spark of change. It might have been because Daddy tells her there's no danger in watching an old game made new, but Mama grants permission. Next Saturday morning, clouds hang heavy and threaten rain, but our attitude is sunny. Bert and I dress with extra care and put on a teeny bit of Patricia's makeup, but Mama notices and shakes her head. "Put on regular clothes. Wash that stuff off your faces. This isn't a social call. It's marbles." And we acquiesce because we have to.

Daddy and Grady slide in the front seat of the car, and Bert and me sit in back with Cora and Lydia on our laps. Helen wasn't even asked to come. We grin on the ride to a forbidden place we've only passed in the truck. Captain Toots meets us at the gate. Bert and I feel funny walking into a place where nothing feminine abides. The attention we garner is thick like sugar syrup but tickles our skin like spider feet. Somebody whistles, and Byron calls out, "Knock it off." We remember the power Patricia and her A team bestowed upon us at tobacco market last August, so this feeling isn't completely new, but it still makes us giddy. The silly thing is I don't know where to put my arms and look natural. By my sides? Folded over my chest? Behind my back? It's a problem I struggle with till I forget to.

Ringers begins, and it's simple enough but challenging. We watch the shooters, but the prisoners watch us. Daddy sees the glances and the grins from the prisoners that don't require knowing German to understand. Didi wins the match, and Grady's got work to do, but I regret leaving the electricity of the compound. Hundreds of eyes watch us walk away.

We don't ask Mama if we can go back next Saturday. We act like it's no big deal.

Grady practices. He studies on Didi.

We bide our time.

CHAPTER 44
BERT: ALL'S FAIR

Today Grady is gonna beat the Nazi. Mama's gonna come watch, too. Nobody wants to miss the fun cept Helen. Mama says we can bring the sunshine right to Helen's door, but only she can open up and let it in.

Tiny Junior's got on an army jacket from Captain Toots cause he's the camp mascot. He's a friend to everybody, but today he's on Grady's side. His uncle Terrell's empty lawn chair sits at the tree line, turning to rust. It's the only thing to remember him by. Terrell Stucky's name was on everybody's lips after the murders last fall, then me and Lu never stumbled over another clue after Tiny Junior said he saw his uncle that last morning. I mostly forget him. I mostly forget Larry Crumbie, too. It's only Frankie Tender I don't forget.

Today, we come through the gate on Mama's heels. Lydia and Cora got dropped off at Aunt Fanniebelle's to play with new paper dolls. Irene stands beside Captain Toots like she belongs. The Germans are polite with Mama here. Nobody whistles at me and Lu, but we feel the buzz.

Grady's buddies are outside the gate. Ricky, Jamie, Donnie, and Russell — they want Grady to make us proud. Whiz Mayhew is there looking lots better than he did at his homecoming party. Sugar, too, and more children. Word has spread round the county that today Grady goes knuckle to knuckle against the German. This is the first time a townie faces off with a prisoner. Grady might become champion of the world.

Inside the gate, me and the Browns stand in front of the Germans to see good. Grady and Didi shoot to a line to see who goes first, and Grady wins, and a strange pride fills my heart. He drops to his knee. He rolls his shoulders. He blows on his favorite Clambroth shooter for luck, the one with red and white stripes like the barber pole on Main Street. He sets his sight and sends his taw sailing, and it strikes one of the marbles on the line, but it don't go outside the ring like it has to. Grady nods to Didi like a gentleman and steps back. Grady lost his lucky lead.

The German kneels and fires his shooter like Grady said he could. Didi hits a marble out while his shooter spins inside the circle. He makes it look easy. Grady chews on his bottom lip. The German shoots another one out. And another. My heart sinks when mibs number four and five go flying, because the first one to knock out seven marbles wins.

Then Didi's shooter barely crosses the line, and Grady gets another chance. *Lord'a mercy, Lord'a mercy,* I pray hard with my eyes closed, waiting to hear the clack of Grady's marble on marble. When I do, I open one eye. A marble is outside the ring, and the shooter is inside. He shoots again — and again — until he *ties* with Didi, five to five. Didi don't look so proud. He thinks he's playing a farm boy, but Grady ain't no ordinary farm boy. Byron shouts the tied score so friends outside the fence know, and they chant, "Gra-dy, Gra-dy . . ." He shoots and misses, and Mama turns away.

Didi smiles all cocky while Grady cusses under his breath. Marble number six for Didi flies outta the circle and bumps my shoe. Didi's eyes travel over the wide ring to my feet and slowly up my legs, my soft hips, and my full chest till our eyes meet. I wink and pout my lips the way the college girl Patricia taught me to.

Didi clears his throat and rubs his hands on his trousers. He only needs to knock out one. It's a wall of prisoners behind us. Everybody's watching. We stand like stone and listen to the chant, "Gra-dy, Gra-dy."

Didi lines up his shot, then stops, stands up quick, breathes in deep, and rolls his neck.

"Gra-dy, Gra-dy."

The German gets back on his knee, blows on his shooter, takes aim, and shoots. The marble rolls straight and steady and clicks and goes outside the circle. But his shooter goes out, too.

Grady's belly must hurt something terrible. Like the time I got the gall to read *The Velveteen Rabbit* to thirty-one folks and thought I'd puke. This is way bigger. When Grady strikes number six, I sink to my knees, and my ears don't work right, and I suck in air and hold it till I get dizzy.

Grady wins.

CHAPTER 45
LUCY: GOLD STAR

Mama and Daddy drive from the camp to Main Street, but the crowd of Grady's peers walks River Road to the soda fountain to celebrate with our international champion. Ricky Miller and Donnie Gibson lift Grady onto their shoulders, and the chant of his name grows. He is a hero of an unparalleled distinction I don't recollect ever seeing. The crowd fills up the soda fountain, and Uncle Nigel's there because he watched Grady win, too, and he shouts, "Ice cream on the house," and he rolls up his sleeves and goes behind the counter to help Judy, the overwhelmed soda clerk. He asks me to carry out cones for Whiz and Sugar and the others outside on the sidewalk looking in. Lydia, Cora, and Aunt Fanniebelle squeeze through the crowd up to our world champion, and the very air sparkles around my brother. For a moment, I don't recognize us. Or maybe I recognize us from another lifetime. This amazing moment gives me hope that levity hasn't been destroyed by war.

Grady and Irene stay in town, but our carload of happiness heads home to tell Helen what she missed. When we pull up our lane, we see a green army car with a crisp white star. A man gets out, straightens his uniform, puts on his cap. He is not disheveled like John T. Booker, who brought beeswax news two years back. This man is a honed professional as somber as an undertaker.

A strange sound from somewhere deep comes out of Mama's chest. She struggles to open the car door and tumbles out in the yard, barely able to stand. Helen is on the porch, wrapped in Wade's old sweater and his wool cap she wears most days. The lot of us stumble across the yard to Helen, but the soldier reaches her first.

"Miz Wade Sully?" he says, likely guessing by Helen's age and demeanor that she's the one he's looking for. She nods with a quick jerk, and he hands her a telegram. It's heavier than the first piece of paper she received with Wade's name on it.

Mama and Daddy have reached her side. Daddy opens the telegram and reads, "Dear Madam, we regret to inform you . . ."

Daddy takes out the gold star that will replace a blue one in our window.

My sense of sight is heightened. Each family member is propped up like Lydia and Cora's paper dolls, two-dimensional, lifeless. An easy wind could blow us over. This is what it feels like to have death come to your door.

The government car leaves as Trula Freed comes up the drive, wrapped in a muted coat the color of sorrow, a pale scarf fluttering behind like a thin flag. I don't see Uncle Nigel's car, so how did she get here? She walks up to Helen, who smiles an empty smile like she's forgotten where she is or who she is or what has happened.

"She's in shock. I have tea," Trula says.

We limp into the house with little Lydia walking in front of me. Does the girl remember her own premonition a year ago? The smell of Oma's Dentyne chewing gum. Her question about Wade looking for Oma in heaven. How did Lydia know? Weeks back, I asked my little sister if she still had night visits from Oma, and she said, "Sometimes." When I asked if Oma gave her another question to ponder, she nodded. Oma asked her to watch over Tiny Junior. Now what in the world kind of foreboding is that for a little girl? Today, I look at Lydia with more than a pinch of wonder.

For a body of people trying to be quiet in the wake of bad news, we make a lot of noise. A sniffle, the creaking floor, the slide of the bench, water in the kettle, muffled wool coats on pegs, standing bodies bending to sit.

Helen starts. "Betty Gail is a good enough name, I guess, now that we're used to it." Her voice is empty.

The tea steeps in the pot. Trula's blend holds golden root, ginseng, St. John's wort, and valerian. She brought it in a mason jar. The herbs are listed on the side. She rubs lavender oil on Helen's wrists and her limp hands, and Helen lets her.

"I think Wade would like that name. Do we know a Betty Gail, Mama? Don't we have an Aunt Betty Gail over Winterville way?" My widowed sister looks around the room at each of us, her eyes large and confused, her voice calm and detached after all the emotion we've witnessed since Wade went MIA. We hear Betty Gail in the next room stir from her nap, crawl out of her crib, and pad into the kitchen, dragging the rabbit Vetee by his ear. She's fifteen months old tomorrow and is the easiest child this household ever raised. She sleeps when she's tired, eats when she's hungry, and rarely complains. She's funny and sweet.

Today, she crawls into her mama's lap and puts her hand on Helen's cheek. "Hey," she says and giggles, all dumplin pudgy cute.

"Hello, sweet Betty Gail, my precious girl."

Daddy goes to town to find Grady and Irene and take the joy out of their day. He talks to Byron, too, and asks him to help piece together what happened so we know more. Next day, he brings us news. Helen listens, too.

"Army rangers raided the prison in the Pacific where Wade had been held. They won't say where, so I won't speculate. It was a gutsy assignment that carried great risk for the rangers and the prisoners. The POWs didn't know help was coming, of course, but the rangers freed a hundred and nine American soldiers that day. But sadly," he says as he looks at Helen, "by the time they got there, Wade was too weak to survive. He died on the way out, but he died a free man, surrounded by Americans, hearing English spoken, knowing he was headed to safety. Maybe that counted for something."

Lydia and Cora hardly remember Wade. Bert has only seen a picture of him. The rest of us spit out our grief in snippets instead of letting it flow. Wade was Helen's one and only sweetheart, and he was reliable and tenderhearted. Now we take our cues from Helen. We listen when she talks. We hold her when she cries. We shed our tears in private. I never told anyone what Lydia said about Oma looking for Wade Sully in heaven. I didn't even tell Bert. The timing is off by months, but I'm not sure heaven time and Riverton time are the same, so maybe it happened when Lydia said.

Five days later, the government casket holding Wade's fragile remains is delivered to Baylor's Funeral Home. Helen is told it arrived, but she's still frightfully detached. "Daddy, you go sign papers for me. I'll go to the funeral, so let me know when it is," are her strange words, spoken without weight.

The day of the funeral dawns crisp and clear. I don't like hard funerals on clear days. I like funerals on rainy, stormy days when the world cries with you and you don't have to pretend. Today, the weather makes fun of the months leading Wade Sully to his death. Or maybe it celebrates his release.

In church, the Brown family surrounds frail Helen. The Sully family sits behind us with Wade's mama leaning on Wade's daddy, both of them so spent from grief they can't see. Betty Gail sits on her mama's lap. The top of Wade's casket is blanketed with the starched American flag. His military burial is formal. I see Whiz Mayhew wearing his army uniform in the last pew in back of the crowd, needing only a single walking stick now. It's a handsome stick with a lion's head carved on top. I think it's one of Trula Freed's walking sticks. The eyepatch he wears gives Whiz a rakish look that suits him. Sugar's got on her eyepatch, too, and holds her brother's hand. For all the world, it looks like Whiz Mayhew is moving back into himself.

At home, with friends filling every corner of the house, Whiz sits alone in the chilly sunshine on our back porch on the top step. I go out to sit beside him and Sugar comes, too. She sits on one side of her brother, and I'm on the other.

"Hey, girls," he says and clears his throat because it's heavy with emotion. "We buried a good one today. That was some fancy coffin."

I nod and try to think of something notable to say about the finality of death when Whiz asks the big question. "I can't help but wonder why I'm alive and Wade's dead." He studies his open palms for answers. "By all accounts, I should be the dead man, but I'm not, and there's gotta be a reason, don't you think? A reason I'm here and Wade's dead . . ."

The hum of voices is steady behind us. Spoons rattle and pots and platters clatter on tabletops. It's as busy as a beehive inside our house, but out here under a cloudless blue sky, the big question floats on the air.

He goes on. "I don't know much about destiny. Maybe it's real. Maybe it isn't. Ma tells me God anointed me with life for a mighty reason, but then I wonder why wouldn't he anoint Wade, too? What makes me worth saving? Do I really have a destiny? A reason to be here?"

Sugar says in a small voice, "So you can be my brother, maybe?" and Whiz grins in a heartbreaking way and pats her knee, but he is so forlorn.

I offer some of Mama's wisdom because I don't have much of my own. "Mama says hope is a road in life, and it's easier to travel than despair. Sometimes a new perspective is all you need to make it through. So I wish you hope and a new perspective."

Whiz leans forward, reaches in his back pocket, and for a second, I worry he's reaching for the bottle of moonshine. Instead, he pulls out an envelope. It's from the North Carolina College at Durham. A teaching college for Negroes. He holds it in both hands and starts crying.

"What'd it say? Did you get in?"

He wipes his nose on his sleeve. "Too scared to open it." He turns it over in his hands. "It came yesterday, and I can't bring myself to see what's inside. Not on the heels of Wade being buried."

"Wade would be tickled if you got in. He'd be so proud. We all would."

"What if it says no?"

"What if it says *yes*? You've got to open it."

Whiz takes his sister's hand and lays the letter in it. "Would you open it for me, Sugar?"

Carefully, she slips her finger under the flap and pulls out the folded paper. Whiz is wound as tight as Oma's cuckoo clock. Sugar unfolds the paper, and it crinkles like giftwrap. I can see the letter is dated March seventh, a week back. Sugar reads aloud, "Dear Mr. William Mayhew, we are pleased to inform you . . ."

CHAPTER 46
BERT: TOBACCO CLOTH

Now that we know Wade won't come home, Mama worries extra bout Everett, and that puts my mind on him, too. I saw his army picture, but it doesn't look like a boy who tells riddles. He looks like a man gone to war. What was he thinking when that picture got took? He doesn't look scared. He doesn't look worried. He looks like a soldier man.

The last riddle that come in a letter was this: *What has a foot but no leg?* Lu says she knows right off but won't say. When we go to bed that night, I can't help myself. "What's the answer to that riddle?"

She says, "A ruler."

I say, "What's a ruler?"

And she says, "Forget it."

The next morning, the air is cold as Christmas, but it's early March. I come outside and see the streak of red peep over the horizon. Me and Lu walk up on Mama and Daddy standing at the edge of the field, worried. They look out at the new tobacco seedlings standing straight in rows. "Almanac didn't say a thing about frost coming." Daddy's words come out in little puffs. "One almost came last night," Daddy says. "The seedlings are in danger."

"I believe it," Mama says and turns to me and Lu. "We need everybody. Gertie and Sugar, and maybe Clara can help. And Grady, too."

"But I don't want to miss school," Lu whines.

"Cora and Lydia will go, but the rest of you are needed here. School can wait. We got gauze to lay."

I'm glad to stay home, cause I don't like school one bit. When I learn one thing, there's something else to know. Questions give me a headache, so I'm glad to stay home. I saw fat rolls of gauze in the hayloft when I first come and wondered bout it. Lu called it tobacco cloth and says it comes out when tobacco is young and a freeze comes late. The bolts come outta the loft and lay beside the field.

Daddy says, "We'll work in teams of four. Unroll the gauze, then take metal pins" — he holds up U-shaped wire — "and stick em through the cloth into the ground to hold it in place. Space the pins three to four feet apart so we have enough. We got till sundown to beat the freeze. Careful not to disturb the baby plants."

Irene and Wolf hold a bolt of gauze, and me and Lu take the ends and start unrolling. The light fabric flutters like butterfly wings, and when the hundred-yard bolt is spent, we walk down each side and stick pins through the cloth. Then we get another bolt and do it again.

I say to Irene to be talkative, "They still looking for Terrell Stucky?"

She straightens and tucks hair behind one ear. "Funny you should ask," she starts and makes Lu pay attention. "Trotter Langley was picking up a load of oysters on the coast when he thought he saw Terrell Stucky. He wasn't positive it was him, but it was the pearl-handled knife the man whittled with that made him take notice. He was whittling outside the fish store, but his hat was pulled low so he couldn't see his face."

"What'd Trotter do?"

"When he got back, he told Sheriff Cecil."

"And?" Lu says. "Then what?"

"That's all I know. I guess somebody went to check it out."

Lu puts her hands on her hips. "Irene Rebecca Brown, you work for the *Mercer*

County Reporter, for heaven's sake. You have to be more curious than that. Finding a missing man who's likely a murderer would be big news."

"Sorry, *Miz Nancy Drew,*" Irene says. "But that's all I know."

"Anybody heard from Frankie Tender or Larry Crumbie?" I add quick before Irene gets in a mood.

"No," is all she says, then Mama rings the dinner bell, and I straighten my back that aches from bending and pushing in pins, and there's dust from my hair to my toes. I don't wash up with the men at the barrel and don't sit at the yard table in the chill. I go inside to the kitchen sink and use a washrag to clean my face and arms and hands. I carry out platters stacked with ham biscuits, bowls of canned corn and tomatoes, and rows of deviled eggs, then I eat in the kitchen where it's warm. Mama has made two three-layer cakes. It's her basic one-two-three-four cake I love. The recipe is so simple even I remember. You take one cup of softened butter and one cup of milk, two cups of sugar, three cups of self-rising flour, and four eggs. One of the three-layer cakes has white icing and the other caramel.

After noon dinner, when we head back to the fields to lay more gauze, Lu says, "I wish

I was at school."

I say, "I wish there was more cake."

But we lay down gauze till the field is covered, and my fingertips bruise, and my back burns from bending, and Lu looks as wore out as me, and we climb the stairs and fall across our bed. I don't think about cake. I bet Lu don't think about school.

CHAPTER 47
LUCY: GHOSTS

Daddy was right. The killing frost did come late in March, and it would have taken out our baby tobacco plants before they got started, but we saved them. And a few days after the freezing nights pass, the gauze was rolled up again and stored in the rafters, but I didn't have to miss school. There's no urgency in putting gauze away. Only in putting it down.

With the coming of April, Bert gets nervous. She says, "I'll kill myself if a swing band comes to town like a year back. Or I'll run away and change my name."

"What name would you pick?"

"That's not the point, Lu. The point is I don't ever want to see a singing man in uniform again. If I do, I'll die on the spot."

I don't believe that fate will happen to Bert, but it happens to our president. He was having his portrait painted and died on the spot. We get the telephone call from the switchboard operator, Lillie, but we already heard from Aunt Fanniebelle, who gets news from a higher source. Mama says it's no surprise FDR died. I ask her why'd she say that and she says, "President Roosevelt led us out of the Depression, through the Dust Bowl, and into this tangled war. He was serving an unprecedented fourth term. There's only so much a body can endure — God rest his soul."

So tonight, the half of America with radios has the other half in to listen, and we huddle and pray for a good connection, hungry to hear details about something that has changed history. Mama sends Grady to fetch the Mayhews. Our parlor is packed. Children on the floor, grown-ups in chairs or leaning against the wall. Lydia and Cora cry softly next to Mama. Whiz puts his arm around Sugar's shoulders. He waits for college to start in September, but for now, he helps Miz Elvira in the back room of the library.

The last time my family was this grief-stricken was two months back over Wade Sully dying. This is a different kind of grief, where the weight of a mourning nation presses in . . . *President Roosevelt, at age sixty-three, recovering from exhaustion at Warm Springs, Georgia, on his doctor's advice, collapsed as he sat for a formal portrait.*

"What happens now?" Bert says.

Mama says, "There'll be a big funeral. A chance for folks to say goodbye."

"No, I mean to us and the war."

Daddy says, "Vice President Truman steps into the president's shoes. Not sure if he knows what he's doing — few vice presidents do — but he'll learn fast. He'll have advisors, but Lordy, I hope he's not weak-willed."

Daddy is cynical of politicians. He doesn't think they live in the real world. *They only pretend to be in touch with the working man's problems* I've heard him say after taxes were raised, the gold standard eliminated, and tobacco regulations tightened. Now our president has been worn out and died. America has a new president. Harry S. Truman, *born into a simple farming family in Independence, Missouri. Mr. Truman was sworn in by Chief Justice Harlan Stone today on April twelfth at 5:47 p.m. as the thirty-third . . .* The radio announcer speaks from far away.

We listen till we can recite the news by heart. Daddy clicks off the radio, and Mama says, "Mr. Truman. He woke up this morning never knowing what was coming before

379

sundown. Sounds odd to say his name, doesn't it? President Truman."

I say, "It sounds like *True-man* to me. President True-man. With him coming from Independence, maybe he came with the right name from the right place at the right time."

I catch sight of Sugar rolling her eyes, making fun of me, but Mama says, "What a lovely thought. I hope you're right." She takes a pin and sticks it in Independence, Missouri.

Listening to the radio took storytelling time away, and it's late so our visitors leave, and we head to bed. As soon as the lights are out, Lydia and Cora come crawling into bed between us.

Bert complains, "Why can't you girls sleep in your room? Y'all are getting too big."

I say, "I like them sleeping with us. Especially tonight after the sad day we've had. One day, they'll be too big but not tonight." I tickle them to hear them giggle.

The bed full of bodies turns quiet, then Bert says, "I don't get it. The whole dead president thing and everybody being sad over a man they never set eyes on. What good's a president anyway if he can't stop a war? Or grow back missing arms and legs on menfolk who come home hurt? He can't save farms from being sold off or stop the hate that got milk cows and Assassin killed. He can't save Aunt Violet from being locked away. So what good is he?" Bert is getting worked up.

"He's only a man. He's not a wizard or God."

"What does the president living or dying have to do with us on a tobacco farm? *Nothing,* that's what." Bert turns her back on us, mad at something. She says, "If I was in my mountains, we might not hear bout a dead president for a long time. And when we do, we don't cry. He's too far away."

Lydia cuddles against Bert's stiff backside then she starts softly, "Sto-ry, sto-ry," then Cora joins her, "Sto-ry."

Bert knows they'll keep on till she gives in. She doesn't have a choice but to say, "Did I ever tell you bout blue ghosts?" And the girls clap and squirm with happiness, and Bert says, "Y'all settle down and be quiet, and I'll tell you a love story," and she rolls onto her back and faces the dark ceiling. She clears her throat but speaks softly so Mama won't yell at us to go to sleep.

"Once upon a time, in the dark of my holler, we don't have wolpertingers like Oma, but we got something special all the same. We got blue ghost fireflies. They rise up from the ground, turn on blue lights, and dance above the forest floor, looking for love. First time I seen em, I was smaller than Lydia. Pa woke me and my sister, Ruth, and told us to come with him. Ma stayed in bed, but Ruth and me got up, rubbed our eyes awake, and walked barefoot behind Pa cross the clearing, past the cemetery, through the apple trees, into the woods. There weren't no moon showing, so Ruth held tight to Pa's sleep shirt, and I held on to the tail of her bedgown. The night air was soft as I ever recollect.

"Pa didn't talk while we walk, and he takes me and Ruth to a big rock. We climb up and sit on top and look down on dancing fairies swirling and floating. Pa says they're called blue ghosts, and he never saw them anywhere but in our dell. Been said they're the souls of Union and Confederate soldiers what died long ago in battle fought in our dell, and they never got to go home. The blue ghosts come in early summer to find mates. The boy fireflies are the ones keeping the light on so long, and the girl fireflies blink on and off. We three stayed there till they stop blinking and we were chilled clear through, and we went home holding on to each other."

Bert stops talking, and the quiet settles on

us, then Cora whispers, "Is that the end?"

"For tonight."

"Were the ghosts trying to get back home? Is that why they blinked?"

"I guess."

"Like Morse code in the war? Talking to their mama and daddy fireflies?"

When Bert doesn't answer, Cora says, "I bet their mama and daddy misses them."

Bert starts crying low, then she cries like a well divined that rises from within her chest. Maybe she cries for her ma and pa and that baby brother who never had a chance to be. Cries for her blue mountains rising into the clouds where you can wash your hands without soap and water. All we can do is put our arms around Bert and hold her tight and let her cry.

CHAPTER 48
BERT: RENDERING

Rendering wax breaks my heart every time cause we steal everything the honeybee has. We done it back in late summer of '43 when I first come and two times in '44. Now it's June of '45, and the war in the east is over cause the Germans gave up but not Japan. Daddy says Japan is hanging on out of stubbornness, but they gotta give up soon. We don't ask Weegee when peace will come. Till the west surrenders, our government buys our beeswax.

Every livelong day, we make the bees live on sugar syrup Gertie makes, and even when the flowers are gone from the fields and the orchards, they eat sugar water. They don't roam free like usual. They mostly stay in the hives and work and don't sleep, and the frames get heavy till it's time. We watch for wax moths since they the only thing that'll eat beeswax.

The first time I see a piece a beeswax up

close with no honey or baby bees inside, I think it's the purest thing I ever did see. It was like lookin in the face of God, the cells was so perfect, and I wish I had Lu's ten-dollar words to say what I see.

Once, long before I come to Riverton, me and my sister Ruth was hunting blackberries two ridges over and come upon a cabin stuck back in the holler. A old woman was on the porch, sitting in a grapevine rocker working at a wicker table. A wore-out quilt was on the floor like a rug. We asked what she was doing and she said, "Making Venise lace for a wedding dress for a rich lady. This quilt on the floor keeps it pure from stain." We watched and stayed back so as not to soil that lace she was makin. There was white silk thread and lots of colored bobbins and pins sticking in a pillow. It was so much over-under-around that my brain got discombobulated seeing the miracle she made, but it spilled out over the table and was hard to look away.

"How'd you learn that?" I asked, and she said it was her memaw that showed her. There won't nothing fancy bout the cabin or her person, but she made the prettiest lace to beat all.

Lu's rich cousin Patricia had her a wedding dress made with Venise lace. She's the one who come down from the North with her college friends to market and turned us into movie stars. Last week, Lu got a letter from Patricia telling bout her fancy wedding and new life. I wonder if Patricia got her Venise lace from that mountain woman? That wedding lace is pretty enough, but it pales next to the miracle of beeswax. And bees don't even have bobbins or pins or patterns.

Like other rendering times, me and Lu and Daddy wear bee suits every day for a week and pull frames from the hundred hives. We smoke the bees first so they get sleepy, but they're flummoxed at what we do, so every time I say thank you. I never work harder than at rendering time, but bee work never stops.

I don't tell Daddy that I feel shame for taking so much from our bees, but I come close. I find him in the barn one evening near the end of rendering. It's after supper but before story time, and he's putting out feed. A lit Lucky Strike is stuck in the corner of his mouth, and the smoke rises into his eyes and he squints.

"You sorry for taking everything from our bees?"

"If we don't, I don't think we'd make it."

We both say, "Thank God for bees," and that tickles us, talking the same words.

CHAPTER 49
LUCY: HOMECOMING

On a regular Tuesday when the workday is done, and Wolf and Joe have gone back to prison camp, and evening chores have started, Aunt Fanniebelle calls with extraordinary news. "Y'all come to town quick. That Japanese Himoto is giving up, turning tail, and the whole dern war is over." Mama holds out the receiver so we can hear about Emperor Hirohito's surrender, skewed Fanniebelle-style. "Everybody's running out their houses and hollering to beat all, and horns are honking and bells a clanging, and somebody shot off some firecrackers that startled my heart. Y'all come to town, you hear?"

As usual, my aunt speaks as though she's omnipotent and sees everywhere at once. Germany surrendered three months back, but it took drastic actions to convince Japan to stop fighting. Mama says, "Ring the dinner bell, and don't stop till everybody's in the yard." Then to Bert, she says, "Turn the radio up so we can hear the news for ourselves."

Everybody within the sound of our bell collects in the front yard. Mama yells from the porch, "The whole war is over. Japan surrendered. We won. We won, and *it's over.*" Her voice catches on emotion that threatens to sink her to her knees. Bert comes from the house and grabs her arm to help her down the steps. Daddy throws his hat in the air and runs to pick Mama up in his arms. Helen has Betty Gail, and they dance in the yard beside Lydia and Cora, everybody a little drunk on happiness of this magnitude. I feared peace would remain a chimera, a castle in the air, but it's here, and we won, and it doesn't feel real.

Lydia tugs at Mama's dress. "Is Everett coming home tomorrow?"

Mama says, "Give your brother time. He'll be home soon. But now we celebrate."

Grady hitches the tractor to the flatbed wagon and all us Browns and Mayhews climb on so we can ride together. With the sun setting on a pink horizon, we head the two miles to town to experience the full rapture. We see Cornell, Rosalee, and baby Amee walking to the celebration and they get onboard with us, and we cross the

Roanoke River with every church bell ringing like Christmas morning. The cacophony is exhilarating. Grady pulls off the side of the road so we can mingle with our friends. Everybody wears a fresh layer of joy, and the streets are full of people clapping each other on the backs. Some bring out fiddles and banjos. Some pull harmonicas from their back pockets, and they play for people doing jigs in the streets, and we almost get drunk from happiness. Peace has come too late for some like our Wade Sully. The Turner girls lost their brother Skip, and Ricky Miller's cousin from Robersonville lost his leg, but everybody's glad the war is over.

But the POWs? What are they thinking?

I say, "Mama, can Bert and I run to see our Germans?" And because she can't deny anything on this day of bliss, she says yes, and we run to lower Main Street and down River Road to the locked gate at the prison camp, leaving the celebration behind.

The scene is different here, and the Germans are quiet. Some are lined up somber against the tall fence looking toward town, hearing remnants of the party they're not part of. We call Wolf's and Joe's names, and they come up to the fence, and Joe says, "Move down more," and we go to the far end where we can talk and link our fingers through the wire fence and stand a foot apart.

"You heard, didn't you?" and they nod, and there's nothing else to say. Their homeland surrendered months back, but with the fall of Japan, the dismantling of war begins in earnest. America has five million soldiers to bring home. War-torn countries need rebuilding from the ground up. It's a daunting prospect I cannot fathom.

Our Germans are downcast. Their future is uncertain. Wolf and Joe won't have a tender homecoming waiting for them like Everett will. I'm not sure they have a home to go to at all.

The next Sunday, after church and the jubilant sermon on victory and the Lord's answer to our prayers, we walk in the door with the phone ringing. Daddy answers it and listens and looks at Bert, "It's for you."

"Who is it?" Mama whispers.

"Her sister, Ruth."

Bert hardly ever talks about Ruth or her pa. She's only gotten two letters since she's been here. She wondered who wrote them since Ruth can't read or write. One said her granny passed, and the other, five months back, said her sister Ruth got married to a widow man with two little girls, and to neither of those events did Bert go home. We stay in the parlor to give her some privacy, but we listen.

"What happened?" she pauses. "When?" and waits. "Okay," she says and hangs up.

She comes to the parlor door. "Pa died last night. Ruth says it was pneumonia that took him, and I need to go home for the burying."

Bert's death-news sucks some of the jubilant air out of our day, and her usual wild glory is compressed. The only other time I saw such sadness come over her was after Frankie Tender left scars on her heart. Those scars haven't healed fully since Frankie was never found. Larry Crumbie and Terrell Stucky haven't been found either, but nobody cares about them.

"We'll get you on tomorrow's earliest bus so you can attend the funeral. Lucy, you should go, too, as support."

I barely register the surprise bus trip before Irene's car pulls in the yard and brakes hard. She hurries across the yard shouting and we step out on the porch. "Got another missing man."

"For heaven's sake," Mama declares in disbelief. "Who in the world is it this time?"

"Tiny Junior. Flossie hasn't seen him since yesterday morning, and she's beside herself." Irene is now at the steps and pats her chest to catch her breath. "He's always home by dark, but last night, he wasn't. She didn't worry much until he wasn't there this morning. She's spent the day looking in all the usual places, but it's time to put together a search party. I thought Daddy and Grady would want to help."

"Course we do. Let's get out of Sunday clothes."

"We'll help, too." Bert adds us to the lot and saves thinking about her pa for later.

I whisper "Trula Freed" in her ear, and she nods. With alacrity, we jump on our bikes and ride with our gingham dresses billowing out. We ride down the dirt road toward the painted cottage with the red door. We pedal hard with the rush of wind sweeping back our hair and muffling our ears. My heart thuds with worry for Tiny Junior, already fearing we may never see him again. But I'm angry, too, at a fate that might take a pure soul before his time. The other missing men were spiteful. Tiny Junior doesn't have a cunning or conning bone in his body.

Bert rides beside me and I see her lips moving. "What?" I shout.

"— be looking for his bicycle. Let's check Aunt Violet's place."

I shout back, "What in the world would he be doing there?"

"We need to look somewhere the others won't."

I want to hear what Trula Freed has to say first, but I don't argue. We pass the cutoff and ride to the abandoned house that was Bert's pitiful welcome to Mercer County. We haven't been this way in a long time. Windows are broken, and the screen door is ripped from its hinges. It was likely boys who made a mess of a place that's not a home anymore. We pass the garden plot grown wild and the chicken coop caved in on itself. We circle the back lot, looking for Tiny or his bicycle.

We see it. In the tall weeds. Lying on its side. The spokes of the front wheel point to the sky. Beside an abandoned well with the rotten boards broken through.

We lean over and look down the well, and there he is. Sitting in the bottom of that muddy hole. Waiting. Grinning.

"Told you so," Bert whispers, feeling rightly proud of herself. She shouts, "You okay down there?"

"Hey, Miz Bert. Hey, Miz Lucy. I'm hungry, and my leg got hurt."

"Hold on," I say. "We'll get help and get you out of there. Your mama's going to be so happy. Everybody's going to be so happy."

Bert stays with Tiny so he's not scared, and I ride home so Mama can call the sheriff's office with the news. Then everybody starts converging at Violet's place, a ladder is lowered down the well, and we are heroes. We stand off to the side and Bert says, "That's the way *The Mystery of the Missing Man* should go. You look for him, you find him, and it's done."

I was looking for a shortcut. Bert thought like Nancy Drew.

The next morning at first light, Bert and I are at the bus station with round-trip tickets, one suitcase between us, Mama's food to fortify us, and ten one-dollar bills from egg money. Soldiers crowd the aisle, manly and kind. They wear the air of relief, their hats under their arms. Their glances linger on Bert. They try to connect with her faraway gaze, but her grief isolates her.

We'll be gone three days to mountains I've only heard about. We will retrace Bert's journey across the expanse of North Carolina. I hide my excitement under a layer of serious because Bert has lost her ma and her pa. How is she going to take seeing him dead when she last saw him in hard times?

How can she mend a bridge that doesn't lead anywhere anymore?

Hours away from Asheville, the mountains appear. They hover on the horizon like a mirage in pale hues different from the blue of the sky. Bert sleeps against my shoulder, and I don't want to rouse her, but Lord am I excited. The bus window is open and, like Bert said there would be, cooler air comes from those far-off mountains. It thrills me to feel her stories come true.

The bus climbs on Route 70, and the mountains grow taller. I see lush green on the lower elevations and hints of reds and golds above, and a chill in the air has me close the window and waken Bert with my movement. "Do you know that your Appalachian Mountains are the oldest in the world? Some scientists say the crystalline rocks found in the mountains are a billion years old. Guess how many zeroes there are in a billion." Bert doesn't guess, so I tell her, but she isn't impressed.

But I am captivated by the other side of North Carolina. I didn't expect to fall in love with a place so different from my birthplace, but I know this is *home* before I ever set foot on terra firma. Trula Freed spoke about other lives lived, and I wondered if she was spinning tales.

Bert stands to pull the suitcase from the top rack, and three men jump to their feet to help, bumping into each other, laughing and apologizing, hoping to catch the pretty girl's eye and earn a smile. She pays them no mind but pulls out two sweaters she knew we would need. I pull mine around, relishing August goose bumps.

With eyes riveted out the window, I say, "How could you stay away so long?"

"From here?"

I glance over to her. "Of course, from here."

"It's pretty. Real pretty. But I thought I was being banished for being a *thoughtless girl.* I buckled under the weight of Ma's words back then."

"You were thirteen," I say, an age that sounds terribly young compared to fifteen. I shake my head. "But what am I saying? If you'd come back here, you'd never have become part of my life. So for every loss, there's a gain, and I'm grateful you belong to us."

The bus pulls into the Asheville station, air brakes hiss, and the door snaps open. We shuffle down the narrow aisle toward the steps with Bert leaning down, looking through the windows. She catches sight of her sister Ruth and squeals, then jumps down from the bus and takes her sister in her arms in a homecoming hug that brings tears to my eyes. I wasn't prepared for them to look alike — the same beauties with auburn hair and golden skin and womanly shapes I still can't lay claim to.

Bert turns to include me in the welcome, and I get a hug, too, smelling a different earthiness on her sister's skin. Ruth's husband stands behind her, a short man with burly arms and kind eyes, unruffled in this sea of flushed joy. My first thought is *You can count on this man.* His name is Homer Sykes, and he holds out his big hand to shake mine. I love the firmness of it for Ruth's sake.

Married . . . with *children.* It's hard to wrap my head around it, a girl two years older than Bert and me, married with her pa's blessing. How could she stay a girl and bury her granny, nurse her pa to death's door, and embrace Homer's two little girls needing a mama? She's already pulled hard time and seems suited for it.

Homer puts our belongings in the bed of a rusty truck. Bert and I climb in back while he tells me where we're headed. "We gotta ways to go," he says quietly and points to the steep side of a mountain that sucks the breath out of me. I had no idea that rugged beauty like this existed in my birth state or what it felt like to breathe high air.

It's midafternoon in sunshine when we leave Asheville. The winding paved road turns to gravel, then to a narrow dirt trail wide as the truck. We go up and up with Bert and me leaning against the tailgate. I pull my sweater tight, and Bert unfolds an old quilt to wrap around us. August in the mountains is not August in Riverton.

Daylight fades and the blackening forest presses snug against the trail. I think of the hair-raising tales Oma told us that were set in the Black Forest, the world of the Brothers Grimm. I think about her wolpertinger, once stored in her trunk in our attic that now lives in Lydia's room, and how I believed it was a composite of three animals skillfully sewn together to create a fantasy creature that never breathed on its own. Now I'm not sure. This loamy richness and crisp air I inhale is as foreign to my side of North Carolina as walking on the moon. It's different enough to breed real magic. Is this the secret place my heart has been yearning for without knowing? Will I see wolves and minks or even a wolpertinger? I don't ask. I want this fairy tale to unwind in its own good time.

The road forks left, right, left, then I'm

lost. We end up in a field on a knoll that holds a cabin on its peak, a neat garden, chickens, goats, a small stand of gnarled fruit trees, and a scattering of horses and buggies. We're surrounded by the outline of mountains like jagged teeth. Tears sting my eyes. This is where Bert was born.

I reach for her hand to give her comfort and wonder for the hundredth time what's going through her mind and hope it isn't only pain. It's over two years back when *Bert the girl* was banished and carried her obstinance bound in muslin to the humid land she has made her home. In the distance, headstones dot the landscape. A picket fence falling over in places encircles a cemetery. Bert's roots were always here.

CHAPTER 50
BERT: THE WAKE

Going up the mountain, my insides turn hollow like they was gutted with a rusty fork. My pain is ragged, and I'm light-headed. Some of that comes from being in high country. Some of it comes from not belonging here no more.

Homer's truck pulls outta the dark onto Pa's land when the sun sets on Mount Mitchell, the tallest mountain in all of North Carolina. The truck stops, and me and Lu climb down from the back and get our footing on the mountaintop. Pa's wake has been going on two days with relations and church family watching over him, but the burial waits on me. Tomorrow, Pa's soul will be released to heaven, and the pine box holding his body will be set in hallowed ground. Jacob Bartholomew Tucker was one of the chosen, so I don't worry bout where his soul is headed.

Ruth whispers, "Pa's waitin in the parlor.

Ready?"

I lie and say, "Ready." A sharp wind whips my hair and cuts through the sweater and cotton dress. Is it Ma's restless spirit-ghost wanting to pierce my soul? This is a haunted place. I am haunted here.

I point to a empty chair in the yard. My eyes stay on the front door. I say to Lu, "Wait here. I'll get you when I'm done."

I follow Ruth's straight back. Her thick braid falls neat. Uncle Bud sits in the porch rocker. "Evening," he says when I pass. Aunt Beulah's likely in the kitchen tending to food. The folks inside the front door part to let us in. The shuffling feet are muffled on worn floors. I nod to Mr. and Miz Davis, the Harker family, pass the McDonalds and the Beirnes. Reverend Aloysius stands by the casket holding his worn bible. The people are the same color and same thinness and wear the same dusty clothes. Candles light Pa's open casket. I bout faint till somebody touches my elbow and holds out a glass of branch water. It's Sam Logan — the boy everybody thought I'd settle with once upon a time — and I look up to meet his kind eyes.

"Thank you," I whisper.

He whispers back, "You different." His breath smells of sassafras he chews.

I go to the casket, and Sam stays back.

Pa was tall but not big, but the man in the casket got all the living seeped outta him. His face got a cloth soaked in soda water to slow darkening. There's likely quarters on his eyes to keep em closed. I pray Pa can't see in the dark of my heart and judge me harsh.

Ruth says, "He died peaceful. He won't never alone. Me and Homer or his mama Marcella was always with him."

I'm shamed to say, "Did he ask bout me?" but I want to know.

"That he did."

"What kind a words did he say?"

"At the start, he say, 'Bert, lend me a hand,' but you won't here to tote wood or water. Then one time he say, 'You look like Bert standing there.' " Ruth throws scraps to me. Last time I hear Pa's voice was two years back when Lu's daddy found a way to reach him. Pa was on the other end of the line, sounding deep in a hole.

Ruth knows my mind. "He don't put blame. The Good Lord called Ma and the baby, that's all." She offers comfort words, but they weigh heavy. "Sam Logan asks if you was moving back and staying. I don't answer for you cause I ain't got the right, but the homeplace is yours if you want it.

CHAPTER 51
LUCY: CLOSURE

I stand in the growing dusk, looking for the privy. I see it off to the side near a lean-to shed. A girl about my age waits at the door, and I walk over. "Evening," I say and nod in respect, and she nods back, then faces the wooden door with the crescent moon cutout. Without turning around she says, "You reckon Allaburt's gunna stay fer a spill? Be wither kin?"

It takes a moment to understand that she's asking about Bert, Allie Bert, *Allaburt.* The girl asked me if Bert is going to stay, and I'm speechless. Unlike last time when she rode across the state with a one-way ticket, Bert has a return ticket leaving in two days, and it never crossed my mind she wouldn't need it.

The privy door opens, and a child steps out adjusting her flour-sack dress that almost touches the ground, then she takes the older girl's hand and they walk toward the house where they belong, like everybody else, except me. I've never been an outsider before, knowing no one, understanding little, standing on unfamiliar land. I've lived such a harbored life, sticking pins in a map on a wall, collecting ten-dollar words, pretending a story in a book was an introduction to life.

After I do my business, I sit in that chair like Bert told me to, a stranger stranded on an island, watching life flow around her, cut off from her normal footing. The dialect of Bert's people strikes my ears as peculiar, and I remember I'm still in North Carolina, the land of *my* people, but not these people. This must be more like Oma's Germany I never knew. I understand her better coming here. I know now that our dense air was hard to breathe. She must have missed her homeland terribly.

Ruth crosses the yard carrying a plate of food and a glass of water. Two little girls trail behind her. One sucks her thumb, and the other carries a piece of blanket. "You gotta be hungry," Ruth says and places the plate on my lap. With a weary sigh, she sinks to the ground beside me, and the girls sit on the far side. She must be worn out from all the change her life has seen.

I lean forward and say "Hey" to the little

girls, but they duck their chins shy and nudge up against Ruth's side.

She says, "They called Hattie and Nell. They mama went to Jesus a while back. This one, Nell" — she puts a hand on the girl's tiny head — "turned sickly two months back bout the same time Pa had a sinking spell. It was a healer from Baines Creek who come all the way here to help. Miz Birdie done right by Nell, and she grows stronger, but Miz Birdie can't help Pa make it through. We be staying at this place these weeks, but Homer got his own homestead for us to work. I hope Allie Bert might want this one."

I had put food in my mouth when Ruth delivers the second dose of possibility about Bert staying here that makes me sick to my stomach. Why hadn't she said anything to me? It takes effort to swallow the food.

"That's for her to decide," I say evenly, though my heart gallops. "I'm sorry we kept her to ourselves all this time."

But *am* I sorry? Would I want to turn the clock back to that summer day at the bridge but have Bert stay sequestered at Miz Violet's home? Our paths may have never crossed in Riverton. Her aunt may have gone crazy, and Bert would have found her way back here to a land I'd never see. She wouldn't learn to read and write. Or do numbers and tend bees and dance the jitterbug. There would have been no return today of the prodigal daughter.

Ruth reaches for my plate of food I've neglected and says, "You gotta be tired. Let me take you to yor sleepin' spot."

My sleeping spot is up the ladder in the kitchen to a feather mattress and quilt under cramped eaves. The murmur of prayers and footsteps on plank floors below and dishes being washed mingle. As I drift off to sleep, I hear, "That's some kind a city talk from that girl, ain't it? Sounds book smart to me." Another says, "Think Allabert done gone above her raising?"

I think they don't know the half of what Bert Tucker can do.

The whiff of dying seasoned with fried chicken and faith flavors my restless sleep. I wake to the sound of rain pounding the tin roof a foot above my face. Water drips from holes. I climb down the ladder into the dry warmth of the kitchen. Ruth slaps a plate of eggs and thick bacon in front of me and pours a cup of strong coffee.

"Morning," I say.

She says "Mornin" back.

"Where's Bert?" I ask between mouthfuls.

Ruth nods toward the parlor.

408

"Still there?"

"Been keeping him company all night."

"What's your pa's Christian name?"

"Jacob Bartholomew Tucker, but folks call him Tuck, and that suits him."

"That's a fine name. He must have been a fine man." I sound like Mama when she gives comfort, but my appetite wanes with the thought of seeing a body three days dead. I pick at the rest of my breakfast. Finally, I scrape the leftovers in the slop bucket when Ruth's got her back to me, then wash and dry my plate to buy a little time. I head outside and run to the privy through the misty drizzle. When I come out, I stand in awe. The drifting clouds squat low, and the mountain peaks jut high. It's like Bert said that first night at supper. I *can* wash my hands in the clouds. They snake over and around these blue, undulating hills.

Ruth comes out of the house and throws scraps to the chickens. At first glance, I think it's Bert, only more serious. She comes to stand beside me.

"Bert talked about this place, but my imagination couldn't conjure it. Where I come from, the land is so flat you can see a wall of rain march across the field. And when the rain falls, it lies like a shallow lake on the land. It's a different place that's hot and sticky in the warm months. These mountains have names?"

Ruth nods. "That's Mount Mitchell." She points to peaks and reels off names as foreign as Oma's world. I think I hear *Roan, Big Bald, Big Butt,* but her accent throws me. I could be wrong about Big Butt. I look back at the cabin that Mr. Tucker likely built to house his family. It's time I paid my respects.

Bert's in the parlor. The open pine coffin sits on sawhorses against one wall. An odd mix of chairs placed here and there around the parlor hold people with heads bent in prayer. Bert stands beside the coffin, holding the cold hand of her dead pa. My stomach turns sour.

"Bert?" I step beside her. "You okay?" is my trite question.

She takes her time. "I missed all em days with Pa. Can't never git em back." The pain has made her slip into her childhood vernacular. "I won't never know if he forgive me killing Ma."

Ruth comes up beside us and puts her arm around Bert. "He love you, little sister. Pa love you. Weren't no blame. Weren't no sin. Rest your weary heart. He be waiting on you to come home so he can go to

410

heaven. You coming is a gift."

The two sisters cling to each other, and the people in the room stand and gather the girls in the folds of their arms. I'm to the side, looking at Mr. Tucker in his pine box, his scarred hands lying still, his legs like broom handles under the fabric of slick-worn trousers, his chest empty of a beating heart. Bert puts out her arm from the knot of people and pulls me into their warm center, and I let her.

Then the serious job of putting Mr. Tucker to rest begins in earnest.

Like square dancers following calls, the people in the parlor move with defined purpose. The coffin is closed and nailed shut. The pallbearers take their places and struggle to get the coffin through the front door. The swirling clouds drift away, and the sky clears as if on command. More people appear as if summoned by the tolling of a bell only they can hear. From all points around the meadow come more men in clean overalls and hats worn low, women in gingham dresses, and quiet children who line up behind the procession with the pallbearers at the lead. They walk to the graveside and stand in a square around the waiting grave. Bert steps into their midst and gives tonal pitches as starting points. She leads a powerful harmony that bursts forth from this clan of her people. Her arm keeps beat to the somber tempo that unifies the believers sending Mr. Tucker to heaven. It is an ancient farewell grounded in faith as old as these hills and I quiver with emotion.

A young man I saw yesterday from a distance stares at Bert with *broken heart* written all over his face. He sings strong, but his eyes pull at Bert with a wanting she doesn't see or chooses to ignore. Opposite him stands the girl I saw outside the privy last night. She looks at the young man with *broken heart* written all over her face. She sings strong, but her eyes pull at the man with her wanting he doesn't see or chooses to ignore.

Why didn't I know that Bert was loved and missed? Why had I conveniently forgotten she had a life before us? I know Bert doesn't belong here, not with her hunger for more and her taste for different and her love for our family of Browns. A life beyond these blue hills was the thing that pulled at her, and I'm confident that despite a family cemetery, her sister Ruth, and Sam Logan, she won't be staying.

Mr. Tucker's casket is lowered. The last

thing we do is drop handfuls of dirt on the pine box. I pick up two handfuls, throw one on the coffin, and put the other in my pocket. I want to take a piece of this place with me. *Here* makes my heart soar like the eagle drifting over thermals. Its haunting tune calls to me. I miss it already.

CHAPTER 52
BERT: LETTING GO

I missed his last day and his last breath and the tolling of the bell thirty-nine times to tell of his dying year. I missed the washing of his body and dressing him in burial clothes. I missed lining his casket with his quilt to add comfort to his final journey. I missed the start of the wake when folks and food showed up and filled his home with mourning. I was sent away and come back too late.

Now Pa's friends stand round his casket built by my sister's husband, Homer. Folks talk kindly about the dead man inside. *He was a good farmer, a servant of God, a fair man, a family man* — until his family was mostly gone.

Before he died, he told Ruth his first sacred harp song would be "King of Glory, King of Peace," and I was to take the lead. It's been a long spell since I sang the Lord's words on this mountaintop in front of a square of believers. I sound the pitch and set the tempo like I was taught long ago.

Out their mouths comes the power of Shape Note singing that thrives in these hills. It presses against me on all four sides and holds me upright in my hour of loss. The powerful sound washes over me and over Pa's plain box. We sing "Love Divine," "Sons of Sorrow," and "Leaning on the Everlasting Arms" until legs are weary and voices are spent and his coffin is put in the ground. My eyes stay away from the tug of Sam Logan, who turned into a man while I was away. He belongs here. I don't. I throw a handful of dirt on top of the casket, and everybody throws a handful of dirt on top of the casket. They drift away from the graveyard and walk to the house for a meal spread out on planks and sawhorses and to talk about the goodness that was my pa.

My feet won't move.

Ruth stands on one side of me, and on the other, Lu slips her arm through mine. I start shaking and can't stop. My hollow bones and teeth rattle, and my belly burns, and my chest fills up with rememberings that squeeze the air outta me. If it won't for Ruth and Lu holding onto me, I'd fall on top of Pa's coffin. I can feel his eyes. They burn through those coins and that soda cloth and the bare pine and into my thoughtless heart. Before they closed the coffin, I slipped into his hand the pocket-knife I stole long back. *Have mercy on me,* I say inside my head, ashamed to beg out loud. So ashamed . . .

". . . too much for her, I reckon." A cold rag is over my eyes. I hear Ruth's voice while I lie on a soft bed. But what bed?

"Is this Pa's dying bed?" My voice is raspy, parched. I struggle to my elbows, for I need to know.

"This ain't his bed. Lie still."

"How'd I get here?"

"Homer. He spotted you sinking and he run back. You been up all the night and all the livelong day and ain't had a speck a food neither. You weak as water. Let Lu get you some vittles, and you eat and rest. Burying Pa's done. Stay here while I see to folks leavin'."

My best friend, Lu. What does she make of this strangeness? Of the old harp singing? Of my weak heart? Does she see why I had to leave? Why I don't belong? And Sam Logan. He tried to lay claim to me once upon a time, him making plans built on sand. He deserves more than me.

The hum outside the door and the shuffle of shoes and the light of day fade away. The house grows quiet, and so do the noises inside my head. The sun is low when I sit. Lu is slumped in the chair napping, but she hears me stir.

"Hey," she says and stretches.

"I never asked Weegee if Pa was okay. I won't thinking bout him one bit," I confess.

"You think you could have saved him? Think you could have stopped him dying?"

"No."

"That's right, so stop punishing yourself." Lu's voice is soft. "But you gotta be hungry. I know I am."

"Yeah. Let's get some food and watch the sun set. You gotta have questions."

"A few." Lu grins.

The platters of food are covered with a sheet to keep flies off. We fold back one end and find fried chicken, angel biscuits, field peas, turnip greens, and sweet potato pie. These'll do. Plates of vittles and spring water in hand, we head to the yard and sit facing Mount Mitchell. The red ball nears the ridge and turns the clouds and us to gold. I bite into a chicken leg.

"Tell me about Sam Logan," Lu says.

I chew and chew and take my time. "Not much to say."

"He couldn't take his eyes off you. He was all moony-eyed."

"He's eighteen."

"Tell me about him," she says, then eats on a biscuit.

"He was a boy I used to know. He was sweet on me. I won't sweet on him. The end."

Lu keeps eating, but I stop. The sight of the clothesline, the woodpile, the scratchy hinge on the screen door, takes my hunger away. The path in the distance to my thinking spot and to the dell where blue ghost fireflies rise up in June. The sun is going down on the second hardest day of my life.

Lu reads my mind and says, "Wanna talk about it?" like she did when I needed to talk about Ma dying. And me getting throwed out of Aunt Violet's place in the storm. Lu is good at listening, but I'm not good at sorting things yet.

"Not much to say. Ma died, I went away, Pa died, end of story."

"Do you hear yourself, Bert Tucker? Every answer you give me is *not much to say,* when I know you're hurting. Don't make it simple. Life isn't simple. It's messy with a lot of heavy layers. We don't have to be old women to know that."

"You sound like your mama."

"*Our* mama. And is that good or bad?"

I grin for the first time all day. "Both, I

guess. She's smart, but she's hardheaded."

"And you're not? Maybe we're both like Mama." We laugh in the waning light that has come with only the outline of mountains backlit. Lu says, "Ruth said one of these mountains is called Big Butt. Did I hear right?"

"Uh-huh. And there's one named Little Butt, too, but we can't see it from here. It's behind the other side of Mount Mitchell."

"*Behind. Little Butt.* Cute, Bert."

"Don't forget Big Butt," I say, and we laugh for real and keep laughing the kind that makes breathing hard but not like that muslin round my middle. This laugh feels new.

CHAPTER 53
LUCY: TRANSFORMATION

Bert's sister comes out of the house carrying a lantern in one hand and in the other, the feed sack of gifts Bert brought. The little ones walk close beside this woman who's now their comfort. The younger girl looks to be close to the age of Violet Crumbie's little boy, who would be a toddler now.

Ruth sets the lantern on the ground and the three of them sit in the pool of light with Bert and me. Five girls. Two who don't have a clue about what's coming and one who stepped over the line into womanhood on her own accord. Then there's Bert and me, getting closer to the line every day.

Bert made these gifts for Ruth and the girls a while back and was going to mail them, but then the funeral came and changed things. When she unties the bag, Hattie and Nell get up on their knees eager to see better. The first present is an apron for Ruth made by Bert with Mama's help.

It has big pockets to hold things and rick-rack around the edge, likely fancier than Ruth has ever seen. Bert said they like plain up here, but she snuck in a touch of green on the ties.

"Reach in the pocket," she says, and Ruth's face lights up when she finds a tiny bottle of Emeraude perfume. Cousin Patricia gave it to Bert last year when she and her friends made us movie stars. Bert saved it for Ruth. She unscrews the tiny cap and holds the bottle near Ruth's nose so she can smell orange and lemon and a vanilla sweetness unlike any flower that grows wild on the mountain. Bert tells her, "Put a tiny dab on the insides of your wrists — right here — and rub your wrists together. Now smell." The little girls lean in, sniff, and get the giggles.

Next comes two stuffed rabbits Bert and I made from scraps and modeled after the velveteen rabbit Oma made years ago. These ears flop, and their button eyes and noses are black, and we stuffed them with cotton batting and used tiny backstitches on the seams so they'll hold up to heavy handling. The two rabbits are alike except for heart-shaped velvet patches — one is red and one is purple so they can tell em apart. The children hug and kiss the bunnies.

Then Bert pulls out her favorite book, a thin book written twenty-three years ago by Margery Williams. My friend once told me that the lines on page five were written for her. *Becoming. It takes a long time. That's why it doesn't happen often to people who break easily.* Bert has learned she doesn't break easily.

"Would you like me to read the story about your bunnies?" she says, and the girls rush to snuggle up beside her and put tiny arms round her shoulders like they belong there. The lantern lights the page and their delicate profiles and their anticipation, and Bert begins. "There was once a velveteen rabbit, and in the beginning he was really splendid . . ."

Here so high — watching the girls watching Bert read to them in this moment close to heaven, with stars almost within reach — I am so very proud of my best friend. She has become a masterful storyteller. She stresses and pauses and pulls them along at the perfect pace. She is so much more than she was. When the book ends and she looks up, Ruth is crying.

"What?" Bert says, unaware of the magic she spun.

"You kin read." Ruth's voice is one of awe. "I can't cipher them words, but you kin read. How'd that come to be?"

"I don't rightly know."

I say, "She worked hard. We read after supper every night and have a stack of books by our bed. Tell em how many books you've read on your own in only two years and three months."

"Seventy-seven," Bert admits, only half willing to brag, likely thinking how different her world is from this one. "At the start it was mostly picture books. I got some in here for y'all to start your own library."

"Thank you for thinking on us," Ruth says and nods at the girls. "Where your manners. What do you say to your Aunt Bert?"

Timid thank-yous come out of the girls, hugging their bunnies like they've always belonged in their arms.

Ruth says it best. "You different, Bert. That fairy in your bunny book did a spell on you, too. She turn you *real* somewhere else. I love you, but you don't belong to us no more."

CHAPTER 54
BERT: RESURRECTION

The bus ride back is familiar. Lu and I stay on our side of the faded white line on the bus floor, the mountains grow flat, sweaters get put away, and the wet heat of August climbs back on my skin. Lu hogs the window seat again and looks at the passing land. She's likely surprised that a state she's called home can be so different from one edge to the other. Like her and me. We both Carolina girls, but I come from jagged rock and dark hollers. Lu's coated in honey, and sandy soil buffs her feet to pearly smooth. That sand's got a ways to go on me.

Mama and Daddy are at the station. When their eyes find us, they look happy at our coming. Like they worried the mountains won't let us go, but I'm here where I belong. I don't even mind going to school tomorrow to fill my head with stuff I don't need.

They say the war is over, but Riverton stays the same cept we don't make sugar syrup every day and the bees get to fend for themselves. Our soldiers don't come home right away. The Germans still work the fields. Tobacco market comes like always, and every Friday for six weeks the auctioneer comes to Mercer County to pull top dollar for hard labor.

Then word comes that Aunt Violet's puny patch of land got sold to a builder. He's gonna put up kit houses. Every four-room house will be the same, with two bedrooms, a living room, a kitchen, and a inside toilet. Daddy says each one will use ten thousand pieces of wood that are numbered and delivered by train. The pieces will fit together like a jigsaw puzzle. Lu and me ride our bicycles out to see for ourselves. A sign at the road reads

COMING SOON
ALADDIN KIT HOMES FOR
RETURNING HEROES

It's October of '45, long after Aunt Violet went crazy. Gone is her garden fence, the chicken coop, and the plate that held the perfect cherry pie. Gone is the dry well Tiny Junior fell down six weeks back and give us a fright. The land is swept clean, and stakes mark where each house will sit on new roads. We count twenty-four squares sitting neat.

"Got a mathematics problem for you," Lu says.

"Okay."

"If each of these house takes ten thousand pieces of wood to build, how many pieces of wood will it take to build twenty-four houses?"

I figure that in my head easy cause I know the trick with zeros. "Two hundred and forty thousand pieces of wood," I say, and that pleases Lu. Then I say to Lu, "How many trees you reckon they cut down to make them puzzle pieces?"

She grins. "A lot."

The next day is Saturday, and Lu and me do the selling at the farmers market. We get back for noon dinner, when Aunt Fannie-belle telephones and shouts through the mouthpiece. "David, hold on to your britches, cause I got big news to tell."

Lu and me step closer to hear the news, and Daddy holds out the earpiece.

"You know they been working at Violet Crumbie's place, building cracker-box bungalows for our soldier boys. Heard tell they're going to cost near bout six hundred dollars. What soldier boy is going to have six hundred dollars in his pocket to spend on a cracker-box house? They ought to give it to him is what they ought to do."

"The news, Aunt Fanniebelle . . . you were saying?"

"Oh that. Well, this morning, they were setting up to dig a new well back at the woods. They use a drill that does the work of ten men, but they still need men with shovels. They don't even get started good when they find bones."

"Bones? Animal bones?" Daddy says.

"Human bones. In shallow graves."

It's all everybody talks about. Human bones buried on poor Violet Crumbie's farm. Some folks speculate that one body is likely the missing Terrell Stucky, cause they heard tell a bullet hole went through the skull. The next body wears scraps of white, so it might be the missing Frankie Tender. The last grave holds a square box crammed with pieces of bones. But not the head. The head is buried beside the box.

All this news tumbles in on me. I don't waste grief on the skull with the bullet hole or the box of bones with the head chopped off, but if the white cloth is Frankie Tender's uniform, that's different. I don't tell Lu how much thinking I done since April a year back, remembering that night behind the

427

warehouse and the feel of that man and what he done to light up my insides. If he'd only asked my name. If he'd only laid me down tender, I would have give myself to him, and he might be alive.

Two weeks after the bones get sent to Raleigh, Irene brings news to the supper table. "Lord, what a mess out at the Crumbie place," she starts, and Mama pinches her lips, not liking gory details when we eat. "The coroner's office confirmed that it was three bodies buried. The bones in the box with the head beside it belonged to a six-foot-tall man. Larry Crumbie was six foot, wasn't he?"

Mama puts down her fork. "I thought Larry Crumbie left town years back."

Daddy rattles the ice in his glass, and Lu slides the pitcher of sweet tea to him. Irene goes on. "That's what we thought, but we could have been wrong. The girls found his truck hidden in Mr. Otis's barn, so we know he didn't drive off. And without his truck, how would he get far? Hitchhike?"

I feel a puff of pride at Irene giving us detective credit while Lu says, "A head weighs eleven pounds."

Grady grins and says, "With or without the neck?" He gets *the look* from Mama.

Then Lydia says, "How much is eleven

pounds?"

But Mama puts up her hand. "Enough. Let's talk about something else so we can properly digest our food." But we don't talk about something else. We turn quiet.

I'm gnawing on a chicken bone when I remember what Trula Freed said: *Larry Crumbie, he go nowhere.* Weegee said Larry Crumbie was HOME and Frankie Tender was HOME, and I thought she meant Frankie's hometown or the army barracks where he lived. I look at Lu and see she's thinking the same thing. All clues point to Aunt Violet's *home.* Larry Crumbie's *home.* My first *home* and now shallow graves.

Lucy and me stay quiet till the dishes get done, then we go upstairs, Lu closes the bedroom door and whispers, "You thinking what I'm thinking?"

I hold out my arm. "You see these hairs standing up?"

"Trula Freed told us Larry never left home, but it didn't make sense till now. I never thought he was dead and buried on his own farm, did you? I thought he was having himself a high time as a free man. But his head chopped off? Do you think your aunt had anything to do with that? And if the other bodies belong to the other miss-

429

ing men, why were they buried in the same place?"

"Hold on, Nancy Drew. That's a lot of questions. We don't even know it's Larry yet. It could be somebody else. But I wonder if the police are gonna talk to Aunt Violet? She used to blab all the time bout her missing husband I never laid eyes on."

"You want to see Trula or Weegee?" Lu whispers. "Maybe one of them can shed clearer light on who murdered three souls."

I shake my head. "I wanna go to Primrose."

"Primrose Mental Hospital? Why in the world? Your aunt doesn't know diddlysquat about the other two bodies. She was locked up when those troubles came to town."

"I think Larry Crumbie is the key. He was the first missing man, and my aunt might know something. It might be the thing making her crazy. We've only been to see her once."

"I don't think she hardly knows her name, Bert. And that's a long drive over there, and if Mama goes, she'd put a stop to us upsetting your aunt with questions about bones. And you remember how she was that day. She may not even know her name."

"That was then. This is now. We're going, Lu. That's settled."

CHAPTER 55
LUCY: VIOLET PRIMROSE

The next day is the first Friday in November, and no matter what Bert says, I don't think we're going anywhere near Primrose. At breakfast, she says in her sweetest tone, "Mama, I got to thinking bout my poor Aunt Violet last night. It's been a long while since we saw her, and I'm feeling neglectful. She don't even know her brother passed. Can we go for a visit tomorrow?"

Mama doesn't look suspicious. She probably doesn't think that box of bones and other bodies have a thing to do with Violet Crumbie. She says, "I'm up to my ears in work for the church raffle, but maybe Grady would take you."

My mouth falls open, and Bert says in all fake innocence, "That'd be great. Can you ask him for us? We'll help with dinner, then be back by suppertime." She links her arm in mine, pulls me from the room, and whispers, "Close your mouth before a fly gets in."

Saturday afternoon, Grady gets behind the wheel of the car. Bert and I sit in back, and we pull out of the driveway on a blue sky day with clouds like meringue. I say, "How did you know asking Mama directly would work?"

"I didn't."

"What would you have done if she'd said no?"

"Think of something else."

"Like what?"

"Why do you have to question everything, Lu? It worked, and we're going to get answers."

"But what are the questions?"

She giggles and looks embarrassed. "I hadn't thought of that. Let's make a list so we don't forget anything important."

"Assuming your aunt hasn't forgotten *everything* important." I find a scrap of paper and pencil. "Okay. What's the first question? *Violet, do you remember Larry Crumbie?*" I joke.

Bert says, "That's not a bad first question. If she don't remember him, how could she know anything about his demise?"

Demise. It tickles me to hear Bert use a ten-dollar word. It's a far cry from her confusion over *bibliophile.*

432

While Grady drives to Primrose, clouds thicken, and it begins to rain. Bert says, "Does it always rain at this place?" I think it's an odd coincidence, too.

Grady pulls into the parking lot. "I'll wait here," he says and pulls out the latest *Popular Mechanics* from under the seat.

"Suit yourself," I say, and Bert and I dash through the rain to the front door and slip inside and shake the water off our hair.

"See what Grady's reading?" Bert whispers.

"*Popular Mechanics.*"

"No, the other one. I bet it's a girly magazine. He's got it inside *Popular Mechanics.* I told you all the boys want to look at what we got."

"Where would he get such a nasty thing?" I whisper.

"Pictures are everywhere. Under store counters, in back rooms, under featherbeds, in privies. Grady's only doing what comes natural. How do you know it's a nasty thing if you never saw one?"

"I don't need to see one to know." I sound prim. I sound old.

Bert shrugs.

"You think Mama and Daddy know? About Grady?"

"They not blind and they not stupid, and

Grady's not asking permission. If it won't necked girls he's looking at, it'd be necked boys."

"Ooh *gross.*" I wrinkle my nose and wonder how Bert knows about such unnatural things. Am I walking through life wearing blinders? Is my brain wrapped in cotton batting? And why am I defending Grady? Why do I care? I do find it curious that Bert and I walk the same road every day but see different scenery and come to different conclusions. And where is the *truth* about right and wrong in all this morality grown-ups preach? It's ironic that we're heading into a mental hospital deliberating truth as if it's debatable. The poor souls inside debate truth every day. Are we all one tragedy away from crazy?

The place looks the same and smells the same, and the nurses sound the same with squeaky shoes on bleached linoleum. Bert speaks to the lady at the front desk. "We're here to see Violet Crumbie."

"One moment, please," she says, then slides the sign-in sheet toward us and picks up the phone. She speaks in a chipper voice in the mouthpiece like we're friends who've come for tea. "Two young ladies are here to see Miz. Crumbie. Is it okay for me to send them up to the fourth floor?"

I thought she was on third.

There's a pause while the receptionist listens, and her mouth moves into a perfect *O*, and her eyes grow wide. She carefully hangs up the phone and says, "I'm so sorry, but it's not possible for you to see Miz Crumbie today. Can you come back another time?" She adds a forced smile.

Bert says with the voice of authority. "I'm Violet Crumbie's niece, Allie Bert Tucker, her closest relative. We've come a long way to see her. Can I speak with somebody in charge? I need me some answers."

Bert plays her cards right, and the lady says, "Well, take a seat. Let me see who can talk to you."

We're the only ones sitting on the plastic-covered chairs waiting. The lady shoots us a sad smile. As soon as she walks away from the front desk, Bert turns to me and whispers. "I think the police have been here."

"Why would you say that?"

"What else could it be? It's only been one day since we heard the bones belonged to a six-foot-tall man. The police would have known longer. They can put two and two —"

The tap of footsteps grow near, and from around the corner a thin man in a gray suit walks toward us with his hand out and his

435

voice well-oiled. "I'm Edsel Rutherford, the supervisor."

Bert stands and introduces us.

"Miz Crumbie is not well today and is resting." Mr. Rutherford's tone is patronizing. "It's best we not interrupt her. I'm sure you understand and don't mind coming back another day."

Bert has one shot to fire, and she makes it count. "Mr. Rutherford, did you know the police found three bodies buried on Violet Crumbie's farm? One of them is a box of bones from a six-foot-tall man with his head cut off."

The supervisor's composure cracks, and his head bobs like a chicken. Nancy Drew would be proud of Bert's surprise attack. "Heavens no. When did this come to light? She's been here for *years* . . ." He's come unsettled and drops in the chair.

"So the police have not been to see her?"

"I am *certain* they have not. I would have been informed of something that *extraordinary*." He punctuates his words for effect, then calls out to the lady at the front desk. "June, have the police been to see Violet Crumbie?"

June overheard the conversation and absorbed the shock. She is composed when she says, "No, Mr. Rutherford. Not on my watch."

"Please check with the head nurse. It might explain today's episode." And off June rushes to do his bidding.

"What episode? Has something happened to my dear aunt?" Bert appears to be the loving niece.

"Surely, you're not suggesting that your sweet aunt is mixed up with . . . *bones.*"

"I don't know," Bert says. "Maybe Aunt Violet knows more than we think. It was her property they were found on. Some of the bones have been there a long time. Back to when she lived there." Bert stretches the truth further than we know for certain.

Mr. Rutherford purses his lips and obviously struggles with how much to say. "Well, she has been acting strange."

"Is that why she was moved from the third floor to the fourth?" Bert says. "Who's on the fourth floor?"

"Now, I can explain, Miz Crumbie —"

"Tucker. I'm Allie Bert Tucker. My pa was Violet Crumbie's brother."

"Well, Miz Tucker . . ." Mr. Rutherford forgets Bert's question. He needs prodding.

"The fourth floor?"

"Oh, the fourth floor . . . It's for people we need to watch *closer.*"

"You mean the dangerous ones?"

"I don't like to put it like that. It's for their own good."

I speak for the first time. "You mean Violet Crumbie is tied up? Chained?"

"Chained? Heavens no. We don't want her to hurt herself. That's all" is his indirect answer.

Bert straightens her back. "Mr. Rutherford, what is going on with my aunt?"

"I can only tell you so much. Miz Crumbie has been yelling the same word yesterday and today." He looks off into space as if permission will come from beyond. He continues cautiously, "One word, over and over. The doctor has given her a sedative to calm her, and she's sleeping. That's why you can't see her today. She's resting."

"*What* was she saying?" Bert asks.

Mr. Rutherford closes in on himself. He says more formally, "It's not unusual for the mentally ill to fixate on one thing. I'm sure it's nothing in Miz Crumbie's case." The gray man in the gray suit in this gray world stands looking composed once more, clearly having made up his mind not to share more with us. "I'm not at liberty to say, Miz Crumbie —"

"My name is *Tucker.* Allie Bert Tucker.

Violet Crumbie is . . ." She repeats the explanation in full to shame Mr. Rutherford.

He doesn't even look embarrassed about being a poor listener, but he is firm with his decision. "Excuse me. I have business to attend to," and he disappears around the corner at an efficient clip, going somewhere else, when June returns to her desk.

We stand in this drab place, confused about what to do next. It wasn't how we planned the visit to end. Bert says in a voice loud enough to carry, "I sure wish we knew what Aunt Violet has been saying. The whole family is so worried about her." Bert stretches truth again for sympathy.

June takes the bait and calls to us in a low voice, "Psst, girls." She motions us over conspiratorially. She has a glint in her eyes, being the holder of a secret that's bursting to be released and giving her status.

"I *know* what Violet Crumbie's been saying. The word she's been saying over and over till she's hoarse." Then she adds as an afterthought to show compassion, "The poor thing."

"What is it?" Bert whispers and leans close to her new friend June with the secret. "We won't tell a soul. Cross our hearts and hope to die, right, Lu?" She includes me in her

439

charade.

June looks around to make sure no one is within earshot and also to stretch out her role in delivering this nugget. She puffs out her chest. "That pitiful woman keeps swinging her arms over her head up and down, saying . . . *chop, chop, chop.*"

CHAPTER 56
BERT: UNRAVELING

Me and Lu is shaking. We run out the door, cross the parking lot, get in the car, and slam the back doors at the same time. Grady's dozed off with his hand at his crotch. When he moves, *Popular Mechanics* spills on the floor. So does the inside magazine with a picture of a necked girl with bosoms smaller than mine. He kicks the magazine under the seat. Me and Lu got bigger worries than girls with no clothes on.

Grady drives, and I look back at the sad place that's likely the forever home for my poor aunt. "Did she kill him? Cut off his head?" I say. "Is that what she meant?"

"We got to be careful not to connect dots that are too far apart, but what do we do now?" Lu is being careful.

"We tell Mama," I say. "We say why we don't get to see her today. We'll ask her to tell the sheriff, since he pays us no mind."

441

"Will he arrest her and put her in jail?"

"I don't think they put crazy people in jail. It would be terrible after losing her baby and her mind if my aunt got put in jail."

"Unless she cut him up."

Grady says, "What are you two yammering about?"

"My aunt might've killed Larry Crumbie."

"Really?" He scoots up straighter and looks at us in the rearview mirror. "Why do you think that?"

So I tell Grady what we know as practice for telling Mama. When I'm done, he says, "Miz Crumbie's a little woman, and she was pregnant then. She wasn't strong enough to get the jump on Larry and chop off his head. That takes muscles she never had."

"Even if she's angry?" Lu says. "Wouldn't that make a difference if they were fighting?"

Grady says, "Well, that means Larry Crumbie would be angry, too, making him stronger, not weaker."

I say, "Could she hit him over the head with a iron skillet while he was asleep? If he was knocked out, she could do what she wanted with him."

Grady says, "But how would she move his body all the way out to the edge of the woods? Larry was a big man." Grady puts another hole in our thinking.

"Maybe somebody helped her," Lu says.

"Like an accomplice? Who would kill a man for a poor country woman and not stick around for the woman or her farm? There'd have to be some reward there that I can't see."

Then I wonder, "Maybe she saw the killer. Maybe that's why she went crazy."

Grady goes on to say, "You sure nobody's told her about the box of bones?"

We don't know. Maybe we should have asked Primrose June more questions.

Grady adds, "And that doesn't explain the other two bodies. If they're Stucky and that singer, they were put there after she went loony. The big question is how all three bodies are tied together."

We tell Mama bout *chop chop chop* but nothing happens. She says leave it to the authorities to handle. At bedtime, while Lu brushes her hair a hundred times, sitting in front of the mirror, I say, "I get a headache thinking bout Larry Crumbie. He's a no-account man giving nothing but grief. I hope no more bodies turn up."

Lu stops brushing. "What did you just say?"

"Bout what?"

"About bodies turning up." She turns to face me. "That's what Trula Freed said at the very beginning. That Frankie Tender and Larry Crumbie would *turn up.* Did she mean like dirt from a burial ground?"

Oh, sweet Lord'a mercy.

Next day, after church, after dinner, after dishes, we go see Trula Freed. We walk on plowed dirt in our field that crunches under shoes with an early November frost. Then through pines on brown needles, to the red door where Biscuit sleeps. We're almost on top of him before he raises his head and thumps his tail. There's gray in his muzzle and clouds in his eyes. Before we even knock, Miz Trula opens the door. She's got her walking sticks and hands me a folded muslin sheet and Lu the scissors. She says, "Bittersweet," and we follow her long cape and two walking sticks thumping on the ground.

Lu says, "When did you know you had the gift?"

"Didn't know it was a gift at first. I thought everybody saw what I saw, knew what I knew."

"But what did you see?" I say.

"I dreamed and told my granny the places I'd go. It was a magic ride where I saw dead people and souls not born yet, and they talked to me."

"Lydia has the gift," Lu says matter-of-fact.

Trula Freed nods. "She's a bridge to the other side."

I'm miffed at them knowing big news I'm hearing for the first time. "How come you know this?" I ask, wondering how Lydia got to be a bridge.

"She told me Oma comes and whispers in her ear while she sleeps. She knew Wade Sully was dead before we got the telegram."

"When was that?"

"Early last year."

"And you didn't think to tell me?"

"I didn't know it was true. It sounded weird till we found out Wade was really dead."

Trula Freed says, "It's hard explaining the unexplainable, Bert."

"She coulda tried. Lu shouldn't keep secrets from me."

Miz Trula says, "Best friends don't have to share everything," but Lu sees I'm upset.

"I'm sorry, Bert, but would you have believed me? Would you have treated Lydia differently knowing she foretold?"

"I'd a believed you. Why wouldn't I?"

"And Lydia? *Will* you look at my sister differently now?"

"She's a little girl."

"A little girl with a big power. Well, now you know."

We come to the bittersweet, and Miz Trula stands off to the side while we cut the vines and wrap them in the muslin sheet, careful with the berries. We carry the vines between us when Lu asks the question we come for. "You know who those three bodies are, don't you?"

The old woman nods.

I say as fact, "Larry Crumbie, Frankie Tender, and Terrell Stuckey."

Miz Trula nods again.

I say, "I know they're bad men, but how did they end up in one place? Frankie Tender never even met the other two."

Then Lu says, "Were they killed by the same person?"

Trula Freed chuckles but not in a funny way. Like the truth is standing right in front of us and we're too blind to see.

CHAPTER 57
LUCY: SILK WORMS

Ending the war is taking forever to get done. Normal is taking its sweet time returning. Everett's last letter said we wouldn't set eyes on him till next summer. "Why?" I ask Byron one supper as he scoops out more mashed potatoes.

"It's a monumental task to take inventory, get paperwork in order, organize transportation, dismantle war factories, collect our POWs. The list goes on and on."

"When will Wolf and Joe and the others be leaving?" Mama says. "What's going to happen to them?"

"I haven't heard a release date, but they won't head home right away. Rebuilding a shattered world will take a long time. The Americas are one of the few lands not ravaged. Our German prisoners will be sent to do cleanup in England and France. At some point, they'll go home, but not anytime soon."

Mama reaches for another pan of biscuits on the stove and holds it out for takers. "Where will you go after camp is closed?"

Byron glances at Irene. "I'm not sure, Miz Brown. I might stay in the service. I might apply for a teaching job at East Carolina in Greenville." He clears his throat, suddenly nervous. "Wherever I go, I want Irene to go with me" — he kisses the back of her hand and looks at Daddy, then Mama — "if you grant me permission to marry her."

My parents look stunned, though they can't be too surprised since Byron is here every day that he's off. Still, the silence stretches like warm taffy, and the light in Byron's exuberant face dims. Mama whispers, "David, are you going to answer the man?"

And just like that, my sister snags a bona fide fiancé with a musical name.

The wedding will be held on New Year's Day. Aunt Fanniebelle insisted the ceremony take place at the Hollingston mansion. We have three weeks to plan Irene's special day.

Ever practical, Irene says she wants to wear a tailored blue suit. One she can wear again after the wedding. She's going to try on the suit today and wants Mama, Bert, and me to go along and give our opinions. Now we stand on the sidewalk looking in Yetta's clothing store window with our reflections looking back when Irene points. "That's the one."

The one is a basic gabardine suit with a notched collar and cinched waist. It looks like a uniform, and I say outright, "That doesn't look like a wedding outfit."

This gets Irene's dander up. "Well, I know it's different, but I don't like long white dresses that cost too much and never get worn again. I don't have extra money to burn for something frivolous. Plus, it's on sale." She looks at Mama, hoping for support. "What do you think, Mama?"

"You'll look pretty in anything, honey, and Byron would marry you if you wore a feed sack. But we've come to the end of some trying years, and an uplifting celebration is just what we need. Do you think that suit is uplifting?"

In the window's reflection, we see Uncle Nigel's Chrysler glide down Main Street, pass us, then back up. The passenger window is lowered, and Aunt Fanniebelle yells, "What y'all gawking at?"

Mama steps off the curb to the car. "We're looking at that dark-blue suit in the window. Irene thinks it would look nice for her wedding day."

"For the ceremony? It looks almost black from here. Whoever heard such a thing." Aunt Fanniebelle shouts to Irene, "Don't even waste time trying it on. Y'all come on to the house. I been meaning to show you something," and they drive off.

"Mama," Irene whines. "She's gonna take over like she usually does. This is my wedding day, and I want it simple as spit, with no lace, no sparkles, no pearls, no frills."

"It won't do any harm to appease her. Your aunt has a generous heart. She's excited for you. We all are. After our visit, you can try on that navy suit."

It's a short car ride down three blocks, across train tracks, and past the church, but Irene is miffed that her practical plans are being threatened. I'm sorry Bert and I tagged along since my sister is turning into a sourpuss. We pull in the driveway and park beside the Chrysler. Uncle Nigel is helping Aunt Fanniebelle out of the car, and the lot of us enter the side door. Uncle Nigel heads to his study, and we walk through the dining room, past the sunroom, into the parlor where Weegee lives in the bottom of the walnut secretary and the grand piano holds silver frames of special moments.

Aunt Fanniebelle picks up the largest

frame, the one that sits beside the photo of Glenn Miller in New York City. It's a picture of Patricia's magnificent wedding party that rivals royalty. Twelve perfect bridesmaids and twelve perfect groomsmen surround the perfect couple with a castle in the background. It was taken last June on the Hampton estate that was given to Patricia and Julian Sanders the Third as a wedding gift. The mansion sits on five acres of oceanfront. The gardens were designed by landscape architect Frederick Law Olmsted, who has his own entry in the *Encyclopedia Britannica.* The elaborate pool was built by Italian artisans at the turn of the century. The pool is lined with a million blue mosaic tiles. Patricia got lost twice in the mansion the first week she lived there. She wrote me such things in a letter.

"You see that wedding gown?" We lean in to look closer. "Julian's mother picked it out. Patricia said it was heavy with a thousand pearls and miles of handmade Venise lace that trailed behind. The veil was ten feet long and appliqued with white roses to match the Winchester Cathedral roses she carried. My daughter almost buckled under the weight of that dress on her summer wedding day, but Julian's mother was firm on what was proper in the Hamptons. At the start, Patricia didn't want to go against her mother-in-law's wishes, don't you know."

Aunt Fanniebelle stops talking and touches Patricia's image in her heavy wedding dress. I always envied my cousin's lavish life. I never knew there'd come a reason to pity her, but I'm looking at it. I lean in closer to study her face and mostly see a smile. But there's a hint of fear I would have never noticed unless I knew her wedding dress was heavy.

My aunt resumes talking. "But I didn't ask you here to see this picture. There's something upstairs in Patricia's room." The climb up the carpeted staircase is at a snail's pace because of Aunt Fanniebelle's stiff joints. I walk beside her, and she holds my arm and the handrail. The others walk patiently behind.

We walk down the carpeted hallway and enter my cousin's room.

We are stopped still. By a wedding gown. Hanging on the armoire door.

A column of white silk, simply exquisite and exquisitely simple.

Aunt Fanniebelle says, "Patricia had two wedding gowns made, and this was her choice. It's made of mulberry silk, the best money can buy."

I want to say, "Do you know how they make mulberry silk? For four weeks, those silk worms get fat on mulberry leaves, then they spin their silk cocoons. When they're snug inside waiting, they're dropped in boiling water to die, and the cocoon of raw silk unravels, and the strands are woven into fabric." But I don't say this truth. Today, I use restraint. I don't want to spoil the wonder on Irene's face.

"But this dress wasn't fancy enough for Julian's mother. I was thinking maybe this dress was made for you, Irene."

"Oh my stars," Irene gushes.

Bert whispers, "I thought she didn't want a long white dress."

I whisper back, "That was then. This is now."

Gone is my sister's wish to wear a blue suit on sale from Yetta's display window. Gone is her ridicule of brides in long white dresses. Off comes her winter coat and plain dress, and over her slip goes a ripple of silk cut on the bias that compliments Irene's slim figure. When she looks in the tall mirror at her beautiful self, she is speechless. We are speechless. Mama clutches her heart and starts to cry. Bert and I cry, too, and Aunt Fanniebelle reaches up the sleeves of her dress for hidden handkerchiefs she

CHAPTER 58
BERT: THE GIFT

It's Christmas Eve, and Grady gives me his hand to help me down from the truck. It's the first time he's touched me on purpose. I look up at him grown tall, and he smiles down on me, and I blush. River Road is full of cars and trucks and wagons cause of the invite in the newspaper. Folks talk and walk by flashlights and lanterns and head to the prison camp. We catch up with Mama and Daddy with Lydia and Cora, who came by car. Some folks are here cause the Germans are their friends. Some are here curious about the gift. Others got nowhere better to be.

Flossie Rose walks beside Sheriff Cecil with Tiny Junior behind, and she waves. Tiny's got on the army hat Byron Toots gave him. They look like a family. Trula Freed is dressed in red finery and has come with her church friends and Preacher Perlie. Miz Elvira the librarian walks with a soldier man I don't recollect seeing before. Cornell walks with his year-old daughter on his shoulders and his wife by his side.

The camp gates are open, and the guards' guns are shouldered. Fat colored lights are strung across the top of the fence. A Christmas tree holds paper chains and painted pecans and strung popcorn. The crowd of town people wait in the road. A German steps in the light wearing an oversized red coat. He shouts, "Meddy Chrismaass, Riverton." The crowd claps and whistles cause he is happy.

"I chosen to say since Anglish iz goot." He bows, and we clap again. "Today, twenty month for now, ve come here to you. Ve come defeat, scart, tired, and German and work hard for you. Ve not forget you. Tonight ve gif to you a present so you not forget us ever." He bows again and steps back.

Wolf comes out with Daddy's fiddle. I cry right off, and Lu cries, too, us welling up before he starts. We miss him before he's gone. We know this about Wolf. He comes from a town called Mittenwald. His family makes violins. His homeland is like my mountains. Maple and spruce trees grow there and make good violins. His sweetheart is named Olga. We hope Olga waits for him.

He plays my favorite Christmas song,

"Silent Night." People hum. Then he plays it again, and the prisoners sing in German. *"Stille Nacht, heilige Nacht, Alles schläft . . ."* Men bring out wooden forms, people size, painted by camp artists. A king. A shepherd on one knee. A manger with baby Jesus is put up beside Mary with a shawl over a blue gown. The pieces keep coming — sheep and cows — till they are sixteen across. They look real except they're flat. Then the Germans sing "Silent Night" in English, and Wolf's violin plays on, and we sing, too. Voices without a mean bone among us. There's not a dry eye neither. My throat gets a knot, and hardly a sound comes out.

How did we get here? How did something that don't make a lick of sense turn into *this*? I wish Helen was here to see. She closed herself off and missed the whole thing. Maybe tonight would change her.

We sing, and flecks of white start falling from the sky. The bits land on hats and hair and shoulders. "Is it snow?" someone says, and the word *snow* runs through the crowd in wonder. It snows in my mountains but not here. Not with stars shining bright.

Then somebody shouts "Fire, fire" from the back of the crowd, and fingers point at smoke swirling above the trees. It's not snow. It's ashes. But what's burning? We move up River Road to Main Street, and the gate stays open, and the Germans come with us. The fire truck clangs, and people in front can see.

It's the newspaper building where Irene works.

She's with Byron, but she pushes to the front, and we go, too, and we see the fire above bare trees. Then we're a block away. Flames lick out the second-floor windows. Irene screams Drake Cunningham's name, her boss, her friend. "He worked late," she sobs to everybody close. "Is he inside? Did he get out? Have you seen Drake Cunningham?"

Everybody looks for Drake Cunningham with gray hair and scratchy voice and a cigarette always dangling from his lips.

Nobody sees him. The Ford firetruck comes. The fire gets hotter. Firemen unwind the water hose and hook it to the hydrant. One shouts, "Step back everybody. Move back." The water comes on and runs through the hose and pushes out the end, but it's a puny spout next to a fire burning stacks of paper and dry wood.

Irene wails for Drake Cunningham inside the burning building. She fights to break away from Daddy and Byron holds her back. Does she want to rush inside a burning building? "It's only burning up there," she says and points to the second floor. "It's smoke on the first floor, so let me go. Let me go in. Somebody please help," she wails.

Tiny Junior watches Irene's grief. He starts crying for his worried friend. He pats her on her shoulder with his big hand, then steps in front.

He walks past the firemen.

Into the door.

Swallowed by smoke.

Flossie cries, "Oh, Sweet Jesus. Somebody stop my boy. *Stop.*" She pushes to the front of the crowd and sinks to her knees — but she's too late. Tiny Junior is outta sight and outta time, and the second floor falls, and the heat slaps us back.

The crowd is flabbergasted. Those in back didn't see Tiny Junior walk into the burning building. Words get passed around, and hearts are clutched, and Flossie faints. Irene's mouth hangs open in horror. Then she looks over my shoulder, and her hands fly to her face, and she falls to her knees. What does she see?

Drake Cunningham. At the back. Up on his tiptoes. Trying to see what's going on up front.

CHAPTER 59
LUCY: SAINT TINY

Drake Cunningham is alive, but Irene wants to die. She is a broken woman we carry home on Christmas Eve. "I'll never forgive myself," she says. "Never, ever." Irene is put to bed in Helen's room, away from the silk wedding dress and lace veil hanging in Irene's room. Byron comes quietly on Christmas morning to see Irene, but she doesn't come out of the bedroom, so he sits in the parlor and waits. The air in our home is somber and chilled no matter how much heat the woodstove pumps out. We barely slept since the unthinkable happened.

Last night Irene called herself a killer and wanted the sheriff to arrest her. Then Sheriff Cecil does come, but he brings Flossie Rose to our door. Flossie is pale and weak but says, "I must see dear Irene."

I don't know how Flossie stands upright. How she carries her grief, the loss of her only man-child who was good and noble.

Where does she find the courage to reach out to my sister in her desperate hour of need?

Flossie taps on the bedroom door, steps inside and closes it. Irene wails and beats against the wall like a trapped animal. Flossie's voice is soothing. We can't understand her words, but we feel her kindness emanate through the walls. Irene's screaming eventually morphs into raspy sobs that dull to whimpers of exhaustion. Gradually, the crying stops and the two women come out.

Sheriff Cecil has been sitting with Daddy and Byron in the parlor, waiting without talk, because what can you say on a day like today? Helen and the little ones went to Aunt Fanniebelle's since it is Christmas, and they will be spoiled there as best this tragic day can deliver. Grady is in the barn. Mama steps to the parlor. "They're coming out," she says, but the men stay in the parlor and don't crowd Irene. Bert and I are at the table, and Mama is at the stove. Flossie helps Irene walk like she's an invalid, and Mama pours cups of strong tea for them. Irene has come undone and been turned inside out. Her face is bruised and swollen with pain. The tendons in her throat are stretched tight. The curve of her shoulders bends more than Oma's ever did. Grief and guilt are appalling punishers. Flossie leaves to plan her son's funeral.

His wake begins the day after Christmas. Everybody comes. They witnessed or heard about the sacrifice that rivals war heroes, to walk fearlessly into harm's way for a mighty cause, necessary or not. My family goes to pay our respect at Flossie's house. We wait in line with everybody else to enter the small house that requires friends to rotate in and out. Grady holds the door open for Bert but then walks in front of me. The cold foods are set outside on plywood tables under a tepid sun. The warm foods are inside. It is more bounty than can be eaten, but that's how we comfort one another in the South — with food. Mama brings Oma's German marble cake she made for Christmas that didn't get eaten.

Irene would not be left behind, and I'm proud of her. To shun Tiny Junior's wake because of her broken spirit would have been a sin to my way of thinking. Everybody here is kind to her, knowing the sorrow she bears. Soldiers who knew and loved Tiny Junior arrive with Byron. He comes to Irene's side and hugs her, but she is despondent and he is patient.

Stories about the gift of Tiny Junior ripple

through the crowd. Everyone has one, and they're shared in low voices. He always seemed to be where he was needed . . . *a quiet boy with a sweet smile.* Folks with men away at war could count on him showing up on that old bicycle of his, lumbering from side to side, doing what needed doing. In our memory, this man was an innocent, a pure soul who gave without taking. If we were a Catholic town instead of Baptist, we would call him a saint. We'd erect a statue on his behalf.

Ricky Miller comes with his parents, and when he sees Grady nearing the cinder block steps, he takes off running across the yard. His mama yells, "Arthur Richard Miller, stop running this instant." I never knew Ricky's first name was Arthur. Or that his initials were A.R.M. I watch him closer.

Tiny Junior's casket is closed. There was nothing Baylor's Funeral Home could do to make the body right. I smell charred ashes when I pass the casket. Bert and I stand in the kitchen up against the wall on each side of frail Irene. We can see the closed casket through the doorway. We each hold a slice of marble cake on a paper napkin and nibble at it. I wipe crumbs from my sister's pale lips. We stuff the napkins in our coat pockets. The mourners grow tighter. It's hot in the house with so many bodies, and Irene looks peaked and close to fainting.

Off the kitchen is the one bedroom with a blanket hanging down the middle to divide two sleeping spaces. The room is empty. Bert and I steer Irene through the doorway to gain a little air. We don't want to rush our visit and leave too quickly, looking disrespectful. The left side of the room is Flossie's, her single bed covered in a faded quilt in the star-block design. Two worn dresses hang from pegs, and a cracked mirror is on the wall. Under the mirror, a washbasin sits on a stand.

On the right side of the partition is a narrow iron bed made with neat military corners. The army blanket Byron gave Tiny Junior lays folded at the foot. Familiar flannel shirts and overalls hang on pegs. I smell Tiny Junior's Black Jack chewing gum but don't see any. I think of the Dentyne that Lydia smelled when Oma whispered in her ear. Maybe a spirit can cast their special scent to let you know they're close by. Maybe Tiny Junior sees today that he is loved. That everyone is here to honor him. He might wonder what all the fuss is about.

Irene tears up standing in his space, and I slip my arm around her for support. She whispers, "I can't believe he's gone," her voice ragged and raw. "Was I ever unkind to him? Did I ignore him because he never required anything? I can't remember, and it bothers me. If I was ever curt or mean to him . . ."

I say what she needs to hear. "You're a good person." I don't say she can be harsh, but that's just Irene getting things done. And being loved has changed her. Tiny Junior would never take offense. He never looked for hidden agendas.

The three of us are shoulder to shoulder in Tiny Junior's personal space that holds little except a narrow shelf made of bare wood mounted above the bed. I step toward it, curious about what he would put on display. Bert and Irene move with me, away from the murmur of mourners and into our dead friend's room, which seems too small for the large heart of him.

Until we stand in front of that shelf.

It holds three scraps of paper.

REAL. BAD. MEN.

Words Tiny collected at different story times. Words he wanted to see written down, then put in his pocket.

The shelf holds three things: a can of Dapper Dan pomade. A tarnished belt buckle. A pearl-handled switchblade.

"Oh, dear God in heaven," I whisper, and

we look wide-eyed at one another, flushed of sorrow replaced by shock. Did Tiny Junior do what we think he did? Has *The Case of the Three Missing Men* been solved?

In each instance, Tiny Junior would have had opportunity and motive. He likely wanted to protect pregnant Violet from a husband who beat her. Maybe the burying box was too small for Larry's body and the head was chopped off because it didn't fit.

And Frankie Tender. Did Tiny Junior defend his friend Bert being battered when she cried out in the dark for help?

Did he deliver swift justice for his two German friends when his uncle confessed to killing them?

And if he did what we think he did, what do we do now? His souvenirs are in the open. Anybody could deduce the truth. The town might turn against the memory of someone who kills so easily. They might turn against Flossie Rose because of her son.

Irene decides how Tiny Junior's story will end. She reaches into her pocket for her paper napkin holding crumbs, wraps it around the can of pomade and slips it into her deep coat pocket. I use Bert's napkin for the army buckle and mine for the pearl-handled switchblade. They go in Irene's other pocket. Bert takes the BAD scrap of paper and crumbles it into a wad, leaving only REAL MEN.

We carry his damning tokens and push against the incoming tide of friends, out the front door, down cinder block steps, past the line of mourners telling their personal Tiny Junior stories. Uncle Nigel's Chrysler is parked on the side of the road, and he comes toward us, walking Aunt Fanniebelle to the wake. Trula Freed has stayed beside his car and waits.

She wears a cape of violet purple that is the color of spirituality and rare honey and healing mystery. A strange wind scurries across the fallow field and whips her cape like a kite wanting to take flight. Trula Freed watches us with an easy calm, for today is the loosening of a secret she's known all along. An enigma revealed when it can do the least harm. A bittersweet secret we'll take to our graves.

AUTHOR'S NOTES

The German POW campsite I visited was located in my birth-town of Williamston, North Carolina, in Martin County. In this work of fiction, the town and county names were changed to Riverton and Mercer County to avoid confusion or misrepresentation. Were it not for the many contributions of the generous citizens of Williamston, this book would not be nearly as interesting.

In Chapter Five, the movie *Lassie Come Home* plays at the fictional Majestic Theater in June of 1943, but the movie wasn't released until December of 1943. This exception was taken to parallel the movie's theme of exile and loss with Bert's exile from her home and loss of family.

Chapter Twenty-One about the Brown's gall-double-dang flu relating to the Spanish Flu of 1918 was written in early 2019, more than a year before the Covid-19 pandemic affected the world. It was strange foreshadowing.

The plot in *All the Little Hopes* is entirely fictional, but the book is peppered with historical truths the author uncovered. Here is an alphabetical list of some of the little-known facts: the beeswax contract in WWII, blue ghost fireflies, German glass marbles, German POWs, Glenn Miller's disappearance, purple honey, Russian test pilots in Elizabeth City, Shape Note singing, the Spanish Flu of 1918, and folklore wolpertingers in Bavaria.

A TASTE OF HOPE
OMA'S GERMAN MARBLE
CAKE

A LIGHT, MOIST, SLIGHTLY SWEET CAKE

1 cup butter (2 sticks), softened
1 3/4 cups sugar
2 teaspoons vanilla extract
5 eggs, room temperature, separated
3 cups all-purpose flour
2 teaspoons baking powder
1 cup + 2 tablespoons whole milk
3 tablespoons sweetened cocoa powder

Heat the oven to 350 degrees, and grease and flour a 10″ tube pan. Cream the softened butter and sugar in a large mixing bowl. Add the vanilla and the egg yolks and beat for 10 minutes. Combine the flour and the baking powder in a separate bowl. Alternately stir the flour and milk into the sugar/butter mixture. Beat the egg whites in a separate bowl until soft peaks form, then fold into the batter.

Put 1/4 of the batter in a separate bowl and thoroughly mix in the cocoa powder, and set aside. Pour half the remaining butter batter into the prepared tube pan, then add half the cocoa batter, and swirl through with a knife. Pour the last of the butter batter into the tube pan, add the rest of the cocoa batter, and swirl with a long knife to create marbling throughout. Bake for 50 to 60 minutes, then check for doneness with a toothpick. Cool in the pan for 10 minutes.

LACY CORNBREAD

(Aunt Susie Made it Best)

1 cup white cornmeal, sifted*
1 1/4 cups very cold water
1 to 1 1/2 teaspoons salt to taste

In a pourable container, mix the ingredients with a fork until smooth and runny. Heat a generous amount of cooking oil, enough to cover the bottom of a well-seasoned cast iron frying pan. Stir the batter briskly with a fork while pouring into the center of the pan. Tilt the frying pan and make sure oil touches all sides of the hoecake. Cook a few minutes and watch for lacy edges to brown, not burn. Turn over with a wide spatula and cook 1 to 2 minutes more. Flip the hoecake

*Use quality stone-ground cornmeal like that made at Old Mill of Guilford in Guilford County, NC. Keep cornmeal refrigerated after opening. Oldmillofguilford.com

one or two more times, looking for even browning. Drain on paper towels. Serve hot with butter.

READING GROUP GUIDE

1. Lucy's mother points out that language is meant to communicate, not separate, which discourages Lucy from overusing her enormous vocabulary. Throughout the book, how do you see language used to communicate? To separate?

2. What do you think of Bert's desire to stay a girl instead of growing into a woman? How do we see Bert and Lucy accept growing up throughout the book? What are the chief differences you see between childhood and adulthood back in the 1940s as compared to today?

3. Describe the role of the Browns in their community. What are the broad effects of being a bibliophile?

4. Bert tends to blame herself when things go wrong — her mother dying, her father

sending her away, Violet locking her out. Why do you think that is? Is it more of a female trait? Are there things you blame yourself for that really aren't your fault?

5. What do you think about the mystery of Trula Freed? Was her magic plausible? Have you ever had an experience with a spiritualist or medium?

6. Lucy and Bert argue about treating Nancy Drew like a real person. Can you think of any literary characters that you wish were real or who felt as real to you?

7. Though purple honey in North Carolina is rare but real, what role does it play in the book? Did it arrive just to cure the mysterious flu, or is it a symbol for something larger?

8. Whiz Mayhew comes home from the war with what we might now call PTSD, and his homecoming is difficult. In his drunken state he confesses that the Nazis didn't shoot him when given a chance because they *didn't think he was worth it.* What was he confessing in that statement? How did his community help him heal? Do we have better options today to help

soldiers with PTSD?

9. Describe the relationship between the Riverton community and the German POWs. What effect does Terrell Stucky have on the reputation of the POWs? How do the Germans come to be an accepted part of the town?

10. When Bert was *almost compromised,* her greatest sorrow was that Frankie Tender never asked her name. Discuss the importance of that missing question and the consequence for Frankie Tender. If he had asked her name, would the evening have ended differently or not?

11. Helen refuses to interact with the Germans in any capacity. What do other characters think of her stubbornness? What does her stubbornness cost her? Do you think you would be as resistant in her place?

12. During her father's funeral, Bert realizes how much she's changed since she left home. Do you agree with her sister that she doesn't belong to the mountains anymore? How is "home" defined throughout the book?

13. None of the vanished men are particularly missed, and each presented a certain kind of danger to the community. How does Larry Crumbie's domestic abuse compare to Frankie Tender's callous seduction? To Terrell Stuckey's hate mongering and murder? Do you think these men deserved their fates?

14. Did Lucy, Bert, and Irene do the right thing when they found Tiny Junior's souvenirs? Would you have done the same?

15. What do you think comes next for Lucy and Bert and the rest of the Brown family? How do you think their experiences and decisions will affect their futures?

A CONVERSATION
WITH THE AUTHOR

Eastern North Carolina comes alive throughout the book. How do you give the landscape a voice?
I was born in the land where this book is set, and lived there until I was ten years old. Then we moved five hours north to Virginia to be with my daddy's people. In those early years, I was surrounded by Mama's sprawling family of fifteen siblings, my aunts and uncles who begat cousins. They were a kind and hard-working lot who stayed close to their roots. Only Mama moved away. I remember featherbeds, the outhouse, the ice box, the hand-cranked ice cream, and "putting in tobacco." Dinner was at noon, supper was at six, and everybody had well-tended gardens. Recreating the book's setting was as natural as breathing.

What inspired this book?
Before Mama died in 2005, I had begun

"interviewing" her about her childhood years. My first published stories were about her memories. But, specifically, it was her comment about German POWs helping at tobacco markets in '44 that planted the seed for *All the Little Hopes.* I learned that between 1942 and 1946, forty-five states had POWs working farms, fertilizer plants, and in timber and canneries. Wikipedia estimates half a million prisoners were shipped to camps and governed by the humane laws of the '29 Geneva Convention. Seven hundred camps stretched across America. Eighteen camps were in North Carolina. One was in my birth town of Williamston.

Did you know much about apiarists before you started *All the Little Hopes*? How did you learn about beekeeping, honey, and wax production? Did you invent purple honey, or is it really possible?

My husband, Dave, began tending bees in 2017 and maintains three hives. I've absorbed some of his enthusiasm and research for bee knowledge and have come to understand the challenges. Then on a trip to Williamston, Rita Harden gifted me with three little-known facts from her childhood: Russian test pilots trained in Elizabeth City, her daddy's beeswax deal with the government, and purple honey that appeared one summer and was sold to bootleggers. I now know purple honey has been found only in central and eastern North Carolina, and is a genuine mystery. Two hives side-by-side can yield purple honey in one and amber in the other. I chose to make purple honey the medical salve for the Brown's gall-double-dang flu.

How did the mythical wolpertinger find its way into the book?

Research about Oma's birth place in the nineteenth century, her connection to German handmade marbles, and the Brothers Grimm and masterful storytelling from the Black Forest led me to an image of a wolpertinger. I was enchanted by its mythology, its appeal to tourists back then willing to pay to "hunt" them, and knew my storytelling Brown family would benefit from having one. Who could doubt Grimm's fairytales were true after they saw a "real" wolpertinger?

Both Bert and Lucy resist growing up in their own ways. Did you have any similar experiences as a teenager?

481

I don't remember being enamored of my childhood enough to want to stay there. In contrast to the 1940s of my mother's time, my transition from girl to woman happened in the sixties when the Women's Rights movement was making strides. Naïve, I looked forward to being a grown-up only to discover it was challenging, harder than I dreamed, and even boring. What I gained from my experiences over the ensuing decades is perfect 20/20 hindsight, and my writing benefits from those lessons learned.

Lucy would be best friends with Nancy Drew if she could. Are there any characters you wish you could bring into the real world and befriend?

I, too, loved Nancy Drew. I still have nineteen of my childhood Nancy Drew books (the blue book edition) and occasionally re-read them for nostalgia's sake. In my carefree summers in the late fifties, I spent days lost in Nancy's world. I'd sit in the shade of an oak tree and be so transported that I didn't hear Mama calling for supper. I yearned for the respect that Nancy garnered and the confident risks she took. I think all girls' dreams should hold those qualities.

You bring up interesting questions about redemption when it comes to the German POWs and the Real Bad Men. Is there a difference between redemption and forgiveness? Do you think it's always possible to make amends?

Redemption and forgiveness are gifts, aren't they? We can choose to give and receive salvation and mercy, but it takes wisdom to know they even exist. And for amends to be healing, it should never be a game of manipulation or win-lose. Bert learned that truth when she returned the things she stole. Helen was slow to forgive, and she suffered more than she had to. And who would have thought that German POWs could live peacefully among us?

Reading and writing are often seen as lonely activities, but throughout the book they bring people together. How do books foster connections? Who's in your book community?

I write stories to be read out loud like the Brown family tradition, and I encourage readers to sharpen that skill. Then there's the energy and connection through book clubs. I have five wonderful girlfriends in my club (Sheila, Shannon, Sally, Dominique, and Glennys), and we meet once a month, drink wine, eat good food, and talk books. We don't always agree on what books are best, but disagreement makes for interesting discussions. We all agree that when we meet an unforgettable character in an unforgettable book, it brings pleasure of great magnitude.

Do you come from a family of bibliophiles?

I come from a family of readers and conversationalists. My dad was a thinker who read about religions, philosophy, and history. My mother loved books that transported like the Mitford Series, *Roots,* and *The Thorn Birds.* My parents believed reading expands understanding, dispels prejudices, and teaches empathy. Mama didn't trust people who didn't like to read.

Do books have a designated place in your home? What's in your reading stack these days?

I have overflowing bookcases and messy stacks of books here and there (not the alphabetized order like the Browns). I love historical fiction and relish Southern voices like Vicki Lane's *And the Crows Took Their Eyes,* the unique writing style of debut novelist Ashley Blooms's *Every Bone a*

Prayer, the 2020 Southern Book Prize winner *Magnetic Girl* by Jessica Handler, and everything by journalist/writer/Pulitzer Prize winner Rick Bragg. In my yet-to-read stack is *Sold on a Monday* by Kristina McMorris and *The Only Woman in the Room* by Marie Benedict. So many books, so little time . . . a wonderful quandary to have.

Do you see yourself in your characters? How do you get from the first idea of a character to the person who lives and breathes in the final draft?

I didn't publish *If the Creek Don't Rise* until I was seventy, and it was my age that gave me a broad scope of experiences to draw from. As a writer, I take the liberty to make characters wiser and smarter or more daring and tender than I'll ever be. *All the Little Hopes* is dear to my heart because I got to turn back the clock and immerse myself in Mama's world. I had two names for the main characters early on, but Lu and Bert are uniquely their own literary voices. I don't pretend to speak for my mama, Lucy, or her mama, Allie Bert, who were extraordinary women in different ways.

What has changed for you as a writer

since the publication of *If the Creek Don't Rise?*

I coincidentally retired when my debut book was accepted by an agent, and I had abundant time to devote to a new career. My extrovert nature has made the journey a pleasure to meet the reading public and hear how strongly they react to characters spun out of words. But it is my equal love of solitary time that has made me a better writer. My greatest surprise is my patience to do the tedious work to complete a book and not to rush the process. My greatest joy is the self-imposed purpose that drives my free time.

HOW THIS BOOK CAME TO BE

Beyond my mother Lucy's nugget of WWII history about German POWs working tobacco market in '44, it was longtime friend Bill Davis who found historian Ila Parker in Williamston, North Carolina. Ila showed me photographs and articles about the POW camp that had housed three hundred and fifty-five war prisoners. The men were more than Nazis; they were farmers, musicians, artists, and teachers. Before leaving Williamston at the end of the war, they presented a thank-you gift to the town — a sixteen-piece life-size wooden nativity scene. Sadly, that gift was destroyed in a fire in 1958. I have a brass Christmas ornament commemorating that scene, and it reminds me that war doesn't only breed fear, hatred, and conflict.

I traveled many times to Williamston developing this story and staying with Marti and Bill Davis. Ann Phelps shared local history books, and Laurie Irwin-Pinkley arranged a meeting with people who remembered POWs working on family farms. Ila Parker joined Rita Harden, Raymond Silverthorn, his brother Irvin "Skeebo" Silverthorn, and Skeebo's wife, Fernande, to talk about their unique memories. Becky Mills Sanderlin was the baby picked up and comforted by a German prisoner. LouAnn VanLandingham granted permission to spend a day in the *Martin County Enterprise* newspaper stacks reviewing 1943–1945. Bonnie Robertson sent me a copy of her sister's POW camp menu of '44 and told me where the mess hall still sits near the river. Faded paint on interior walls resembles a theater curtain. There, meals were eaten, plays performed, and music sung, but it now houses irrigation equipment. These memories became the heart of this novel.

Billy Yeargin's book *Remembering North Carolina Tobacco* refreshed the hard life of "puttin' in *t'bacca.*" Sergeant Walter Juopperi's WWII account for his family in *A Soldier's Life in Battle* helped me stand in his young, frightened shoes. Bear Moore answered my bee questions and Bill Tucker gave me a bee article he compiled from Robert Morse, Sue Hubbell, C. P. Dadant, and Sue Monk Kidd. Harold and Jenny

Beirne patiently waded through early drafts to understand the tedious process of writing a book. Lara Turchinsky advised me on tarot cards and my sister Glo Swann cast a careful eye when I needed it most. She remembered Mama's risqué toast that both shocked and tickled us (*Here's to the Girl in the little red shoes . . .*).

When I was wrapping these facts in fiction, my patient agent, Rebecca Gradinger, and her assistant, Elizabeth Resnick, challenged me to move from the character-driven format of my debut novel, *If the Creek Don't Rise,* to a plot-driven format for *All the Little Hopes.* Then my talented editor, Shana Drehs, and her extraordinary staff comprised of MJ Johnston, Jessica Thelander, and Sabrina Baskey, helped hone the book's sense of direction. They asked insightful questions and double-checked my facts. Added to my gratitude for inspiration is the Wildacres Writing Workshop founded by Judi Hill (wildacreswriters.com) and the faculty there who help unlock creativity.

So many people contributed to this book in invaluable ways over multiple years, but it is my husband, Dave, who makes the writing journey easier. He is a gentle and supportive partner who understands without

ABOUT THE AUTHOR

Leah Weiss is a Southern writer born in eastern North Carolina but lives near the Blue Ridge mountains of Virginia. *All the Little Hopes* is her second novel. You can follow her on Facebook and her website, leahweiss.com.